WICKED
WAYS

Books by Lisa Jackson

Stand-Alones

SEE HOW SHE DIES
FINAL SCREAM
RUNNING SCARED
WHISPERS
TWICE KISSED
UNSPOKEN
DEEP FREEZE
FATAL BURN
MOST LIKELY TO DIE
WICKED GAME
WICKED LIES
SOMETHING WICKED
WICKED WAYS
SINISTER
WITHOUT MERCY
YOU DON'T WANT TO KNOW
CLOSE TO HOME

Anthony Paterno/Cahill Family Novels

IF SHE ONLY KNEW
ALMOST DEAD

Rick Bentz/Reuben Montoya Novels

HOT BLOODED
COLD BLOODED
SHIVER
ABSOLUTE FEAR
LOST SOULS
MALICE
DEVIOUS

Pierce Reed/Nikki Gillette Novels

THE NIGHT BEFORE
THE MORNING AFTER
TELL ME

Selena Alvarez/Regan Pescoli Novels

LEFT TO DIE
CHOSEN TO DIE
BORN TO DIE
AFRAID TO DIE
READY TO DIE
DESERVES TO DIE

Books by Nancy Bush

CANDY APPLE RED
ELECTRIC BLUE
ULTRAVIOLET
WICKED GAME
WICKED LIES
SOMETHING WICKED
WICKED WAYS
UNSEEN
BLIND SPOT
HUSH
NOWHERE TO RUN
NOWHERE TO HIDE
NOWHERE SAFE
SINISTER
I'LL FIND YOU

Published by Kensington Publishing Corporation

LISA JACKSON
AND
NANCY BUSH

WICKED
WAYS

KENSINGTON BOOKS
www.kensingtonbooks.com

KENSINGTON BOOKS are published by

Kensington Publishing Corp.
119 West 40th Street
New York, NY 10019

All Kensington titles, imprints, and distributed lines are available at special quantity discounts for bulk purchases for sales promotion, premiums, fund-raising, educational, or institutional use.

Special book excerpts or customized printings can also be created to fit specific needs. For details, write or phone the office of the Kensington Special Sales Manager: Attn. Special Sales Department. Kensington Publishing Corp., 119 West 40th Street, New York, NY 10018. Phone: 1-800-221-2647.

Kensington and the K logo Reg. U.S. Pat. & TM Off.

Library of Congress Card Catalogue Number: 2014934221

ISBN-13: 978-1-61773-415-1
ISBN-10: 1-61773-415-2
First Hardcover Printing: October 2014

10 9 8 7 6 5 4 3 2 1

Printed in the United States of America

WICKED
WAYS

Prologue

Near Deception Bay, Oregon

"She's never going to leave," Lena muttered, thinking this was a bad idea. Just because they'd heard that the woman and her missing husband hid money in their house was no guarantee that they would find anything.

"Shhh!" Bruce shushed sternly. "Just wait."

"I have been waiting. For nearly an hour." Catching an angry glare from her boyfriend, Lena bit her tongue. Darkness had settled in. A thick fog, smelling of brine, was creeping through the crooked and pockmarked streets of the unincorporated town inhabited by what the locals called "The Foothillers." It wasn't much of a place in the daylight, only a few steps up from a shantytown in her estimation. With the coming night, the cul de sac looked foreboding, nearly malicious, as only half the houses on the street were occupied and those that were had overgrown lawns and staring, dark windows. Not exactly a place one would expect to find a cache of thousands of dollars hidden in the mattress or in a secret cubby in the floor, but the old guy in the bar last night had insisted that the people who lived here only looked poor. And, well, it was true that the vehicle sitting in the drive was a newer model Volvo wagon.

Still . . . Lena was cold to the bone, the gusts chilled by the ocean as they rolled into town on the fog. For stealth purposes, the fog itself was a good thing, she decided. But did it have to be so friggin' cold? Shivering, she blew on her gloved fingers. *Come on, come on,* she thought.

According to the geezer in the Sand Bar, the woman, whose husband was often away, left every Tuesday night to have dinner with her sister somewhere south of Tillamook, so Lena and Bruce would have plenty of time to search the place and get away.

"Here we go," Bruce muttered, pulling down his ski mask. She did the same and watched as a tall, willowy woman came out of the front door carrying an infant seat, a diaper bag slung over her shoulder as she turned to close the door behind her. She hurried down the single concrete step and along a cracked walkway, heading to her vehicle, which she unlocked before strapping the baby carrier into the back seat.

Finally!

Lena just wanted this to be over. Yes, they'd robbed homes and cars before, but tonight was different and more dangerous. She felt it intuitively. Their plan didn't seem as well thought out, and the crummy one-story house with its peeling paint and sagging porch didn't give her any confidence that they would score anything, not even a bag of weed or ounce of cocaine, much less a cache of serious money.

"Damn," Bruce whispered frantically. "Get back!" He yanked her farther into the shrubbery and threw her face down as a car turned onto the dead-end street and slowly drove by. Lena managed to peek up and her heart nearly stopped as she recognized a yellow and black cruiser for the Tillamook County Sheriff's Department.

Oh, Jesus.

Closing her eyes, she lay motionless, facedown in the carpet of pine needles.

Headlights cutting through the fog, big engine purring, the cruiser rolled slowly around the arc of the deserted street.

Lena chanced another look. The woman whom they intended to rob had her driver's door open. She'd halted in the act of getting inside as the Crown Vic rolled past her drive.

Neither Lena nor Bruce moved for long moments. They huddled in the salal bushes beneath the low branches of a contorted pine. As the cruiser passed by a second time, they could hear the officer talking on his radio. Suddenly, he gunned his engine and, with a chirp of tires, sped away, blue and red lights strobing the area until the vehicle disappeared around the corner.

Lena's heart was pounding so loudly she thought everyone in the entire county could hear it. This had to be over and soon. Maybe they should abort. But they were out of cash and Bruce was sure the house would be a big score.

God, she hoped so.

The woman took a last look at the baby in the back, then slid into the driver's side just as a phone started ringing from inside the house. She glanced up and looked back toward the front door. Muttering something unintelligible, she climbed back out and hurried toward the front stoop, unlocking the door, and rushing inside. Lights snapped on and through the window they watched as she picked up the phone.

Bruce was on his knees, straining to see. "Why the fuck can't she just leave?"

Lena looked up at him. "This feels wrong. We should just go."

"And do what?"

"Pick a pocket at the bar, scoop up a purse—"

"Didn't you hear the old man? He said *tens of thousands* are hidden inside."

"How does he know?"

"He's an uncle or something. I don't know. But it's worth a shot, babe." Bruce placed a gloved hand around her arm. "It could be like winnin' the fuckin' lottery. Change our lives."

She liked the sound of that and stole a glance at the house. Through the front window she could see the woman pacing, holding the receiver to her ear and shouting loudly.

"This could take a while," Lena said.

"I know, I know." Bruce, too, was nervous.

"And that cop. What was he doing here? What if he finds our car?"

"He won't." Bruce glanced at the house where the woman was so engaged in her conversation, so agitated, that she was gesticulating wildly with her free hand.

Lena doubted she was aware of anything other than ripping the person on the other end a new one. "It's dangerous," she muttered.

He rubbed a hand feverishly over his masked forehead. "I got this." He looked at the window one more time and must've mentally calculated how long the mark would be engaged in the conversation. "Stay here."

"What?"

"I'm gonna get the kid."

"*What!* No!" Bruce was teasing, right? "You're not serious." No way would he kidnap the baby. But the set of his jaw and determination in the eyes staring deep from the slits in his ski mask said otherwise. "Bruce . . . God . . . No. Don't even joke about—"

"No joke."

"But she'll be out any second and what will we do with a baby?"

"Sell it."

"Oh, dear Jesus."

"I know a guy, who knows a lawyer in LA somewhere. Does private adoptions. Asks no questions and the fee is astronomical."

"But the woman . . . the cops . . ." Lena shook her head, disbelieving, her hands clammy. "You can't just steal a kid!"

"Oh, no?" he countered, his lips twisting into a cold smile. "Just watch me." He stole quickly toward the car, opened the back driver's door, unhooked the car seat, and pulled the baby out.

CHAPTER 1

Twenty-five years later
Southern California

Elizabeth watched through her front window as two police officers trudged up her walk. She knew what was about to come. She'd seen this walk to the door before in varying incarnations on television dramas. It seemed like every cop show had at least one scene where officers came to talk to someone and deliver the bad news. A death, she guessed, her heart hammering, but whose?

A wave of fear enveloped her. After closing the plantation blinds, she hurried away and down the hall to the room where her daughter was sleeping. She knew Chloe was safe in bed, but she had to *see* her. Pushing open the door to Chloe's room, she gazed in fearfully, her pulse racing with premonition. Her daughter's golden-brown curls were splayed on the pillow. She saw the sweep of her eyelashes, the way her arms lay flung around her head in the abandonment of deep sleep, the soft puffs of her breath.

Knock, knock.

The sound was so loud she jumped. Gently closing her daughter's door, she race-walked back to the living room to flip on the exterior light before cautiously opening the door and eyeing the two officers through the screen.

They stood in a circle of yellow light, their expressions grim.

The woman spoke first. "Mrs. Elizabeth Ellis?"

"Yes." Her throat was dry as dust.

"I'm Officer Maya, and this is Officer DeFazio." They already had their badges out and Elizabeth's eyes traveled toward them as Maya continued. "We regret to tell you that there's been a car accident."

Car accident.

"Is it Court?" Elizabeth whispered.

"Ma'am, may we come in?" the male officer asked.

Elizabeth wordlessly opened the door fully. Their faces blurred in front of her. She was seeing something else. The entire last week in bullet points. . . .

On Monday, she reluctantly kissed her husband Court good-bye as he left for yet another business trip. They had that fight . . . again . . . about what she referred to as her ability to foreshadow.

"You really think you can sense danger?" her husband of six years demanded. The face she once thought so handsome stared down at her in scorn, his brown eyes simmering with fury, his lips twisted into a snarl. "Don't act like a crackpot, Liz. I'm about to make partner at the firm, and I swear, you better not get in the way."

"I'm not going to tell anyone else," she assured him. She was scared, worried. After she'd predicted Little Nate's accident on the monkey bars before it happened, her friend Jade had gazed at her with wonder, awe, and maybe a little horror. But when she'd tried to tell her husband about Little Nate and other times similar things had happened, incidents she'd dismissed as coincidences—because honestly, what else could they be?—he'd shut down completely. Their marriage was disintegrating, had been for a long time. She knew it, but was unable to put her finger on what was wrong.

"Make sure you don't," he said, then left in anger.

On Tuesday, Chloe had a fainting spell at school. It was troubling, because she seemed to be having more and more of them. Elizabeth picked up her daughter and brought her home. Chloe assured her that she was fine, fine, fine, in a loud, five-year-old voice that never seemed to have any volume control.

Nevertheless, on Wednesday, Elizabeth kept Chloe home from school and took her to the doctor who checked her out and pronounced her good to go, a fact that made Elizabeth slightly uncomfortable. Something was going on with Chloe that no one seemed to be able to diagnose. But maybe that was just Elizabeth being paranoid again, a helicopter parent, as Court had accused her of often enough.

On Thursday, Elizabeth took Chloe back to her preschool class, then met with one of the women from her Moms Group for lunch. Tara Hofstetter was the closest to a real friend Elizabeth had in the group that had been formed online and consisted of women in the area who had delivered babies around the same time. Court had wanted Elizabeth, who'd always been somewhat introverted, to meet people around the Irvine, Costa Mesa, and Newport Beach cities where he worked as an attorney in a high-rise business center near the Orange County airport. Dutifully, she had gone outside her comfort zone and joined the newly formed group after Chloe was born. Since that time, a number of women had left and entered the group, but Elizabeth and Tara were two of the original members, and Tara's daughter, Bibi, played well with Chloe.

Elizabeth was running late. She blew into the sandwich shop and could tell by the look on Tara's face that something was wrong. Before she could even ask, Tara reached across the table and grabbed Elizabeth's hand. It was a surprise as Tara, with her bleached-to-hell blond hair and taut dancer's body, wasn't exactly known for demonstrative displays. "I saw Court with Whitney Bellhard yesterday."

"Whitney Bellhard . . . where? What do you mean?" Elizabeth asked. Whitney Bellhard was an aesthetician who gave Botox parties around the area and her picture was plastered on flyers she passed out in every neighborhood around the school. Whitney was big-breasted, big-eyed and about as subtle as a Mack truck.

"They were holding hands at this bistro I go to whenever I'm in Santa Monica," Tara revealed.

"Santa Monica?" Elizabeth repeated faintly. "Court's in Denver." Santa Monica was at least an hour away from Irvine in good traffic, and it wasn't a city on Court's recent itineraries.

"Elizabeth, they were staring at each other so hard they didn't even see me. I ducked out and watched a little while from outside the window."

"Maybe they were . . . just . . ." But she hadn't been able to come up with any reasonable excuse for them being together in a city far enough away that they wouldn't expect to be seen by someone they knew.

"They were acting like they couldn't wait to get the bill," Tara finally said in a reluctant voice, her blue eyes regarding her friend regretfully.

At that, Elizabeth nodded and silently accepted the unwelcome realization that her husband was having an affair.

On Friday, Court got home late after Chloe was already tucked into bed. Elizabeth was lying in bed with a book, reading one page over and over again as her mind worried about what she was going to say when she saw him. She'd run the gamut of disbelief—fury, despair, and a kind of angry acceptance. She tried to self-assess, asked herself if she cared enough to try to save the marriage. For Chloe, she wanted to, but for herself? That was a trickier question.

By the time Court entered the bedroom, loosening his tie and telling her he'd come straight from a meeting, really wanted a drink, and did she want something, Elizabeth put down the book and was simply waiting, her hands folded on her lap. Court didn't wait for her answer. He went into their living room and she heard the squeaking hinge that indicated he'd opened the bar which was hidden inside a tall chest made of ebony wood. Next, she heard him slam a glass on the counter.

She walked into the living room as he pulled out the stopper to a bottle of scotch and splashed a healthy dose into the old-fashioned glass. She watched silently as he bolted it down and she could almost read his mind as he considered the bottle, wanting to pour a second drink but thinking it might not be prudent based on his wife's uncertain mood.

"What's wrong?" he asked sullenly, rolling the glass between his palms.

"Is it true that you met Whitney Bellhard in Santa Monica?"

Court jerked his head back as if he'd been slapped, then tried to cover up the tell with a bunch of bluster.

Detached, she watched his florid face turn brick red and knew he was going to lie to her.

"Who the fuck told you that?"

"Someone from the school," she lied right back.

"I wouldn't have that plastic bitch on a dare," he declared.

"No one said you had her. They just said you met her for lunch."

"Whatever nosy bitch told you that should just mind her own fucking business and stop trying to stir up trouble."

"It's not true?"

"Of course it's not true!" He slammed his empty glass down on the bar and reached for the bottle of scotch again, his misgivings gone in the face of bigger issues.

"So, if I check, I'll find out you were still in Denver on Wednesday, like it says on your itinerary."

"Since when do you check on me?" he demanded, his dark eyes glittering as he shot her a vituperative look.

Elizabeth almost lost her nerve at that point. She'd never challenged her husband before. Court Ellis was a master arguer, a born lawyer, and she couldn't compete with him in any discussion. He loved talking circles around her, and she hadn't realized how little affection was left between them until that very moment.

"What's the name of the bitch who told you those lies?" he demanded as he took another healthy sip of scotch.

"What's the name of the hotel where you supposedly stayed in Denver?"

He slammed out of the house after that and didn't come home the rest of the night.

Saturday afternoon he returned, but they didn't talk about Whitney Bellhard or Santa Monica or if he'd been in Denver at all. They lived in icy silence throughout the day. Chloe, picking up the tension, cried and fussed, and it was a relief when it was finally late enough to put her to bed. Elizabeth told herself that she should talk to Court some more, but she never found the energy and in the end, while Court slept on the couch, she lay awake in their king-sized bed alone, feeling a cool breeze come through the open window, smelling the menthol scent of nearby eucalyptus trees, watching palm fronds wave in the soft landscaping lighting of their backyard.

About five AM Sunday morning, Court entered their bedroom and stood at the foot of their bed. Aware something momentous was about to happen, Elizabeth sat up and pulled her knees up to her chest under the covers, automatically bracing herself.

He was perfectly sober, the anger seemingly drained out of him. "I didn't want it to happen this way," he said, his voice curiously tight as if he might break down, though Court Ellis never showed any emotion. "I'm in love with her," he said, shocking Elizabeth so much she actually gasped. "I've been meaning to tell you for months. Whitney and I have been meeting at a place in Santa Monica at the end of my business trips. I wasn't in Denver. I haven't been in the final cities on any of my itineraries for almost a year."

It was such a bone deep betrayal that Elizabeth couldn't find her voice. There was no love between her and Court; maybe there never had been. But she was shocked, hurt, and cold. Frozen to the core. She stared at him and thought terrible thoughts—*I wish I'd never met you. I wish I never had to see you again. I wish you were dead.*

"Get out," she ordered through gritted teeth.

"Elizabeth, you know I never meant to hurt you."

"Get the hell out and don't come back."

"Jesus." He stared at her as if she were being unreasonable. "You're such a bitch. When did you become such a goddamn bitch?"

"You need to leave," she said woodenly.

"This is my home, too, and—"

"This is not your home," she corrected swiftly.

"Be careful. Don't push me. I can make your life a living hell."

"You didn't just say that." She was stunned by how quickly he went on the offensive.

"I have a daughter, too, and when I get back from this next trip—"

"You don't have a daughter anymore!" she shot back in fury. "You're never going to see her again. Get the hell out and never come back!"

"Cut the dramatics, Elizabeth." He came around the bed so swiftly it scared her.

She tried to scramble away. When he placed his hands on her shoulders and glared down at her, she felt threatened. She sensed that he wanted to put his hands around her neck. They held each other's gaze for a moment, then he suddenly released her and left the room. They suffered through the rest of Sunday not speaking to each other.

Elizabeth shook her head to clear away the memories. Now it was Sunday night and two police officers were standing in her living room. In a hollow voice, she said to Officer Maya, "Court's dead, isn't he?"

Her careful expression said it all. "Yes, ma'am."

You wished this on him. You made this happen. It's happened before . . . Elizabeth swallowed. "You said it was a car accident."

"That's right." It was Officer DeFazio who answered her. "A single car accident."

"So, no one else was hurt?" she asked, hopeful.

Maya, who was somewhere in her thirties with blunt-cut dark hair, shared a look with DeFazio who was at least ten years older and a whole lot grayer, before turning back to Elizabeth. "There was a second fatality."

Elizabeth's head swam. "Oh, no . . ."

"It appears your husband was driving and another person was in the passenger seat."

Feeling like everything was coming at her at once, Elizabeth held up her hand and said in a strangled voice, "Excuse me. I have to check on my daughter." She left the two officers hanging as she hurried on rubbery legs down the hall to Chloe's room and opened the door a crack. The night-light bathed the room in a soft circle of illumination. Of course, Chloe was still breathing easily, sleeping soundly, but Elizabeth clung to the doorknob for support, fighting down a rising panic.

It can't be your fault, she told herself. *Things like this don't happen.*

But she knew she was lying to herself.

She carefully shut the bedroom door and returned to perch on the edge of the couch. The two officers were still standing in the center of the room.

Elizabeth wasn't sure what emotion they could read on her face. Grief? No. Not yet. Maybe not ever. Numbness? Definitely. Fear? Yes . . . a little of that, too, though she would never be able to explain why. Even if she could, she knew they'd look at her as if she were stark raving mad.

"Who . . . ?" she asked, picking through the words that seemed to be shuffling around in her brain, not connecting in sentences. She thought she knew already and didn't want to hear the name yet, so she changed direction. "Wait, no . . . how did it happen?"

They'd been about to tell her about the other victim; she could see the way both drew a breath, but they checked themselves.

DeFazio said, "That's still to be determined. It looks like your husband lost control of the vehicle. A BMW. It appears to be his car."

Elizabeth nodded. Court loved his silver BMW while she was happy with her Ford Escape.

"The car was found near San Diego," Maya supplied.

"San Diego?" Elizabeth half-expected to hear Santa Monica, thinking maybe Court had decided to meet Whitney Bellhard at the beginning of his trip, not the end.

"South of San Diego. Almost to the border," Maya said.

"Court wouldn't go to Mexico," Elizabeth responded with certainty. "He got a bad case of Montezuma's revenge once, and he swore he would never go there again." *And he would never drive his beloved car across the border, either.*

"We have a receipt from a Tres Brisas Hotel in Rosarito Beach from last month," DeFazio stated.

Elizabeth could feel herself staring and had to force herself to drag her gaze away. "You sure it was Court?"

"A man and woman were registered as Mr. and Mrs. Bellhard," DeFazio told her.

Elizabeth felt near collapse. He had been with Whitney again. Of course he had. What had she expected? Clasping her hands together and squeezing so tightly it hurt, Elizabeth asked, "The other fatality is . . . ?"

"Mrs. Whitney Bellhard," Officer Maya confirmed.

Not only Santa Monica, Elizabeth thought dully, though why she should care she had no idea. If Court had been meeting his lover from Los Angeles to Mexico and beyond, what did it matter? They were gone now.

"One of our detectives will be here soon," DeFazio said into the silence that followed.

Elizabeth felt dissociated from the action around her, as if she were far away looking down on them, watching a play, maybe. Someone else's troubles.

"We spoke with Mr. Bellhard before we came here," Maya said. "He told us he'd suspected his wife was having an affair with someone for about a year. He apparently followed her to Rosarito Beach and saw her with your husband, but he didn't know who he was. So, he tailed her again today. She left her car in the parking lot of your husband's law firm and got into his vehicle. Mr. Bellhard then followed them to the juncture of I-5 and the 405 south, then turned around because he had a dinner meeting with his boss at the Bungalow in Newport Beach. He was still at the restaurant when officers contacted him. Detective Bette Thronson has taken a statement from him. She sent us ahead to contact you." Maya hesitated as if she were deciding if she should say anything more, and then added, "Mr. Bellhard followed them because he wanted to use their affair as leverage in the pending divorce between his wife and him. They've been separated for several years."

Elizabeth didn't give a damn what happened between the Bellhards. She was having trouble processing that Court was dead. Gone. Never to trouble either her or Chloe again. She should care more that Chloe had lost her father but couldn't summon up the emotion. "A detective is on her way here?"

"Yes. Detective Bette Thronson," Maya repeated, her dark eyes studying Elizabeth. "Can you tell us where you were today?"

"Me?"

"Yes, ma'am," Maya said.

"Well . . . uh . . . I was home with Chloe in the morning, but I went into work for a while. Misty—she's our babysitter—she was here. She . . . um . . . she lives down the street."

"You're a real estate agent," Maya said.

In a distant part of her mind, Elizabeth realized the officer was stepping outside her bounds a little. It wasn't part of her job, but maybe she wanted to be a detective herself. "I was at the office for a while."

"From when to when?" Maya questioned.

They want me to account for my hours. "Umm . . . I went to a couple open houses . . ." she said vaguely.

In truth, she'd been at the office for a short time and then had gone to a local park and sat at a table under a tree, lost in thought. When she got home, Chloe had practically been done in from all the fun she'd had with Misty who was fourteen going on ten and who had lots of energy. Elizabeth had fed Chloe and put her to bed at seven-thirty, her thoughts still on her fight with Court. She'd thought about leaving him a text on his cell that he could read once he'd landed in Chicago but hadn't gotten around to it. Now she knew he'd never made it to Chicago.

Of course.

It was another thirty minutes before the detective finally showed and the officers departed. Detective Thronson was tall, iron-jawed and intense. She had short gray hair and a body built like a barrel. She didn't stand on ceremony and almost immediately began asking questions that made Elizabeth feel like she was under attack. She asked the same questions Officer Maya had, then started in on her family.

"Your daughter goes to school?" Thronson also chose to stand and took center place in the middle of the room while Elizabeth was once again seated on the edge of the couch.

"Preschool until this fall," Elizabeth explained.

"She was with a babysitter this afternoon while you were working?"

"Yes."

"Did you know your husband was heading south of San Diego, possibly to Rosarito Beach?"

"He was supposed to be flying to Chicago. That's what his ticket said."

"Did you know Whitney Bellhard?" A trick question said off the cuff as if the answer didn't mean that much to her, but Elizabeth knew the detective was keyed into her response.

"I knew of her. She . . . advertised around the neighborhood with flyers."

"Her husband said she was an aesthetician."

"Yeah . . . she advertised Botox and facials and skin peels. I never went to her."

Elizabeth's mind was starting to wander into dangerous areas again. *You wished him dead . . . just like you wished bad things on Mazie . . . just like you wished ill on that other cop, Officer Unfriendly . . . and they both died, too . . .*

But how could thoughts *kill*?

Detective Thronson asked questions about her relationship with Court, which Elizabeth answered dutifully. Yes, there were some problems in the marriage. No, she hadn't known he was having an affair with Whitney Bellhard until . . . She stumbled and lied, saying, "Until the officers told me." She didn't bring up Tara's revelation, nor her fight with Court, nor the true deteriorated state of their marriage. It didn't take a rocket scientist to determine something was fishy about the accident. The probing questions the detective was asking indicated something wasn't right.

Finally, Detective Thronson wound down and slowed her questions. When she ended the interview, she told Elizabeth she would be in touch with her later.

Elizabeth thanked her and showed her out, then nearly collapsed against the door panels once the woman was out of her house. With an effort, she gathered her strength, then made her way to the bathroom, staring in the mirror at her own drawn face.

You shouldn't have lied. You should tell them, right now, what you know. Before they learn it some other way. Let them know he's dead because of you. That you knew it was going to happen. That it's your fault. That it's happened before. Tell them before it's too late.

But it was already too late, and she knew she wouldn't say a word.

CHAPTER 2

The funeral for Courtland Ellis was scheduled for eleven A.M. on the Friday following his death. Despite being stunned and feeling as if she were living in an unreal world, Elizabeth had started planning a memorial service, but on Monday Court's estranged sister Barbara had flown in from Buffalo and insisted on orchestrating her brother's funeral. She took charge as if she'd just been waiting for a chance to bully her way back into her brother's life, or death, as the case may be, which seemed odd as Court and she had suffered a falling out years earlier.

Elizabeth, still dealing with her own reeling emotions as well as Chloe's seeming lack of them, gratefully let Barbara make all the arrangements. Fighting her sister-in-law would take more energy than she could spare, and she needed to take care of Chloe. Take care of herself. As for the details of burying her husband, she didn't much care one way or another how he was interred. Memorial service . . . funeral service . . . the only thing that mattered was keeping Chloe's life on track, making certain it was as normal as it possibly could be.

That was Elizabeth's aim, and she had been monitoring Chloe all week. Apart from an initial sadness when she'd learned the news of her father's unexpected death, Chloe had been pretty much business as usual. There had been a few tears the first night and several nightmares where Chloe had ended up in Elizabeth's bed, but all Chloe's night fears had seemed to evaporate. Elizabeth hoped it meant her daughter was coping with her grief, not burying it, but it was hard to say. Chloe, like Court, was adept at hiding her feelings.

And what about you, Elizabeth. Aren't you the master of repressing your emotions? Maybe your daughter learned to maintain tight control because she'd witnessed it in you.

Whatever the reason, when Barbara blew in, Elizabeth was relieved to let her take over. Barbara was tall, brown-haired and brown-eyed and looked a lot like Court, but where Court had been smooth and polished, Barbara was raw, socially awkward, and had a tendency to stare at people a little too hard for any kind of social comfort. Fortunately, she'd decided to stay at a nearby hotel, keeping Elizabeth apprised of her plans as if it were a duty, which, Elizabeth supposed, it might have been.

On Friday, Barbara came over at the crack of dawn, rapping loudly on the door until Elizabeth, in her bathrobe and balancing her first cup of coffee, let her inside.

Barbara's gaze swept over her as she headed into the kitchen. Barbara followed and spied her niece.

Chloe, hair mussed, still in her pajamas, was eating breakfast at the kitchen island.

"You need to get dressed, sweetie. We don't have time to dawdle." Barbara was dressed all in black—black dress, black shoes, black hat with a veil.

"Not dawdling," Chloe said, frowning, her little eyebrows pulling together as she stared at her aunt.

Barbara glanced at Elizabeth. "We can't be late!"

"I know." To her daughter, Elizabeth said, "You can finish your pancakes first, Chloe."

"I'm not going to the funeral," Chloe said, unconcerned. She was scooting a mini-pancake around her plate, soaking up as much maple syrup as possible.

Barbara's gaze turned frosty. "This is something we need to do."

Elizabeth frowned. "I don't know that—"

"I'm not going with you," Chloe interrupted.

"Of course you are," Barbara bulldozed over her, walking closer to the island where Chloe rolled her eyes upward to hold her stare. "We all need to say good-bye to your daddy, honey."

"I'm going to preschool to see my friends," Chloe said, forking a big chunk of pancake into her mouth, though her gaze didn't leave her aunt's.

"Not today, you're not." Barbara told her tautly.

"Mmmmhmmm," Chloe mumbled.

Elizabeth could see the way her jaw was starting to jut out in the stubborn way that warned of a battle to come. An Ellis trait that Court and Barbara also possessed.

"Today you're going to the funeral," Barbara told her flatly.

"Nope." Chloe was unmoved.

Barbara, who had no children of her own, turned to Elizabeth and demanded, "You tell her that we're going to the funeral."

Elizabeth bristled. She'd already had a run-in with her father, whom she rarely spoke with for too many reasons to count, one of them being that he hadn't liked Court at all. Luckily, he hadn't offered to come to the service when she'd called to give him the news, so the only person she had to deal with was Court's sister who was determined to throw her weight around. "I'm going to let her go to preschool," Elizabeth decided, taking a sip from her cup.

Barbara's gasp was loud enough to be heard through the whole house. "She needs to be at the service. Courtland was her *father!*"

"It's been a tough week for all of us. If Chloe feels more comfortable at her school, let her go."

"Yeah," Chloe said, finishing her last bite and reaching for her cup of milk. She took several large gulps and climbed down from the barstool.

"Chloe, you need to change your attitude," Barbara said.

"You sound just like Daddy." Chloe stalked off to her room and slammed the door.

Barbara turned to Elizabeth in outrage. "What are you going to do about that?"

"Give her a little room, Barbara. Please."

"You're letting her walk all over you!"

"I'm letting her deal. She just lost her father and it's been tough on all of us, her included. I don't really care whether she's at the funeral or not."

"But—"

"I'm not sure how much she's grasped of Court's death. And she's been having these flu-like bouts that the doctor can't seem to diagnose." Elizabeth admitted. "Feverish, loss of appetite . . . anyway, I'm just worried, and I don't—"

"I can't believe you're giving in to her again!" Barbara was aghast.

"This is my call. I just want my daughter to be okay." Elizabeth felt her anger rise and steadfastly tamped it down.

"It's a mistake, Elizabeth. That child runs this place. I've seen it since I've been here. You make her lunches and she gets to choose whatever she wants to eat. She stays up till eight o'clock every night, and she wears whatever she wants from her closet even though she looks like a ragamuffin." As if she realized she'd crossed an invisible line, Barbara stiffened a bit. "I'm sorry, Elizabeth, I know things are . . . difficult right now, but someone needs to speak their mind around here."

"So I guess that would be you, right?" Elizabeth said, not hiding her sarcasm.

Barbara barreled on. "You're just letting her do whatever she wants and she's rude! You're not doing her any favors, you know."

"Her father died in an auto accident less than a week ago," Elizabeth pointed out more calmly than she wanted. "I give her three choices for her lunch and she picks one. She's always gone to bed at eight, and she likes to do it herself so I let her select her own clothes. I think it shows independence."

"Well, she needs to go to this funeral, and she needs to be dressed appropriately." Barbara swept up her purse, headed toward the front door, stopping to examine her reflection in the hall mirror. "We should get there early, so chop-chop. Time to get Chloe dressed. And you, too," she added, eyeing Elizabeth's bathrobe.

In a controlled voice, Elizabeth said, "You go on ahead. I'll meet you there."

"What about Chloe?"

"I told you. I'm not taking her."

"Oh, please, Elizabeth. Court would want her there."

Elizabeth's jaw tightened and she almost blurted, "Court didn't want her at all, if you want to know the truth," but managed to stay her tongue.

"Go get dressed, and *I'll* get Chloe," Barbara said, heading down the hall toward Chloe's room.

"No."

Barbara turned her neck to give Elizabeth a look, but kept moving forward.

"I said no, Barbara. She's my child and she's going to preschool,"

Elizabeth stated firmly as she tamped down her outrage at her sister-in-law's high-handedness. "I'll meet you at the funeral later."

Barbara stopped short and heaved a huge sigh. "Do we have to have this drama?"

"Nope. That's why you're leaving." Elizabeth walked to the front door and held it open.

Barbara hesitated.

Elizabeth waited.

"Oh, for the love of God. I can't believe you're doing this. This is so childish." Barbara reluctantly walked back toward Elizabeth.

"I'd agree with you on that." Elizabeth was firm and as soon as Barbara was across the threshold, she closed the door hard.

Good riddance, she thought, closing her eyes slowly. She counted to ten, releasing her anger, reclaiming whatever bit of equanimity she could grasp. It wasn't the time to let her emotions run wild.

Finally calm again, she walked to her bedroom, rifled through her closet and found a dark gray dress with a matching bolero jacket edged in black piping, her most somber outfit. Once she was dressed, she helped Chloe pick out pants and a shirt for school, along with closed-toe shoes, a preschool requirement, then bundled her into the Escape.

They drove to the school in silence for most of the trip. As they turned into the parking lot for the school, Chloe announced from the back seat, "I don't like her."

"Who, honey?" Elizabeth asked, though she guessed.

"Aunt Barbara. She's mean."

A bully. "I don't like her much, either," Elizabeth said, and met Chloe's eyes in the mirror. The tentative smile on her daughter's lips was the first she'd seen in a long, long time, and Elizabeth grinned back.

"I'll go if you want me to," Chloe said. "To Daddy's funeral."

Elizabeth's heart cracked. She had to blink back tears. "It's up to you."

"I don't want to."

"Then go to school," Elizabeth urged and cut the engine. As she helped Chloe out of the car seat, she said, "I'll tell you all about it later, if you want to know."

"I love you, Mommy," Chloe said, taking Elizabeth's hands as help for the first time in weeks. Glancing up and squinting, she wrinkled her nose, then swung her mother's arm as they walked toward the front doors of the preschool.

"Love you, too, pumpkin." Elizabeth answered, trying to remember the last time her independent daughter had held her hand, let alone told her she loved her.

Seated next to Barbara in the front row at the funeral home and throughout the director's long and sonorous recounting of the life of Courtland Ellis, Elizabeth could feel waves of anger emanating from her husband's sister. Court hadn't been a man to forgive easily and apparently Barbara wasn't a forgiving woman, either.

Several rows behind her, one of the women who worked with Court sobbed as if her heart were broken. Hearing that, Elizabeth assessed her own feelings and knew she felt sadness, numbness, and a sense of total displacement. Still, she wouldn't have been able to manufacture a tear if her own life depended on it, and she wondered what that meant to Detective Thronson whom she'd seen in the back row when she'd entered after everyone else had been seated. Did the detective think she was disaffected? Did that make her seem guilty? The investigation into Court's death was ongoing. Though no one was saying it was anything but an accident, Elizabeth sensed the police were leaning that direction.

You aren't responsible. You didn't kill him. You couldn't have.

She shivered. She couldn't help it. Barbara looked over at her and scowled and just for just a moment Elizabeth's temper flared. She'd about had it with Court's sister and could hardly wait for her to fly home. With a concentrated effort, she tamped her negative feelings back down.

Barbara had insisted upon a graveside service as well, so an hour later, Elizabeth stood beneath a canopy next to the open grave and watched as the coffin was lowered into the ground. A ring of King palms fluttered in a brisk breeze and gooseflesh rose on Elizabeth's skin.

Barbara had made noise about having an open coffin and a viewing, but on that Elizabeth had put her foot down. She'd identified Court's body and though his face hadn't been damaged, she felt that was enough. At that point, she hadn't known which way Chloe would fall on going to the service for her father and Elizabeth wasn't going to have Court's dead face be the last image in her daughter's mind. Barbara had acquiesced with ill grace.

Rain fell fitfully, making soft *ponk-ponk* sounds on the canvas canopy. The wind picked up, swaying the palms high overhead and a sudden *thunk* startled everyone when a huge frond dropped onto the pavilion just as a woman began to sing a hymn. Her voice warbled for a moment, but she pulled herself together and sang on with strength.

And then it was over. Elizabeth greeted people who walked by and offered sympathy, watching as Barbara began hugging everyone as if they were best friends. As soon as she could, Elizabeth escaped the crowds and picked her way toward the parking lot over somewhat soggy grass from a surprisingly hard rain the night before. The wind was gusting and rain began to fall again.

Her friend Tara met up with her. "I'd be happy to pick up Chloe today. She and Bibi can play together, and you can come get her whenever you're ready. Will that work?"

"That would be terrific. Thanks, Tara," Elizabeth said, heartfelt. "I'll call the preschool." The children of a number of Elizabeth's Moms Group friends attended Bright Day Preschool with Chloe. Tara's name was on the list of people who were allowed to pick up her daughter.

"Not a problem."

Several other of her Moms Group friends caught up to her as they all headed toward their vehicles. Honey-haired, green-eyed Deirdre Czursky gave her a fierce hug. Her son Chad was in Chloe's home room and a good friend to her.

"How're you doing? The truth now," Deirdre said, finding an umbrella and clicking it open.

"So-so."

"Well, you look great, if that means anything to you. Hang in there," she advised.

Vivian Eachus, her blond-streaked, curly hair banded into its ubiquitous ponytail poof, looked alien in a dark skirt and sweater as Elizabeth almost always saw her in Lululemon workout gear. Vivian's daughter Lissa was bolder and louder than Chloe, a little stockier and slightly taller. With her straight brown hair forever falling out of the glittery clips Vivian forced her to wear, Lissa was bossy and head-strong, even more so than Chloe, which made the two girls wary friends.

"I'm so sorry about all this," Vivian said, also giving Elizabeth a quick hug as the rain started in earnest.

"Me, too. It's just awful," said Vivian's friend Nadia. She some-times joined their meetings even though she didn't have a child. Ac-cording to Vivian, Nadia had been trying to conceive like mad for years, but it just hadn't happened. There had been talk of in vitro, ap-parently, but Nadia still was slim as a reed. Elizabeth couldn't pull out her last name no matter how hard she tried, so she just gave up; it had been that kind of week.

Nadia bit her lip, then gazed at Elizabeth through stricken blue eyes. "Look," she said and squeezed Elizabeth's hand hard. "If you need anything . . . ?" She left the question open.

"Thank you." Elizabeth gave her a crooked smile.

It had to be difficult for Nadia to be part of their Moms Group, given her situation, but she had insisted she wanted to join and be with them all and had made it clear that she didn't want them to hold back, or make concessions for her just because she was childless. She had assured them more than once that it was therapeutic for her to be around the kids, so they all tried not to tiptoe around Nadia's feelings. The truth was, she didn't always come to their gatherings. Then again, none of them could make all the events.

The women who'd attended the funeral were only a faction of the larger group, but they were closest to Elizabeth, the ones she hung out with, the ones she considered her friends.

Bending her head against a fresh gust of wind, she walked quickly through the rain, only to hear her name shouted above the wind. "Liz?"

She turned to spy Jade Rivers, the final member of her closest friends, the only people who shortened Elizabeth's name.

"Hey, wait up." Jade was flagging her down. A tall, statuesque African-American woman, Jade was six months pregnant with her second son, whom she planned to name Liam. Her firstborn, Little Nate, as everyone called him, was nearly a year younger than Chloe and therefore in the class behind her in school.

Catching up to her, Jade hugged Elizabeth fiercely, her voice catching. "Oh . . . God, this is so awful. I mean I . . . I can't believe it.

I'm just . . . just so sorry, Liz. You know I'm there for you. Whatever I can do to help, you just call me, okay." She blinked back tears and held her friend at arms' length as the rain peppered the ground.

"I will."

"Promise?" Jade demanded. "I mean it, Liz."

Elizabeth nodded. "Believe me, I'll let you know."

"Good." Jade ducked her head against the rain and dashed for her SUV, just as Elizabeth hit the remote to unlock her own.

It was over. At last.

As the wipers swiped at the rain, she drove home lost in random memories of her marriage to Court.

It had been so hot on their wedding day, and he'd been in a bad mood. She recalled how he battled back and forth with the people they purchased their house from, insisting that she keep going back to the other agent with yet another demand. He'd been unhappy when he learned they were having a girl. He'd flirted outrageously with attractive, twenty-something women, then pretended that she was the one who had a jealousy problem.

Yeah, their marriage had been dying for a long while she decided as she drove into the garage and walked into the house they'd shared. Funny, it didn't seem any emptier than it had when Court was alive, but then he'd rarely been home.

She understood why her vague suspicions, those worries she'd buried deep in denial, had finally been unearthed.

Once in her bedroom, she glanced at the racks of his clothes neatly pressed and hung in the closet—jackets and slacks, suits and ties. Her throat clogged for a second, not so much for the death of the man or the marriage, but for the demise of the dreams. Her dreams.

Before she could go any further down that dark emotional path, she changed into fashionable sweats of her own; Vivian wasn't the only one who wore Lululemon and the like.

Later in the afternoon, she found a bottle of Sauvignon blanc in the fridge. Opened a few days earlier, the bottle was less than a third full. She poured a glass and tasted the wine. Satisfied that it was still good, she carried her glass and the bottle to one of the sea grass chairs that faced a wide window to the backyard. The window was open a bit, a little breeze slipping into the room. Sipping the white wine she observed the rain spatter between the slats of the white wooden portico that shaded the corner of the slate patio.

I'm going to have to sell, she thought. During the week, she'd taken a very brief look into their accounts and finances only to learn that Court had been stealing from Peter to pay Paul and they were virtually broke.

Well, except you have Mazie's clients now, don't you?

Elizabeth swallowed hard. Mazie Ferguson, her boss, the hard-driving, bitch-on-wheels whom Elizabeth had also wished dead. Mazie, who'd also died in an auto accident. The difference was that Mazie had been way over the legal alcohol limit when her Lexus had sailed off the edge of the Fifty-Five freeway. Luckily, she hadn't killed anyone on the street where her car had landed in a crumpled heap of twisted metal. Only Mazie had died. But then, she was the only person Elizabeth had silently wished dead.

"I didn't kill her," she said aloud, smelling the eucalyptus, watching the shivering, finger-like green leaves of the rafus plant dance in the breeze.

CHAPTER 3

The doorbell rang and Elizabeth thought, *what now*? She walked to the front door, recognizing the shape of Barbara's hat through the translucent glass panels inset into the thick panels of her front door. *Great*.

Reluctantly, she opened the door to her sister-in-law who bustled inside.

Immediately and with disapproval, Barbara eyed Elizabeth's half-drunk glass of Chardonnay. "People are talking about you, you know," she warned once in the foyer.

It had begun to pour outside again and Elizabeth watched Barbara shrug out of her dripping coat, rain puddling onto the travertine of the entry floor. "The rain's supposed to be gone by tomorrow," she said distractedly.

"Elizabeth," Barbara snapped in annoyance and started in again. "Chloe should have been at her father's funeral."

"I'll hang your coat in the closet. It'll drip on the floor, but it's travertine, too, so it should be okay."

"For God's sake, are you deaf?"

"No, I was just tuning you out. Chloe didn't go and I don't want to talk about it anymore. It's over."

"Give me the hanger. You've got a glass of wine in your hand and I don't want you to spill it—"

"I won't." Geez, her sister-in-law was a workout. "But have it your way." She slapped a hanger into Barbara's outstretched palm then watched as her sister-in-law carefully hung her coat in the closet and placed her hat on the shelf.

Perfect.

She nearly slammed the door to the closet shut, then reminded herself to be cool, not get emotional, not to lose control. "So, Barbara," she said forcing a calm she didn't feel, "How about a glass of wine?"

"What? No, I don't . . ." Barbara lifted a hand in frustration and dropped it back down as Elizabeth walked to the kitchen, her sister-in-law following and still jabbering at her. "Elizabeth, we haven't really talked about what happened to Court. I know he was in an accident, a horrible accident, but not much more. With all the arrangements for the funeral, you and I haven't really had a chance to talk. But now . . . Do you know how that damned accident occurred?" She paused for a moment. "Or do you not want to talk about that, either?" An undercurrent of accusation ran through the question . . . as if Elizabeth were somehow holding out on her sister-in-law.

Elizabeth forced herself to ignore Barbara's tone.

"Well, just so you know, I'm in the dark here because *no* one's telling me what the hell happened!"

"It was a single car accident. But that's all I really know, too." Elizabeth glanced out the window again. The rain was letting up a bit.

"What about that woman detective?" Barbara said, standing on the other side of the island and snapping her fingers in frustration. "Oh, what's her name?"

"Detective Thronson."

"That's it." The finger snapping stopped. "Hasn't she said anything. She knows what's going on. She has to."

"I'm sure she has a better idea than I do, but—" Elizabeth lifted her shoulders and tried to ignore the headache that had been threatening her since the funeral. The truth was, the police had been pretty tight-lipped about the accident and the circumstances surrounding Court's death.

Even while escorting her to the viewing room in the morgue, Detective Thronson had been quiet, regarding her solemnly. It had been a traumatic day. Elizabeth hadn't wanted to go, and she still remembered how it had felt.

She walked along the shiny tile floors of the hospital's basement and was led to a window. On the other side of the glass, an attendant stood over a draped gurney. With a nod from Thronson who

*stood next to her—ready to catch her should she swoon, she sup-
posed—the coroner's assistant pulled down the sheet.*

*She mustered all her strength to gaze down on Court's face after
the coroner's assistant lifted the sheet. Surprisingly, Court just
looked like he was asleep, except for his skin tone—a mottled gray-
ish color. The damage to his crushed chest was kept under the sheet,
thank God, but it was still an effort for her to strangle out, "Yes,
that's my husband. Court Ellis."*

She felt a painful squeeze in her heart.

*Until that very moment when she saw her husband's lifeless face,
the accident and his death had held a dreamlike, unreal quality.
Yes, he hadn't come home, but that hadn't been abnormal and yes,
she understood what everyone said, but the reality that Court was
gone forever hadn't really pierced deep into her soul until she identified his body.*

*Her knees did not give out, though she felt sorrow for the demise
of the man whom she'd married, whom she'd once believed, fleet-
ingly, was her soul mate. But as the attendant drew the sheet over
Court's head, hiding him, a small, wayward thought skittered through
Elizabeth's brain surprising her.* I'm free. No, wait, Chloe and I are
both free.

*Her throat tightened at the notion and she told herself she was
an awful person, but the idea lodged deep.*

"So you've talked to her? Thronson?" Barbara said, breaking into
Elizabeth's reverie. "She's phoned?"

A day after the viewing, Detective Thronson had phoned. And another time or two since. Oh, yes, Elizabeth had taken several calls
from the police and none of them had been comfortable.

Barbara was glaring at her, her lips twisted again in disapproval.

"Why don't you call the police yourself?" Elizabeth suggested and
took another sip of wine. She was tired of the badgering and second-
guessing. "Talk to Detective Thronson."

Barbara considered, eyes narrowing. "Maybe I will."

"Good."

Unfortunately, the conversation wasn't finished. Barbara asked,
"So who was the woman Court was with again?"

"Her name was Whitney Bellhard."

"Why was she in the car?"

Elizabeth lifted a shoulder and finished off the wine. She didn't want to talk about this. Not now and probably not ever, at least not with Barbara.

"Well, it's all very suspicious and didn't I hear something about them racing?"

"I mentioned it." Elizabeth had already relayed everything Detective Thronson had told her about the accident to her sister-in-law, but Barbara had been so focused on the funeral, she clearly hadn't paid attention to the details.

Elizabeth told her again, "The detective said that several other drivers thought Court was in some kind of car race, that several witnesses reported a dark SUV weaving in and out of traffic about the same time Court's BMW was doing the same thing. It's just a theory."

"What kind of SUV was it?"

"Barbara, I really don't know."

"Well, was it a big one, or smaller, like your black Ford?"

Elizabeth felt a shiver slide down her spine and she gave Barbara a long look. "I said I don't know," she repeated.

"Did this car hit Court's, maybe?"

"Or Court just lost control."

"He didn't just lose control," Barbara snapped. "That wasn't Court."

Like you knew him so well, Elizabeth thought. But then, neither had she, apparently. "All I know is the investigation's ongoing and no one's located the driver of the SUV that was supposedly involved." She leaned a hip against the counter and let out a sigh. "That's all I know, Barbara. Really."

"When you learn something, call me," Barbara ordered. "Better yet, give me that detective's number. She's with the Irvine Police Department, right? Maybe I will call her."

"Good idea." Elizabeth found Detective Thronson's private number and scribbled it onto a sticky pad she kept in the junk drawer, then ripped the page off and handed it to her sister-in-law. *Have at,* she thought.

Barbara glanced at the number, then folded the paper and stuffed it into an outside pocket of her purse. "I'd better get going. My flight's tomorrow. I should get back to the hotel and frankly I don't see that there's anything else I can do here." She walked to the closet and grabbed her coat and hat.

Elizabeth, trying not to appear to relieved at her departure, opened the front door.

After shrugging into her coat, Barbara started to step across the threshold, but stopped mid-way and slowly pivoted on one heel until she was facing her sister-in-law again.

Elizabeth automatically braced herself and gripped the edge of the door more tightly.

Barbara didn't disappoint. "Let me give you some advice," she said as she adjusted the brim on her black hat. "You might try acting like you care more, or someone could get the wrong idea."

"The wrong idea?"

"You know what I'm talking about."

Of course she did. Elizabeth leaned against the open door. "I wish he were still alive, Barbara," she said as a breath of wind rushed through the palm fronds high overhead. "Believe me."

"Right." Barbara slung the strap of her purse over her shoulder. Lips pursed in disbelief, she added, "You know, you're going to have to be a hell of a lot more convincing than that." With one last condemning glance at Elizabeth, she stepped through the doorway.

Good.

Elizabeth let the door slam shut behind her. A second later, she twisted the lock, securing the deadbolt. Only then did she let go. Sagging against the door and squeezing her eyes shut, she fought tears, not only of sadness but indignation and yes, anger. With an effort, she pushed back her battling emotions, refusing to cry, attempting to quiet her slow-burning rage, ignoring the pain. Her fists balled at her sides, but she wouldn't let the flood of emotions consume her; she didn't dare allow the passion within her free. It was just too dangerous.

She heard the sound of an engine sparking to life and slowly let out her breath as she stretched her fingers and counted to ten, then twenty. The storm within her passed, thank God, though she knew it was only for the moment.

After peering through the window to see that her sister-in-law truly was gone, she headed back to the kitchen and the bottle of wine still sitting on the end table near her chair. Without a second thought, she poured herself the last glass from the bottle. After taking a calming sip, she rinsed and recycled the bottle, then walked to the wine rack and drew out another of Chardonnay, which she intended to place in the refrigerator to chill. As her fingers curled over the neck her gaze fell onto the bottle of red wine Court had purchased several years earlier. He'd told her he wanted to save it for a special night. "When we have something to celebrate," he'd said with a smile. She'd agreed, glad for his good mood, which had become exceedingly rare in those days.

"Why not?" she asked herself.

Sliding the Chardonnay back into the rack, she pulled out the Merlot, uncorked it and poured herself a healthy glassful. She then dumped out the glass of Chardonnay and took the Merlot to the couch, tucking her bare feet beneath her. Holding her glass, staring at the blood-like color of the wine, she thought about the past few months and the changes those months had wrought. A lot of changes. Despite telling herself she wouldn't slide into the dangerous territory that surrounded the death of Mazie Ferguson, Elizabeth again mulled over the woman's death. So sudden. Like Court's.

Don't go there.

Taking a swallow of the Merlot, she tried to corral those wayward notions. It was not the day—especially after Court's funeral—to run through those disturbing memories again, but she failed, as she always did.

"It's not your fault," she said aloud, her fingers clamped around the glass. "It's *not* your fault."

But her mind and fearful heart refused to listen.

CHAPTER 4

Mazie Ferguson's memorial service had been three months earlier and Elizabeth had felt nearly as dissociated, shocked, and afraid then as she did now. The circumstances of Mazie's death and Court's were different, yet surprisingly similar. They'd both died in car accidents, though Mazie had apparently been driving while under the influence and Court had lost control of his car while stone cold sober.

Elizabeth's throat grew tight and she gulped at the wine, remembering.

As she stood around silent and motionless at the reception afterwards, her hand gripped around a glass of club soda and lime like it was life-giving elixir. She suddenly recognized that she was willing people to die. That it was her fault Mazie was dead, and also Officer Daniels—dubbed Officer Unfriendly—before her. It was impossible, of course. Elizabeth knew it was impossible. But Mazie had died and so had the police officer. Both times it was after Elizabeth had wished them dead.

A couple sales associates in her office and other realty agencies had tried to poach Mazie's clients away even before her body was cold. Though Elizabeth had worked with most of the clients as Mazie's assistant, she was too shattered to put up much of a fight. All she could think about was that somehow, some way, it had been her fault that Mazie had died. At night, she dreamed of the accident, the nightmare crawling through her subconscious. During the day, she struggled with the doubts that plagued her, so profiting from her boss' death was the farthest thing from her mind.

But as it turned out, Mazie's clients were unwilling to give up Elizabeth. They knew her. They trusted her. She worked with them before and after she'd obtained her own real estate license, helping out whenever Mazie needed her, which was fairly often since "Crazy Mazie" as she was dubbed by some of the more envious agents, always seemed to have a million things going at once. So Mazie's clients gravitated to Elizabeth.

She backed away from them, unable to profit from a tragic situation she felt was somehow her fault. She explained that she didn't think it was right for her to be their agent. They doubled and redoubled their efforts to keep her. Maybe they sensed how upset she was and wanted to save her, make her feel better. Maybe they appreciated that she was just generally a nicer person than Mazie. Or, maybe they just didn't want to be fobbed off. Whatever the case, Elizabeth found herself with a plethora of new clients and she was busier than she'd ever been.

The memorial service was on a sunny October day. Elizabeth felt like a Judas and didn't want to go, but there was no way she could say no. She felt physically sick but made herself attend all the same, even though she was certain everyone could read the guilt on her face.

Everyone treated her like she was Mazie's good friend because she'd been her assistant, when in truth, Mazie hadn't even really liked her any more than she liked anyone else. The feeling had been mutual.

At the service, Elizabeth smiled and nodded and accepted condolences she felt she didn't deserve. Eventually, she escaped the claustrophobic hall where the service took place to the reception room at Lemon Tree, an airy restaurant near to the Suncrest Realty offices, a spot where Mazie often met her clients for lunch.

Elizabeth tried to tuck herself into an out of the way corner where she hoped to hide out until she could politely and unobtrusively leave. The only place available was near the back end of the bar, which ended up being right in the middle of the action.

A server plopped down a tray loaded with mini-croissants, wedges of cheddar and Havarti, and wheels of brie cheese right be-

side her, and the appetizers served as a siren's call to the milling crowd. Elizabeth found herself a reluctant focal point as people moved closer to order drinks and grab a small bite. Suncrest's owner had wisely rejected the idea of a hosted bar suggested by one of the dumbest sales associates—dumb because Mazie's blood alcohol had been enough to kill her on its own—and offered food and soft drinks instead. If anyone wanted a drink, they could buy it themselves.

Elizabeth held onto her club soda and tried to move out of her spot, but she was trapped by the crush of people mingling around the bar. Paddle fans swirled overhead, but still the room, filled as it was, seemed close. Stuffy. People dressed in black swarmed around the bar, keeping their voices low. Though Elizabeth would have preferred a glass of wine or two to help dull her senses, she stuck with her soft drink and silently counted the minutes that dragged by until she felt comfortable saying her good-byes.

Elizabeth shook her head at the memories, realizing how similar her feelings were at both services. At Mazie's, she had counted the minutes till she could leave just as she had at Court's funeral. Unwillingly, her thoughts returned to what had happened next at Lemon Tree.

In her corner, she sipped slowly, waiting and trying not to think too hard about how angry she'd been at Mazie, but her mind worried the problem like a dog with a bone. Her last confrontation with her boss had been at the office with the owner of the company. Mazie had cut off a suggestion that Elizabeth had been making and had sneered at it, acting as if Elizabeth were a moron. During the awkward silence that had followed, a malicious gleam had appeared in Mazie's eyes and a slightly satisfied curve had appeared on her full lips. She'd put her underling in her place. Along with a hot wash of embarrassment, Elizabeth had seen red, anger streaming through her bloodstream as she returned to her desk.

You didn't ply her with drinks, *she reminded herself from the corner.* All you did was wish her dead. She drank too much and got behind the wheel. That's what killed her.

But that didn't make sense. Although Mazie certainly liked her vodka tonics, Elizabeth had never seen her have more than one or two at any event, had never witnessed Mazie more than faintly buzzed. The woman was always selling, selling, selling. Inebriation was simply not part of her real estate game plan.

So, how had she gotten so drunk? *Elizabeth asked herself. How? Mazie had apparently been at home before she took off on the wild drive that ended her life.* Had someone been with her, drinking with her? *No one seemed to think so, or at least Elizabeth had never heard that Mazie had been with a companion before her ill-fated launch off the freeway.*

You did it, *her mind accused once more. Elizabeth shook her head, set her drink on the bar, and tried to force her way through the crowd in search of air and elbow room.*

Connie Berker, one of the sharks who'd tried to grab Mazie's clients from the moment of her death, caught her before she could reach the door and escape. "Elizabeth," she called, holding up a hand to stop her as she wended past a crush of bodies. "You're not leaving?"

"I am." Elizabeth kept moving. "I've got a daughter at home."

"Tragic, isn't it?" Connie said, ignoring the fact that Elizabeth had one hand ready to push open the restaurant's side door. "Mazie going airborne like that." She gave a full body shudder.

"Yes, it really is."

"Seems so un-Mazie-like, though, doesn't it? She was always so rigid about everything." Connie scowled into her own glass. "You know, I just can't see her getting sloshy drunk."

"I guess she did, though," Elizabeth said, forcing herself not to steal a glance at the oversized watch on Connie's wrist. She just wanted to leave.

"We're all sorry she's gone. I mean, it's terrible. Truly terrible." Connie made a face, then looked slyly at Elizabeth and whispered, "But, let's face it. We all know Mazie was a total bitch."

Elizabeth's heart started pounding a heavy beat. "Well . . ."

"She was sure hard on you," Connie went on as if sensing the protest forming on Elizabeth's lips. "Everyone saw it, but I guess you were smart to hang in there. Get your real estate license. Handle her clients. Never let her get to you."

Elizabeth made a noncommittal sound even though Connie had been wrong on that score. Hatchet-faced Mazie had definitely got-ten to Elizabeth more than once. The older real estate agent would smile warmly at her clients, then, as soon their backs were turned, she'd bare her teeth and snarl invectives at any and all coworkers she thought had screwed her in some way—and she always thought she'd been screwed in some way.

As Connie floated away, waving to another colleague, Elizabeth pushed the door open and left the restaurant.

Elizabeth didn't move from the chair facing the window. Not wanting to think about Court or her marriage, she let more memo-ries of Mazie flood her brain.

Mazie believed her younger assistant was trying to usurp her clients, which made helping her a double-edged sword. Though Mazie needed someone to run interference for her, she was highly suspicious of anyone who did, certain they were just humoring her while they tried to steal her clients.

Elizabeth was attempting to help a woman as demanding as she was rich, but Mazie had the idea that Elizabeth was trying to poach on the woman and the potential sale.

"Don't think I don't know what you're doing," she warned, her black eyes boring into Elizabeth.

"I'm not doing anything," Elizabeth answered carefully, sensing Mazie was about to erupt.

Somewhere in her fifties, Mazie always told people she was in her mid-forties and was able to pull it off owing to hours at the gym that kept her thin and tough as rawhide. The fact that Elizabeth was in her mid-twenties grated on Mazie who always assessed everyone around her as competition, whether real or imagined. She glared at Elizabeth as if she were deliberately goading her. "You met with the Sorensons when I wasn't here," she accused.

"They asked where you were. They came to the office to see you, but you weren't here."

"I already had another appointment!" Mazie practically shouted. "I can't be in two places at the same time!"

"I said you would be back in the office later."

"You made them wait for me?" She sounded aghast.

"They wanted to, Mazie."

She pointed a bony finger at Elizabeth. "And then you talked to them and talked to them and talked to them. So friendly. They just love you now, don't they?"

Elizabeth didn't answer as her blood pressure rose. She realized that someone had been blabbing to Mazie about the Sorensons, probably Pat, the gossipy receptionist, and selling the older woman a bill of goods about Elizabeth's intentions. "They asked if they could wait, and I said it was okay, that's all," Elizabeth said through her teeth.

"I'm sure."

"If you don't want me to work with them, I won't."

"I don't want you to work with them," Mazie snapped back.

"Then, you're on your own." Elizabeth stalked away, boiling. Die, *she thought.* Disappear. Evaporate. Go away permanently.

Now, Elizabeth shuddered. She set the empty wineglass on the table next to her without realizing it.

The next afternoon she related the story to her Moms Group, though she didn't tell them her childish wish that Mazie die, of course. The moms were sitting on outdoor benches while they watched their kids playing on Bright Day Preschool's outdoor equipment. It was the mothers' custom to convene about the same time every school day and meet with their friends while their kids packed in a last few minutes of playground time before everyone went home.

Deirdre listened to Elizabeth's complaints about Mazie and said, "Old bitches like that create misery and mayhem, and then they die."

Remembering Deirdre's words startled Elizabeth for a moment, they were so prophetic. She realized her glass was empty, poured more Merlot, and took a sip, lost in her memories.

"Hopefully." Vivian made a face and bobbed her ponytail in agreement. "She sounds like a total nightmare."

Elizabeth agreed. "She is *a nightmare."*

Springing to her feet, Vivian called sharply to her daughter, "Lissa, be careful!" The little girl was trying to climb up the slide's ladder on Little Nate's heels, all the while nudging him to move more quickly. "Lissa! Do you hear me?"

From a bench nearby, Jade yelled, "Nate, watch out!"

Elizabeth turned to see Chloe stomp to the ladder, pump her fists onto her hips, and give Lissa a piece of her mind. Unhappily, Lissa backed down, making a mean face at Chloe before racing to the monkey bars.

Jade glanced over at Elizabeth and she knew Jade was thinking. About another time when, from behind a post, Elizabeth had seen Little Nate slip on the jungle gym and get his foot caught, hanging precariously. At Elizabeth's scream of warning, Jade had rescued him in the nick of time before he fell headfirst.

"How did you know?" Jade had asked in wonder.

Elizabeth hadn't been able to come up with a plausible answer. Because there hadn't been one. "I just caught a glimpse," she'd lied to her friend.

Jade's eyebrows had pulled together, puckering her forehead as if she didn't understand, but she'd let it go.

Oblivious to the look Jade sent Elizabeth, Tara said, "Karma will get bullies like Mazie every time." She shaded her eyes with one hand, stood and watched the jungle gym where a group of kids had gathered.

"Maybe," Elizabeth muttered.

"Things'll change. They always do," Jade said. "Just when you think you can't stand it one more minute, something always happens."

Elizabeth wasn't so certain. "I hope you're right. It's a mystery how Mazie ever makes a sale. She's like Jekyll and Hyde, nice to the client but god-awful to anyone else. Before I got my license, I was seriously thinking about quitting."

Deirdre's green eyes were serious. She warned, "You do that and she wins. End of story."

"That's right," Vivian agreed.

"I just meant quitting the agency," Elizabeth had assured them, "not giving up on real estate altogether." That was a bit of a lie. In truth she'd been close to taking a break from her career to concen-

trate on home life as things were rocky with Court. Make that rock-ier. Their marriage had never run smoothly.

At a meeting with the half dozen other moms who belonged to the larger Moms Group, Tara had cornered Elizabeth in the conference room of the preschool. "So how's it going with Crazy Mazie?" she asked.

Elizabeth mentally kicked herself for ever mentioning the nick-name.

Several other of the women tuned in, all wanting to know what had happened at the real estate agency.

More than a little miffed at Tara for bringing up the sensitive subject in front of everyone, Elizabeth downplayed her answer. "Surprisingly a lot better," she said with a smile she didn't feel. "She's been a lot nicer lately, so maybe we were just going through a rough patch."

Everyone except Jade seemed to buy her story. She regarded Elizabeth with questions in her dark eyes, but the conversation turned back to the next preschool function—"fun night"—a type of carni-val aimed at securing more donations from the parents and nearby businesses. At least for the moment, the subject of Elizabeth's relationship with her boss was over.

Six days later, Mazie was dead.

According to all reports, Mazie had driven her car off I-55, her Mercedes going airborne to crash on the road below. She'd been rushed to a local hospital, but succumbed to her injuries a few days later. Mazie had never awakened from her coma.

Elizabeth was shocked, sick, and disbelieving. She immediately thought back to her conversation with her friends in the Moms Group and cringed inside.

When Vivian called later and whispered, "Oh, my God, Eliza-beth! Oh, my God," Elizabeth held her phone in a white knuckled grasp and tried with all her might to pretend that she thought it was just an odd and sobering coincidence.

"It's . . . it's horrible," she whispered. "I can't believe it." Staring at her pale reflection in the window over her kitchen sink, she added, "I guess, bad things just happen." But she'd hung up shaken.

And bad things happen when you wish them so.

The thought made her nearly throw up in the sink. She splashed water over her face and somehow pulled herself together as she mentally repeated the mantra it's not your fault. It's not your fault.

When her other friends called, she dealt with them as she had with Vivian, whispering words of shock and horror as those emotions were real.

As she sipped Court's "special" Merlot, Elizabeth stared out the window. Neither she nor Jade had brought up the jungle gym incident again, but sometimes she felt Jade's gaze lingering on her as if puzzling her out, questions forming in her mind. Jade had half-guessed about Elizabeth's gift of foreshadowing.

But she hadn't a clue about Elizabeth's gift for causing death.

Do bad things just happen? Elizabeth wondered. "Bad things like *that?* Did they? If so, what about Officer Unfriendly?" she whispered.

She watched the storm clouds scud across the sky and felt the same coldness inside that had enveloped her the first time someone had died and she'd wondered if she'd been at fault. Impossible, right? Crazy. And yet eight months earlier . . .

Officer Seth Daniels of the Irvine Police Department pulled her over when she was traveling five miles over the speed limit. Really? Five miles over the speed limit? In southern California? That was hardly worth stopping someone. Elizabeth almost laughed. It felt like it was breaking some unspoken, sacred code to pull her over for such a minor offense.

She said as much to him as he stood near the open window of her car, traffic moving behind him. Her comments brought a cold smile to his face that was a little spooky. When her easy, half-joking persona failed to get results, she tried reasoning with him, but he just gazed down at her implacably, that icy grin never quite leaving his face, as if he were enjoying the show.

She got the feeling he savored her discomfort, so she dropped all pretense of friendliness and said, "You're kidding, right? Five miles over?"

"Not kidding," he responded, writing her up a four-hundred dollar ticket and handing it to her with a flourish.

What an asshole! *Her blood pressure hit the roof. Feeling her lips compress, she snatched the ticket from his hand and threw it to the passenger seat, never taking her eyes off the officer.*

Daniels, a man in his late forties with male pattern baldness marching over his scalp and hiding beneath his hat, said with a faint sneer, "You beautiful women think you can get anything you want."

Elizabeth almost ripped up the ticket in front of him but had somehow managed to hold herself back; he would've probably arrested her on the spot.

Shaking his head, he added, "Have a nice day," and headed back to his cruiser.

All the way home she fumed, her head filled with vile forms of retribution for Officer Unfriendly.

When she went to court to have the amount of the ticket reduced, there he was, still smirking. She forced herself to make eye contact with him, giving him her coldest glare packed with negative thoughts, the uppermost one being she wished he would just disappear forever.

She got that wish.

A month to the day of her traffic court appointment, he pulled someone over who then yanked out a gun and shot him straight through the heart. Just hauled off and popped him. The killer then sped away. Did the deed, drove off, zigzagging through side streets, the stolen plates that had been on the vehicle tossed onto the road, no fingerprints recovered. No arrests had been made to date, though the crime had gotten plenty of press and the police were determined to catch the cop-killer.

Elizabeth, standing at the kitchen island, nearly collapsed as she read about Daniels' death in the newspaper that Court tossed aside before going to work one morning. The headline jumped out at her and she went into a state of shock, her heart galumphing once, then pounding so hard in her ears she could scarcely hear.

She had trouble reading the article as her hands were shaking violently and she was forced to drop the pages onto the counter where she steadied herself. Her breath came in fast gulps while her vision telescoped down to a black dot.

You wished him dead and now he is!

She didn't quite pass out, but almost. She told herself it was a co-

incidence, that was all—nothing more sinister than an officer pulling over the wrong person, a maniac with a gun. . . .

Elizabeth bit her lip and set her wine on the side table. Officer Daniels's death was long *before* Mazie's accident, which had shaken her further. She'd tried to convince herself it was another situation that had nothing to do with her. She'd almost believed it.

Until Court's death.

What were the chances? Three people she'd wished would disappear had died. It just couldn't be coincidence.

I'm normal, she told herself as she had so many times over the last year. *I'm completely normal. I lead a normal suburban life.*

Except now I'm a single mother because my husband's dead.

Suddenly tired, she got up from the couch, took her glass to the kitchen, rinsed it out, and put it in the dishwasher. She glanced down to the pile of papers on the section of counter that she used as her catchall. Detective Thronson's name and number lay on a piece of paper atop the various recipe books, coupons, junk mail, and bills strewn in an untidy pile.

She ignored it all and put a call in to Tara as she opened the refrigerator door and peered inside, hoping to spy anything within that nutrient-bleak interior that she could pull together and create some kind of good meal. Impossible. She'd have to come up with plan B.

"Hey," Tara answered. "How's it going?"

"Fine, I guess. Or fine as it can be. My sister-in-law left and I think I'd better go grocery shopping or Chloe and I might just starve. Okay if I pick her up on the way back?"

"Perfect," Tara said. "Everyone's getting along."

Elizabeth smiled for the first time that day. "A miracle."

"Yeah, it might not last long."

"I'll hurry," she promised, clicking off her phone, then snatching up her keys and purse and heading to the garage. As she climbed behind the wheel of her black Ford Escape, she hesitated, key about to be jammed into the ignition. *What had Barbara asked?* If the SUV that had been reported to have been racing with Court's BMW had been dark, like Elizabeth's. *Another coincidence?* The car that maybe had been playing some kind of freeway tag with Court was similar to hers?

A drip of cold fear slid down Elizabeth's spine.

Don't even go there.

Setting her jaw, she jammed the key into the ignition and switched on the engine. As the garage door lifted and the gray light of the afternoon spilled into the gloomy interior, she told herself that she was being paranoid, searching for connections that probably didn't even exist.

She pulled out of the drive and hit the automatic switch, closing the garage. Staring into the leaden sky, she couldn't shake the feeling that something bad was happening to her. Something very, very bad.

CHAPTER 5

January in southern California was a revelation to Ravinia Rutledge. The weather was usually sunny and warm in the dead of winter. Even when it rained, it wasn't really cold, although at night the temperature could sure as hell plummet; she knew that from sleeping outside more times than not.

It had rained hard the night before and she'd taken refuge in a local Starbucks, sipping hot coffee until the storm had passed.

The morning had dawned bright and clear with white fluffy clouds floating across the blue sky. As she sat with her back propped against a palm tree in Santa Monica, she thought about her long journey from Oregon and the comparative safety of the locked gates of Siren Song, her home near Deception Bay. It had been weeks since she'd started on the quest that led her ever southward, but she hoped she would finally find her cousin, Elizabeth Gaines, the reason she'd started the journey in the first place.

Ravinia suspected the good weather wouldn't last. She'd learned January was the rainy month in southern California. "The rainiest month," one know-it-all type SoCal-er had declared when he'd realized she was from Oregon and had never been out of the state before.

She hadn't even been five miles from Deception Bay before this trip, but she'd declined telling him that as it would have been another reason for him to go off on the wonders of California. She liked the state, but Mr. SoCal kind of pissed her off with his better-than-thou, know-it-all attitude. He was just someone she'd met on the train and they'd parted as soon as they'd reached the Los Angeles station, but she'd had hours of listening to him.

She'd arrived in downtown Los Angeles about four days earlier, having come from the San Francisco area. Though she was careful with her cash, she'd seen no way to get to Los Angeles by hitchhiking unless she worked her way down Highway 101 and she was pretty sure that would take forever, time she didn't have. Instead, she'd caught a train that had taken her across the California countryside, through Modesto and Stockton, then into Bakersfield, where she'd been transferred to a bus, which finished the trip and dropped her off at the Los Angeles train station, a bizarre fact, but there it was. When she'd asked why the train didn't go all the way from San Francisco to LA, Mr. SoCal had quipped, "This is the land of cars. Get used to it."

If she'd had a driver's license, she might have taken his advice. As it was, she was a slave to public transportation and she'd found San Francisco a whole lot more workable in that department than LA. But then, she was altogether new to traveling, having spent the greater part of her nineteen years inside the gates of Siren Song, the lodge located outside the town of Deception Bay on the Oregon coast, where she'd been hidden from the world along with her sisters. Her Aunt Catherine, the woman who'd chosen their particular way of life, had always claimed it was to protect them from the evil forces that had destroyed their mother, Catherine's sister, Mary, whom Ravinia didn't even remember. Ravinia had rebelled against the restrictions and had always felt that the whole *keep us all safe* mantra was a manifestation of Aunt Catherine's own fears and basic weirdness . . . well, until recently. Now she knew there really were evil forces at work. Evil people, anyway . . . and that's why it was urgent that she find Elizabeth and warn her, make sure she wasn't being targeted by those who wanted to harm their kith and kin.

In San Francisco, she'd searched for her cousin's adoptive parents, the Ralph Gainses, who'd lived around the Bay Area. That was all the information she'd had to go on except for what they'd named their new daughter—Elizabeth.

Ravinia had managed to track down two Ralph Gaineses, both in San Francisco, and a third in Sausalito, but none of the men were or had been married to a woman named Joy. Frustrated, Ravinia had thought she'd come to another dead end, but her luck turned.

When she'd finally connected with Sausalito Ralph Gaines, he'd told her, "Might be the couple you're looking for moved to Santa Monica. I had a confusion once over a prescription at my pharmacy. They kept calling me and saying Joy's prescription was ready. I didn't know who Joy was, so I went on down there and said I was Ralph Gaines and what the hell were they talking about. They asked for ID and then handed over Joy's prescription. Had a different phone number on it. Don't know how they mixed it up with mine. So, I wrote down the number, handed 'em back the bottle, then later on I called up this Joy and told her she'd better make sure those fools down there didn't hand out the wrong pills to any Tom, Dick, or Harry. She thanked me and said it wasn't gonna matter as they were moving to Santa Monica. Pretty sure that's where she said."

Ravinia had been jubilant. She'd thanked him and then booked passage on the next train south, which was scheduled for the following morning.

She'd boarded bright and early while a thick layer of fog cloaked the bay and filtered through the city streets. Settling down in her seat, she'd closed her eyes, intending to rest, but she'd inadvertently picked up threads of surrounding conversations. Through half-closed lids, she'd watched the twenty-something college kid work his smartphone to play games, text, and connect to the Internet. Though she'd only briefly used that kind of high-tech equipment on her unsupervised forays outside Siren Song, she had the kind of mind that understood technology. She knew deep down that she could use a tablet or a phone to help in her search. So as the kid in his hoodie and baggy jeans rapidly thumbed the phone's tiny keyboard, she started thinking that she needed a smartphone as well.

In Los Angeles, the winter sun was pale and the layer of heavy fog she'd witnessed in San Francisco had been replaced by a higher, thin tier of smog that gave a slightly yellow hue to the city, at least in Ravinia's eyes. She hadn't wasted time, but had made her way to Santa Monica, a community west of LA where the air was clear, the breeze blowing off the ocean cool and fresh, the beach long and white, and the place where she'd hoped to locate her cousin.

To save money, she'd been sleeping in the park on a ridge that looked out over the Pacific. She wasn't alone, as the park was used for the same purpose by the homeless, men mostly, who cradled their heads on rolled up clothes and slept on the grass. Nothing much disturbed them until they wanted to be disturbed, not the early morning joggers, tourists carrying coffee cups, or anyone else who might meander along the path that ran along the cliff's edge.

The warm days turned to cold nights and Ravinia slept in three pairs of pants, a long-sleeved T-shirt, sweatshirt, and jacket. She always kept her back toward a tree and a hand on her knife, just in case she was accosted, but so far she'd been left alone.

There had been a minor incident when she'd first headed out, walking along the road. A car had stopped in the growing dusk on a stretch of highway south of Tillamook. As one man sat behind the wheel of his idling vehicle, the bruiser in the passenger seat had opened his door and stepped a foot on the gravel shoulder as if intent on forcing her into the vehicle when she refused their offer for a ride. She'd sensed they meant her harm and wondered if she was going to have to use her knife. Fingering the blade, she'd tensed then suddenly felt a wraith move up beside her. In that instant, her would-be attacker backed up, scrambling into the car. The driver had hit the gas, and they'd burned away as if the hounds of hell were on their heels.

She'd turned her head and spied the wolf. Standing near her on the side of the road, the wind ruffling its fur, its yellow eyes following the vehicle as it had disappeared.

Unafraid, Ravinia had asked in a whisper, "Friend or foe?"

The shaggy animal had only turned and padded away into the forest. She thought she'd caught sight of him later as she'd made her way to a motel where she'd taken refuge for the night, but she hadn't been certain.

Sitting nearly a thousand miles away, she wondered if the wolf had even existed. That eerie encounter had been weeks ago and she hadn't seen him since. She'd been told there were no wolves in the Coast Range. She would have said the same if she hadn't *seen* him, but she was beginning to wonder if the beast had been in her mind after all, a specter she created when she needed help.

Those two men at the side of the road near Tillamook had certainly blasted away in their car as if they'd seen something that scared the liver out of them.

Now, she got to her feet, dusted herself off, then undid the dark blond braid that hung just past her shoulders, raked her fingers through her wavy hair, then quickly replaited it. After stripping off the top two layers of sweats, she shoved them into her backpack, stretched, then hiked the straps of her backpack over her shoulders and started walking. She wore sneakers—a new purchase since she'd arrived in Santa Monica—her favorite olive green dungarees, one of her three long-sleeved T-shirts, and a black jacket over a gray sweat-shirt. As the day wore on and the sun became warmer, she would shed more garments.

She headed toward the nearest Starbucks, thinking about Aunt Catherine. Her aunt needed to be brought up to date. The problem was, communication was nearly impossible. Aunt Catherine didn't have a cell phone and there was no land line at the lodge. The disposable cell Ravinia had purchased wasn't much of a help. The older woman only called when she went into Deception Bay to use the phone.

Pain in the ass, Ravinia thought. It had been one of the favorite expressions of the twenty-something women she'd sat behind on the train, and she'd adopted it as her own.

The Santa Monica Pier with its iconic Ferris wheel was up ahead, but Ravinia turned away from it, crossing Ocean Avenue, having to skirt a curly-haired little dog straining against a leash and the woman holding tightly onto that leash with a death grip. The woman wore tight short-shorts and a long sleeved hoodie that was cropped below her breasts, leaving her abdomen bare. Her outfit was a far cry from the long, print dresses Aunt Catherine had made all of Mary's children wear after Mary herself had lost her wits and somehow opened Pandora's Box to all manner of ills, putting the residents of Siren Song in direct peril.

As Ravinia passed by the woman, who held a cell phone to her ear with her free hand, she caught information about Botox, another one of the twenty-something's topics. LA had a whole different language from Deception Bay where the main topics were the weather, fishing, crabbing, and well, her odd family.

For most of her life, Ravinia had believed Aunt Catherine was either just plain wrong or paranoid about the dangers to her and her sisters. Maybe a little of both. Recent events had caused her to re-assess, and she thought there was a very good chance her aunt wasn't completely off base. It was true that Ravinia and her sisters had been born with certain traits—supernatural "gifts"—that defied explanation unless the strangeness of their ancestors was known and believed in. Those gifts, Aunt Catherine had insisted, put them all in danger, and Ravinia now accepted that as truth.

The Starbucks she'd visited during yesterday's rain shower was two blocks ahead. Though she was watching her cash pretty closely, money Aunt Catherine had given her for her mission, Ravinia found if she started off with a muffin and a coffee she could go nearly all day. Besides, coffee shops offered up a steady stream of people who were sources of information. Once in a while, when eavesdropping didn't help, she could ask a patron to look up something for her and learn a bit about the Internet and her surroundings. She wasn't always lucky in this regard, but occasionally someone would take the time to show her how to research different kinds of information.

Ravinia had discovered fairly quickly how little she knew of life outside the gates of the compound. Her knowledge was eclectic, learned through lessons from Aunt Catherine, from the old television that they were allowed to occasionally watch, from the few townspeople she knew around Deception Bay, and from people she'd recently met on her journey south. But the more she learned, the more she needed to know. She was like a visitor from another planet, observing the ways of the beings who populated a foreign world.

As she entered the coffee shop and smelled the rich scent of the brewing coffee mingled with the aroma of sweet pastries, her stomach growled. In reaching into her pocket for her money, she noticed the dirt around the edges of her fingernails. What she needed was a shower. Her last one had been in a rundown motel that was way more money than she'd wanted to spend for a night just before she took the train south. Lodging sure wasn't cheap, and that's why she'd resorted to sleeping in the park. She needed to re-up the minutes on her phone, too, or when Aunt Catherine finally deigned to phone, she might get cut off in the middle of the call.

Pain in the ass.

Ravinia stepped out of line, walked to the rest room, and once inside, used the toilet, then stood in front of the mirror. Not only did she scrub her hands until any bit of dirt beneath her fingernails had washed away, but she also washed her face, ignoring the fact that someone angrily rattled the locked door handle. *You can just wait,* she thought, gazing critically at her reflection. Her hair needed washing, her clothes should be laundered, and all in all, she had to find a place to stay, despite the state of her finances. And she needed help. Searching on her own was taking too long.

When she dried her face and hands and finally left the restroom, a woman in sunglasses and a grim face shot her a disparaging glance before hurrying inside and locking the door.

Ravinia walked to the back of the ever-growing line to order coffee, taking her place behind a woman in black leggings and a long khaki tunic who, just like everyone else, was studying text messages on her phone. Once again Ravinia considered her options for food. A pastry? Breakfast sandwich? Just a cookie or piece of coffee cake? Everything looked good as she was flat out hungry.

Hunger was becoming part of her lifestyle, she reflected dourly, as she was counting her pennies. The train trip had cost her a lot more than she'd expected, but there it was. At least she'd learned a few things from the people on the train with her—the college student with the smart phone, the women she'd sat behind, and then Mr. SoCal.

The women had given her a lot of information, she reflected. Not all of it worthwhile, but definitely interesting. It was when she'd learned that their ultimate destination was also Santa Monica that she'd tuned in. Hour upon hour, they'd discussed the best bars and restaurants, the best places to shop for clothes, even the best street in both of their biased opinions—Montana. They couldn't live without a daily trip to Starbucks, and standing in line at coffee shops was the best way to meet interesting people and guys with good jobs. Finding these same guys with good jobs at bars was iffy. Men in line at a coffee shop were a much better bet, but that didn't mean that you stopped going to bars. You just had to know what you were looking for.

Well, huh.

Halfway through the trip was when Mr. SoCal had boarded the train and seated himself across from Ravinia. His gaze had studied her with frank admiration and she'd wondered what the hell he was seeing because she was in her dungarees and sweatshirt and well, it had been a while since that last shower. But he was in long shorts and a sweatshirt, too, and he'd stuck out his hand and introduced himself as Doug.

With nothing else to do in the slow-moving line, Ravinia's thoughts wandered back to the man she'd named SoCal and her life since arriving in Santa Monica.

He wanted to know all about her, but all she told him was that she was on a trip to visit her cousin. Mr. SoCal—Ravinia just couldn't think of him as Doug—told her he worked at a restaurant hotspot in Santa Monica as a bartender, though mostly it sounded like he was a kind of beach bum. He shared a place with two other guys who also worked in the restaurant business. By the way he'd talked, she sensed every night was a party . . . and maybe every day.

"Where's your cousin live?" he asked her. "You got a ride, or do you need a lift?"

"I might," she said, then changed the subject quickly before he could ask for an address. No way she was giving out more information than she had to. Until she knew whom to trust, she was sharing as little as possible, and one thing she knew for sure was that she wasn't going to tell anyone about her and her sisters' "gifts". Aunt Catherine had pounded that into her head before she left, though that was a "no brainer" as Mr. SoCal would say. The people around Deception Bay who knew skirted the women of Siren Song. Besides, her own gift wasn't all that spectacular—she could look into the heart of a person and know if they were good or bad.

She looked inside Mr. SoCal as a matter of course and got a squishy feeling, like he was made of jelly instead of stone, weak and prone to take the easiest path rather than to fight for what he wanted. Not criminal qualities, just not worth knowing.

She left Mr. SoCal and the college student and the twenty-somethings at the train station, then went in search of transportation to Santa Monica. Mr. SoCal had a car, and the twenty-somethings took a taxi, but the price was too prohibitive so Ravinia eventually learned which bus would take her toward the ocean.

Once she was inside the Santa Monica city limits, she was able to ride a Big Blue Bus and figured out how to maneuver her way around the city without having to walk everywhere. She found a place to sleep in the park and hung out at Starbucks. Her investigation was stalled in her search for Ralph and Joy Gaines because she didn't have a smartphone or a driver's license, two very important pieces. She tried looking up their names in telephone books, but that hadn't worked out. Few phone booths were left and very few of them had books that hadn't been ripped off. The best way to find out information was the Internet, but she had no way of accessing it just yet.

"*But soon,*" she told herself as the line moved forward a bit.

The danger to Elizabeth was real enough, as it was to the rest of them. But Elizabeth had no concept of what was coming for her. It was Ravinia's job to inform her and find a way to keep her safe.

CHAPTER 6

"Can I help you?" a cheery voice asked.

Ravinia was pulled out of her reverie and found herself at the register where a girl about her age with a broad smile was ready to take her order. The woman in line ahead of her was still texting as she moved farther along the counter to the spot where she'd pick up her order.

"Yeah," Ravinia answered, nodding and finally making a decision. "Sure. How about black coffee, and uh, maybe a bran muffin and water . . . not bottled?"

To hell with bottled water. Why pay when Starbucks would give her a plastic cup filled with water for free? The whole bottled water phenomenon was beyond her. Siren Song lodge had a well, as did most of the Foothillers, the descendants of mainly Chinook Indians who lived in an unincorporated town nearby, and everybody just drank out of the tap.

Not so in Santa Monica.

After carefully meting out her change, Ravinia carried her drinks and muffin through the crowded seating area where she found a small table that had been recently vacated. Listening to people's conversations had proven interesting and sometimes even fruitful, but only a man reading a newspaper was seated nearby. Pulling her phone from her pocket, she made a face, realizing it was nearly out of battery power. She needed to get a room to take a shower and charge up the phone, then add more minutes unless she could find a way to get a smartphone.

She sipped from her coffee and made short work of her muffin. Still hungry, she considered getting in line again, but decided to wait.

Glancing around the room, she marveled a bit that she was so far from home, a world away from the cosseted life she'd known.

Of course, she'd been the one to leave. She'd always been the most vocal and outwardly mutinous of her family. Maybe it was because she was the youngest of Mary's daughters, at least the youngest living at the lodge. But she wasn't the only one who had been outside the gates. Some of her sisters had escaped by being purposely adopted before the gates slammed shut, and the boys Mary had given birth to were immediately dispensed with by Mary herself, adopted to families unknown . . . at least unknown to Ravinia.

The only boy allowed to stay had been Nathaniel, Ravinia had heard, a son who'd never been right, apparently. He was long dead.

Ravinia wondered about that, but then, she'd wondered about a lot of things. What was truth? What was fiction? Why all the secrets?

According to Aunt Catherine, Ravinia's mother had given herself to man after man, but she hadn't trusted her own boys, hadn't wanted to raise sons. Maybe there was a reason for that. Maybe there was a bad seed within those male offspring. Maybe Mary had been protecting her daughters. Certainly there had been evidence enough of evil lying in wait, something dark and insidious and wanton. Ravinia's skin crawled with memories of sensing *his* presence.

So, because of Ravinia's rebelliousness, her experiences beyond the wall, and her ability to sense the evil ones, Catherine had reluctantly sent her on her mission. To save Catherine's only daughter. The girl known as Elizabeth Gaines who had been adopted out as a baby.

"Let me know she's all right and keep her safe," Catherine had said to Ravinia as she'd sent her on her quest.

Keep her safe.

Aunt Catherine had her reasons. Good reasons. Reasons Ravinia understood better than she ever had. One of them was Ravinia's half brother, one of the boys Mary had dispensed with, who'd returned intent on revenge. That he was currently missing was no reason to feel safe. Aunt Catherine believed he was just lying in wait, planning another attack on her family. That's why she'd sent Ravinia to find Elizabeth and at least warn her.

Ravinia took another swallow of her coffee, strong but cooling as her gaze wondered around the glass walls of the coffee shop and she thought about how she'd actually come to leave her home.

She'd been thinking of getting out of Siren Song for some time— the walls were too high, Catherine's world too archaic, the rules too restrictive.

Her aunt gleaned what was on Ravinia's mind. "When are you leaving?" Aunt Catherine asked as they stood in front of the fire at the lodge. For once they were alone, her sisters in their rooms for the night.

"Leaving? What? For good? I'm not sure I am. What are you saying?" Ravinia responded, slightly alarmed that her half-formed plans to leave Siren Song had been thrown on the table. She intended to get away but hadn't settled on a date, wasn't certain when it would be.

"Cassandra's seen you on the road with a friend. I'm asking you, when are you planning to go?"

Cassandra was Ravinia's sister who had a knack for seeing into the future—her "gift." And the hell of it was, as usual, Cassandra wasn't wrong. Ravinia had met someone. And she really did want to leave the lodge behind her, so she impulsively said, "Tomorrow," finalizing her plans just that fast.

Aunt Catherine answered in her pragmatic way, "Then you'll need some money," and walked to her desk and opened a strong box within. She returned with a roll of bills that damn near blew Ravinia away. "Be wise and frugal," Aunt Catherine cautioned, blinking as if tears were forming behind her eyes. "And most of all, be safe."

"I will," Ravinia promised and tucked the money into her bra.

She shook her head to clear the memories and touched the money belt around her waist that she'd purchased during those weeks in northern California. The friend Cassandra had seen her with hadn't caught up with her again, but Ravinia had the sense that he'd gone north when she'd gone south, first to the San Francisco area, finally landing in Santa Monica. She looked at her phone again, realizing that she had burned up the minutes talking to Aunt Catherine who called her on an irregular basis. She wished her aunt would come out of the dark ages, for crying out loud, but she supposed she should be happy that Aunt Catherine knew how to drive a car. Ravinia was determined to get her license at the first opportunity, but that would have to be after she found Elizabeth . . . and how was she going to do that without an Internet connection? And how was she supposed to get that when she had no credit history? It was a phrase she'd learned when she'd looked into getting her own phone,

She glanced around the dining area again. Nearly everyone in the chairs was using their smartphones in some capacity. Probably connecting to the Internet.

Cash was great, but to really think about getting a smartphone with a phone number she could definitely use credit history. But before she could get credit history, she needed a credit card or some record of payments, like to utilities. The truth was, no one wanted to help her all that much after they learned she was a blank slate. She needed an address for billing, which she didn't possess.

She'd learned all this when she was in the San Francisco area and she'd made the mistake of telling SoCal who'd laughed at her and declared that she must have been living under a rock, which kind of pissed her off. He'd also told her that she must have been "living off the grid" her whole life because she was definitely "under the radar." She'd never heard either of those phrases before, but she'd gleaned that she was an oddity and *that* she'd already known, if for different reasons from those Mr. SoCal realized.

Good riddance that she'd left him at the train station.

Ravinia sipped her coffee and contemplated her next move.

Coffee long gone, she was sitting in the same spot an hour later, still undecided, when a woman somewhere in her forties came hurrying into the coffee shop, bypassing the line.

Frantic, she glanced around the room, zeroed in on the older dude at a table near Ravinia's. "Thank God." The woman made a beeline to the table with the guy who, by the looks of him, was old enough to be her father.

He half-rose from his seat to give her a quick kiss, and then she launched in. "Oh, my God, I'm so glad you're still here. It's just hell with Kayla right now. I could kill her!"

He sighed and picked up his cup. "What happened?"

"Ran away again. Just like I knew she would. Everybody said the teenage years would be terrible, but I had no idea . . . oh, Jesus! Last weekend she snuck out the window to be with her friends. When I discovered her missing, I tried to connect with the friends I knew about, the one's I had numbers for. I called and called. The kids. Their parents. I went to their houses, but no one had seen her. Or at least that's what they said. But they lie. They *all* lie. Thick as thieves those damned teens. Couldn't they see how frantic I was? I mean, I was out of my mind. Literally out of my mind. I was about to start going to hospitals or the police." Reliving her ordeal, the woman was talking faster and faster, her voice rising.

The older guy patted the air, silently reminding her to slow down and maybe not talk so loudly.

But the woman was too wound up to put on the brakes. She barreled on, "I had to hire a private investigator to find her. And when he located her, it didn't matter." The woman was pulling a face and shaking her head. "Kayla still wouldn't come home with me."

The guy looked at her as if she were crazy. "You're kidding."

"Oh, no, I'm not."

"But to hire a private detective?"

"I *had* to. I couldn't find her. Jesus, didn't you hear me?" she accused, then took a deep breath before going on. "This friend of mine, Linda? Her son's got a real drug problem and was missing for weeks, and she called this guy and he found him. The guy's an ex-cop and anyway, he did whatever it is those guys do, and found Kayla right away."

"How?"

"I don't know." She flipped a hand upward toward the ceiling. "And I don't care. He specializes in runaways and family problems. Doesn't matter how he tracked her down. What's important is that Kayla's home and I'm trying to get through to her—which is damn near impossible." Rolling her eyes, she added, "It feels like I don't know her anymore. It's like living with a stranger. One with a really bad attitude."

"Maybe I shouldn't be moving in right now."

"Oh, no." She reached a hand out and grabbed his arm. "That's just what she's aiming for. You have to move in or she'll think she's won and then it'll be even worse. We're moving your stuff at the end of the month and Kayla's just going to have to get used to it!"

Ravinia realized that the older guy was a romantic interest for the younger woman, which made her give him a second look. He was kind of homely with big ears and thinning hair and glasses that sat on the end of his nose. But his clothes looked expensive. *Money,* she decided.

The guy didn't appear all that convinced about the potential move. He took a final swallow from his paper coffee cup, then crushed it, and folded his paper. "Who'd you hire?"

"The private investigator?" Her eyebrows shot up and he nodded. "Rex Kingston of Kingston Investigations."

"Was it expensive?"

She shrugged. Tipped her hand back and forth. Maybe yes. Maybe no. "I guess I should've just waited for her to come home," she said anxiously as if sensing the guy's disapproval. On the heels of that thought, she said, "But it wouldn't have worked. She would have never come back. That's the problem."

Scooting his chair back a bit, he tossed his empty cup into the trash.

In that moment, Ravinia peered into his heart and saw that he wasn't really all that much of a winner. Maybe didn't even have the amount of money he'd led the younger woman to believe.

As if he sensed her perusal, he turned to stare right at her, but Ravinia let her gaze slide away as if she were lost in thought about something else.

Sometimes people sensed something happening when she was checking them out, felt some kind of tingle or had a glimmer of insight, though they generally didn't get it and certainly didn't look at her to be the cause.

The man stood, grabbed his newspaper, and tucked it under his arm.

"You leaving?" the woman asked.

"I've got to get to work." He glanced away a second and cleared his throat. "Have you thought about sending Kayla to her father?" he suggested as she reluctantly stood up as well.

"God, no." She gazed at him as if he were from another planet. "You know that would be a disaster!" Then, after a pause, she said, "Wait a second. What are you saying?"

The man slid a look toward Ravinia, clearly uncomfortable having her close enough to hear every word. Tucking his hand around the woman's elbow he led her purposefully toward the door.

As inconspicuously as possible, Ravinia followed, wandering through the tables, even going so far as to pretend interest in the various mugs, carafes, and bags of coffee on display tables when she was really hoping to hear more about Kingston Investigations. It didn't work. The man was too aware that she was eavesdropping. He opened the door for his companion who was running on about Kayla and her father, who was an asshole, an *asshole,* and there was no way she could trust him to be *any kind of father*.

As the glass door started to close, Ravinia slipped outside and watched the couple walk across the parking area to separate vehicles. She didn't give their continuing relationship much hope, unless the rebellious teen Kayla was actually out of the house.

Ravinia had been a runaway herself, for very different reasons. She knew that once anybody thought their living situation was untenable, they weren't going to stick around.

The man drove off in a older Cadillac, the woman in a compact.

Ravinia turned her attention away from them and back to the crowd of coffee-drinking Internet surfers lounging inside and at a few exterior umbrella tables positioned near the building. It was slightly warmer, the temperature rising a little, the clouds lightening a bit. On a bench near the door, her forgotten drink at her feet, a teenaged girl was texting like mad. Next to her, a boy about the same age was into his phone, too, probably playing some game.

God, she wanted one of those phones, just for a few minutes.

If only I had Google, she thought, taking a recently vacated chair.

Cooing loudly enough to be heard over the morning rush of traffic, a pigeon pecked its way near her table and she absently brushed off crumbs from a previous customer.

She wanted to look up Kingston Investigations immediately and see if the office was anywhere near Santa Monica. She needed help in her mission, and it seemed providential that she'd overheard the people at the next table talking about a private investigator. From the two channels the television at Siren Song had picked up by antenna, she knew what a private investigator was, at least the TV kind. The fact that Rex Kingston had been a policeman first sounded good, like he would know his stuff.

The trouble was, it also sounded as if he might be kind of expensive.

Then again, maybe he was the kind of guy who might negotiate with her a little.

She pulled out her disposable phone to find that it was completely dead. She lifted her head and thought about asking one of the other customers if she could borrow their phone, but a quick look around at the serious expressions convinced her that was unlikely. If she were one of them and someone like her asked for the phone, she'd turn them down flat.

Time to move on.

She lifted her backpack to her shoulder and got to her feet, all the while gazing across the parking lot to the street, thinking there had to be a telephone book in a telephone booth somewhere. Maybe she could go to the library and find some kind of directory. If she—

From the corner of her eye, she spied a black convertible race into the parking lot. The driver gassed it toward a space where a young mother pushing a baby stroller was about to cross.

Ravinia sucked in a sharp breath.

The mother shrieked.

The driver slammed on his brakes.

His car shuddered to a stop.

"For the love of God," a woman at the next table said as the mother hurriedly pushed her child to safety.

"You should watch where you're going!" she cried, clearly upset.

The driver just glared at her as if the situation was her fault.

Shaking her head, she pushed the stroller onto the sidewalk then checked on her baby.

Grimacing, the jerk hit the gas again, his tires chirping and most of the customers went back to their conversations or electronic equipment. Ravinia stared hard at him and as he jumped out of the car, he caught her intent gaze. As he shouldered his way into the shop, she lowered her eyes and turned toward the coffee shop. A few steps behind him, she caught the door that was swinging closed then slipped inside.

In loose shorts and a T-shirt with some surf shop logo on the front and back, he seemed to have already forgotten her as he surveyed the menu mounted high over the barista station. She hung back from him for a bit, surveying him and noticed the tip of his phone peeking from his pocket.

An idea began to form as she pretended interest in the refrigerator case of yogurt and water. As the other people in line were served, he jiggled his leg impatiently, then when it was his turn to order, he leaned forward and started talking intimately to the girl behind the counter.

It was her chance. As if jostled from the crowd behind, Ravinia bumped him slightly and deftly slipped his phone from his pocket. He threw her a dark look, but the girl serving him was cute and he was in the middle of some heavy flirting.

"Sorry," Ravinia muttered, but he didn't notice.

Strolling casually back outside, she immediately tried to access the phone. She hoped to high heaven he didn't have an automatic lock on the thing, which, fortunately he didn't. She knew enough to work the phone and had no trouble pulling up an Internet search for Kingston Investigations in Santa Monica. No luck. But there was an office in Los Angeles. That had to be the right guy. She memorized the address and phone number just as the dude with the sports car came bursting back outside.

Frantic, the drink he was carrying sloshing onto the pavement, he raced past her to his convertible and started searching the interior. "Son of a bitch," he muttered in a panic as he set his drink on the hood and it fell over, the warm contents oozing over the car's shiny finish. "Son of a goddamned bitch!"

Suppressing a smile, Ravinia nonchalantly walked over to him and held out the phone. For a moment, he ignored her as he was so angry about his drink and intent on searching his car.

"This what you're looking for?" she asked.

He glanced over at her and his jaw dropped. "You goddamned thief!" He snagged his phone from her fingers.

"If I were a thief, I'd keep it. You're lucky I didn't call 911 and report you, since you almost ran over that woman with the stroller."

"She was standing in the middle of the fuckin' parking lot!" he sputtered.

"You were driving too fast."

"That doesn't give you the right to steal my phone, you little bitch. I should call 911 on you!"

"Go right ahead," Ravinia challenged. She was bluffing. She had no intention of sticking around and trying to explain herself to the authorities, but this asshole didn't have to know that.

"Look what you made me do, you little freak." He motioned to the mess of mocha-whatever glopped and running in sticky rivulets down the convertible's once-shiny hood. "Just get the fuck out of my way." Red-faced, veins throbbing in his neck, he seemed about to take a swing at her but at the last minute thought better of it. "You're a bitch, you know that?" he declared, his gaze raking over her as if for the first time. "A fuckin' goddamned hippie bitch!" Phone held in a death-grip, he shouldered past Ravinia and slammed back into the coffee shop, presumably for a fresh drink.

"Yeah, whatever," Ravinia said as she rounded a corner and slipped off her backpack. After locating a pen and notepad she kept in the front pocket, she wrote down the address and phone number for Kingston Investigations before she forgot it. Then she hooked the strap of her backpack over her shoulder and went in search of one of Santa Monica's Big Blue Buses.

CHAPTER 7

Get moving! A voice inside Elizabeth's head urged her to quit staring at the ceiling and get out of bed. Make that a nagging, irritating voice.

She glanced out the window. Through half-closed blinds she saw the gray day beyond. She'd been up already and had gotten Chloe a banana, then climbed back into her bed, feeling chilled to the bone. She'd slept poorly and already her pulse was rocketing along at an increased pace. She'd thought, hoped, that after Court's funeral she would start to feel normal again, but that hadn't happened. Barbara's admonition about pretending that she cared more kept rolling around Elizabeth's mind. And she was worried about Detective Thronson, about what was going on in the investigation. Elizabeth had the impression that Thronson didn't trust her and thought she might be lying or covering up something. She couldn't help wonder if the detective thought she'd had something to do with Court's death.

Frowning, she stared at the light fixture overhead. *Had* she? Was she responsible for the horrifying accident that took two lives?

She squeezed her eyes closed. *No. No. Of course not.* With an effort, she tamped back all those same memories that haunted her about Mazie and Officer Unfriendly. The more she thought about them the worse she felt.

Throwing back the covers, she climbed out of bed again, tossed on a light robe, and walked to the window to look out at the skyline of houses, trees, and a winter sun that looked like it might actually warm her frozen insides. It was no good telling herself she wasn't to blame for random acts of violence and accidents. She felt responsible, and though no sane person would point a finger at her for the deaths of Officer Unfriendly, Mazie, and Court—not to mention Whitney Bellhard—Elizabeth felt as if she were holding her breath, waiting for the other shoe to fall. Could all of these violent deaths really be coincidence? Could they? She couldn't help feeling like the common denominator. For months, she'd told herself she was making too much of it, that she was normal, that coincidences do happen, even really spooky ones . . . but with Court's death . . . She shook her head to stop the thoughts.

She had to go to work this afternoon. Misty was coming over to take care of Chloe and give Elizabeth time to show more properties to the Sorensons who were the couple Mazie had fought over so hard. After all the months of viewing every home that came on the market, they'd finally settled on a house . . . only to be outbid. Now, they were deciding between two sprawling mansions and Elizabeth should have been a helluva a lot more excited about the possible sale. In truth, all she felt was anxiety and a deep, dark fear that she might be going out of her mind.

Drawing a breath, she stared out across the backyard fence to the roof of the house next door. She needed to rouse Chloe from her favorite spot, squarely in front of the television set. It was time to start readying the little girl for the rest of her day.

There were other decisions to be made, as well. Financial decisions relating to Court's death, but Elizabeth dreaded the thought of meeting with the lawyer. Just talking to the man on the phone had made her feel weary.

"Mommy?"

She glanced over to see her blond, blue-eyed daughter standing in the doorway. Chloe's nightgown barely reached her knees. Her daughter was growing like a weed, growing up too fast. In the back of Elizabeth's mind she made a mental note to go through Chloe's drawers and donate all the clothes she'd outgrown.

"Hey, there," she said, padding to the doorway to pull her daughter into her arms.

Chloe immediately squirmed to be free. She wasn't much of a hugger and never had been. "When are we going to the park?" she demanded.

"I don't know if we have time. Misty's coming over."

"I want to go to the park *now.*"

"I know. But it'll have to wait. Come on. I'll make you breakfast." Elizabeth was firm. Since Court's death, Chloe, always willful, had been more stubborn than usual. Considering that the little girl had just lost her father, it wasn't hard to understand. Still, letting Chloe always get her way was a slippery slope.

"I already had breakfast," Chloe declared.

"A banana does not a breakfast make." Elizabeth walked past her to the kitchen, pulled out the frozen waffles, tossed them in the toaster oven, then went back to the refrigerator for the blueberry syrup and an aerosol can of whipped cream. Lurching into the room behind her mother, Chloe carried herself half bent over as if the weight of the world were on her shoulders and sighed dramatically.

Elizabeth ignored her. Sometimes the less said, the better.

If this kind of acting out and being argumentative was the way Chloe chose to deal with the fact that Daddy wasn't coming home any longer, it was a small price to pay. Elizabeth figured the obvious rebellion was far better than if her daughter were internalizing, which had never been Chloe's way.

Even when Elizabeth had pulled Chloe onto her lap and broken the news that Court wasn't coming home anymore, that he was, in fact, in heaven—words she'd nearly choked on as she had trouble thinking of Court and heaven in the same thought—Chloe had stared at her long and hard, then said, "No, he's not," and had climbed off Elizabeth's lap and stomped off to her room. When Elizabeth had peered in to ask if she was okay, Chloe had looked up at her guilelessly, big blue eyes round with innocence. "Fine," was her answer before playing with some dolls that were scattered on the floor. She hadn't asked anything further about her father, and though Elizabeth had purposely kept mentioning Court, Chloe hadn't responded.

And then she'd told Barbara in no uncertain terms that she wasn't going to the funeral.

An odd reaction, but one Elizabeth had defended in her true mother-bear style, telling Barbara to back off. As she started the coffeemaker and heard the water hissing through the pump, she was beginning to worry that something else was going on.

Thinking of her daughter's recurring and still undiagnosed illness, she wondered if Chloe's disaffection was hiding some deeper, darker emotion and decided to make another appointment with the doctor. She *seemed* to be adjusting, but maybe she should ask Dr. Werner for the name of a child psychologist, just in case.

Watching her daughter pour blueberry syrup in a thick pool over her waffles, Elizabeth reminded herself they were in an adjustment period and not to look too hard for problems above and beyond normal grieving. Still, she didn't want to miss anything. Most important to her was that Chloe was all right, that her daughter was reacting normally, that Elizabeth hadn't misread a sign of deeper psychological problems.

As Elizabeth watched her little girl tuck into her meal, she was overwhelmed with a sudden terrifying thought. *If you killed those people . . . if somehow, someway, it was because you were angry with them, because you thought dark, dark thoughts, and yes, even wished them dead, that they did perish in horrific deaths, you need to make sure you keep a tight lid on your emotions. Keep things co-pacetic. Stay calm. No extreme mood swings.*

Because, Elizabeth, you don't know whom you could hurt.

With a new fear slithering through her, she stared at her daughter. Elizabeth loved Chloe with all her heart, but that didn't mean she was never angry with her child, didn't mean her temper didn't flair when Chloe disobeyed.

Oh. God.

"What?" Chloe demanded, glancing up as she felt the weight of Elizabeth's intense gaze. Her little eyebrows drew together as if she were confused.

"Nothing," Elizabeth hastily said, her heart in her throat, her insides quivering at the dark turn of her thoughts. "Look, honey, when you're finished, why don't you grab your coat. It's nice out now, but it's supposed to rain again. Maybe we can sneak in a quick trip to the park after all."

The first Rex Kingston learned of the girl was when she walked into his office and immediately rubbed his part-time helper, Bonnie, the wrong way. The raised voices caught his attention just as he was about to send Bonnie home and slip out and start his evening surveillance of the cheating Mrs. Cochran who was quasi-famous for being on two different reality shows, breaking up one of the other contestants' marriage on both, then marrying the producer of an entirely different show who believed she was screwing yet another guy who seemed to be a fitness guru of some kind.

Hollywood. It doesn't get any better than this, he thought dryly.

He'd pulled an Angels baseball cap low over his eyes and changed into gray sweat pants, sneakers, and a black sweatshirt over a T-shirt with a zipper at his throat. He could be a jogger, or someone planning to work out, or just a person hanging loose on a Saturday afternoon. What he didn't plan to be was the man in the casual dress shirt and sunglasses who'd been watching the house from his vehicle the last few days. He was someone else. A stranger in a different car. Just in case Kimberley Cochran or her lover or anyone else was looking.

He turned toward the back door and the parking lot where he kept his own nondescript, several years old, blue Nissan sedan—a car meant for surveillance—and the newer dark gray Hyundai Sonata that he'd rented for the day. Though he was certainly no prize himself, Mr. Dorell Cochran, the producer who'd had the misfortune of marrying the beautiful and wily Kimberley Babbs, had been clear that he was ready to pay almost any amount of money to get the goods on his wife.

"Do what you have to do," the bear of a man had growled. "Just goddamn get it done."

Sleazy work? Well, yeah. Not as satisfying as helping families find missing loved ones? That, too. But issues like the Cochrans' paid the bills, handsomely, and though occasionally dangerous—Kingston did sport that scar behind his ear where a really pissed off football player who hadn't been quite good enough for the pros had taken offense when Rex had convinced his terrified ex-girlfriend to go to the police and testify about all his criminal activities—at least it wasn't boring. Luckily that brute was still in jail and Rex's ear was still intact.

He'd been shot at once, too, though that was while he was still on the force. The bullet had missed by a good six inches. That's what he told himself, though the memory of that still had the power to send a shiver down his back. It had served as one of the reasons he'd left law enforcement, though it was the bureaucracy that was the true culprit of his disillusionment. His current profession had found him rather than the other way around; people wanted help in all manner of family issues without the straightjacket of police policies. Not that Rex worked outside the confines of the law, usually. Just sometimes. In any case, his business had flourished over the past decade. He was at the point where he couldn't do it all by himself and had been thinking of taking on a partner.

As he turned down the back hall, he made the mistake of garnering a look at the newcomer—a young woman in loose, drab clothing, a backpack slung over one shoulder, a dark, blond braid draped over the other, facing down Bonnie as if they were readying for one-on-one combat. Bonnie, who was just as young, but dark-haired, half-Hispanic, and fiery when her authority was questioned was glaring at the newcomer with flashing dark eyes.

Rex immediately turned and headed to the front of his establishment, which was little more than a small reception area, two chairs, Bonnie's desk, and a rather sickly looking plant in a pot near the window. "Hello," he said, greeting the girl.

She regarded him with wary blue-green eyes. She would have been drop-dead gorgeous if she tried at all, but he could sense that appearance was way down her list of priorities. She had a grimness of purpose about her that clearly wasn't going to be put off by the fact that Bonnie had puffed up like a Banty rooster.

"Are you the private investigator?" she asked. "Rex Kingston?"

"It's Mr. Joel Kingston," Bonnie corrected flatly.

"A lot of people call me Rex," he said, seeking to pour oil on troubled waters. Sometimes Bonnie was more trouble than she was worth. "More people than call me Joel."

"Do you find missing persons?" she asked, lifting her chin.

"Yes. Sometimes."

"I would like to hire you to find my cousin."

Bonnie put in tightly, "I told her the agency rates and she swore and said we were criminals."

"I said, 'God Almighty, that's insane. You're all a bunch of bandits down here,'" the girl corrected.

"Down here?" Rex questioned.

She circled the receptionist's desk to shake hands with Rex, watching Bonnie like a hawk. "I came from the Oregon coast, a town called Deception Bay."

"Hitchhiking?" Bonnie asked, wrinkling her nose.

The girl faintly smiled. "Mostly. My name's Ravinia."

Rex shook her hand. "Ravinia," he repeated. "Do you have a last name?"

"It's just Ravinia, for now."

He stared at her. Folded his arms across his chest. "Okay, but if you want me to help you, you have to be honest with me. That's the deal."

Ravinia nodded slowly, her frown saying she was really thinking that one over.

Bonnie's eyebrows shot up and the glance she gave him silently said *See? I told you so. Nut job.*

Ravinia caught the look and her own eyes narrowed at the receptionist before she turned back to Rex, jaw taut.

Purposely ignoring the interplay, Rex asked, "So, Ravinia, you want to find your cousin?"

"I have money." She threw a defiant look Bonnie's way.

Bonnie had lapsed into injured silence.

He could tell she thought he hadn't backed her up enough. "I'm on my way out. Why don't you come by tomorrow morning and we'll discuss what you want to do."

"I'll pay your bandit's rates if I have to, but I'm not leaving," Ravinia said. As if to underscore her point, she dropped her backpack on the ground and sank down beside it, seating herself cross-legged on the floor.

Bonnie's gaze flew to his face as if to say *See?!*

"I'm going out on a job and we're going to close up here," Rex said.

"Is that how you dress for work?" Ravinia asked curiously.

"Sometimes. Surveillance jobs," he added.

Ravinia said, "I'll wait."

"Didn't you hear him?" Bonnie snapped. "We're closing."

"If you won't let me stay inside, I'll wait outside the front door."

"We won't open again until Monday," Bonnie declared, rolling her eyes toward Rex as if to say *Can you believe this?*

"Where are you staying?" Rex asked her.

"I don't have an address."

"You're homeless?" Bonnie asked with scarcely disguised contempt.

Ravinia regarded her coolly. "I have a home in Deception Bay, but I'm not there now, so yeah . . . I'm homeless."

"Maybe you should pay for a motel." Bonnie sniffed.

"I'd rather pay for your services," Ravinia said, turning her attention back to Rex. "If I have to, I'll wait till Monday, but I'd rather get going now."

"Well, you can't stay here," Bonnie huffed, opening a lower drawer in the desk and pulling out her purse.

"Watch me," Ravinia told her, parked on the floor.

"Mr. Kingston," Bonnie choked out, turning to him for help.

He'd had trouble before with Bonnie's territorial streak; Ravinia wasn't the only potential client she'd turned away because she'd made her own judgment call.

"Why don't you come back into my office for a minute," Rex said to Ravinia.

Bonnie inhaled on a hurt gasp.

He knew she felt he'd undermined her, but it couldn't be helped. "You go on ahead. I'll lock up."

"I'll stay," she said hurriedly.

Rex wasn't having it. "You said you had a date for dinner. Go on. I've got this."

Clutching her purse, Bonnie stood. Undecided for a moment, trying to come up with some way to stay, she lifted her hands as if she couldn't understand what was happening, then let them drop. "If that's what you want."

"I do," he asserted and her back stiffened. It was her MO when she felt thwarted.

Rex wished to high heaven that she would just do the job he paid her for, which was manning the front desk, answering the phone, and taking down information. Bonnie was the daughter of a friend of a friend and when he'd first met her, Rex had been grateful for the help. Before Bonnie, he'd run his business by cell phone, but it was better having an actual office telephone and a receptionist as it made him seem more "legitimate" to the sometimes skittish clientele who deemed his profession seedy and full of graft. Too many television PIs, and well, there was some truth there, too.

Apparently unable to come up with another argument, Bonnie threw Ravinia a look of contempt and stalked out the front door, just coming short of slamming it behind her.

Rex locked it behind her, then led Ravinia to his office and gestured for her to take one of the client chairs on the opposite side of his desk, while he perched a hip on the edge and crossed his arms over his chest. "I have only a few minutes, so go fast."

Ravinia stared at him hard for a moment. A dark intensity simmered in those blue-green eyes.

He felt something slide through him, something warm, almost like the heat that came with embarrassment, a flash that was gone before he could define it. *Did she do that?* he asked himself, startled.

No. Way. He wanted to dismiss the notion as ridiculous. And yet . . .

"I'm looking for my cousin, Elizabeth Gaines. She was adopted as a baby by Ralph and Joy Gaines who apparently moved to Sausalito. I went there and found a different Ralph Gaines, a couple of them, actually, but one knew about them because a prescription got messed up. He called Ralph and Joy up to warn them about the mix-up so it wouldn't happen again and he found out that they were moving to Santa Monica." She said it without blinking once. With a shrug, she added, "So, I left the San Francisco area and went to Santa Monica. Then I found you."

"Did you find them?"

"No." she said simply. "That's why I need you."

He eyed her with new respect; there was more to this young girl than first met the eyes. "But you've done some investigating on your own. How did you learn about me?"

"Some lady was talking about you in Starbucks. You found Kayla for her."

"Ahhh . . ." Rex rubbed his nose, hiding a smile. She was so forthright it was amusing.

"I could find Elizabeth myself," the girl insisted, "but I don't have a car or a license to drive one, and my disposable phone doesn't give me the Internet or GPS or anything else. It's dead right now, anyway. I just want to find her fast."

"Ralph and Joy Gaines of Santa Monica?" He glanced at his watch. He needed to get onto his surveillance and was already late.

"My Aunt Catherine wants me to find Elizabeth before anything bad can happen to her."

"She in some kind of trouble?"

"Not exactly. Maybe. We all are."

"Who's we?"

"My family," Ravinia said reluctantly. "Well, mainly Aunt Catherine, but my sisters, too."

Glancing at his watch, he said, "I can look into this tomorrow . . . er, wait, make that Monday." He remembered his promise to spend the afternoon with Pamela, maybe take in a movie, though it was the last thing he wanted to do. How he'd let himself slip from occasionally dating the woman to becoming her weekend partner was something that irritated the hell out of him. What was worse, he only had himself to blame.

"Monday? No. I can't wait that long." Ravinia was firm, her small jaw set. "Can't you get on the Internet and look them up?"

"That's a first step."

"Well?"

He choked back a laugh. "I'll do it tomorrow." *To hell with Pamela.*

"How about later today? After your job." Ravinia flicked a glance at his clothes. "Surveillance."

He almost said, "Maybe," but then shook his head. "I don't know how long this is going to be, and you and I haven't talked price yet. You already think I'm too steep and I don't want to take all your money and keep you from a warm bed tonight."

"I just don't see how it can take you very long, so I don't expect it to cost much."

"You never know." He straightened and waited for her to get out of the chair, which she did so reluctantly.

"I'll come with you," she said.

"Dream on." If nothing else, the kid had moxie. "I'm sorry. But what I do can be dangerous, and . . . no. Just no. I work solo."

"Is it more dangerous than sleeping on the street in front of your door?"

"You really wouldn't do that."

"I've slept in that park in Santa Monica above the ocean for three nights," she said with a certain amount of pride.

"Not my problem, Ravinia," he said, though he did feel a jab of guilt. She was barely more than a kid. Somewhere under twenty, if he had to guess. He walked past her toward the back door and waited impatiently as she slowly sauntered along, deliberately taking her time.

"You're starting to piss me off," he remarked.

"Yeah, well, sorry," she said, clearly unrepentant.

"What's your story?" he asked, the question out before he could even ask himself why he was asking when he had so little time.

"My story?"

"You're going to play coy?" he asked, seeing her tense up.

"It's a long story. I can tell it to you while you're watching whoever you're watching."

"No." They were finally outside the back door and he tested the handle and made sure it was locked.

"Oh, come on. How are you watching these people? Standing outside? Sitting in your car?"

"I'm in my car. For hours sometimes." He added dampeningly, "And nothing happens."

"You're just some guy in a car? What? With a pair of binoculars? If I'm with you, it'll be less weird."

She wasn't wrong, but he was kind of surprised she understood it so well. "It's a stakeout. It could last hours. If you have to go to the bathroom . . ." He spread his hands even while he was asking himself why he was still talking to her.

"I can take care of myself."

In that, he believed her. She had a barbed-wire tough attitude that was in direct juxtaposition to her small frame, wide eyes, and full lips. He had no designs on her; he was pretty sure she was young enough to be his daughter, and he wasn't interested in her romantically, anyway. But she intrigued him and that was a rare thing these days because he was jaded, tired, and pretty well convinced the human race wasn't worth a goddamn. He was, in fact, a cliché of all the old time world-weary PI's.

"I must be out of my mind," he muttered as he turned toward the rental Sonata and yanked the keys from his pocket. He hit the remote to unlock the doors.

Ravinia climbed in the passenger seat without being invited and buckled herself in.

CHAPTER 8

Spending the day with Marg and Buddy Sorenson had been pure torture. Buddy was full of bonhomie and jokes and tales of deep-sea fishing with his pals, while Marg wanted the most lavish home for the least amount of money, and she wanted Elizabeth to find it for her toute de suite. Marg believed, somehow, that it was Elizabeth's fault that she'd lost that first house when in fact Marg had simply dallied too long in making an offer. Part of the problem was Buddy. He had almost less interest in what home caught his wife's fancy than he did in the ballet, which they'd apparently gone to once in their long marriage and which he brought up from time to time as the dullest experience of his life.

"Please tell me again how hard it is to dance that damn dance," he would remind his wife every time she would complain about how she'd tried to introduce him to culture outside his world of fishing, boating, and general good old boy backslapping.

"Ballet is hard," she would snap.

After the spiral into that conversation, Buddy confided to Elizabeth, "I worked on an oil rig when I was younger. Now that's hard."

"No one's disputing that, Buddy," Marg clipped. "All I want is for you to keep an open mind about the house."

"How many millions is it?" he asked.

"We can afford it," she assured him. "Elizabeth is going to work her magic and get them to come down to a reasonable price."

"We?" Buddy asked, raising his brows at his wife who gave him a chilly glare.

"Don't put too much faith in my magic," Elizabeth told her. *Unless it's dark magic*, she thought.

As Marg and Buddy haggled and sparred, Elizabeth drove them to the four grand homes Marg had winnowed down on her list. She kept whining about the house that had been stolen out from under them, but Elizabeth didn't respond to her, knowing Marg hadn't really liked that one until it was out of reach. Then, of course, it had become "perfect," as Marg seemed to have forgotten that she'd said it needed a major remodel of the kitchen, three baths, and master suite.

Elizabeth wondered if Marg would ever pick a place. The woman liked looking, not buying, and Buddy certainly didn't want to make the leap from the mansion they already lived in. Though Elizabeth had a headache from all their bickering, and sometimes she wanted to commit hari-kari rather than listen to them one more second, staying at home and listening to her own thoughts wasn't that much better of an option.

As Marg and Buddy wandered up one side of the entry's double stairway with its ornate leaf and branch wrought-iron design, she felt her fears and doubts creeping back in. As had become her habit, she went through her affirmations again. She was just like all the other moms in her Moms Group. She was going to join the PTA this fall when Chloe started kindergarten at Willow Park Elementary. She was a realtor at Suncrest Realty, not just an assistant anymore, and, courtesy of Mazie Ferguson, she had an impressive client list. She went to a yoga class most Tuesday and Thursday mornings with friends from the Moms Group and they all drank Jamba Juice smoothies together after Tuesday's class. She was married to a corporate attorney who was strikingly good looking and on a fast track to make partner in his law firm.

Was married . . . she reminded herself with a jolt, surprised she'd let that last one slip through. Swallowing, she revised that last thought. She was a single mother, making a good living for her well-adjusted daughter.

Who has strange fainting spells with no root cause.

"Elizabeth!" Marg Sorenson called down to her from the second floor causing Elizabeth to jump. "Come up here a moment."

She trudged up the right hand stairway and met Marg and Buddy in the master bedroom, one of six. A chandelier hanging over the bed and built in cabinetry were fashioned in a baroque style that seemed ill-suited to the rest of the beautifully appointed house. In fact, so much carved woodwork and inlaid silver filigree took the eye away from the cathedral ceiling and massive windows with their view north, up the coastline.

"Don't you love this?" Marg asked.

"The view is spectacular," Elizabeth said.

"The cabinets, my dear. Is there any way to dome this room?"

"Dome it?"

"Christ, woman, you'd have to change the roof line," Buddy grumbled. "Do you know how much that would cost?"

"You just don't know design," Marg sniffed.

Elizabeth said, "You'd really need to talk to an architect about that."

"We're not going to goddamn dome it," Buddy growled, stalking out of the room.

"You see what he's like?" Marg said on a huge sigh.

"Maybe this isn't the right property for you," Elizabeth suggested.

Marg's face clouded. "Half the time I think you're trying to talk me out of things. Maybe we should go back to that one with the little elves."

Elizabeth kept her expression neutral. One of the houses she'd inherited with Mazie's client list was a two-story, near-mansion Tudor right on the ocean with massive grounds and a portico. Mrs. Stafford, co-owner of the property with her husband, was an aficionado of Tolkien's *The Hobbit*, apparently, because she'd made a crèche on the edge of the lawn populated with Hobbits and other Tolkien creatures. Though both Mazie and Elizabeth had suggested the display be removed while the house was for sale, Mrs. Stafford had stamped down her Ferragamo heel on the idea, so the crèche remained . . . and had been dubbed by the agents at Suncrest Realty as "Staffordshire." Marg had liked the house and ignored the tableau, and Buddy had made comments about the owners' state of mental health, so, of course, they'd submitted no offer. To date Staffordshire remained unsold. As the Staffords themselves were currently touring Europe, Elizabeth tried to swing by and make sure everything was secure and locked up tight as often as she could, and now she made a mental note to add that to her to-do list, although the way things were going she could be showing it to Marg and Buddy again very soon.

Marg and Buddy sniped at each other the rest of the time and Elizabeth was relieved when she could take them back to the office and herd them to their own vehicle. She could feel her tense shoulders relax as they climbed into their Lexus and she waved good-bye.

"How'd it go?" Pat asked brightly as Elizabeth pushed open the glass door to Suncrest Realty.

"Better than expected." She wasn't about to give anything away to the blabbermouth receptionist. Pat, blond and efficient and a fashionista who always dressed to the nines, tens, and beyond seemed to consider it part of her job to spread gossip along with sorting the mail, taking phone calls, and dealing with walk-in clients.

"Did they choose a house?" Pat asked, elbows on the reception desk, hands clasped. "Marg and Buddy? Did you find them one?"

"Still narrowing down the list." Elizabeth walked away from her as quickly as possible and into Mazie's office, actually her office if she wanted it, but she'd spent most of her time sharing cubicles in the large room at the end of the hall and hadn't quite changed her habits yet. She picked up a couple files, then headed to the cubicles, feeling more comfortable in one of the squeaky office chairs rather than the supple leather one Mazie had special ordered.

Plucking her cell phone from her purse, she checked her messages and found one from Vivian asking her and Chloe to come over for dinner that night. Elizabeth smiled faintly, touched. Her friends had been rallying around her this week and though Chloe struggled to get along with Vivian's daughter Lissa, she called Vivian back and accepted the offer. "What can I bring?"

"Just yourself. So glad you're coming! I've ordered from Gina's and we'll get the kids pizza, too. I invited a few other people, too."

"Oh?" Elizabeth's heart sank at the thought of a crowd.

"Just some of our group," Vivian said breezily, "and Bill will be here, of course. See you at six?"

"Six . . . sure. Thanks."

Bill was Vivian's husband. Tall and athletic, a golfer with salt-and-pepper hair he kept clipped short, Bill had been to a couple events at the preschool. Elizabeth didn't know him very well, but then when their group got together it was mainly just the women. She wasn't sure she was up for a big dinner party, but she'd already committed and really didn't know how to say no.

She worked for several hours in relative quiet. When she'd finished a couple phone calls and e-mails, setting up appointments for later in the week, she headed outside again.

Of course, Pat was lying in wait, eager to ask her more questions about her clients and their personal lives. Elizabeth murmured something about being late and hurried out the door even though she sensed Pat's seething resentment. For what? Not gossiping with her? Not hanging out with her? Not sharing information about other Realtors and clients? As she walked to her SUV, she felt Pat's gaze boring into the back of her head and a glance over her shoulder confirmed the sensation as Pat, cell phone to her ear, was glowering through the window.

Get a life, Elizabeth thought and wondered who the receptionist was talking to. Not that it mattered. She slid inside the warm interior, slipped a pair of sunglasses over the bridge of her nose and switched on the Escape's engine.

She thought about Pat as she drove home. And though she switched on the radio, she didn't hear the music and drove through the familiar streets by rote. The receptionist's nosiness irked Elizabeth, and she told herself that next time she would use her key to enter through the back door off the alley, just to avoid her and all those prying questions. If only someone else had Pat's job. Someone less . . . annoying. But there was probably no way Pat would resign. She loved her position at the company too much.

If only she would just quit.

Hearing her thoughts, Elizabeth caught herself up short. Was that wishing harm on someone? Hoping they would relinquish their job?

You can't think *harm to someone,* she reminded herself harshly as she slowed for a red light, then cracked the windows to let in some fresh air. *It's not about you.* Besides, Barbara had flown back to Buffalo and as far as Elizabeth knew nothing bad had happened to her sister-in-law despite the fact that Elizabeth had certainly spent this very long week annoyed at her.

Still, there's no need to entertain such negative thoughts toward Pat, she thought, slowing for another red light. Better to err on the side of caution, ignore people's irritating habits, and generally have a sunnier disposition. Condemning other people's behaviors certainly didn't help her. And wasn't that what positive thinking was all about, anyway?

Pat's still a pain in the butt.

"So are a lot of people," she reminded herself.

Her cell rang just as she waited at the light. Quickly, she put in her ear bud, then plugged the cord into her cell and answered before she checked the number.

"Hello?" Then she saw the number. Detective Bette Thronson's cell phone. *Damn.*

"Sorry to bother you, Mrs. Ellis," the cop said, then added, "This is Detective Thronson. I wonder if I might have a word with you."

Oh, great.

"I'm . . . I'm driving."

"Not now. I could stop by this evening if that's convenient?"

"No . . . no. I'm sorry. I'm going out." Elizabeth's eyes were on traffic, but her pulse was thundering, adrenaline rushing through her bloodstream, her insides rattled. She stretched her fingers over the wheel just as the light turned green and she stepped on the gas pedal.

"Ahh . . . maybe tomorrow?" the detective asked.

"Is there something you want to tell me?" Elizabeth asked impatiently.

"I'd like to discuss a few things. . . ."

"Can't you just tell me on the phone?" She heard herself and inwardly snorted. So much for the pep talk on having a better attitude.

Pretend like you care. . . .

"You said you were driving."

"I'm using my hands-free device. I can hear you just fine." It was better to get this over with, right? Move forward?

"Okay," the detective said, her voice sliding into cool, neutral tones. "I interviewed the hotel clerk at the Tres Brisas and he gave me a description of a woman who'd been seen at the hotel a number of times while your husband and Mrs. Bellhard were there."

"Oh?"

"Let's see," the cop said as if she were searching her notes even though Elizabeth thought they were probably right in front of her. "Yes. A blond woman in her mid to late twenties who wears her hair pulled up into a messy bun."

Elizabeth's gaze traveled to the rearview mirror and she looked at her own reflection. Detective Thronson could have been describing her. Heart pounding, she asked, "Who is it? The blonde?"

"Don't know yet. She doesn't appear to have checked into the hotel. The management doesn't video their guests, so we don't have an actual picture of her."

Elizabeth's throat was dry as dust as she eased into the slower lane. Telling herself to stay calm, she asked, "What does she have to do with my husband?"

"We're just following leads. It might not have anything to do with him."

"But you think it does. And you think his death was something more than just an accident, don't you?"

The detective hesitated briefly before admitting, "The reports that his vehicle was 'racing' with another seem to be consistent."

A dark SUV, like your Escape . . .

Elizabeth's palms sweated over the wheel. She wanted to tell the detective that the police department was barking up the wrong tree and loudly proclaim her innocence. She hadn't been anywhere near San Diego the day Court died. She'd been in Irvine and Newport Beach, showing property . . . well, most of the time, anyway. Could this detective really think Elizabeth was involved? *Don't even go there,* she warned herself, but felt her blood pressure and worry escalate. With an effort at concentrating on the traffic, she forced out, "So, what does that mean?"

"It could be vehicular homicide," the detective said slowly as if she were testing Elizabeth, waiting for a response.

Oh, Jesus. "Look, Detective, all I know is my husband's dead," Elizabeth snapped and then decided to end the conversation. "I've got to go. When you find out more, let me know. I'm sorry, I wish I could help you, but I can't." She clicked off and let out a long breath.

What the hell was the detective thinking? What was the real purpose of the call? Was Thronson fishing?

Lost in thought, she nearly missed the turn off for her house and started to ease over to the correct lane, looking over her right shoulder.

In a blur, a dark convertible BMW slashed in front of her.

Instantly she slammed on her brakes.

Her heart froze.

Gasping, she braced herself for the inevitable crash, the crumpling of metal, the spinning into oncoming traffic.

Her Escape fishtailed, missing the BMW by mere inches. "Oh, God," she said, her heart thundering wildly as she gained control of her vehicle.

The prick behind the Beemer's wheel, glared at her through his rearview mirror. His face contorted in anger, he stabbed his middle finger into the air.

Immediately Elizabeth's finger shot up in response. The jerk thought it was *her* fault? His brake lights flashed and she was forced to slow at the next light. Still silently fuming, she pulled to within a hair's breadth behind him, nearly covering up his license plate, which read GOODGUY.

"Good guy my ass," Elizabeth muttered, still seething.

Holding her gaze in the mirror, he started making a disgusting pumping gesture with his hand down by his lap.

Yuck! Seriously? Seeing red, anger pumping through her bloodstream, she mouthed *asshole.*

The light turned.

He hit the accelerator.

She tromped on the gas.

Pissed beyond all reason, she drove like a maniac, right on his tail.

He zipped in and out of lanes and she followed recklessly behind the bastard.

Are you nuts, Elizabeth? What the hell are you doing? For God's sake let it go! He's just a jerk, one of a million behind the wheel. Stop this! You're a mother, for crying out loud!

In a blink, her brain kicked in and she came to her senses. "No," she whispered, easing off the gas, deccelerating and sliding into the slower lane. Her heart was still pounding a crazy tattoo, but her fury was spent and she was horrified by what she'd done, how an idiot had goaded her into such erratic, uncharacteristic behavior. She could have hurt someone, or killed them, or herself.

She trembled inside.

As she found a spot to turn around, she could hear the rushing in her ears, the pounding of her heart, the stutter of her own breaths. *What's wrong with you?* her mind screamed.

He reminded you of Court, didn't he? That's what this was all about. Well, it's crazy. Elizabeth, pull yourself together! You're Chloe's only parent now. You can't afford to fall apart.

Shaking inside, trying to understand the instant, unlikely rush of pure fury that had overtaken her, she pulled over to the side of the road. As cars streamed by, she took in deep, calming breaths. Finally, when she felt in control again, she flipped on her blinker and driving with extra care, eased into traffic again and found a safe spot to turn around as she'd long before passed the turn-off to her house.

Still trembling, she drove the rest of the way home extra carefully and pulled into her garage. She'd never done anything like that. Ever.

She cut the engine and hit the button so that the garage door closed, slowly blocking out the daylight. As the engine cooled, ticking and darkness surrounding her, she rested her head on the steering wheel. Never had she experienced that white-hot level of road rage. Never had she chased down an idiot who had cut her off.

What was the report on Court's accident? *Several witnesses reported a dark SUV weaving in and out of traffic about the same time Court's BMW was doing the same thing. . . .*

Dark SUV. Like hers.

BMW. Like the one she'd just chased within an inch of her life.

Oh. Dear. God. Elizabeth swallowed hard and closed her eyes.

The detective thinks you were there. That you killed him.

"But I wasn't on the freeway with Court. It wasn't me!" she said aloud, wondering what in the world was happening to her?

The door from the house burst open, light spilling into the dark garage. Chloe, blond curls bouncing, raced into the garage. "Mommy?"

Pulling her thoughts up short, Elizabeth came back to the here and now. She pushed open the driver's door and climbed out, but her knees shivered a little, threatening to give out. Forcing a smile, she leaned against the hood of the car. "Hi, sweetie."

"Mommy, Misty's been on the phone all day," Chloe complained, her little arms folded over her chest.

"Has she?"

"I wanted to play with her, but she's mean. I don't like her!"

This was a new tack, a ploy for attention. "Oh, come on, Chloe. You adore Misty. Let's go back inside." Forcing her legs to move, Elizabeth pushed off the car, then bent down to give her daughter a quick unwelcome hug.

"I don't adore her," Chloe maintained as she slithered out of her mother's arms.

"Fine. You don't." Placing her hand between her daughter's shoulder blades and guiding her into the house, Elizabeth said, "Let's just go inside, anyway." She pulled the door shut behind her and found Misty in the kitchen..

Coltish, with big brown eyes and a penchant for temporary tattoos—bound to be the real thing once she turned eighteen—Misty set down her cell phone onto the counter as if caught in some nefarious act.

"See?" Chloe crowed triumphantly as she pointed at the girl.

"I wasn't on my phone the whole time," Misty defended herself even before Elizabeth could open her mouth. "We played together."

Chloe muttered, "Barely."

"A lot," Misty argued and adopted a hurt expression, as if her young charge had betrayed her. "We always do."

"Nuh-uh!"

"Enough," Elizabeth interjected. "It's over." While Chloe flopped sullenly on the floor, Elizabeth hastily wrote the teenager a check, thanked her and, as Misty let herself out the front door, called a hasty, "Good-bye."

Chloe's head was turned, watching the sitter leave, but as soon as the door shut with a soft thud, she whipped back to her mother. "She was on the phone the whole time. She *lied*."

"Maybe she was on the phone today more than usual." Elizabeth pulled a bottle of water from the fridge, cracked off the top and took a long swallow.

Chloe jumped up from the floor. "She was!"

"I'll have a talk with her about it." Still shaken from the road rage incident, she didn't have time for Chloe's petty squabbles. To change the course of the conversation, she said, "We're going to dinner at Lissa's house soon, so—"

"When?"

"In a little while. I—"

"No! When are you going to *talk to her?*" Chloe's fists were on her hips and she had that stubborn look in her eye.

So the ploy to detour her child didn't work.

"Misty?" Elizabeth asked, taking another long swallow as Chloe nodded her head wildly. "Probably the next time she babysits."

"I never want her to babysit me *again*!"

"Chloe," Elizabeth admonished on a heavy sigh.

"She's mean. She's a mean girl."

"No, she's not. She's self-involved. All teenagers are."

"What? What's self-devolved?"

Elizabeth almost smiled at the mistake and was reminded how young her daughter was and how much she'd been through in the last week or so. No matter how she was reacting, Chloe was dealing with a major issue with the loss of her father. Even if Elizabeth's love for her husband had shriveled, the same wasn't necessarily true for her child. "Never mind. I need you to get ready to go."

"To Lissa's house?"

"Yes."

"For dinner."

"That's right." So she had gotten through.

"What are we eating at Lissa's?" Chloe demanded suspiciously.

"Pizza for you girls."

"Yuck."

So this was how it was going to be, Chloe obstinate.

"You love pizza," Elizabeth reminded her daughter. "Now, come on, squirt. Go comb your hair. You look like nobody loves you."

"But you do. You love me."

"Very much." And to prove it, she gave her daughter another hug, holding her fiercely, the memory of the road rage on the dark edges of her mind. Chloe actually giggled before wriggling away.

Elizabeth forced out, "And find your shoes. I've got to . . ." She didn't finish her sentence as Chloe had rushed out to, hopefully, do as Elizabeth had asked.

Only when she was alone did Elizabeth let go. Her legs buckled and she knocked over her water bottle, spilling it onto the counter. Quickly righting the bottle, she didn't bother wiping up the mess because she had to sit down at the kitchen table or fall down.

She covered her mouth with her hands and stared blankly ahead, watching the water drip from the counter to the floor and unable to do anything about it. She heard the ticking of the clock mounted high over the cupboards, in an almost eerie counterpoint to her own heartbeats.

Something was happening to her. Something bad.

I'm normal. I'm totally normal.

But it wasn't true.

CHAPTER 9

Rex slid a look at his companion as he eased his seat back and dropped the baseball cap farther over his eyes. He'd parked in the shade of a Madrone tree a block over from the Cochran's drive and had told himself he wasn't completely out of his mind by allowing Ravinia to come. She was right about the fact that his surveillance would be more camouflaged by having her in the car. He'd been outside the Cochran home enough times to be remarked on, and that "pull date" when someone finally noticed the man loitering in the car and the alarm went out was always a possibility.

Surveillance was a tricky thing and he had to be cautious. Having Ravinia in the car with him could be good or bad. God knew she could certainly blow the whole thing if she wanted to, though he suspected that wasn't how she was made. He considered himself a pretty good judge of character, most of the time, and apart from a few epic fails in his personal life, he usually knew about people, their habits and their motivations. In that, he'd been a pretty decent policeman throughout his twenties, but deep into his thirties, his skills worked best in private investigation.

Ravinia turned her head, feeling his perusal. She was sensitive that way, though her personality was anything but. She was prickly, confrontational, suspicious, and determined, so when she came out with, "I'd be good at your job," he gave a bark of laughter.

"What?" she demanded.

"We've been here all of ten minutes."

"You just have to wait around and watch people."

"There's a little more to it than that," he remarked dryly as a slow-moving truck, its cab scraping the branches overhead, rumbled by.

"And ask questions and gather information and chase people down. If I had a car and Internet access—a smartphone would really do it—I'd be ready to go."

"You also need a license," he pointed out.

"If I had my license, I could be driving on my own car, and I could maybe have already found my cousin."

"A private investigator's license," he corrected.

She frowned at him. "You have to go to school for that?"

"Take some classes, sure."

Casting him a leery glance, she said, "I have my GED."

"Did you go to high school?"

"I was home schooled by my aunt."

"Aunt Catherine?" He was looking through the windshield, his binoculars in his lap, his gaze on the door of the Cochran home.

Kimberley had a fairly specific routine. To the gym in the mornings, coffee with friends—a lot of air kissing went on among them—and then back to the house. Tennis on Monday, Wednesdays, and Fridays. Dorell Cochran had moved out and so her time was her own, but she hadn't met any paramour as yet.

He could feel Ravinia's attention sharpen on him. "Yes, Aunt Catherine."

He kept his gaze centered on the end of the long drive, which curved up the hill to the Cochran home. They were in Sherman Oaks. A number of expensive homes perched on the ridge above him. Parking was prohibited on the four lane road that led past the drive, but he'd found a few places on a side street that offered an unobstructed view. He'd been pretty lucky so far in finding an observation point, but Dorell Cochran was impatient to learn whom his wife was seeing and was making noise about cutting off funding. If he did, so be it. Rex couldn't manufacture results. A lot of PI work was a waiting game.

"Who are you waiting for?" Ravinia asked.

"A woman whose husband thinks she's having an affair."

"Is she?"

Rex shrugged, shifting in the driver's seat. "Maybe. He thinks so. I haven't seen any evidence of it yet."

"How long are we going to be here?"

"Told you it'd be boring." He glanced her way. She'd pinched her lips together and was glaring through the windshield. "What's your story?" he asked her again.

"I told you. I just want to find my cousin."

"So, tell me something about yourself."

She raked him with a sideways glance from suspicious blue-green eyes. "I'm from Oregon."

"You already told me that. You lived around a town called Deception Bay on the Oregon coast. What else?"

She thought that over. "Okay," she said as if she'd decided something. "If I tell you something about *my*self, you have to tell me something about *your*self."

Rex raised the binoculars to his eyes and swept them across the front of the Cochran house. "Fair enough."

"All right. Well then, I guess I'll tell you that . . . my aunt is worried about her daughter, my cousin. My aunt gave her away at birth but feels that she might be in danger."

When she stopped abruptly, Rex put down the binoculars. "From what?"

"Oh . . . you know . . . forces of evil."

"Like in a video game?"

Frowning again, Ravinia shook her head. "No, Aunt Catherine thinks it's one of my brothers."

"One of your brothers?" he repeated.

"Yeah. There's the good one and the bad one, and well, he's the bad one."

It was starting to sound a little far-fetched. Well, a lot far-fetched. And it must've registered on his face.

She said, "I told you it was a long story. Anyway, it's my turn. Are you married?"

He hesitated, not wanting to give insight into his personal life, then said, "No."

"Ever been married?"

"Yeah . . . once," he admitted reluctantly.

"Doesn't sound like it was good."

"It was for a while." Rex had no interest in continuing this line of questioning. He'd been married to Allison for six years before her infidelity came to light, and it was after he'd learned the truth that he left the LAPD. He'd been itching for a change for a while, but it took the impetus of Allison's betrayal to finally get him to act. That and the fact that she'd taken up with one of his fellow officers whom she'd married almost before the ink was dry on the divorce decree. That was nine years ago, and Allison and Kurt had popped out two daughters in quick succession. He hadn't even come close to marriage since the divorce and he kind of regretted the fact that he had no children, but life was full of twists and turns. He might not have much of a family life himself, but he'd become the go-to man for sorting through other people's domestic chaos—cheating spouses, runaway kids, missing kin. Good ol' Rex was your guy when it came to dysfunctional families.

"What happened?" Ravinia asked.

"We grew apart," he said brusquely, cracking the window a little farther, allowing more of the late afternoon breeze to filter through the car. "So, tell me, why do you think your evil brother is after your cousin?"

"I don't. My aunt does. It's because he's threatened us and he killed my mother."

"He *killed* your mother? Truly?"

"That's what Aunt Catherine thinks."

"And he got away with it?" Rex confirmed, realizing that Bonnie was right. This girl was certifiable.

"It's true!" she said as if reading his thoughts.

"So now he's on the loose and after your cousin?"

"He's after *all* of us. It's the nature of who we are." She slid down in the seat, her voice growing softer. "My turn."

"No, wait. All of you? Your . . . family?"

"My sisters and I live with our aunt in a lodge. We're kind of well-known around Deception Bay. They all think we're crazy."

"Yeah?" Rex half-smiled. This was bizarre. "I assume the police know all this. That if this is true—"

"It is!"

"There's a warrant out for this guy's arrest. By the way, does he have a name? And the other one, the good brother. What's his name? How does he figure into all of this?" Even as he asked the questions, Rex realized it was all for naught. She was spinning fantasies.

"My turn," she insisted, her eyes narrowing as if she expected him to lie. "How many cases have you solved?"

"Wait a sec. We were talking about the bad brother who killed—"

"How many?" she demanded.

"Oh, for the love of God." He shrugged. "I don't know and I'm not sure I'd even call them cases." He stared through the binoculars again, adjusting the focus. "Sometimes I'm just searching for kids who've run away from their parents and it ends up that they were really just away for the weekend, staying with a friend, not bothering to tell their folks. Sometimes it's a lot more and takes some time. Like what we're doing now." He pulled the glasses away for a sec. "So how many sisters and brothers do you have?"

Ravinia shrugged.

"You don't know?"

"Not really," she admitted. "Some I know of, some I don't."

"But one brother's threatening the rest of you?" His skeptical tone had obviously reached her.

"My family's not normal."

"I'll buy that."

She threw him a look. "But you don't believe that my brother is evil?"

"I don't know enough to make that call."

Ravinia said flatly, "I'm telling you the truth. I can't make you believe it."

He lifted his hands in surrender. "Go on. Explain about your family."

She drew a breath. "My mother must have been pregnant most of her adult life, but I just have vague memories of her. I've heard stories, though. She had a lot of lovers and a lot of children from those lovers. I have a couple sisters who were adopted out as soon as they were born. Two, I think. No, three . . ." She shook her head and then started ticking off her fingers. "I just learned I had a couple brothers who were also adopted out as babies. We just got information on their adoptive parents and Ophelia's helping Aunt Catherine find out more about them. Ophelia's one of my sisters still at the lodge— Siren Song. That's where most of us live. Anyway, after Natasha ran away Aunt Catherine really put us in lock down."

"Natasha is your sister."

"Yeah." Ravinia looked out the passenger window. "I thought Aunt Catherine was crazy and, you know, kind of a warden. It seemed unfair and I just couldn't handle being locked up like that."

"This Siren Song was a prison?"

"No, no. More like a fortress if you have to label it. But it didn't matter to me. I had to escape, so I kept sneaking out, climbing over the wall and leaving."

"But you said she sent you to find your cousin."

"She did . . . after she realized the danger and knew that I had the best chance of finding Elizabeth as I'd been out enough to understand what I had to do. Some of my sisters . . . well, they're kind of naive, I guess you'd say. They wouldn't know what to do and Aunt Catherine had to stay and take care of them."

"So you were elected."

Ravinia shook her head. "I *wanted* to find Elizabeth. So that's why I'm here. I don't agree with Aunt Catherine on everything, but I get where she's coming from now. She's not half as crazy as some of the rest of my family. It's just that she was always so secretive. She thought she was protecting us, but she would never tell us anything, so I gave her a hard time and just wanted out. Now . . . it's just all kind of murky. The past. She tells it in bits and pieces, kind of on a need to know basis."

Ravinia turned her attention away from the window and leaned against it so she could look straight at him. "Anyway, I also know one of my brothers, Nathaniel, died as a baby. He was kind of mentally slow, I think. His grave's at Siren Song, like my mother's. I don't know exactly what happened to him. There's some mystery about his death, and Aunt Catherine isn't talking."

Fun group, Rex thought, but held his tongue. Her countenance had become pensive, so he asked, "Something else?"

Her gaze lifted, finding his. "One of my cousins was a homicidal maniac." She said it in that *Oh, I almost forgot* kind of voice.

"Another cousin?" Rex questioned and thought she was really off the rails. Her story got more fantastical by the second.

"Like a second cousin." Ravinia seemed to think it over as if she wasn't sure she wanted to go into it, then said, "His name was Justice. He breached the wall, climbing over to get at us, once."

"And?"

"I stabbed him." She held his gaze, nearly daring him to ask.

"You stabbed him?" He found it hard to believe she was violent.

"Yeah."

Rex couldn't help but ask, "What happened?"

"He survived. But not for long. He's dead now, too."

"Because of the wounds you inflicted?"

Shaking her head, she said, "No."

Rex had to drag his gaze away from her and turn his attention back to the Cochran mansion. He couldn't tell if she was a tall tale teller, a mental case, or if some truth was buried in what she was saying. He felt it might be the latter, but he couldn't say why. All the talk of stabbing and death and murderous intent was stretching his ability to believe her. "So, your aunt's worried that your brother is coming after you and your family."

"My half brother," she clarified.

"And she sent you out to find her daughter, your cousin, because she's worried about her."

"Aunt Catherine thinks we're safe at Siren Song but nowhere else. She's a little bit of a control freak. Well, a *lot* of one."

"But she let you leave the . . . fortress where your sisters and brothers are and head south."

"She didn't think she had much of a choice. She wanted me to find Elizabeth. And it's just my sisters at Siren Song with Aunt Catherine—Isadora, Ophelia, Cassandra, and Lillibeth." Ravinia shot him a look as if she didn't think he'd been paying attention. "I told you my brothers were adopted out."

"Except Nathaniel," he reminded her.

"He wasn't right somehow. He was a lot older than the other boys, and that was before they all really knew about the gifts." She pushed some wayward strands of hair into her braid.

"Gifts?" Rex asked dubiously.

"You're not going to believe me so I'm not going to tell you." She let her braid fall and stared at him with those intense eyes again. "My turn for a question."

"No, wait. You can't stop there. You're dying to tell me. What gifts?"

"Psychic gifts," she said after a long moment.

Rex looked at her hard and laughed out loud. "You sure you're not from LA?"

She let out a disgusted breath. "I know how it sounds, believe me. Next thing, you'll want me to prove it to you."

"Well, that would be the natural next step."

"The thing is, my gift isn't one you can really assess."

Rex had to force himself not to goad her further. He'd heard a lot of stories in his business. Some pretty outlandish. But this one was right up there. "All right, I'll bite. What's your gift?"

"I can look into someone's heart and know what kind of person they are, good or evil."

The smile died on Rex's lips as he remembered the heat he'd felt in his chest when her gaze had first landed on him. "And have you looked into mine?"

"Of course." She nodded, holding his gaze.

"Did I pass?"

"I'm here, aren't I?" she countered. "Ever read mythology, Mr. Kingston?"

"Rex. Call me Rex, and no, I can't say that I have."

"Well, you should. Anyway, in myth, Cassandra could predict the future, but she angered the gods and therefore was cursed. From then on, it didn't matter that she could tell the future, the curse made it so no one would ever believe her. I have a sister named Cassandra. She used to be Margaret, but when my mother realized she had the gift of prophecy, she changed her name."

"Your sister has the gift of prophecy?"

"Yep. Except we believe her."

He shook his head, trying not to smile though it was a losing battle.

She, however, was dead serious. "How come you grew apart?"

"What?"

"You and your wife. How come you grew apart?"

She'd woven such an unbelievable tale that he'd forgotten for a moment where his story had left off. His marriage. "She wanted more than a cop's life."

"You're not a cop anymore."

"Close enough." He picked up his binoculars and once again focused them on the Cochrans' house.

"You weren't that sorry when the marriage failed."

She'd got that right. But maybe it wasn't that much of a stretch. "I thought you said your sister was the seer."

"You don't have to be psychic to read people."

That was probably true enough. He slowly scanned the perimeter of the Cochrans' estate, but so far no action. He dropped the glasses again. "What about your other sisters and brothers?"

"I don't really know what they all can do. We don't talk about it much because it's dangerous."

"Dangerous? How is it—?"

"Is that the woman you're waiting for?"

Rex swung the binoculars to his eyes again to see that the gates of the Cochran estate were sliding open and Kimberley Cochran's silver-blue Mercedes was idling. She was behind the wheel waiting to enter the road.

Finally. Show time.

Tossing the field glasses into the back seat, he clicked on his seat belt and twisted the ignition. "Buckle up," he ordered as he started the engine.

"Why? Are you going to drive fast?"

"It's the law and I don't want a ticket."

"Do you believe what I told you?" she asked, reaching for the shoulder harness, "Or do you think I'm a complete wacko, like everybody else?"

He slid her a quick glance, then eased into traffic. "I'm leaning toward complete wacko." He turned his attention to the Mercedes slowing for a stop sign at the cross street and felt that little tingle of anticipation he always did when he was on the move and following his quarry.

CHAPTER 10

It took longer than she'd expected for Elizabeth to pull herself back together and get Chloe cleaned up, then dressed in clothes that didn't look as if she'd been wearing them for a week. Combing her daughter's hair was a nightmare as Chloe thrashed and moaned and screamed, "You're hurting me!" as soon as Elizabeth put the brush to her scalp.

"Sorry," Elizabeth apologized, though she knew she wasn't hurting her child. Chloe was just being Chloe and she lived her life out loud all the time. Elizabeth figured her daughter's outspokenness would be an asset when she was older, though hopefully she would temper it a bit. However, it seemed as if no one was going to run over Chloe or tromp all over her feelings or give her a complex; she just wouldn't let them.

"There ya go. Take a look in the mirror," Elizabeth said once Chloe's wayward curls had been tamed. "All set."

Chloe had to grin at her reflection of rosy cheeks bright eyes and finally, tangle-free golden locks. "But I don't want to go to Lissa's," she complained after one last glimpse in the bathroom mirror before hopping off the counter.

Elizabeth silently agreed. She, too, would have loved to bag out. The fact was, she was just plain tired after a very long, very stressful week, and was mentally kicking herself for agreeing to have dinner at Vivian's. She would have much rather stayed home with Chloe and let her daughter be a bundle of loud energy away from a crowd. But that wasn't what was going to happen.

Less than half an hour later, Elizabeth wound her way up the curving street to where Vivian's house stood on the crest of the hill. She pulled up to the curb about two blocks away from the imposing residence. Located in a pocket of houses with a Newport Beach address, the Eachus home was a sprawling California ranch that had a second floor added sometime in the nineties. Vivian and Bill had remodeled once more on a grand scale, courtesy of Bill's company and the place was huge, surrounded by manicured grounds. Bill was in real estate development and had been savvy enough to skip over the recession and land on his feet. Currently his company was building rows of houses in developments in Irvine just east of I-5.

As she and Chloe walked up the palm lined street, Elizabeth eyed the exterior of the massive structure. Though it wasn't quite dusk, palm and eucalyptus trees were already bright with strands of outdoor lights, the gardens manicured. Elizabeth guessed from the sheer size of the home, six, possibly seven bedrooms were tucked inside.

She had been to Vivian's grand home once before, but it had been for a quick drop in and she hadn't been given the tour. She hadn't seen the upper floor, but thought she'd probably get her chance. No doubt Chloe would barrel upstairs and down, so Elizabeth was probably going to get her chance to see a lot of house just trying to corral her daughter.

Lissa met them at the door almost before Chloe pressed her finger to the bell. The two girls looked at each other for a second, then Lissa said, "Come to my room," and they were off, laughing and thundering up a wide staircase. If only they would stay happy with each other, Elizabeth reflected as she stepped across the threshold into a grand foyer, but she didn't hold out a lot of hope as the two girls' personalities were bound to clash. They always did.

"We're in the kitchen!" Vivian yelled.

Elizabeth followed the sound to a wide kitchen with a broad bank of windows and what seemed like acres of granite glimmering under recessed lighting. Through the windows, she viewed flagstones that led to a shimmering pool and the tended grounds surrounding it. Deirdre and Les Czursky were seated at one of the tables scattered around the patio, their son, Chad, a classmate of Chloe's, occupying one of the chairs and the younger son, Bryan, on his mother's lap.

"So glad you could come," Bill said from the bar where he was pouring ice from a plastic bag into a bucket. Tall and lean, with dark hair and eyes, he stopped filling an ice bucket to round the end of the counter and gave Elizabeth a friendly kiss on the cheek. "Sorry about Court. I . . . I just don't know what to say."

Neither do I. "It's okay," she said, forcing a smile she didn't feel as he stepped away. "Here." She handed him a bottle of red wine. "Thanks for inviting me . . . er . . . us."

"Anytime!" Vivian pulled a bake-your-own pizza from one of the double ovens and slid it onto the counter. "Glad you made it," she added as her husband Bill added the Merlot to a grouping of about six other bottles already situated on the bar. The hot pizza smelled like heaven. Curling rounds of pepperoni floated on a sea of melting cheese.

"Have an hors d'oeuvre." Vivian gestured to the tray of cheese, grapes, crackers, and what looked like fig jam positioned on one counter while an array of salads had already been positioned on the island.

"Deirdre and Les are outside," Vivian said as she searched in one of the drawers and scowled as she came up with a plastic pizza wheel. "With their boys. I guess Chad and Bryan don't want to mingle with the girls." She started working with the pizza wheel. "Geez, is this the best we can do? Bill, don't we have another cutter somewhere? I've got to start in on the steak."

He shrugged and Vivian shot Elizabeth a look. One that suggested all husbands were useless in the kitchen. "You'd think we could afford a real pizza wheel, something stainless steel, you know, one that didn't come as a freebie the last time we ordered from Domino's or something." Frowning, she added, "Oh well, this will just have to do." She worked the plastic wheel, dragging it through the oozing cheese, long strings of mozzarella trailing after it. "God, what a mess." She looked up at her husband once more and sent him another look. "Maybe Elizabeth would like a glass of wine."

"I would," Elizabeth said and walked to the bar.

"Sorry. I was just about to offer you one," Bill said. "Red?"

"Sure." As soon as the stemmed glass was full, she plucked it from his fingers and stepped outside.

Elizabeth had never met Deirdre's husband before, and when she was introduced to the short man with the receding blond hair, she was surprised by the warm hug he gave her.

"Sorry about your loss," he said, sounding like he meant it.

"Thank you."

"Can we go in the pool?" Chad asked.

Standing, Deirdre placed her younger son onto the patio and said to Chad, "No, honey. It's not that kind of party."

Lower lip protruding, Chad hung his head, but Deirdre ignored him as Bryan stayed close to her. "So, glad you decided to come," she said, and like her husband before her, gave Elizabeth a hug.

"It's good to get out," Elizabeth lied, once disentangled. The truth was she was counting the minutes until she could politely collect Chloe, return home, and collapse.

The doorbell rang again, dulcet chimes pealing just as they were heading inside.

Lissa called from upstairs, "I'll get it!" With a clamber of footsteps and flashing legs, Lissa and Chloe raced madly down the steps to the front door. "It's my house!" Lissa shrieked.

"I'm here first!" Chloe yelled back.

"You can both open the door," Vivian called, rolling her eyes.

Bill said dryly, "Like Lissa's going to let that happen."

"They're so competitive," Elizabeth said and glanced at a clock mounted high over the bar. If she could just go home. Everyone was nice, but she was just overwhelmed, and she didn't want to spend her energy trying to keep Lissa and Chloe in their separate corners.

Nadia Vandell. Elizabeth suddenly remembered Vivian's friend's last name as she entered the foyer. She was the last member to join their Moms Group as she hadn't been around when they first formed and she didn't have any children. Vivian had asked if she could join and everyone agreed as there was no exclusivity. Their common interests had been their children in the beginning, but as the years past they were simply friends. Nadia's husband, Kurt, another spouse Elizabeth had yet to meet, was out of town, Nadia explained, so, for the night, she was a single, too. "We can stick together," Nadia said, flashing a smile as she plucked a glass of wine from Bill.

Within seconds, before the door could close again and there was another fight about who would answer it, Tara arrived with her daughter Bibi, and her husband, Dave. Elizabeth remembered Dave as she'd met him a couple of times before, once when he popped in on one of their Moms Group Happy Hours, and another time when Tara and Bibi had stopped by after a dance class that Chloe and Bibi had taken. When Tara's car had refused to start, Dave came to pick them up.

An impromptu barbecue had ensued, where Dave went to the store for all the fixings for hot dogs and hamburgers, and Elizabeth served gin and tonics to the adults and lemonade to the girls while they waited for Triple A to come and recharge the battery in Tara's car.

Though she'd called to warn Court that they had company for dinner, he'd come home in a dark mood, turning down offers of all the food and sipping his gin and tonic with a tight, angry look on his face. After the Hofstetters had left, Elizabeth had braced herself for a lecture, but Court simply said he wanted more notice next time and had gone to the bedroom and shut the door while she cleaned the kitchen. As bad as things had been between them, Elizabeth figured she'd gotten off easy.

No, she thought, sipping her wine in Vivian's grand kitchen, *I really don't miss my husband, at least not his bad moods and sharp comments.*

As Bibi zipped upstairs to join the other girls, Dave greeted Elizabeth with a hug, too. "I wish there was something I could do." A gym rat, he had a compact, athletic body, kind face, and hair that was turning prematurely gray.

"I'm fine, really. It's . . . hard, but . . ."

Try to pretend that you care. . . .

She *did* care. She cared that Court was gone. She cared that he'd been lying to her. She cared that she'd wished him dead. Any sadness she felt was for a love lost, promises broken, a dream shattered, all which had occurred before her husband's death.

"Are you good with that?" Dave asked, inclining his head to the barely touched glass of wine she held in her hand. In the kitchen spotlights, his crown glimmered with strands of silver.

Court had displayed the beginnings of gray hair, too, but he'd been death on admitting it and woe to anyone who had the bad form to make a comment about it.

Elizabeth took a sip of her Merlot and gave Dave a thumb's up. He was tall, like Court and Bill and had a strong chest and muscular arms. She wouldn't have had to be told he was into working out; it was stamped all over him.

That reminded her that she should cancel her membership to Fitness Now! Oh, God, there were so many things to do, so many loose ends to tie up, so many reminders of Court.

Vivian rounded up all the kids and got them situated on the covered patio with juice boxes and slices of pizza on paper plates. The temperature was pleasant enough that coats and sweaters had been shed.

"If anyone's ready for dinner, pull off the plastic wrap." She signaled to Bill to do just that as she stuffed her hands into oversized mitts, then bent to the oven and pulled out a broiler pan with two large flank steaks sizzling away. "Five, ten minutes and we'll be ready to serve."

"I'm liking the hors d'oeuvres," Les said, spreading brie and fig jam on a cracker.

"You're like Kurt," Nadia said. "He loves the appetizers."

"Who doesn't?" Deirdre piped up as she replicated her husband's choices.

They slowly moved to the dining room table and seated themselves. Vivian directed Elizabeth to sit at one end and Bill to sit at the other while she took a seat to her left, which gave her ease to get up and down to the kitchen.

Throughout the meal, the conversation stayed with small talk, nothing serious discussed until talk inevitably strayed to the memorial service. The kids had already rushed back inside and ran like a herd up the stairs, the boys joining the girls. Elizabeth had finally made it to the bottom of her wine glass and Bill, who'd gotten up to bring the bottle to the table, was quick to give her a refill before she could demur.

"I invited Jade, but she's just feeling too pregnant," Vivian said, cutting off a bite of steak and popping it into her mouth.

"When's she due again?" Nadia asked. She was on Elizabeth's right and when Bill lifted his brows in query she held up her wine glass for him to top off as well.

Her question reminded Elizabeth of Nadia's inability to conceive and it seemed to catch Vivian up, too, as she hesitated before saying, "Ummm . . . six weeks or maybe eight?"

Nadia looked straight at Elizabeth. Her eyes were the same shade of blue as Chloe's and had the same piercing quality. A line drew between her brows. "Are we having a baby shower for her?"

"Nah." Deirdre shook her head. Her honey blond hair was pulled into a loose ponytail.

Blond woman with a messy bun . . .

The wayward thought slid through Elizabeth's mind like a snake and for a second she felt her stomach clench. She had purposely worn her hair down tonight and clipped away from her face.

"Nobody wants to go to a shower for a second one," Deirdre went on. "We should just have a kind of open house after the baby's here." She waved a hand over the table. "Wine, appetizers, small sand- wiches . . . this kind of thing."

"Good idea," Tara said. Her hair had been recently bleached again, but she'd battled its dryness with a lot of product and it lay smooth and stiff at an angle to her chin.

Vivian's poof of hair was corralled into a tight bun this evening, and for once she'd given up her workout gear for a blue shift that showed off her tanned arms and legs.

Blondes. We're all blondes. Elizabeth's throat tightened. Funny, she'd never noticed that fact before.

Because it doesn't matter. Don't go all psycho just because your friends are comfortable with L'Oreal.

Elizabeth forced down what she could of the meal and once everyone was finished and had complimented Vivian a dozen times over on the food, Vivian got up and went to the freezer, pulling out a mud pie. "I can't take credit for this," she said, slicing up the dessert and putting it onto small plates.

Elizabeth's stomach was still in knots and she begged off, though everyone else had a piece, the women sighing as if the dessert was somewhat orgasmic. Elizabeth just wanted out.

At last, they pushed away from the table and walked onto the patio to drink coffee with or without Baileys, Elizabeth followed, wondering how to escape.

Vivian clinked her cup with Elizabeth's, then said sheepishly, "I got a chance to get my aggressions out after I left the grave site today." She leaned back in her patio chair and cradled her cup. "Some damned asshole cut me off when I was driving home and I just laid on the horn. God, I swear it was a full minute. He was pissed as hell, but it made me feel so great." She sighed. "Dumb, huh?"

Elizabeth could barely speak for a second, but managed to squeak out a "No." Deirdre, Tara, and Nadia agreed.

"Sometimes it feels good to just blast someone, you know?" Tara said.

The men were in a group a few feet away, all wrapped up in some story. Dave glanced over his shoulder at Tara, but whether he heard her or not Elizabeth couldn't say.

"So many idiots on the road." It was Nadia, this time.

Elizabeth was nodding. "I had an incident like that today, too," Elizabeth admitted, lowering her voice so the men couldn't hear.

"You?" Nadia sounded disbelieving.

"Yeah, me. It's kind of embarrassing." She went on to tell them about her run-in. "I was so mad that I actually chased him for a while. Easy to follow. His license plate said GoodGuy. Like, what did I think I was doing? I'm a single mother now, and I'm not a moron, at least most of the time. It was . . . kind of unreal." She let out a long breath. "No, *very* unreal. I can't believe I did that."

"GoodGuy." Nadia shook her head. "My Kurt really is a good guy, but he'd never have a license plate that said so."

Deirdre snorted. "Nobody would, if they had any sense."

"Guys with vanity plates, right?" Tara muttered, rolling her eyes.

"Court had one for a while," Elizabeth said. "The number four plus words *the law*. But he felt it was too noticeable so he got rid of it. He liked being under the radar."

There was silence to that. Everyone knew what Court was like, about the secret life he'd been leading with Whitney Bellhard, and, Elizabeth thought, perhaps others. Whitney could have just been the latest in a string of lovers . . . but she wouldn't go there, not tonight.

Vivian straightened in her chair. "GoodGuy?" she repeated. "I know I'd seen that license plate, but I couldn't remember where. But . . . I think, no, I'm pretty sure I saw it in the parking lot of Fitness Now! Maybe he's a member!"

"Oh, no," Elizabeth said.

"You're a member there, right?" Nadia asked.

"Yes. But I was thinking of dropping. Now I know I will," Elizabeth said to a chorus of "No," "Don't," and "That's the last thing you should do."

Embarrassed, she said, "I think I don't have much of a choice, anyway." She explained a little about her finances, finishing with, "Apparently Court was just turning a blind eye to the state of our financial affairs."

"Don't give up your membership yet," Vivian insisted. "We'll figure something out."

"But now that you know where he is, you should leave a note on his car or something," Tara said.

"Key it," Deirdre suggested dryly, her eyes flashing.

"Whoa. Let's not get her arrested," Tara said, holding up a hand and sending Deirdre an *are-you-kidding* look.

"I like the note idea," Nadia said.

"What are you girls talking about?" Les asked, ambling over and placing a hand on his wife's shoulder.

"Nothing, dear," Deirdre singsonged back to him.

"I think I'll just stay away from him," Elizabeth said, knowing the best thing to do was leave well enough alone.

At that moment, an ear-splitting shriek reverberated down from the stairs.

Elizabeth stood up. "Uh oh."

Bibi raced down the stairs, her hair flying, her legs nearly tripping. "Lissa and Chloe are fighting," she tattled, throwing herself into Tara's arms.

Finally, it was time to go.

CHAPTER 11

The silver blue Mercedes wheeled to a stop in front of Ivy at the Shore on Ocean Avenue, a hot-spot Ravinia had learned was frequented by Hollywood stars. Immediately, the car door opened and the woman Rex was following stepped into the street and handed a valet the keys to her convertible. Tucked inside a tight, white dress that showed lots of cleavage and was stretched around one of the roundest butts Ravinia had ever seen, the woman headed into the restaurant.

Ravinia couldn't help but stare when she thought about the long dresses Aunt Catherine had fashioned for them. High collars, sleeves to the wrist, hems that swept the wooden floor of the lodge. "Some dress. What's wrong with her?" She continued to stare even as the door closed behind the woman in white.

"What?" Rex asked.

"Her rear end doesn't fit the rest of her."

"Probably butt implants," Rex said.

"That was a *choice?*" Ravinia couldn't believe it.

"I guess." But he really didn't seem to be paying much attention to the conversation as he drove slowly past the restaurant. "You know, this would be about the last place for a rendezvous," he muttered, frowning.

Ravinia agreed. The area was crowded with cars lining the street and pedestrians walking past—women with strollers, joggers, joggers *with* strollers, and skate-boarders. "So where're you gonna park?"

"There isn't anywhere," he said as they circled the block again, not a single spot open. "Maybe I'll valet my car and stick around a while." But he scowled as if the idea didn't appeal to him. "Don't know if it's worth it."

"You gonna follow her in?" Again Ravinia eyed the doors where the woman in the white dress had entered.

"I'm not ready to get that close to her. Don't want her to remember my face."

"I could go in," she offered.

He seemed to come out of a fog and gave a hoot of laughter. "You? You look like a skateboarder." He shook his head. "No. You're not going into the Ivy. Look, I shouldn't have taken you on this stakeout in the first place. It was a mistake and so, this is probably a good time for us to separate. There's a motel up the street. I don't think it's too much money. You could rent a room there."

"I sleep in the park," she said, a little wounded at being dismissed. They'd circled around to Ocean again, and she pointed toward the area where she'd camped. "Right over there."

"No, you don't," he said, but she could tell he believed her and was slightly horrified at the thought.

"Sure I do." She reached for the door handle and hitched her chin in the direction of the Ivy. "So, I'll just go in and take a look around, see who she's with."

"Not a chance. Everybody'll look at you in there, notice you. You'll stick out like a sore thumb. First order of surveillance? Fit into your surroundings."

"What's her name again?" Ravinia asked as he pulled the car as close as he could to the entrance and a valet appeared with a ticket.

"I never said. That was a choice, too."

As Rex was talking to the valet, Ravinia opened the car door. Backpack slung over her shoulder, she headed for the front door.

"Hey!" Rex called.

"Gotta use the bathroom," she said over her shoulder, and breezed her way in and found the ladies' room. She did draw a few long stares, but she acted like she owned the place and no one stopped her. A good thing as she did, in fact, need to use the facilities.

Pushing open the door, she caught a quick glimpse of two women who were freshening up their makeup. A redhead was applying gloss to extremely full lips. Next to her, a tiny Asian woman in impossibly high platform shoes was turning her head this way and that, surveying her image. They barely gave Ravinia a glance as they were in a deep discussion about the audition process.

"I actually saw Frank Milo and *said hi to him!*" the redhead said importantly.

"No, fucking way. What was the producer doing there?" her friend demanded.

"One of the casting people is his daughter, Natalie."

"No!"

"Yeah, who knew, right? She's about my age. Looks way too natural, though. Birkenstocks."

"Oh."

"She'd be kinda pretty if she actually did anything with herself, but you know . . . it looks like she's making a statement."

"One of *those.*"

Redhead added, "She was nice enough, though. She even thanked me."

"But they all do. That's just a way to get you to move along."

Click. Sounded like a compact or clutch purse closing.

"I know. But I think this might have been different." There was a pause, then the redhead added, "If I could just get on a hit show like *Dragonworld*, my God . . ."

Their voices faded away as they left the restroom, the door opening and closing.

Ravinia flushed the toilet, then washed her hands. Nothing like a good clean bathroom. She glanced at her own reflection, plain and dreary compared to the other women who couldn't have been much older than she. Not that she wanted to be anything like them. Still . . . she saw the smudge on her chin and scrubbed it off, irritated that Rex hadn't said anything. Then she turned on the hot water and washed her entire face. With a glance at her clothes, she frowned. A few stains, but mainly just wrinkled. Tucking a few wayward wisps of hair into her braid, she admitted to herself that she might need to find that motel Rex had mentioned, after all.

But first she had a job to do—to prove herself, if nothing more.

She slipped out of the restroom and wandered back into the main part of the restaurant where she observed the two women she'd overheard join a table with two guys, twenty-somethings in slacks and polo shirts, both on cell phones. They barely acknowledged their dates.

Figured.

Her gaze swung around the room. She didn't immediately see the woman in white, so she moved into a second room. *Bingo!* The woman they'd been following was sitting by herself. She, too, was talking rapidly into a cell phone.

Ravinia narrowed her eyes, thinking about her next move. When she flicked a look toward the maître d's stand, she caught a glimpse of Rex who was apparently asking about a table. Jaw set, he caught her eye and shook his head slowly, warning her off.

She could tell he was pissed.

Ignoring him, she wended her way through the tables, slowing her steps when she was directly behind the woman in white and making a point of looking around the room as if searching for someone.

"Not that simple," the woman was saying. "I have a life, you know." A pause, while a tinny voice spoke, then, "You think I haven't been thinking about *you*? One more week. I promise. That's all or I'll go crazy. I just have to make sure. I'm meeting him now and we're just talking. He wants the split to look like it's both of us. Gotta save face, you know. I'll see you Tuesday, and we'll work it all out. Casa del Mar. Be patient."

"May I help you?" a waiter asked, sneaking up behind Ravinia.

She turned sharply and gave him a look. His hair was medium brown with blond tips and he had dark eyes filled with suspicion. A sneer threatened his lips.

"Just trying to find my father," she said breezily. "Frank Milo? You know him?"

Still suspicious, he looked her up and down, a line forming between his brows. "I don't believe I do."

"You should." She leaned in and whispered with meaning, "The producer . . ." Straightening before people at other tables keyed into their conversation too closely, she added, "I don't see him, but if he shows, tell him Natalie was here."

"Well . . ." he said uncertainly.

Why Natalie might be carrying a backpack and looking like she'd been camping for two weeks was a question Ravinia didn't want him asking, so she beat feet back to the front door. Rex was nowhere to be seen, so she gave the maître d' a smile and sailed back outside.

She was debating on what to do next when Rex suddenly reappeared from a side exit.

His lips were compressed as he approached.

Uh-oh.

Grabbing her by the arm, he propelled her away from the front door and kept his voice low. "What the hell were you doing?"

"Investigating," she said, then quickly added, "She's here to meet her husband and try to work things out. She said he just wants the split to look like it's from the two of them. To save face."

"How do you know this? She was sitting alone."

"She was on the phone to lover boy." Ravinia yanked her arm from his grasp. "I heard her side of the conversation, or at least part of it. She said she'd see him Tuesday at Casa del Mar and to give her a week. She said she won't be able to stand it any longer."

"Huh." Rex handed a valet his ticket and watched as the valet hurried off in search of the car, "What else? Anything?"

"You know a producer named Frank Milo?

"I think I've heard of him," Rex said thoughtfully. "He's got a couple hit TV shows."

"Dragonworld?"

He stared at her as if he didn't believe this backwoods girl who'd been locked inside a lodge in Oregon could know anything about Hollywood. "Yeah, maybe. But I don't get it. Is that who Kimberley was talking to?"

"Nope. Auditions are just going on. It was the talk in the bathroom."

He muttered something under his breath and shook his head.

"But now you have some time," she pointed out with a lift of her chin, "when nothing's going to happen with her. So, you can start helping me."

"If I believe you."

"I don't lie."

He made a sound in his throat she couldn't quite decipher, and then said, "You and I haven't written up a contract."

"What kind of contract?"

"A business contract. That's how this kind of thing works. I give you a contract with my rates, and you sign it and give me a retainer."

The valet showed up with the gray car and Rex handed him some bills.

It didn't take a genius to figure out that he was annoyed with her, so before he could leave her on the street, which Ravinia sensed wasn't that far out of range, she slid into the passenger seat and dutifully buckled up. "And after I sign this form, you'll find Elizabeth?" she clarified.

"I'll try."

She hesitated. "What's a retainer?"

He rubbed the first two fingers of one hand against his thumb. When Ravinia regarded him blankly, he said, "*Money*," as if she were dense.

She threw him a dark look.

As they pulled away from the curb, Rex looked in his rearview mirror. "Well, you were right about one thing," he admitted and she twisted, craning her head to peer out the back window. "That's Dorell now. Her husband. He must be meeting her."

"I was right about everything," she corrected.

His answer was a snort.

Forty minutes later, Rex walked Ravinia into the motel office of the Sea Breeze Inn, a two-level motel on Santa Monica Boulevard that looked like it could use a little less sea breeze and a little more TLC on the peeling paint and cracked pavement of the parking lot.

"I can book my own room," Ravinia said testily.

He didn't know what the hell he was doing with her. It was like she was the daughter he'd never had and he felt responsible for her in a way that defied description. One minute she seemed streetwise and sly as a fox, the next naive as a lamb.

"Yeah, but will you?" he asked.

"I have money. I just don't like using it."

"I'm not leaving you on the street so you can sleep in the park."

"Fine, fine. We're here, aren't we? I'll take the room."

He'd tried several other motels first, but she'd shaken her head and been completely obstinate until he'd pulled into the Sea Breeze, which was a few rungs down the ladder on luxury.

He held open the door and she swept under his arm, her back stiff. No one was at the desk and so Ravinia, spying a bell, rang it half a dozen times, slapping her palm on it so rapidly that it jumped and jangled and looked like it had a will of its own.

"Are you going to start tonight?" she asked, not looking at him.

"Looking for your cousin? No. I'm going to go home and have a drink and think for a while."

"Where's home?" She turned and looked at him with those blue-green eyes.

"About an hour away in good traffic, so most of the time an hour and a half away, maybe two."

"But where?"

"Costa Mesa," he said reluctantly. *You should just lie to her.*

"You live with anybody?"

"No. And I'm not planning to, either."

"I wasn't asking to move in," she said tightly.

"Good. Because I don't need a roommate, and if I did, I'd choose someone with better credentials than yours."

"What do you know about my credentials?"

"Nothing. From what I can tell, you don't have any."

"I'm truthful, and I'm not crazy."

"Good for you."

"Slow down, slow down, honey!" A middle-aged woman in black sweats and bleached, spiky blond hair appeared. Waving Ravinia away from the bell, she glanced over at Rex and smiled. "You want a room?"

"She does," he said. "Alone."

"I have cash," Ravinia told her in that straightforward way he was growing used to. "No credit card."

The woman eyed Ravinia sourly. "Well, then you're gonna have to put down a cash deposit, just in case, you know."

"No. What do you mean?"

"Now, don't get all riled up," the woman advised, holding up her hands, palms out. "Just in case you skip out, that's all I'm sayin'."

"I'm not going to skip out," Ravinia said huffily.

Rex had to fight the urge to put his own credit card down. What the hell was that all about? It wasn't like him to want to fix a situation, but in Ravinia's case, it was almost like she'd put him under some kind of spell that made him act out of his usual cynical character. Then again, according to Ravinia herself, a spell wasn't that far outside of her or her family's "gifts." Oh, hell. He was starting to actually listen to her fantasies.

As she and the woman behind the reception counter hashed out the details of the transaction, Rex hung around, not leaving until the business between Ravinia and the Sea Breeze was concluded. After he saw that she was being handed a key, he made his escape by walking across the parking lot to his car. He didn't get far.

She was right on his heels. "Wait up!" she called.

"What?" he asked, stopping short and turning to face her.

"I need a way to make money, and I could help you."

"No." He kept walking, but she stayed in step with him.

"I know what you're like," she announced, shifting her backpack from one shoulder to the other. "Tough on the outside, but all gooey and soft on the inside."

"You don't know anything about me." He ignored the memory of their first meeting when he'd thought for just a second that she could see into his soul.

"You like me and you don't know why because you're basically suspicious and really don't like anybody at first. I don't blame you for that. I get it. And you want to think I'm a whack job, but you're half-convinced I'm not."

He dug his keys from his pocket, and using the remote, unlocked the car from a distance. But she didn't stop.

"You won't admit it, but you want me to help you. You weren't as pissed off at me as you feel you should have been after I went into the Ivy and got information you didn't. You've been looking for a partner and here I am."

Rex's mouth dropped open, more at her attitude than her accuracy. "How old are you? Twenty? Twenty-one?"

"Nineteen," she admitted after a moment.

"For the love of God."

"This was the best day you've had in a long time," she insisted.

"You don't know anything about me," he repeated, not quite believing it himself.

Her chin inched up a notch and those intense eyes stared at him. "I know you were bored with your job and now you're not."

"I gotta go," Rex said, the hairs on his arms lifting. "You're damn eerie, you know that."

"Yeah. It's kind of a family trait."

He held up his hands to ward her off and give himself some space as he reached the car. "I'll look into your cousin's whereabouts, I promise. See what I can find out."

"Elizabeth Gaines."

"Got it."

"You have my cell number?" she called as he turned away.

"Yep." He climbed into the rental and started the engine. As he backed around, then shoved the gears into drive and hit the gas, he saw her in the side-view mirror.

She hadn't moved, her arms crossed over her chest as she watched him leave.

CHAPTER 12

Twenty minutes later, Ravinia stepped out of the shower and dried herself with one of the Sea Breeze's thin towels. The room was foggy as the fan didn't work, but she felt refreshed, her skin and hair clean, her mind already racing ahead to her next move.

As she swiped at the condensation on the mirror, she heard her cell phone ringing.

Naked, she ran to where she'd plugged it in and left it on the faux wood desktop. Snatching it up, she looked at the screen. *Rex already?* Her eagerness was blunted when she saw it was a number she didn't recognize it. "Hello?" she answered cautiously.

"Ravinia?"

Aunt Catherine.

Ravinia felt more anxiety than elation. Though she really, really wanted to talk to her aunt, Ravinia also needed some time to process her day with Rex Kingston and everything she'd learned. Something was happening. She could feel herself being pulled in the right direction for the first time in a long while, as if some unseen presence was holding her hand and making sure she found the right path. *Maybe I have a guardian angel.*

"Did you get a cell phone?" Ravinia asked. She couldn't hear the background noise she always associated with the Drift In Market, the store where Catherine usually used the phone, so it sounded as if her aunt was somewhere else.

"I'm using your sister's," she said primly.

"Ophelia? She's got a cell phone?" That kind of pissed Ravinia off for reasons she couldn't quite name. Maybe it was because Ophelia was the only one of her sisters at the lodge who was living in the twenty-first century. Or, more likely, it was Ophelia's superior tone, the one she used as if she were somehow in charge—which, of course, she wasn't. Ophelia had told Ravinia she'd gotten her driver's license and she was all about modernizing the lodge, and that was all for the good, but she'd blithely gone and done all sorts of things—privileges—with nary a word to any of the rest of them, except, of course, Aunt Catherine. Ophelia had known how much Ravinia had wanted her own driver's license and it was almost as if her older sister had been lording it over her.

"Yes." Aunt Catherine was short. She hated being interrupted. "How are you doing? Are you all right?"

"Fine," Ravinia said, eyeing her bleak surroundings, the stained blue carpet, faded bed spread that didn't quite match the curtains, the TV that was about the same age as the one at the lodge. "I'm fine." She unzipped her backpack with her free hand, finding her underwear.

"So, have you made any progress?"

"I made it to Santa Monica," she said, struggling into her clothes. "I haven't found Elizabeth yet, but I've got some ideas."

"Ideas? Nothing concrete?"

"Not yet. But I haven't been here long." When her aunt didn't respond, Ravinia asked, "Has anything changed? Have you heard from Silas or—"

"No. Not really."

"What's that mean?" Silas was her brother, the good one, the one she considered her friend, one of the few people in the world she trusted. Juggling the phone, she pulled on a pair of jeans.

"We haven't been bothered. No one's come here," her aunt assured her. "But that doesn't mean we're safe, nor you, nor Elizabeth." She sighed loudly. "I'm afraid it could be just the calm before the storm."

Ravinia's insides clenched. "But you're still sure Elizabeth's a target?"

A pause. "Yes," Aunt Catherine whispered softly, her worry audible. "I just want to make sure she's safe."

"I'm working on it. Really. I don't want anything bad to happen to her or anyone else," Ravinia said, feeling her aunt's urgency as if it were directly transmitted to her.

"Me neither. Please. Stay safe."

Ravinia's throat clogged at her aunt's concern. She felt tears touch the back of her eyelids but pushed them back as she found a nearly clean long-sleeved T-shirt. "I've got this number now, so I can call you or Ophelia back."

"Yes. Good. Phone when you find Elizabeth. Or if you just learn something."

"I will."

"And make it soon." Aunt Catherine added, "Please," as if hearing how demanding she sounded. "Be careful, Ravinia."

"Will do," Ravinia answered, hanging up and praying Rex was going to get on the job ASAP. She wiggled into her T-shirt, then walked to the window and peered through a slit in the curtains. Dusk had given way to night, but the darkness was kept at bay by the street lamps and security lights that cast bluish shadows over the parking lot in front of the units. In a weird way, this night-turned-day seemed more dangerous to Ravinia than the complete darkness that surrounded Siren Song at night. There, she heard the dull roar of the ocean in the distance, the rush of wind through the fir boughs, the pelting of rain in the crushing darkness, but there was a safety in the Stygian depths of the Pacific rainforest.

In the city, not so.

She felt an unlikely shiver run through her and for a second, she longed for the safety of her home, the tall walls surrounding Siren Song, the quiet hoots of the owls, the soft purr of bat's wings, the familiar security of her family, her aunt and sisters surrounding her.

Steadfastly, she tamped those emotions deep into the back of her consciousness. No room for maudlin nostalgia or second-guessing. She had a job to do, a mission she embraced.

She let the curtains fall into place, wishing to high heaven tomorrow wasn't Sunday because she wanted, no, she *needed* Rex Kingston on the job.

Sitting on the edge of her daughter's bed, Elizabeth closed the book she'd been reading. Chloe was already out cold and snoring softly. Her daughter ran at full speed and slept so hard a cannon could practically shoot off next to her and she would sleep through it. "Good night," Elizabeth whispered, kissing Chloe's crown and drawing the cover over her shoulders. "Love you."

Flipping off the light, then softly closing the door behind her, Elizabeth turned toward her own bedroom, then detoured to the third bedroom, which had been turned into Court's den. A modern desk with a glass surface resting on curved metal legs sat in the center of the room. Upon the desk, next to the files she'd brought from the office, was her laptop. She ran a finger over its cover before glancing to the row of industrial black file cabinets that rested beside the window and against the wall. Court had kept the cabinets locked, but in the past few days she'd found the key and opened all of them one by one, searching quickly through the documents and finding nothing sensitive inside, at least as far as she could see.

She'd found piles of paid bills and various and sundry desk items—a stapler, a box of pens, paperclips, scissors, and such in the desk. One drawer was filled with stacks of unused printer paper, which fed the printer that sat atop a credenza across the room. The credenza wasn't much more than two smaller file cabinets stuck together with a painted black metal top, but she remembered Court insisted on purchasing it despite its cost—a small fortune—and now the damned piece of office furniture had outlived him.

Something inside her broke and for a second, a few tears burned in her eyes, though she knew they were more for her small family, her dream of what it should be and not really for the man. The three of them, Court, Chloe, and her, had been a family once, if only briefly, though in truth, he'd never been much a part of it. Clearing her throat, she brushed aside the single tear that had tracked down her cheek and concentrated at the task at hand.

A number of unpaid bills had come in over the last week and she'd tucked them aside as she hadn't felt like tackling them. She sat down at the desk, slit open the envelopes, and laid the bills on the desk beside the work files, then switched on her computer. Court's laptop had been with him the day he'd died, and though she'd asked for it, the police hadn't given it to her yet. They clearly believed there was foul play involved in the accident, though nobody, including Detective Thronson, would come out completely and say so.

Elizabeth paused, her hand poised over the keys as she thought about the police. It was bothersome and aggravating and she couldn't help but feel a low grade fear whenever she thought about Detective Thronson's call. *A woman who looks like you was at Tres Brisas and in some kind of race or game on the freeway with Court and Whitney Bellhard.*

Elizabeth adjusted the desk chair, thinking about that. Was there a possibility that the accident had been more about Whitney than Court? Whitney's husband Peter had admitted to following them to Rosarito Beach, but no one was saying anything about that. Maybe he was more upset about their relationship than Elizabeth had been. In life, Whitney had been pushy and tough. She'd rubbed a lot of people the wrong way. If foul play had been involved, if a crime had been committed, could Whitney have been the target, and the horrible deaths of Court and Whitney the result of that?

Elizabeth sat back in her chair. Court had been at the wheel, yes, but if someone had been chasing them down, forcing an accident . . .

A blond woman in a dark SUV.

Elizabeth almost bought into her new theory when two faces— Mazie's and Officer Unfriendly's—flitted across the screen of her mind. They, too, had died violently . . . seemingly because of her. She shook her head, putting Court's accident and the reasons behind it aside for the moment and concentrated on what she could do, which was get her life back on track, starting with the finances.

Court had paid all their bills online, but he'd been a stickler for keeping paper records, thank heavens, and he'd actually made a list of passwords, which he'd taped to the inside of one of the bottom drawers of the desk. Looking over that list, she accessed the Internet and clicked her way to their joint bank account. She'd seen paper statements sporadically; Court had never deigned to go green and well, there'd been nothing "eco-friendly" about him, but she'd never seen all of their accounts together on one screen before.

All six of their accounts, she thought, counting them up and beginning to feel slightly ill. None of them had more than a couple hundred dollars, and most were closer to a zero balance. She looked at recent payments made and saw there were hefty chunks paid to Court's credit cards. She stared at the screen for a long time. As she scrolled through the last few months of online statements, she realized he'd been paying for his affair on credit, which had grown increasingly expensive. And he'd been sending the statements to his office.

His office . . .

For the most part, his coworkers had stayed away from her at the funeral. She'd recognized only a few of them anyway, so it hadn't seemed strange. Of course, she realized that some of them could have known more about his private affairs than she did. In fact, that was a pretty good guess.

Not that it mattered anymore.

Several of the bills next to her computer were close to past due. She paid the ones she could via the Internet. She'd always run their household on the money Court had transferred from his account to their joint account, but unless there was cash in some other bank, she was close to destitute.

She did know how much they owed on the house, and though it was enough to make her stomach tremble, she also knew the house was worth far more than the mortgage. She just had to sell quickly as the bill collectors were going to be at her door.

As for life insurance, she hadn't known Court to carry any. A quick look through the filing cabinet again revealed no policies, of course. During their marriage, they'd never discussed the need for insurance on his life. Or hers, for that matter. She'd have to rethink that, for Chloe's sake.

Not having a huge life insurance policy had one good side, at least as far as the police were involved. Without the big financial win from Court's demise, there was less of a motive for his wife to have killed him.

Oh. Dear. God.

She stared at the stack of unpaid bills that remained and wondered how she could possibly pay them before the house sold. Impossible with the money in their accounts. Just trying to figure out how to get by in the next month or two made her head hurt.

"Maybe I can wish him back alive," she said on a half laugh, half sob.

Except she didn't want him back. Not now . . . not ever. She was sorry he was dead, but she wasn't sorry he was out of her life, out of her daughter's life. In truth, he was a lousy husband and even worse father.

Fate or whatever or whoever had killed him, had done her a favor.

The room was quiet and dark with only the diffused dot of the tension lamp illuminating the vellum stationary. The hand clutching the pen was taut, squeezing.

Emotion. Too much emotion.

Calm down.

Breathe deeply.

Let go . . .

Finally, the pressure was released until the pen was held in a manner that allowed the words to be written. Important words.

Elizabeth,

It's all for you. Do you understand yet? I've been hiding my feelings for so long, but now finally, I can let you know. I'm sick, you see. Sick with love for you. Heartsick. Soul sick. I'm going to give you everything you desire. I am your slave, your genie in a bottle. Command me, and I will deliver. I grow stronger because of you. You don't see me yet. I'm just a flicker in the corner of your eye. But you'll see me soon, my love. Very, very soon.

CHAPTER 13

It took longer than expected to find the trail that led to Ralph and Joy Gaines of Sausalito and then, supposedly, to Santa Monica. Rex had searched public records and finally found a business license in Costa Mesa registered to Ralph and Joy Gaines for an independent insurance agency, formerly Gaines-Connett, now Harper Insurance Agency.

Well, that's convenient, since I live here, Rex thought as he stood in his kitchen and sipped his first cup of coffee.

Further investigation was just a matter of showing up and asking the right questions. As far as a residence however, he'd struck out. A number of Ralph Gaineses were listed throughout southern California, but Rex couldn't find anyone associated with a woman named Joy.

Staring out the sliding door of his two-bedroom house, he watched as a robin hopped through the damp grass, pecking as it made its way across his lawn.

Ralph and Joy could have divorced or she could have died. Those records would be easily located and confirmed.

He thought about whether to give Ravinia the information on the phone, meet her in person, or make a trip on Monday to the insurance agency by himself before actually contacting her. He commuted from Costa Mesa to his office in Los Angeles three times a week on an average, depending upon where a case led him. Of course, he could live closer to his business but had found it didn't really matter where he called home; he was contacted by people from all over the southern half of the state. Sometimes northern, too, and that covered a lot of territory.

The question was, did he really want to report to Ravinia yet? They had paperwork to complete, and he knew better than to start working on a case before he had a contract in hand. A couple deadbeats had taught him that lesson long ago. Still, he felt like going against his instincts and calling her, which made him shake his head at himself. That damn girl made him feel like he'd fallen down the rabbit hole.

And she also got your juices flowing, didn't she? About the case? As bizarre as it sounds, it's more interesting than following Kim Cochran around.

His cell phone rang and he eagerly snatched it up until he saw Pamela's number. For half a second he considered not answering it. *Chickenshit*, he told himself and made a point of saying with false cheer, "Good morning."

"Hey, there, handsome," she greeted him. "What do you want to do first? Breakfast? Or, I could come over to your place and we could start in bed?"

The day with Pamela. He'd promised it and promised it and here it was. Inwardly he groaned, then realized spending time with her shouldn't feel like such an obligation.

There's nothing wrong with her. She's fun, energetic, fairly optimistic, attractive, and smart. There's absolutely nothing wrong with her. What do you want? The earth to move every time you're together?

He caved. "How about I pick you up and we do breakfast? I want to drive by a business off Seventeenth, then we can go to that place you like."

"The Breakfast Plate."

"That's it," he said, making note of her cool tone.

"Well, okay as long as it's the *only* work-related thing of the day."

The steel behind the words gave him pause. "There could be one more thing," he tried, thinking of Ravinia. He knew he should leave well enough alone but couldn't help himself.

"No more things, Joel," she insisted. "No more things. Today's just for us."

He felt himself grimace. Yes, *Joel* was his name, but he never used it. He didn't think of himself as a Joel, but Pamela had glommed onto it as if it made some kind of difference. "You know my job's not a nine-to-fiver."

"All I want is today. One Sunday. Can't you give me that?"

Why did it feel like a noose was tightening around his neck? From the corner of his eye, he caught movement out the window, a flutter of feathers as the robin pounced, snapping up the worm and flying into the low-hanging branches of a tree. "I'll try," he said into the phone, already knowing that it was a lie.

Looking like she just rolled out of bed, Misty came over to the house about eleven o'clock. Slipping her cell phone into the front pocket of her jeans, she eyed Chloe warily as if she knew just how much the little girl had complained about her babysitting skills.

Elizabeth half expected Chloe to reprimand Misty, but her daughter had seemingly forgotten, or at least chosen to ignore her own pique at the teenager. In fact, Chloe ran to Misty as soon as she entered and dragged the reluctant teenager to the kitchen table where diamonds, stars, and circles cut from colored paper were in abundance. Chloe had been working to make some kind of collage.

"Hi," Elizabeth said, already scooping up her purse and a jacket.

Misty nodded to her as she tried to feign interest in Chloe's art.

With a glance at the clock, Elizabeth said, "Lunch stuff is in the fridge. Fruit, cheese and there's always peanut butter sandwiches. I've got to get a move on." She hugged Chloe who barely noticed. "Be good. Love you." To Misty, she said, "I'll be back by around four-thirty."

Scrounging in her purse for her keys, Elizabeth was walking to the back door when Misty called after her, "Can you make it back on time today?"

Elizabeth paused, keys dangling from her fingers. First on her agenda was a quick meeting with Marg and Buddy. Marg wanted to see one more house and that was about all Elizabeth could manage before she was scheduled for an open house from one to four.

Misty said, "I've got semester finals coming up."

"Sure. Of course," Elizabeth said positively. "Yes. The open house ends at four and I'll come straight back."

"Good." Misty turned her attention back to Chloe and the art project.

On her way out, Elizabeth checked her cell phone and saw a text from Barbara who was just letting her know she'd made it home. Elizabeth felt a moment's relief as she walked into the garage. *See? Being angry at Barbara didn't bring her any harm.*

For a moment Elizabeth felt a little foolish. *You didn't really think you brought about Court's death, did you? Seriously?*

"And Mazie's . . . and Officer Unfriendly's . . ." she muttered as she climbed into her car and switched on the ignition, then pulled out.

Those were aberrations. Nothing to do with you.

She headed out of the neighborhood toward the office.

And what about the precognition with Little Nate? What was that all about?

With a glance in her rearview, she caught the worry in her eyes. "Not today," she told herself. "Not today."

With an effort, she pushed aside all her guilty thoughts and snapped on the radio to drown out the nagging voice in her head. She wheeled into Suncrest Realty, parked, and hurried inside. To her surprise, Jade was seated in a chair near the circular desk, where, as usual, Pat was sitting, headset in place, fingers poised over a keyboard but not typing.

"Hey, there. What brings you here?" Elizabeth greeted Jade warmly.

Pat, as always, was avidly listening in and pretending to be busy. Her interest in everyone else's business beyond annoying.

Inwardly, Elizabeth groaned, but she ignored her for the moment.

Jade flashed a quick smile. "Hi." The deep green sweater she wore looked great against her dark skin, her belly bump protruding. She sighed and apologized. "Sorry I missed last night. Things have just been crazy."

"Tell me about it. And anyway, you're pregnant. Everything feels kind of crazy at the end."

"I know, but seeing everyone at Vivian's would have been fun." Jade's dark eyes were sober. "So how're you doing, girl? I wanted to say more at the service, but . . . you seemed kind of like you wanted to just not talk."

"You read that right." Elizabeth turned her back to the reception desk, hoping that Pat wouldn't overhear. "I was . . . in a fog . . . a state of disbelief. I still am, I guess, but I'm okay." Of course, the last statement was a lie and even sounded false to her own ears.

"You can't be." Jade shook her head, hooped earrings catching in the light. "When things like this happen—"

"Yeah, I know. It's weird having Court gone," Elizabeth admitted, a shiver feathering down her spine. "But anyway, what are you doing here?"

"I'm just squeezing out some time this morning for myself, you know? Byron's taking care of Nate to give me a little time to myself."

"Want to come back to my office? I've got some clients coming in soon, but they're not here yet." Elizabeth pointed to the hallway.

Jade waved the offer away. "I should have known you'd have clients. I talked to Deirdre and she told me you said you were coming in around eleven today. I just thought I'd drop in and just say hi, and see how you were." Again she grinned. "You look fabulous, by the way."

"That's a joke."

"No, seriously. You look great. But you always do."

Elizabeth rolled her eyes. She felt as if she'd been through the wringer backward and forward. "You're a liar, but thanks."

"I hoped we'd have time for coffee, you know but no big deal. Another time."

"Maybe later?" Elizabeth said. "I've got an open house in University Park, but if you're around, maybe . . . ?"

"Don't I wish." Jade grinned again, showing a dimple. "I've barely been gone an hour and Byron's texted me twice. I swear that man is helpless when it comes to taking care of his own child. Wait till this one gets here." She dropped a hand to her rounded belly and patted it gently.

"The Sorensons just pulled up," Pat announced loudly from her desk then sent Elizabeth a quick, admonishing glare.

"Another time. It's a date!" Jade got to her feet and headed toward the door. "Oh, by the way, Deirdre told me about GoodGuy." Elizabeth felt her muscles tighten as Jade went on, "You know, I'm pretty sure I've seen that license plate at Fitness Now!, too, but, really, Elizabeth you can't let some jerk force you into giving up your membership. I mean it. I need to get this body back in shape as soon as Abercrombie shows up, and you need to be there."

"Abercrombie?"

"Or Fitch," Jade said, "depending on how I feel."

Elizabeth chuckled.

"You're not quitting," Jade insisted again. "There are too many *bad* guys with road rage just like GoodGuy."

"He's not the reason I'm quitting the club," Elizabeth assured her as they walked outside together. "It's more a matter of . . . getting my finances in order."

"Oh, honey." Jade hugged Elizabeth, who felt a sting of tears that she fought back.

As her friend walked toward her car, she pulled herself together and went to meet Buddy and Marg.

The morning crawled on and by eleven-thirty Rex had lost all interest in trying to appease Pamela. Somehow he'd made it through breakfast and had ended up at her condo for a quick regrouping, but already, the day was stretching long. The problem was, Pam didn't appear to be happy unless he was showering her with attention, and keeping up the pretense was not only exhausting but out of character for him. He'd never been the type to pretend interest or fawn over a woman.

He had to break it off with Pam; he knew it and had been considering how to end the relationship for a while, but until today it hadn't been so painfully obvious that they were wrong for each other. Once Ravinia, odd kid that she was, had shown up, his interest in his work, in his damn life had picked up. He *wanted* to help her, to find out more about this outré fantasy, sort fact from fiction. For the first time in months, he was jazzed about a case, interested in the twists and strange turns, even if they were all in Ravinia's head. She was a little wily, had a few street-smarts, and was certainly bullheaded, but she was refreshingly sincere and guileless in her own way. She intrigued him, was a mystery, and he wanted to help her.

Probably put me under her damn spell, he thought with a glance down the hallway to the closed bathroom door where Pamela was freshening up.

Pulling his cell phone from his pocket, he leaned a hip against her kitchen counter and started searching Web data bases. His thumbs flew over the keypad in his search for Ralph and Joy Gaines, all the while expecting Pam to return and, no doubt, voice her disapproval.

Yeah, the relationship wasn't working.

Pamela wanted to go for a long walk on the beach while Rex felt an urgency to keep working on finding more about Ravinia's cousin's family.

When his cell buzzed in his hands, he shot a glance at the number, saw it was Dorell Cochran, and ignored the little bit of disappointment that it wasn't Ravinia. "Hello, Dorell," he said, as Pamela came out of the bathroom and stopped short, frowning and shaking her head at him.

God, she is a pain.

Turning his back to her unhappy glare, Rex listened to Cochran tell him all about what he already knew—that he'd met his wife at the Ivy.

Undeterred, sandals slapping the floor in loud annoyance, Pamela came around to face him, arms crossed, wedging herself between Rex and the slider to her deck. The pissy look on her face prickled him a bit, but he didn't hang up. With Pamela listening in, he didn't feel like explaining to Dorell that he'd seen his client when he'd been following his wife, so he wrapped up the conversation. "I'll call you later," he told the man before switching off.

Pamela held out her hand. "If we're going to have a day together, maybe you'd better give me your phone."

Really?

Rex actually laughed. "Forget it."

"What is it going to take to get your complete attention?" she whined.

"You've got as much of me as I can give. This is how I work. You know that."

"Every goddamn day? Can't you take even one blessed day off?" she demanded, then crawled her fingers up his arms in some kind of sexual foreplay meant to dispel the argument.

The ploy didn't work. "I've got a couple jobs that need tending to. They don't care that you want an uninterrupted day."

"The point is, you *could* give me a day, if you really wanted to. You just don't want to."

She was right, of course.

He peeled her fingers from his arms. "I don't know what you want to hear."

"This is *our* day and you're going to be with me. That's what I want to hear!"

"I am with you. It's just that I have things I want to do, too."

"Joel . . ." she whispered.

He took a couple steps backward, away from her. "Come on, Pamela."

"Come on, Pamela?" she repeated, not liking the sound of that. "So now, this is my fault? That I just want to spend time with you?"

Rex could feel his temper escalating and he tamped it down. "I don't think this is working," he said in a cool voice.

"I *know* it's not working. And I know *why* it's not working."

"I mean the whole thing, Pamela. You and me. We're not working."

Her eyes widened, a shaft of pain visible.

"And I think it's time for me to go."

"What? Go? Because I asked for one day?"

He could hear tears forming in her voice. His jaw tightened. "You know what I mean."

"If it means that much to you, go ahead." She waved an arm dramatically. "Get on your cell phone. Leave. Do you what you have to do. *Work*."

"I'm going home." He turned toward the door.

She flew at him in a panic, grabbing his arm again, tightly. "No . . . Don't leave. Joel . . . Rex . . . please. I didn't mean it. I said you could use your phone, so . . . just use it."

"I don't want to feel like I have to ask permission." He gently pulled her hand from his arm. "I think you might be looking for someone else."

"No, no. I want *you*," she argued, visibly upset, tears glistening on her lashes as the weight of what he was saying sank in. "You know I want you."

"I'm not that guy." He turned away from her again. He didn't want to make her feel bad, but the break up had been coming a long time and he knew that if he didn't stick to his guns, this conversation would be repeated at some future date.

"You're really just going to walk out that door?"

"I'll call you later."

"Don't do me any favors. You don't want to, so don't."

"Good-bye." He walked through the door and closed it behind

him, bracing himself for the sound of something thrown against it, a shoe, a vase, or something, but it was eerily quiet inside her apartment.

He hoped to hell that was the end of it, and though he felt bad for letting things go on as long as they had, he was relieved that at least one problem in his life was resolved.

CHAPTER 14

Elizabeth texted Barbara back as she was showing Buddy and Marg yet another wildly extravagant and expensive, though outdated home. It was an over-customized nightmare. Every modern convenience available circa 1962 and nothing updated or even still working, since. While the couple was poking around upstairs, Elizabeth thanked Barbara for helping out and said she was glad she'd made it home safely. *Of course she made it home safely.*

"You can't wish someone dead," she muttered under her breath at herself.

Marg came bustling down to the living room where Elizabeth was waiting, just tucking her phone into her purse. Buddy came lumbering after his wife.

"What do you think of this one?" Marg asked Elizabeth, then didn't wait for an answer as she added, "It really needs to be updated. You think they'll come down some?"

"They'd have to come down about five million," Buddy grumbled as he stuffed his hands deep into his pockets and jingled his keys.

"It's not *that* bad," Marg snapped.

"Pretty bad," he argued.

Elizabeth said, "These sellers don't seem that eager to bargain. They already had an offer that fell through. I don't know all the details, but I do know they weren't budging on price."

"Termites," Buddy said. "Betcha it was termites and it came out in the home inspection."

"You don't know what you're talking about," Marg declared, her lips compressing.

"I know I ain't buying this termite-riddled piece of garbage," he retorted and started making his way to the front door.

And so it went. By the time Elizabeth got them back to the office and into their vehicle, Marg and Buddy weren't speaking to each other at all.

Par for the course, Elizabeth thought as she hurried to University Park, a neighborhood of about two hundred homes in an Irvine Company development just off the 405 freeway where her open house was scheduled. The area had a newly reconstructed community center, pool, park, playground, and tennis courts within easy walking distance of the house she was holding open for another of Mazie's clients.

After placing directional signs at the entrance to the development and on the corner of the street that led to the open house, she parked across the street and down two houses to keep spaces available in front of the home. Another sign indicating the house was open was placed near the driveway. Once inside, she added a stack of her business cards next to the flyers listing the home's specifications and amenities, then opened the blinds and turned on lights. If she'd had time, she would have purchased small bottles of water to set out for the "lookie-loos" who might cruise through, but she'd been too distracted all week to remember. Luckily, being January, the weather wasn't beastly hot and for the moment, the rain was still being held within the gray cloud cover overhead.

A good day for an open house.

Suddenly, Elizabeth felt tired to the bone and the thoughts she'd kept at bay came crashing back. One moment she was hustling around plumping decorative pillows, the next she was completely done in. She'd been trying to outrun her own thoughts with limited success. She sank into one of the leather chairs that faced the television in the room off the kitchen and tried to rev up some energy and dissuade herself from her uneasiness.

Officer Unfriendly and Mazie and Court . . .

She literally shook her head, trying to dislodge those thoughts, then her brain switched to Jade stopping by the office and that reminded her of Little Nate and how she'd seen him falling even though he hadn't been in her line of sight. She'd tried to deny the truth at the time of the accident, but Jade had known, had told her that she couldn't have seen him even while Elizabeth insisted she had—which had been a bald-faced lie. Though Elizabeth had pretended that Jade was the one who had been mistaken, she'd known the truth. And seeing Little Nate's near-accident hadn't been the first time she'd experienced precognition.

The bridge is falling!

In her mind, she heard the childish voice, her own voice, screaming to be heard. Then she saw her father's face, the awe replaced by a veil of opportunistic greed. She hadn't known then exactly what he was thinking, but she'd gotten the emotional hit and she'd shut down, willing herself to stop receiving such messages.

Over the years, she'd been fairly successful at doing just that. She'd even half-convinced herself none of it had really happened. She had no extra ability, no psychic gift. She'd just been weirdly lucky in her predictions.

But Little Nate, and then these recent deaths . . .

She closed her eyes, clenched her fists, and took a deep breath. Despite denying to herself that anything was wrong, she'd spent some time at the local library, looking up articles on all kinds of inexplicable behaviors. She'd also combed the Internet and purchased books online about incidences of precognition. Nothing she found positively identified her experience. Many people claimed to foretell disasters, but when she'd delved deeper into their stories, something was always off. She'd come to the conclusion that most of them were either charlatans, trying to use their so-called abilities to extort money from gullible believers, or people who suffered from some kind of mental illness that made them see reality incorrectly and believe they possessed special powers.

Nowhere did she find the kind of hard evidence she was looking for.

Or maybe I'm just crazy.

The thought cut through her mind. Even if she were certifiable, she hadn't been the person on the freeway, playing a dangerous game of tag or road rage or whatever it was with her husband and Whitney Bellhard. Nor had she been to Tres Brisas in Rosarito Beach. And she didn't kill her husband . . . or Mazie . . . or Officer Unfriendly. None of that was her doing.

"Of course not," she said aloud just as she heard a knock on the door. It swung inward before she could scramble to her feet.

A male voice called, "Hello?"

Elizabeth quickly jumped up to meet the man who was just stepping inside. "Hi," she managed and swept a hand toward the basket of blue paper booties on the floor. "The owners just redid the hardwood floors and would like you to cover your shoes," she said quickly. "Or you can walk around in your socks, if you prefer."

He didn't immediately do either. He simply stared at Elizabeth as if he were assessing her.

Warning bells clanged in Elizabeth's mind.

He managed a smile that didn't quite touch his eyes as he closed the door behind him. "You're Court Ellis's wife."

"Well, yes," she admitted a little reluctantly. That was the problem with open houses; oftentimes she was alone with a stranger. She glanced out the window, hoping to see someone else parking at the curb or heading up the walk to the front door. "Uh . . . I'm his widow."

"Thought so." The man slipped out of his shoes and walked in his socks toward her. As he approached, he held out his hand. "Sorry to drop in on you this way, but I thought we should meet. I'm Peter. Peter Bellhard. Whitney's husband."

Ravinia picked up her disposable phone for about the fiftieth time, intent on calling Rex, then tossed it down again. He'd said he would call her and she didn't want to be a complete pest, so she'd forced herself to wait all morning. But the waiting was making her want to tear her hair out. Another day, she would be taking a bus back to his office and stomping up to his door, but it was Sunday and she knew he didn't plan to be there.

Even if she knew his home address, which she planned to learn as soon as she could, she had no means to get there fast. She could hitchhike, maybe. Or, take a bus? But he probably wouldn't be there, anyway. He'd said something about taking the day off from work and she'd gotten the impression there was someone in his life he planned to share it with.

Why are you relying on him? Do it yourself. You've managed on your own so far. Keep it up.

The trouble was, she didn't have access to all the information Rex Kingston did. It would take her three times as long to get to the same place he could with a few well-placed inquiries. Unfortunately, she needed help from someone who made it their business to find people and she'd zeroed in on Rex. She'd looked into his heart and learned that he was a decent enough guy. Actually, she knew that within the first fifteen minutes of meeting him, but she'd examined him with her gift as well, searching the darkest reaches of his soul. *It really isn't much of a gift at all,* she thought with a sniff. Common sense worked just as well.

It was after noon when she peered out the window. The sun shone bright as it peeked through the clouds and illuminated the cracked asphalt of the parking lot. A few cars were still positioned, nose in, to the long cement porch that skirted the building and at the far end, a maid pushing a cart of cleaning supplies was unlocking a door.

Ravinia knew it was past check-out time, but she didn't plan on turning in the key to her room until someone insisted. Still, she needed something to eat so she stepped outside right into the teeth of a brisk wind that caused her to shiver. "Brrr," she muttered, hiking up her backpack on her right shoulder as the door shut, locking behind her. Maybe she would still be able to get into the room when she returned, but maybe not. In any case, she liked keeping her backpack close.

When Rex had driven her to the Sea Breeze, Ravinia had noticed a convenience store about four blocks away, so she hiked the short distance in search of food. Inside, she saw some limp-looking pastries behind a plastic case. Against a wall stood a tired-looking Slurpee machine amid a wall of snacks and chips, none of which appealed, so she settled on plucking several pepperoni sticks from a tall jar sitting on the counter near the cash register, and paid for them with some change she found in her pockets.

"Nice day, huh," the middle-aged guy behind the counter said, smiling, showing a gold-capped tooth.

Ravinia grunted a noncommittal response, then pushed through the door and trudged back to the motel, letting herself inside her room, which was just as she'd left it. Dropping the backpack with a thunk on the industrial carpet, she fell onto the bed and stared up at a crack in the ceiling as she munched through first one pepperoni stick and then another.

She couldn't just hang out in the room. Sooner or later the maid, the motel manager, or someone else would show up and kick her out. Besides, she had way too much to do to be stuck inside just . . . waiting. She felt tense and impatient and annoyed.

When haven't you?

She almost smiled. She'd pretty much been the same her whole life. Ask anyone who knew her. She'd never felt comfortable at Siren Song. Had always known something else was out in the real world waiting for her. She just hadn't had the means to strike out on her own, and she'd been too young, too sheltered, and well, too afraid to completely leave everything and everyone she'd known. She'd battled Aunt Catherine daily and it was only when Justice had threatened their lives that she'd finally felt a sense of community with her own family. Solidarity. Yes, she missed her family. And yes, sometimes she ached for the safety she'd once felt at the compound, but that security hadn't existed for some time and she knew she'd never be content to live out her life behind the gates her aunt had erected.

The truth was, the gates weren't strong enough to keep her in, nor solid enough to keep danger out.

Despite Aunt Catherine's bet efforts, the evil had invaded.

First had been Justice, a cousin of sorts and a twisted psychotic. More recently was Declan Jr., her brother, who was no better and maybe even worse in ways. *Half brother,* she reminded herself.

Lying upon the bed, Ravinia closed her eyes and remembered those last few days in Oregon before she'd taken off in search of Elizabeth.

Aunt Catherine was wrought with worry and deigned to take Ravinia into her confidence. With Justice, they'd had their hands full protecting themselves at the lodge, but with Declan Jr. . . . there was just no telling what his plan was or where he would strike next.

Fear made Aunt Catherine confide in Ravinia about Elizabeth, fear for her only child. Ravinia's own mother Mary had dropped babies as indiscriminately as a cat, with about as much interest in them, although at least a mother feline spent a few weeks tending to her young. Not so Mary, from all reports. She had lived for sex and drama and danger, and her behavior had led Aunt Catherine to exile her to Echo Island, the outcropping of rock just outside Deception Bay that was less than a mile across from end to end and whose shores were treacherous enough to discourage would-be afternoon boaters from trying to go ashore.

Catherine was far different from her indiscriminate sister. Catherine's affair had been a love match.

Ravinia gleaned that, though far be it for Aunt Catherine to admit as much.

Mary's revolving door of lovers had eclipsed Catherine's relationship with Elizabeth's father, apparently, and since Catherine had, for the most part, pretended the affair had never existed, it was a well kept secret . . . until Declan Jr. targeted the women of Siren Song and couldn't be stopped completely. Aunt Catherine feared he would go after her only child.

Elizabeth.

Though Ravinia and most of the rest of the world relied on conventional means to locate someone, Declan Jr. had other ways. Evil ways, some said, though Ravinia suspected it was all part and parcel of the same brand of "gifts" the daughters and sons of her ancestors all possessed. Declan Jr. just chose to use his malignantly. Or maybe it wasn't even a choice. . . .

Ravinia shivered a bit at that thought. Maybe neither Justice nor Declan Jr. could really help themselves. And maybe there were more of them out there, too. Tortured souls unable to keep themselves from their murdering proclivities. Whatever the case, Justice was gone, and Declan Jr. was still missing after wreaking havoc upon a number of people around Deception Bay, including Aunt Catherine and those at Siren Song. He'd been less focused than Justice in his deadly mission to rid himself of the others like him, but he was equally vicious, destructive, and determined.

She thought about the other player, her half brother Silas, whom she now considered a friend and who seemed to be working with Aunt Catherine and against Declan Jr.

Ravinia first ran across Silas when she was walking along the ice-crusted highway outside Siren Song and something about him drew her in. He knew who she was, which unsettled her. He gave her a sheaf of papers to take to Catherine.

Her aunt clued her in. "What did he look like?" Aunt Catherine asked after Ravinia handed over the papers—adoption records it turned out.

"I don't know. Dark hair. Blue eyes . . . I guess. Handsome," Ravinia replied reluctantly.

"His hair was dark? Not any shade of blond?"

Ravinia knew what she was asking as all her sisters were blondes, a strong genetic trait running through the family. "He's not one of us, is he?"

Her aunt didn't answer directly, but Ravinia later learned he was her half-brother. Meanwhile, a number of strange incidents had happened that she had been involved with, at least peripherally—all of which culminated in a fire on Echo Island that they witnessed from the lodge—and Aunt Catherine said it was Silas who had set the blaze. He was burning the bones of Declan Jr.'s father, who by all accounts was about as bad as bad can be.

Ravinia stirred. *Bad to the bone,* she thought without humor.

Ravinia knew about the bones as she'd been instrumental in helping dig them up from the Siren Song graveyard, at Aunt Catherine's request. But the casket and bones were missing. Creepy, that. Ravinia didn't understood completely what it was all about, but she was careful not to ask too many questions as she'd never before been privy to any of Aunt Catherine's thoughts and plans, and she didn't want to blow things.

"Why would Silas burn the bones?" she managed to ask, to which Aunt Catherine replied, "It's how you kill the Hydra. Burn it, so it doesn't grow another head."

Ravinia sat up. Mysteries within mysteries . . . Her brother Declan Jr. was still alive and likely still focused on his mission of indiscriminate death and destruction; psychos like him didn't just give up and change course. Like Justice, Declan Jr.'s ultimate target seemed to be the women of Siren Song, Ravinia's sisters and aunt, but he'd taken a more circuitous route to them and had been thwarted in the process.

It seemed that her brother Silas was following Declan Jr. When Ravinia had met him on the road, he'd been heading north while she was going south because her mission was to find Elizabeth, who was unaware of who she was and the threat Declan Jr. represented to her.

Maybe Declan Jr. had gone north initially, but that didn't mean he wouldn't go south eventually and then Elizabeth was a sitting duck. Not exactly Aunt Catherine's words, but close enough. Ravinia was to find her and warn her, although that was bound to be one tricky conversation.

Unless she has a gift, too, and why wouldn't she?

Ravinia thought about laying her whole story on Rex Kingston, but decided against it. He was already balking at the bits and pieces she'd tried out on him. No surprise there. It was best to keep him in the dark, just like everyone else outside of her family.

She exhaled heavily and climbed back to her feet. Aunt Catherine had infected her with urgency and she'd taken off on her quest to find Elizabeth. Not long into the journey she'd seen the wolf. For one wild moment, she'd thought the shaggy animal was Silas in lupine form, but that really was crazy. Still, she'd thought the beast had meant her no harm, and these long weeks later, she wondered if he might have been a figment of her imagination.

Shaking her head, she dug into her backpack for her phone. Oh, to hell with it. She was tired of waiting. Quickly stabbing out Rex Kingston's number, she held the phone to her ear, looking out the window and watching the motel manager trudge her way across the parking lot toward the outside stairway that led to Ravinia's room.

"Pick up," Ravinia said aloud into the phone. "Pick up, pick up, pick up. . . ."

CHAPTER 15

Peter Bellhard's handshake was firm and quick. He dropped her hand almost immediately. "I follow local real estate and saw that you were putting on an open house."

Elizabeth hung onto her smile with an effort even as her pulse sped up. She wasn't sure what Whitney's husband wanted, but she didn't want to find out. Not here. Not now. Not while she was working.

Besides, she really didn't know what to say to the man.

"You're with Suncrest." He walked over to the counter and picked up one of her cards, even though he'd probably seen the Suncrest Realty sign hanging from a post planted into the front yard.

"That's right."

He was tall, taller than Court, and wore a black dress shirt and gray slacks. His legs were long and his body lean and his hair was thick and dark with just the beginnings of salt amongst the pepper. He was nice looking, in a plain sort of way, but she sensed he was on some kind of mission.

"I'm . . . I'm sorry for your loss," she said and he scowled.

"Our loss."

"Yes," she agreed. "*Our* loss."

When he didn't say anything further, just thoughtfully fingered the card, the silence stretched awkwardly.

Finally she asked, "Is there something I can help you with?"

His head snapped up as if she'd brought him out of some kind of reverie. "I just thought we should meet," he explained, focusing on her again. "After what happened, I wanted to . . . you know, see how you were doing." He attempted a smile, but it fell away immediately.

"As good as can be expected, I guess. It's a shock."

"Did you know?" he asked suddenly. "About your husband and Whitney?"

She shook her head. "Not until the last couple days before he died."

"How did you find out? I mean, if you don't mind me asking?"

He sounded merely curious, but Elizabeth really didn't want to talk about Court. "A friend saw them together and told me."

"Saw them where?"

"At a restaurant." Elizabeth felt herself shutting down. Guilt and sorrow were trying to take over again. "I heard you followed them to Rosarito Beach."

He frowned. "Who told you that?"

"The woman detective. Thronson."

He seemed surprised by that. "I thought cops were supposed to ask for information, not dole it out," he said, his lips tight. "Yeah, I followed Whitney. Not that it was some cloak and dagger mission. Believe me, she and your husband were blatant about their affair. Maybe not at first. I don't know. Maybe I wasn't paying attention. But by the end, they sure were. I'd gotten sick of waiting around for her to come home and when she did show up, she'd start in with the lying. I called her on it a number of times, but she always acted like it was my problem. The jealousy." His smile never reached his eyes. "A good defense is a strong offense, but I knew I wasn't wrong. I figured there was another guy in the picture. All of a sudden she's wearing perfume and has sacks of new clothes and lingerie. Black lace bras and panties. I even found a red teddy underneath the ratty pajamas she wore to bed with me."

Elizabeth's mouth was dry. She didn't really know what to say, but out of curiosity asked, "How long did you know before . . . ?"

"A while. I confronted them in Rosarito Beach. Did you know that?"

"I knew you'd followed them."

"More courtesy of Detective Thronson?" He gave a derisive snort. "She's a pretty big blabbermouth for an investigator."

"It wasn't really like that." Elizabeth didn't know why she was defending the detective. "It was when I first learned about the accident. I was trying to take it all in and she said you'd told her that. She'd seen you first."

He shrugged as if it didn't matter, but she could tell it did, at some level. "Better to lay all the cards on the table. I didn't want the police learning from the hotel staff that I'd been there."

There's a girl who looked like you . . . blond hair in a loose bun. . . .

"Have you talked to the detective recently?"

"Not really." Bellhard's eyes narrowed a fraction. "Why? Have you?"

"She's called a few times," Elizabeth admitted, wishing that she hadn't brought the subject up. She'd counted on the fact that Thronson was keeping in close contact with both of them. After all, Bellhard had admitted to following his wife and Court to Tres Brisas. He'd known about the affair longer and had actively stalked them to their love nest in Mexico. Apparently, he had the nerve to actually face his wife and Court.

But it was a woman who played a dangerous game of tag on the freeway.

"You confronted both of them together?" Elizabeth made herself ask, though every instinct told her not to poke the bear in the cage. She might not like the reaction.

"Well, your husband was there, but he saw me and peeled off and ran away. I told Whitney he was a fucking coward." He pinned Elizabeth with a look, almost daring her to defend her indefensible husband.

The front door opened at that moment and a young couple came inside. Relieved, Elizabeth shot them a smile as they read the sign to remove their shoes and immediately slipped out of their flip-flops.

"It's so weird this house is selling," the girl said brightly. "I grew up in this neighborhood, over on Royce"—she waved into the direction of the front of the house—"so I knew the people who lived here."

"Take a look around," Elizabeth invited.

The twenty-something boy moved toward the kitchen to glance up and down the long counter. "You said there'd be cookies," he said in a stage whisper.

The girl elbowed him in the side and they quickly walked down the hallway, giggling together.

Bellhard continued as if there'd been no interruption. "I told Whitney, 'You'd better hope that loser business of yours finally turns a profit 'cause you're getting nothing from me.' You know what she said?" Bellhard's anger, hidden in the beginning, had surfaced with a vengeance. "She said, 'Court and I are getting married and he's got tons of money. Lots more than you'll ever make.'" He was staring at Elizabeth as if somehow she were to blame.

"It's not true," Elizabeth blurted, thinking of the disaster that was her finances. "I mean about the money."

"Whitney always had a nose for cash," he argued, "but hey, if you don't want to talk about your finances with me, I get it. Just don't hide anything from the police. They'll find out."

"There is no money." She didn't want to tell him anything, but she couldn't help herself. Bellhard was ramping up her anxiety level.

Arching a disbelieving eyebrow, he said, "Take it from me. Full disclosure is your only ticket out."

"I've been completely honest."

He clearly didn't believe her. The look he sent her asked, *Have you?*

Awash with anxiety, Elizabeth swallowed hard. *You didn't tell her about wishing Court harm. And Mazie . . . and Officer Unfriendly.*

None of that is relevant, she reminded herself. It was all just . . . coincidence.

The young couple had gone upstairs. Elizabeth heard their clambering footsteps overhead as they moved from room to room. Wracked with conflicting emotions, Elizabeth stepped away from Peter Bellhard.

"Listen, I don't mean to scare you," he said a little more gently. "But take my advice. The police haven't stopped digging around and if Thronson's still calling you, she's not satisfied." The smile he sent her was more genuine. "Maybe we could get together sometime, for coffee or something? I think we should talk some more. You know, hash things out. Like it or not, we're in this together."

Spending more time with Bellhard was about the last thing Elizabeth wanted to do, but before she could even consider declining his suggestion, two middle-aged women entered the house, opening the door and hesitating only a second in the foyer before picking up some of the blue shoe covers, then slipping them over their shoes.

"Excuse me," she said, thankful for the distraction. "I'm kind of busy."

"I'll let you go." He examined her card again. "Is that your mobile number?"

"Yes." Inwardly, she groaned.

Holding up the card, he said, "Thanks. I'll be in touch."

As soon as he was gone, Elizabeth sighed in relief. She hadn't re-

142 Lisa Jackson and Nancy Bush

alized her palms were sweating until the moment the door thudded softly shut behind him.

One of the women cocked an ear toward the ceiling. "Is someone upstairs? Using the bathroom?"

Elizabeth heard the flushing at the same moment and decided it was time to move the lookie-loos along. "I'll check and oh, the flyers are on the counter," she told the two women before heading up the stairs.

Starving, Rex glanced at his watch as he drove slowly through the strip mall that housed Harper Insurance Agency. As expected, the sign on the door indicated that the agency opened at nine Monday through Friday and was closed on the weekends.

Doesn't help much today, he thought, cruising through the near-empty lot, his stomach growling and reminding him it had been hours since The Breakfast Plate. Somehow he'd missed lunch.

At least he had some time to devote to finding Elizabeth Gaines for Ravinia.

Ravinia.

Sheer trouble.

She'd called him right after he'd broken it off with Pamela and had badgered him until he'd finally told her that Joy and Ralph Gaines had been the previous owners of the insurance agency. When she'd learned it was located in Costa Mesa, she'd said suspiciously, "That's the same place you live."

"Lucky," he admitted. " I know. I'll check with them in the morning."

"I want to go, too."

"Well, that's a little tough as I'm already here and you're in Santa Monica. Just sit tight and I'll give you the information when I get it."

"How far is it from where you live?"

"The agency? A few miles. Not too far."

"What's your address?"

"I'm not giving you my home address," he'd stated firmly, seeing where this was going. She still surprised him with her frankness and her bold questions. "I'll interview the owner and hopefully there'll be some information on the Gaineses."

"I'm coming that way."

"No. Ravinia, stay put."

Click! She'd hung up, probably before she'd heard his last command, which, of course, she would ignore, anyway.

He'd actually stared at his cell phone in disbelief. "Idiot," he'd muttered, not sure if he'd aimed the barb at her or himself, before jamming the cell into his pocket.

As he drove away from the strip mall toward the two-bedroom ranch he called home, he squinted through the windshield of his Nissan and considered his life. He was renting to buy the house from an elderly couple, but was having second thoughts about putting down roots in Costa Mesa. He'd lived here more years than he'd intended already, but then if not here, where? Since he'd begun his private investigation business, he'd played things by ear and it had worked out fine. But maybe it was time for a change. His relationship with Pamela, such as it was, had come to an end and he knew he'd been feeling restless for a while, though he'd tried to ignore the symptoms.

Ear bud in his ear, he drove through the familiar streets and tried calling Ravinia, but she wasn't picking up. Maybe she was actually on her way south or maybe her phone had died since their last quick call. Earlier, she'd said she needed to purchase more minutes, but he didn't know if she'd gotten around to it.

Or she could just be avoiding you.

With Ravinia, who knew?

Was she really on her way to Costa Mesa? he wondered. She could probably catch a bus, or would she dare to hitchhike? That thought made him uneasy.

She's not your problem.

"Yeah, then why does it feel like she is?" he muttered aloud while rounding a final corner near his house and determinedly pushing all thoughts of the girl with the blond braid, backpack, and tough attitude out of his mind.

CHAPTER 16

"You're late," Misty stated flatly as Elizabeth hurried through the garage door into the house. Chloe and Misty were parked in front of the television where one of Chloe's favorite animated shows—a hive of bees that solved mysteries—was playing.

"It's four-ten. I said I'd be back after four," Elizabeth told her a bit testily. She slung her jacket over the back of the couch and dropped her bag into a chair at the bar.

Misty shrugged. "Well, okay," she finally allowed. She dropped her attitude completely and admitted, "I don't really want to study anyway, but my mom's been calling and calling." With a roll of her expressive eyes, Misty added, "She's going to drive me insane."

"Insane," Chloe repeated. "That means crazy," she informed Elizabeth.

"Yes," Elizabeth agreed and she found her wallet and pulled out a few bills. "It does."

Quickly she paid the teenager and followed her to the door. The skies were already starting to darken. Misty lifted a desultory hand in good-bye then trudged off. Standing in the doorway, Elizabeth watched for a while and made sure Misty turned the corner to her own street. As she waited, arms folded across her chest, Elizabeth heard little footsteps in the foyer and from the corner of her eye she spied Chloe, barefoot hurrying into the foyer.

"You're making sure she gets home?" she said, standing next to her mother.

"That's right," Elizabeth said.

"She played with me today and wasn't so mean."

"Good." Elizabeth gave her daughter a quick hug as Misty disappeared. She herded Chloe inside and closed and locked the door behind them. "So, pumpkin, what do you want for dinner?"

"Cheese quesadillas!" Chloe declared.

"I think I've got that." Flour tortillas and grated cheese was all Chloe required. Good enough.

"And chocolate milk!" Chloe said, skipping back toward the kitchen.

"Uh-uh." Shaking her head, Elizabeth made her way to the refrigerator. "Regular milk or water. Your choice."

"Yech," was Chloe's response, though she liked milk well enough most days. But she was as changeable as the weather and Elizabeth had learned never to take her daughter's word as gospel. Not on anything.

As Elizabeth sprinkled grated cheese over the tortillas, Chloe plopped down in front of the television again, absorbed by an animated show about farm animals. A black shepherd dog was the main character. "Can we get a dog?" she asked, never taking her eyes off the set.

This—the campaign for a puppy—was her mantra these days.

"Not right now, honey."

"A hamster?"

Elizabeth slid the quesadilla into the microwave and hit the QUICK MINUTE button. "God, no."

"What?" Chloe turned to frown at her.

"Nothing in a cage," Elizabeth said, ignoring Chloe's protruding lower lip. "I think we've had this discussion."

"Oh . . ." Chloe's shoulders slumped. "I want a dog, anyway. A big dog with a black nose and a fluffy tail."

Since this was similar to the animated dog she'd just been watching, Elizabeth smiled to herself. "Someday."

"That means never."

"No, it means someday, just not today." Elizabeth had nothing against adopting a pet, but the timing was off. Currently, her ability and interest in taking care of another being felt about as reachable as the moon. She was struggling with warring emotions in the aftermath of her husband's death, while battling with a newfound fear for her future. *Their future,* she mentally corrected, glancing again at her daughter as the microwave dinged. Using a hot pad, she pulled the plate of hot bubbling cheese escaping from a folded tortilla from the oven.

"Come and get it," Elizabeth called and for once her daughter complied.

Chloe ate her quesadilla at the counter and downed the glass of milk that Elizabeth poured for her. Her earlier complaint about hating milk seemed to have been forgotten. At least for the moment. She found her way to the couch and curled up in a corner as Elizabeth cleared her plate, washing off the melted cheese.

Chloe suddenly asked, "Do you miss Daddy?" Glancing over the back of the couch, she gave Elizabeth a quick sideways look, then swept her gaze back to the television.

Momentarily taken off guard, Elizabeth recovered quickly and said, "Of course I do."

Once again, Chloe turned and looked at her mother in that scrutinizing way she always used when she wanted to see if Elizabeth was lying.

"I do miss him," Elizabeth said as if to defend herself, which was ridiculous. But it was true. She did miss Court. At least some parts of him. "I miss him as much as you do." She slid the rinsed plate into the open dishwasher.

"Do you think he loved me?" Chloe asked.

"Oh, honey, of course he did. Absolutely."

"I don't think he did," she stated matter-of-factly.

"Where'd you get that idea? You're his little girl." Drying her hands on a dishtowel, Elizabeth crossed to the couch and sat down next to her child. "He loved you more than anything. You know that." Heart breaking for her daughter's loss, she hugged Chloe close, but the girl was having none of it and wriggled free to stare at her mother.

"He loved me more than that other lady?" she asked, ignoring the television completely.

Elizabeth felt cold all over. "What lady?"

"The one he killed."

She swept in a sharp breath. "Who's been saying that?"

Chloe shrugged. "I dunno."

"Tell me who's been saying that," Elizabeth insisted, seeing red that someone was heartless enough to say malicious things to her child.

Chloe shrank into herself. "Nobody," she whispered.

"Your father loved you, Chloe. Don't ever think he didn't."

"You don't have to be so mad."

"I'm not mad. I'm just—"

"Mad," Chloe insisted.

Elizabeth let out a frustrated breath. "Okay, but I'm not mad at you."

Chloe sent her a disbelieving look as Elizabeth's cell rang loudly, vibrating against the counter.

Elizabeth pushed herself to her feet and walked rapidly to the kitchen, snagging the phone and catching sight of Deirdre's number on the display. With a last look at Chloe, who'd turned back to the TV, she answered, "Hey, there."

"Did you see Jade today?" Deirdre asked without preamble. "She said she was going by the office."

Elizabeth's attention was still on Chloe, but she nodded and said, "She did. I had a client though, so we only talked for a few minutes."

"Bummer, 'cause she's not available tonight, either."

"What do you mean?"

"I got an idea. Bring Chloe over to our house. I have a babysitter. We're all going out to the Barefoot Bar tonight for dinner."

Elizabeth wrenched her attention to the conversation with Deirdre. "Sounds great, but I can't. It's a school night for Chloe and we've already eaten."

"*I've* already eaten," Chloe corrected, her bright gaze back on Elizabeth as she sensed with unerring accuracy that plans were afoot. "*You* haven't."

"Come on, Elizabeth," Deirdre urged. "Get over here."

"You know you don't all have to try so hard to make me feel included," Elizabeth protested.

"Is that what we're doing? Gee. And I thought it was just that I had this brilliant idea to be with all my friends."

Chloe was off the couch and staring at Elizabeth, her expression pleading.

"I don't know . . ." Elizabeth weakened.

"Come on over," Deirdre insisted. "You can ride with me and Les to the bar."

Ahh . . . the husbands were going. Of course. Elizabeth tried to beg off, not wanting to be a fifth wheel again, but Deirdre was having none of it. Nadia was going to be there and some other people, too.

What other people? Elizabeth wanted to know, but Deirdre was already hanging up, as if afraid Elizabeth would change her mind again.

Despite her better judgment, half an hour later Elizabeth and Chloe were on their way to Deirdre's house. Chloe had brightened considerably and was keeping up a nonstop chatter as if afraid Elizabeth would change her mind given too much time to think about it. Her daughter wasn't wrong. All Elizabeth wanted to do was climb into bed and drag the covers over her head. *Maybe this is what Chloe needs.*

She glanced down at her skinny jeans and tailored blue blouse. A black sweater coat lay in the passenger seat. The Barefoot Bar in Newport Beach had an outside patio with a concrete floor lined with sand. Several fire pits were clustered around the area, each with curved benches and Adirondack chairs. In the summer, the place was completely packed and it was impossible to cadge a seat, but the cool temperature would likely deter the crowds. At least that was Deirdre's contention.

Chloe was dropped off to play with Deirdre's sons, Chad and Bryan; the kids were left in the care of a nanny Deirdre shared with another woman. As Elizabeth slid into the back seat of the Czurskys' dark gray Mercedes, she listened to Deirdre and Les extol the virtues of the food at the Barefoot Bar.

"You've had dinner there," Deirdre stated to Elizabeth as if it were fact, half-turning her face toward the backseat.

"No, I've only been to the patio bar."

"You're kidding. It's great. You'll see. Fresh seafood. Great salads."

"Steaks, too," Les put in.

Elizabeth thought about her dwindling bank accounts, but didn't say anything as Deirdre and Les enthused about their favorite restaurant. No matter what Peter Bellhard had alluded to about Court's finances, there was no secret stash of money. Court may have fooled Whitney, but the truth was he spent anything he made and nothing much was left. Elizabeth determined that she would just order a garden salad or soup, something not too expensive. She wasn't all that hungry, anyway.

While the valet took the keys of their car and parked it, they walked through reception area and outside to the patio. The Eachuses and Hofstetters were already there. Nadia, looking harried, was just arriving, a few steps behind them. "Kurt blew me off at the last minute," she said, clearly unhappy. "It's like I don't even have a husband half the time." She heard herself and stopped short. "Oh my God. I'm so sorry, Elizabeth," she said, abashed.

"Don't even think about it." Elizabeth waved off the apology. As they met up with the other couples, Elizabeth was introduced to the other people Deirdre had mentioned. Actually, it was really just one other person, as Deirdre introduced her to Gil Dyne, who worked with Les.

Dyne was a widower, it turned out, and Elizabeth sensed he'd been invited to even out the couples because she was coming as a single and everyone had expected Nadia's husband to show. Already it was happening; she was the odd woman out. Elizabeth cringed inside.

No wonder Deirdre hadn't taken no for an answer.

Elizabeth was almost glad Nadia's husband hadn't showed. It kept her from having to be Gil Dyne's almost date.

All in all, it was irritating as hell, and it was all Elizabeth could do to smile through it and remind herself that her friends meant well, that they were just trying to help her through a rough transition.

Still . . .

"I heard about your husband," Gil said to her.

She wanted to sink right through the patio. She didn't need this, probably not ever.

"I know how difficult the first few weeks are." He had a friendly face and a nice smile, but he stood a little closer to her than she would have liked. "How're you getting on?"

She shot Deirdre a warning look, but Deirdre pretended not to notice. "I'm working my way through it," she said to Gil as Nadia, who had been mingling with the others, joined them. *Thank God.*

The waiter came by and she ordered a glass of white wine, but when the waiter returned, Gil insisted on paying. Of course. She protested mightily, but he swept away her objections. He made no effort to buy Nadia's drink, however, even though she was standing right beside Elizabeth and had ordered at the same time.

It was uncomfortable and awkward.

Twenty minutes later, she finally found an opening to move away from him and with Nadia in tow, whispered, "I hope Deirdre doesn't think this is a date."

Nadia was a few inches taller than Elizabeth and when she hazarded a glance at Gil Dyne, one of the outdoor lights caught the icy blue of her eyes. "Men prey on single women."

"Oh, I think he's just being nice," Elizabeth said. "Deirdre told me she invited him." It was strange to think of herself as a single woman.

Nadia took a long swallow from her wine glass. "If you ever need anything, call me. You have my number."

"Thanks, yes."

"I mean it," she pressed.

Elizabeth nodded. She didn't know how to tell her friends that she was a little overwhelmed by everyone's eagerness and urgency to help her, that she just needed time alone. To process. To consider her future. To come to grips that she and Chloe were alone in the world.

At that moment, Deirdre swept up to them and said in a conspirator's voice, "I shouldn't have invited him, I know. But Gil's a good, good guy, and he's got loads of money. Loads."

What's that got to do with anything? Elizabeth thought, then remembered confiding to her friends about the state of her finances. Obviously, a mistake.

Deirdre continued slyly, "You know, he might not look like it, but he could buy and sell half the people I know."

Good guy . . . Her words reminded Elizabeth of GoodGuy and she had to force out a smile and a noncommittal response.

Not so Nadia, who asked suspiciously, "What happened to his wife, then?"

Deirdre gave her a long look. "What do you mean?"

"I heard it was suicide," Nadia said.

"Oh, I'm so sick of that. Monica would never." Shaking her head, Deirdre said, "It was a pill overdose. A mistake. That's all." She was clearly annoyed with Nadia.

But Nadia wasn't about to give up. "There was a question about it. That's what I heard."

"Can anyone join in this conversation?" Tara asked. Her husband Dave was with Bill and Gil standing near a fire pit. Les, too, staring at the flames, stood near the men.

Elizabeth noted that Vivian was at the bar ordering more drinks.

"Gil's wife, Monica Dyne, died of a drug overdose," Nadia said to Tara. "Deirdre says it was an accident, but—"

"It *was* an accident," Deirdre snapped.

"There was a question about it." Nadia spread her hands, her lips pressed tightly together. "That's all I'm saying."

"Girls, girls," Tara said, then grabbed Elizabeth by the arm and pulled her away. "You looked trapped."

"I was trapped. Thanks for the rescue. Deirdre seems to have invited Gil so I could meet him."

"It's way too soon for that."

"No kidding."

"I never knew Deirdre was such a matchmaker." Tara guided Elizabeth away from the patio and fire pits to stand near the front door.

Elizabeth said, "Peter Bellhard stopped by my open house today."

"You're kidding." Tara looked scandalized.

Elizabeth gave her the gist of what Bellhard had said to her, finishing with, "There's no money and no insurance."

Tara sighed loudly.

"Anyway, I'm all for full disclosure if it gets Detective Thronson off my back."

"Yeah, but what do you have to disclose that you haven't already?"

Elizabeth shook her head, then looked at her closest friend. Could she trust her with her thoughts, crazy as they were, about wishing Court dead? Could she? "Tara . . . there's something I should tell you."

CHAPTER 17

"What?" Tara asked, looking at her expectantly over the top of her glass of wine.

Before Elizabeth could answer, Vivian sashayed up to them, leading a waiter who held a tray of tropical drinks. "Maui Wowies, the drink kind," she announced. "I've ordered some pupus, too. Don't start making potty humor jokes," she warned loudly to the men who were paying no attention to their conversation.

"You were saying?" Tara asked Elizabeth.

"Nothing." The moment had passed and it was crazy, anyway.

"Gil's buying," Deirdre said as one waiter set the tray of drinks down and another placed a huge tray of different appetizers, from teriyaki sticks to broiled pineapple wedges to sticky rice balls to fish tacos, next to it. Elizabeth had sampled some of the fare the one time she'd been to the bar, but she'd planned on just having a salad or soup and even the thought of either of those didn't stir her appetite. But seeing how everyone was looking at her, waiting for her to choose as if she were the guest of honor, she felt obligated to pick up one of the chicken teriyaki sticks and nibble at it.

As soon as she chose, the women made their selections, then the men descended on the food and drinks in a ravenous horde. Maui Wowies or no, Elizabeth had already decided she wasn't going to switch from her wine, but Gil Dyne brought her one of the glass mugs filled with pinkish-purple liquid and garnished with a spike of mango and a wedge of the white pulp, black-seeded center of dragon fruit. She'd set her glass of wine on one of the scattered tables flanking the benches and Adirondack chairs. She placed her half-eaten teriyaki stick on a napkin beside it and accepted the mug, though she had no desire to drink from it.

"Thank you," she said, finding a spot at the end of the benches.

Immediately, Gil took the nearest Adirondack chair. The flame from the fire pit threw shadows on the faces but not a lot of warmth so Elizabeth wrapped her sweater coat closer around herself, glad she'd swept it up from the car on her way inside.

"I hear you're a member at Fitness Now!" Gil tried as another conversation opener.

"Well . . . yes."

"I lived there after my wife died. Worked out all the time. I don't remember seeing you there, but then, I haven't noticed anything for a while."

"My husband was the one who really used the club." She felt obligated to at least take a sip of the drink, which was heavy with guava and passion fruit, a little too sweet for her liking.

"You use it, too," Vivian said, moving to a seat on the other side of Gil. "We've been there together a lot."

Overhearing her, Tara moved closer. "We used to all go to classes together when we first met each other. But now, well . . . kids, work, and life have gotten in the way."

The couple that had been sitting on the other end of Elizabeth's bench saw that they were being taken over by another group and moved to a different fire pit, so Tara grabbed the nearest spot next to Elizabeth. Nadia sat on the other side of her and Deirdre came to stand nearby while the husbands found chairs on the far side of the fire pit.

"Is that the one off Jamboree?" Nadia asked. Since she hadn't been with their Moms Group from the beginning she'd missed out on joining Fitness Now! at the time the rest of them had.

Deirdre took a large sip from her drink and nodded. "But it's Jade who was the real workout fiend in the beginning, and in between her pregnancies, too. She still makes me feel like such a slacker."

"I might have to join," Nadia said.

"Where is Jade?" Tara asked.

Deirdre replied, "Oh, I tried to get her and Byron to come, but she said she had some family thing."

"She's feeling very pregnant, too," Vivian said.

"We all know what that's like," Deirdre agreed.

"Well, I'd better join the men," Gil said, getting up from his chair, which was a welcome diversion as it covered up Deirdre's gaff. Nadia acted like she hadn't heard her comment, which helped cover the awkward moment.

Gil's gaze lingered on Elizabeth as he circumvented the fire pit to join the guys on the other side and she couldn't help but worry that Gil was thinking about her in ways she wasn't ready for. He'd bought the drinks, and she was pretty sure he'd buy her meal when they went in to dinner if she let him, but she didn't want to give him any encouragement. She felt out of sync and weird. Court had only been gone a week but at times, it felt like ten years. How could that be?

"You're missing him," Nadia suddenly said, her gaze on Elizabeth's face.

"Who?" Elizabeth responded, startled.

"Your husband."

"Of course she's missing him," Deirdre said. "It's weird to be alone all of a sudden."

"It's been a weird week," Elizabeth agreed. Suddenly, she just wanted to go home.

Before she could say anything, the maître d' came and told them their table was ready. They all rose and moved toward the dining room, but Elizabeth wished she'd brought her own car. "I hate to be a party pooper, but I might have to blow off dinner. I've got a lot to do tomorrow."

"A pu pu pooper," Les said, and Deirdre rolled her eyes at him.

"Oh, come on," Deirdre said. "We barely got here and we're your ride."

"I know, but—"

"I'll take you home," Gil put in.

That was the last thing she wanted. "Oh, no. Thank you, but I can call a cab."

"Let me drive you," Nadia said, but Deirdre insisted, "You have to stay just a little while longer. Please. It's a four hour minimum for the nanny, so let's use it up."

"Umm . . . sure . . . ." Elizabeth gave in with good grace and moved with the flow of them into the dining room. She was seated next to

Gil on one side, Nadia on the other. When she just ordered the mushroom soup, everyone tried to get her to get something more, but she wasn't hungry and stayed firm. Gil asked her about her work, and though she didn't really want to talk, she also didn't want to be rude, and she found herself telling him about her plans to sell the house and maybe find an apartment.

"I own a fourplex in Corona del Mar," he told her. "One of the units is coming up this spring."

Corona del Mar was known for its pricey living spaces. "I don't think that's going to work," she said honestly. "I'll be looking for something fairly reasonable."

"You could take a look at it. I wouldn't gouge you. Scout's honor." He lifted two fingers in the Boy Scout symbol and smiled.

"I'm not really sure when I'll be putting the house on the market," she said as a way to dissuade him.

Tara leaned over from across the table "Take your time, Elizabeth." She shot a look of annoyance at Deirdre who lifted her hands in a *who me?* gesture.

They ordered their entrees and the conversation turned to Dave Hofstetter and his golf game. He'd entered an amateur tournament and won. While Elizabeth spooned up her mushroom soup, he regaled them with a hole by hole recap that had Tara groaning and covering her ears in mock torture, saying, "Do you know how many times I've heard this?"

As they were looking over the dessert menus, Elizabeth got up to go to the women's room.

"I'm coming, too," Vivian said, dropping her menu and hurrying after Elizabeth.

Outside the restroom door, Vivian said, "Don't be mad at Deirdre. I know it's too soon, but she just wanted you to at least meet Gil. I guess women are all over him all the time, and he's a great catch. None of us know exactly what you're going through. We just want to help."

Elizabeth pushed through the door. "I feel guilty that I don't feel worse." Once they were alone in the room, she stood near the counter and admitted, "I just kind of wanted to get away from the table for a few minutes."

"You mean get away from Gil. I kind of figured." Vivian hesitated, glanced into the mirror, her gaze meeting Elizabeth's in the glass. "I was going to talk to you. You know that other group I go to? Where I met Nadia?"

"Yes." It was a grief counseling group. Vivian had lost her first child to SIDS and had joined after the little boy died.

"It's all women, and we only go by first names, but we've all suffered in some way, whether it's abusive relationships or sudden tragedy. It's kind of loosely formed, but it's really helpful. Maybe you want to come with me tomorrow." She offered a tentative smile.

"Tomorrow?" Elizabeth shook her head slowly. "I don't know if I really qualify for your group. What I'm feeling seems more guilt than grief."

"It's all mixed up together. Survivor's guilt and sadness and regret and grief. You know that."

"Yeah, but . . ." She trailed off as she thought about her daughter and what she'd said earlier about Court not loving her—which reminded her . . . "Chloe asked me about the woman Court was with, the one he *killed* was how she phrased it."

"What?" Vivian said.

"I was trying to figure out where she heard that. I asked her, but she wouldn't say."

"Oh, God. I think it was Lissa." Vivian held her hand to her mouth for a moment, then bit her lip. "She overheard Bill and me talking about the accident and asked us who was killed. I thought I explained it, but she must've got it wrong."

"It doesn't matter," Elizabeth said.

"It does. I'm so sorry."

"Chloe doesn't think her dad loved her, and I was trying to tell her that I missed him, too, and that he missed her and . . . I don't know. I'm worried about her. She seemed to be taking his death too well, so it's good that she's talking a little bit about her feelings. I don't know what to do."

"Come to the meeting," Vivian insisted. "This is exactly the kind of thing we work out as a group."

Elizabeth held up her hands, palms out. "I'm not that great with groups."

"Are you kidding? You're totally great. You're a founding member of our Moms Group!"

Elizabeth half-laughed and decided that she should do something, anything to help her get past Court's death and the guilt surrounding it. "Okay."

"Okay, you'll come tomorrow?"

"Talk to me in the morning."

"I will."

Vivian went into a stall and Elizabeth washed her hands. She returned to the table alone, walking past the outdoor bar, glancing around the benches and fire pits. Night had long descended. The shadows beyond the flickering flames were deep.

A cold frisson slid down her spine, a warning that someone was watching her, someone hidden in the unfathomable umbra. She shivered a little, then sharply scanned the people on the patio. No one seemed to be paying her any special attention. She squinted into the gathering darkness but saw no glint of hidden eyes.

Huh, she thought, ignoring her accelerating pulse. *Now you're getting paranoid.*

The uneasy feeling chasing after her, she returned to the table and tried not to look over her shoulder to reassess the crowd, but she felt more than a little relief when Les rose to his feet and declared it was time to get going. Of course, no one would take any money from her for the meal, though she tried to pay, and soon she was heading into the cool evening air and across the parking lot to the Czurskys' car.

She never shook the feeling that someone was watching.

Rex's cell phone buzzed around midnight. He was still awake and on his laptop, seated in the leather recliner in his den with one light on and CNN on mute. He picked up the phone and recognized the number.

Ravinia.

"Where are you?" he asked, glancing at the clock.

"Costa Mesa."

He wasn't surprised. She gave him the cross streets to her location and added, "Are you going to come and get me or what?"

"How did you get here? I told you to stay in Santa Monica." He was already up and heading for the entryway table where he swept up his keys, then grabbed his jacket from the back of the overstuffed chair where he'd tossed it earlier. The chair was a bit of a relic, in his opinion. It was a piece of furniture the woman he'd dated before Pamela had talked him into buying, claiming his house was too "bachelor."

"I came by bus. And what good would it do me to stay?"

"I don't know. Save you bus fare." He was relieved she hadn't hitchhiked.

"Are you coming?"

"I'll be there in twenty," he said shortly. Again, he felt responsible for her, which really pissed him off. "Don't talk to anybody. Nobody out this time of night is worth talking to."

"It's not that late," she said on a snort, then hung up.

Feeling like he was being swept along by forces beyond his control, he headed to the garage and his waiting Nissan.

> *Darling Elizabeth,*
>
> *I saw you tonight and you sensed that I was there, didn't you? You're beginning to know how I feel about you, and you're feeling it, too. It's glorious. I'm almost in your sights as you're in mine. The waiting is excruciating, but that's what makes it so wonderful. But you're looking for a sign of my love. I know you are.*
>
> *Soon . . . soon . . . I will send you a message. I will take care of you and you'll know we're right for each other. We're meant to be together. It's just us against the world.*
>
> *Watch and see what happens. A bright, shining flame will write across the night sky. A message meant for you.*
>
> *My love . . . my fairest love . . .*

The hand paused, the point of the pen digging into the vellum, but it wasn't the time to write a signature. Not yet. There was too much to do. Carefully, the nib of the pen was pulled away from the page, leaving a small hole that almost looked like a heart. A growing stack of notes lay on the side of the desk and the latest missive was placed gently on top.

Thump, thump, thump.

The prisoner was angry.

Again.

Well, it was past time to take care of that loose end, too, wasn't it?

Pieces of fate were swirling in the atmosphere and slowly coming together, linking their past, present and future.

Soon, Elizabeth. Very soon . . .

CHAPTER 18

Monday morning and the sky was deep gray and oppressive. Traffic was moving steadily, but if the rain should fall, who knew what the other California drivers would do. Rain didn't bother Rex much, but it seemed to paralyze half of the other drivers on the road.

"Far be it from me to tell you what to wear, but do you have anything else?" Rex asked Ravinia as he drove them to the strip mall he'd visited on Sunday, the building that housed Harper Insurance Agency.

In the passenger seat, Ravinia glanced down at her wrinkled blouse and made an effort to smooth it out with her hands. Her jeans had a dark stain on one leg that he hadn't noticed when they'd been at the Ivy, but at least they weren't full of holes . . . although with current fashion trends that would undoubtedly be more acceptable. As it was, she looked like she'd been camping for a month . . . which was close to the truth.

"I don't have a lot of clothes. And I don't have time to get them clean." *And I don't care*, she could have added.

"I could have thrown them in the wash last night if I'd known."

Ravinia turned her blue-green eyes his way but said nothing. She didn't have to. Her cool gaze said it all. There'd been no time to do much of anything but pick her up and take her back to his house, which of course, he'd told himself he wasn't going to do. But finding her a place to stay at nearly one in the morning had felt like a chore he wasn't up for, so he'd taken her back and shown her the couch in his family room as there was no second bed. She'd curled up instantly, still wearing her clothes and fallen fast asleep whereas he'd spent a fitful night feeling like a heel, wondering if he should have at least offered to swap the couch for his bed.

He'd heard her get up early in the morning and had tensed, but she'd just used the bathroom. After he'd showered and dressed for the day in casual slacks and a dress shirt, he'd found her standing in the middle of his family room. She'd been staring outside to the leaf-carpeted patio, the last stubborn leaves hanging tenuously to bare branches etched against a gray sky.

"I like your kitchen," she'd said, still looking through the window.

He'd glanced at her in surprise, then taken a harder look at the kitchen with its basic U-shape and the island that divided it from the family room. "Thanks."

"Where I come from, we add conveniences at the speed of snail," she said, still gazing outside.

She'd washed up in the bathroom and then they were on the road. Their only stop had been at a diner where he'd ordered huevos rancheros and watched her tuck into a pile of pancakes that looked fit for Paul Bunyan. That her slim body could eat so much defied the laws of nature. While he sipped coffee, she drank a tall glance of orange juice and another of water.

"How much do I owe you?" she'd asked after he'd paid and they were walking back to the car.

"I've got this one."

"Just put it on my bill," she said stubbornly.

He'd shrugged, in no mood to fight with her. At that time, he'd tried not to comment on her clothes, but they were about to walk into an interview that could net them information . . . or not.

"We'll throw 'em in the wash when we get back," he said as he parked the car.

"When we get back. So you're not putting me on a bus to somewhere else?"

"Would you go, if I did?"

She smiled. "Maybe, but now I know where you live."

"That makes you sound like a stalker. People get arrested for that kind of thing."

"I don't see how. I've been a guest at your house."

"Uninvited," he pointed out.

"*Invited,*" she argued. "You picked me up and took me home. And whether or not you can admit it, you like me okay. I don't mean in a weird way. I'm not picking that up from you. But you find me interesting."

"Finding someone interesting is a far cry from actually liking them."

"Now, you're just being argumentative."

"Leave your backpack in the car. Try to look . . . professional," he said, though it was a joke.

"I'll lock it in the trunk."

He nodded and they got out of the car using opposite doors and met at the trunk. Rex unlocked it with his remote and Ravinia dropped the backpack inside, looking surprisingly tense after he slammed it shut.

"That's everything I own," she explained.

"I'm not going to keep it from you."

She nodded slowly, accepting that. Despite their age difference, sometimes she seemed vast eons older than he was, which he found slightly annoying. He pulled on the front door handle of the insurance agency, only to realize it was still a minute before nine and hadn't opened yet.

They waited outside in silence. Rex honestly didn't know what to do with her. The hell of it was, she wasn't completely wrong. For all the aggravation she gave him, he enjoyed her company . . . somewhat.

A rattle of keys came from the other side and the shade went up on one half of the glass doors. They could peer inside to see a woman opening up for the day.

"Good morning," she said, holding open one door before lifting the blinds on the other one. She wore black boots and a red knit dress with a wide black belt, and her hair was held back by a thin black headband. She was chic and trendy, maybe a little overdressed for office work, but her clothes were a far cry from Ravinia's garb.

Ravinia didn't miss that. Her gaze raked the other girl from head to toe.

"I called and left a message. I'm Joel Kingston, here to see the owner." He gave her a smile.

"I'm sorry. Beth's not here yet."

"Beth Harper?" he confirmed.

"Yes."

"We'll wait," Ravinia said, plopping down in one of the two chairs in the waiting area.

The girl looked conflicted. "I'm . . . not really sure Beth's coming in this morning. Today's her husband's birthday."

Rex said, "Oh. So . . . you think she'll be in tomorrow?"

"Maybe. Maybe even today. I don't know. I'd have to check." The woman pressed her lips together and spoke quickly, as if the faster she said it, the less of a betrayal it might be. "Her husband passed away about a year ago, and it's a ritual, you know?" She said it as if she thought the idea was a little crazy. "She could be on her way. I just don't know if I can call . . ."

"This is a business, isn't it?" Ravinia stated flatly.

Rex quickly overrode her. "I could leave a card."

The girl nodded, but Ravinia looked at him as if he were nuts. "I'm not leaving," she told him.

"We'll work it out," he told the girl, handing her a card from his wallet. From the vantage of his height, he could see over the large room, which was divided by a number of cubicles, half of them populated by heads, some with headsets on, others just bent to some task. The *puck-puck-puck* sound of computer keys could be heard, and somewhere a cell phone began to ring. It was cut off quickly, probably snatched up by one of those with a bent head.

"I'll try calling her," the girl relented.

"Thank you." If Rex could've, he would've clapped his hand over Ravinia's mouth. She might be good at surveillance, but the fine art of wheedling information from people clearly escaped her.

"Would you like coffee or water while you wait?" the girl asked as she moved away.

"Water," Ravinia said.

"Coffee would be great," Rex said. "Black, please."

The girl headed briskly down the aisle that bisected the cubicles and led in the direction of a glassed-in office at the back of the room. Blinds like on the front door were pulled down over the windows.

As soon as she was out of earshot, Rex said to Ravinia, "You're not helping."

"You're gonna just wait till tomorrow, or whenever the owner gets back?"

"I'm the lead dog. Keep that in mind. A little tact would be a good idea."

He kept his eyes on the girl in the red dress and watched as she entered the door just left of the office. As it opened, he caught a glimpse of a counter with a coffee machine and a vending machine on the opposite wall. The break room.

"What are you looking at?" Ravinia demanded.

"Nothing. I'm not going to hang around here all day," he warned her.

"I can stay."

He squatted down beside her chair and she gazed at him, her expression careful. In a low voice, he said, "You want this information about your cousin? Then, let me do my job. You can't just bully your way through everything. That works to a point, but you hired me to do a job, so let me do it."

"I just said I would stay if you couldn't."

"What you said was, 'If you can't do the job, Rex, I'll do it myself.'"

"That's not what I said."

"I'm not going to argue with you. We've got to come to an understanding. I'm not—" Rex straightened as the girl returned with their drinks.

She said, "I texted Beth and she said she's going to be here in about half an hour."

"See?" Ravinia said, swiveling to give him the evil eye.

"Thank you." Rex gave the girl a grateful smile.

"No problem." She smiled in return and gave him a lingering look as she headed back toward the mass of cubicles.

Ravinia's gaze followed her, then she turned to Rex again. "You lookin' for a date?" she asked dryly.

"I'm looking for anyone who'll give me any kind of information." He took a drink of his coffee—tepid, but beggars couldn't be choosers—and sat down to wait.

Appearing harried, Beth Harper showed up about forty-five minutes later. She was in her mid-forties, near as Rex could tell. She had a plump figure and a blondish pixie haircut that was currently popular in the Hollywood set, but was harder to pull off after a certain age.

"I'm sorry. I didn't realize anyone was waiting for me until Isabel texted me," she said a little breathlessly.

"We didn't have an appointment," Rex assured her. "I just left a phone message over the weekend. I'm actually looking for someone. Ralph Gaines. You purchased the agency from him and his wife?"

"Oh. Yeah. Years ago." She waved a hand dismissively. Old news. "Jimmy and I were looking for a business to buy and Ralph was getting ready to sell." She peeled a scarf from around her neck and heaved a sigh. "You want to come into my office? I need to sit down for a while."

"Sure," Rex said.

Ravinia popped to her feet and they all walked single file down the blue carpeted runway that led to the glassed-in office. Beth flipped on the lights and hung her jacket and scarf on a coatrack in one back corner. On the desk was a picture of her, and probably her husband, in happier days, the shot snapped in an outdoor setting. They were smiling at each other while behind them dandelion seeds floated upward like little ballerinas.

Seeing they were looking at the photo, Beth said, "We renewed our vows in a field. It was just such a perfect day." For a moment, she stared at the photo and her eyes watered, but then she took a deep breath and said, "You're looking for Ralph Gaines. Can I ask why?"

"I'm his niece," Ravinia said before Rex could answer.

That wasn't strictly the truth, but Rex decided it was as good an explanation as any.

"We've lost touch," Ravinia went on, "and my mother really needs him now, what with Kayla running away again and Dad leaving. It's been hard," she embellished. "But Uncle Ralph's her brother."

Rex stared at Ravinia. *Kayla?* He'd just chased down a runaway teen named Kayla shortly before Ravinia showed up on his doorstep.

Beth Harper looked at Rex. "Isabel said you were a private investigator."

"That's right. Ravinia hired me to help find Mr. Gaines."

"Hmmm. Well, I don't know that I can help you." Beth's eyes slipped over the stain on Ravinia's jeans. "We bought the business from Ralph and Joy, but they were at the tail end of a divorce and she was just a signature on a page. We mostly dealt with him. I believe there was talk of moving to Colorado, but I can't remember if that was Joy or Ralph or both of them. They didn't seem like they were staying together."

"Did you meet my cousin, Elizabeth?" Ravinia jumped in.

That caught Beth off guard and she frowned slightly.

Rex tensed, worried that Ravinia had pushed too hard and blown it, but all Beth said was, "I do recall your cousin. She was a little girl at the time. But . . . well this had to have been, what? Maybe twenty years ago."

Rex was surprised. "But you remember her."

"Elizabeth. Yes. I remember because her name was like mine."

"I really want to find her, too," Ravinia pressed.

"It's Ralph I remember most," Beth said. "He was proud of the business and I think he was suffering serious second thoughts about selling it, so he kept showing up long after it was sold, just to see how we were doing. The divorce forced the sale, and eventually he moved. I didn't really know the wife."

"So he didn't move to Colorado." Rex made it a statement rather than a question.

Beth frowned. "No, at least not then. Really, I didn't keep up with either one of the Gaineses."

"Did you meet Elizabeth?" Ravinia cut in, asking the question again before Rex could ask for a forwarding address.

"He brought her with him a couple of times." Beth seemed to want to say more but didn't know how, so she just shut down.

"What was she like?" Ravinia questioned.

"A little quiet . . ."

Rex gave Ravinia a look and asked Beth, "Do you have a forwarding address?"

"I'm not sure I do," she apologized. "We bought the business outright and Jim wanted it to be just ours, so he discouraged Ralph from coming around."

"But Elizabeth," Ravinia pushed. "What do you remember about her?"

"It's funny you should ask," Beth said, then shook her head as if dispelling something from her mind.

"Why?" Ravinia asked.

"She went to Wembley Grade, which is not all that far from here. Do you know it?" Beth was looking at Rex.

"I do." *How do you remember that, and not anything else?* he wondered, waiting for Beth to explain.

"I don't want to tell tales out of school," she said, "but there was an incident with Elizabeth that sticks in my mind. It's one of those weird things that seemed important at the time, but maybe really isn't."

"What?" Rex asked.

She hesitated, and something about that hesitation made him brace himself for what was to come. Even before she spoke, he found the hair starting to lift on his arms. Rapt, Ravinia learned forward, sensing the change in the atmosphere, too.

"Elizabeth was a pretty child. Fairly quiet, like I said. But one afternoon when she was here with Ralph, she started suddenly shrieking that the bridge was falling down. 'The bridge is falling!' she yelled, standing on one of the chairs in the agency. Everybody stopped and stared at her. It was just so . . . odd, all of a sudden. Ralph tried to shush her, but she was adamant. 'The bridge is falling!'"

"What bridge fell?" Ravinia asked, never taking her eyes off Beth.

"Well, that's just it. We thought it was 'London Bridge is falling down.' Ralph said as much. He played it off like she did this kind of thing all the time, and maybe she did. Anyway, about two hours later a pedestrian bridge not far from here collapsed over a ravine. Nobody was killed, luckily, as it crashed down at night, but it was spooky because of what Elizabeth had said. I called Ralph about it, but he acted like it was just a coincidence, and maybe it was, but . . ." Beth let out a pent up breath. "Anyway, I've thought about it over the years, and I've wondered about Elizabeth. If you find her, I'd like to know how she's doing."

"You don't have *any* address for either Ralph or Joy?" Rex pressed.

"No, as I said. Only the address from when they lived here. It was an apartment building near the grade school. Brightside Apartments, I think. I don't remember the unit number off hand. Maybe I could find it," she said doubtfully.

"That's all right," Rex said.

They talked to her a few more minutes, but Beth Harper was tapped out and losing interest, her gaze drifting back to the picture of her husband and herself in a field of dandelions. She promised to call or e-mail Rex if she thought of anything else.

Outside, Rex cast an eye toward the hovering black clouds overhead, pulled Ravinia's backpack from the trunk, and handed it to her before climbing into the driver's seat and waiting for her to buckle up.

Once they were on their way, he said to her, "We'll get your clothes clean and then I want you to hit Wembley Grade School and ask some questions. You can say you went to school there, or something. Maybe ask about a teaching assistant job. Tell them your cousin went there. Teachers remember former students, especially if there's something about them that's different and it sounds like Elizabeth was different."

"You're going to trust me?"

"I think you're a natural when playing a part," Rex admitted.

"What are you gonna be doing?"

"I'll check Brightside Apartments, find out who owns the complex, see if I can engage the manager into conversation, see how long he or she's been there. Might even be able to do that today."

Ravinia seemed to roll that over in her mind as Rex drove into traffic. "I've never been inside a school," she admitted.

"First time for everything. You look like you could still be a student. Have you got anything besides jeans?"

"You mean like that red dress Isabel was wearing? No, sorry. My wardrobe's a little more limited than that," she said testily. "And I purposely didn't bring one of Aunt Catherine's dresses."

"Aunt Catherine's dresses?"

"Long, old-fashioned ones. She wanted us to look like we were . . ."

"Amish?" When she didn't immediately answer, he asked, "You know about them?"

"Yes, I know about them," she snapped. "We did have a television, though it's nothing like yours. And books. No, Aunt Catherine just wanted to shut the door on all the bad things that were out there. Hide us away. Reverse time."

"I don't think it worked with you," Rex said lightly.

"I guess she did what she thought was right," Ravinia said grudgingly.

They lapsed into silence for a few moments, each lost in their own thoughts.

Then Rex said, "Maybe we can't have you apply for a job at the school. It might be better if you were a student. Check in with a couple of the older teachers as school's letting out. Maybe someone will remember Elizabeth. Beth Harper sure did."

"Maybe they have information about where she went."

"It's getting that information. Privacy laws make it difficult. They're not just going to hand it over."

"We have to sneak the information out of them."

"Well . . . yeah . . . a lot of times."

They drove for several miles through the traffic choked surface streets, and then Ravinia asked, "What did you think about what she said about the bridge falling down?"

"I'm glad it made an impression on Beth Harper."

"I know, but Elizabeth *predicted* the bridge collapse."

"So, what are you saying? She's got a gift, too?" he asked dryly.

"Maybe." Ravinia lifted her chin. "Maybe Elizabeth can see the future, sort of like my sister Cassandra . . ."

"Good, then she can see us looking for her. Maybe she can even help out. Send us a signal."

Ravinia heaved a deep sigh and looked through the windshield as if she found him too, too dense. "I'll go with you to the apartments."

"No, I'll take you over to the school later. Anyway, I've got a lot of other things to do."

"What other things?"

"Other jobs. People other than you. I'm driving to the office tomorrow, so I'll take you back to Santa Monica."

"I'm not going back." She looked affronted. "The trail to Elizabeth is here."

"I should've had you sign the contract when you were in the office."

"Well, bring it on. You want a *retainer*? I've got money."

"So you've said."

"Fine." With that, Ravinia reached down for her backpack and started digging through it.

"Stop. We'll take care of it later tonight." When she set the pack back down, he said, "I take it you plan on staying another night."

"I can find another place to sleep," she said with a sniff.

At that moment, a deluge of rain poured over the car, sheeting the windshield so thick it ran like honey. Rex threw the wipers on full blast. "You might want to rethink that," he pointed out.

Though she looked like she wanted to make some retort, she wisely kept her mouth shut.

Elizabeth dropped Chloe off at school and drove to Fitness Now! She sat in the parking lot for several minutes, flexing her hands on the steering wheel. She'd dressed in workout gear, but her main reason for heading to the gym was to cancel her membership. It was all fine and good that her friends wanted her to stay, but she could sense a tsunami of financial problems rushing toward her and if she didn't start swimming now, she was going to be battered, beaten, and drowned in debt.

She found herself surreptitiously looking around the parking lot for a sign of GoodGuy's convertible and caught herself up. *Let it go. It doesn't do you any good to dwell on it. It's over. There's no reason to tap into negative feelings.*

Pulling out the combination lock she kept in the glove box, she hurried inside against a persistent, cold rain, then made her way to the women's dressing rooms. Grabbing the first available locker, she placed her purse and jacket inside, then spun the lock's dial to erase any sign of the combination numbers and headed into the main fitness area with its treadmills, ellipticals and various other workout equipment.

She chose a treadmill in front of a television that was tuned to an all-day news channel, which was fine with her. She'd barely gotten started when Vivian, whom she'd called to tell that she was heading to the fitness center, appeared wearing a dark orange tank top and black Lululemon pants. She waved at Elizabeth then grabbed the treadmill next to her, which was just being vacated by a man sweating from head to toe.

"So glad you changed your mind about the membership. We should start up yoga classes again," Vivian said as she grabbed a towel and sprayed it with disinfectant from a bottle kept near the machines. "Ugh. Some guys can sure sweat!" She started the treadmill and began jogging. "It's sick the way they never wipe down the equipment after they use it."

Elizabeth was starting to sweat as she'd set a fast, uphill pace. "I'm probably still going to give it up," she answered, puffing a little. "My membership, I mean. I came in to do just that, but I wanted to work out at least once more. I don't know. Everything just feels so uncertain."

"You're coming to the grief counseling group tonight, right?" Vivian asked.

"Yeah . . ." Elizabeth kind of wanted to get out of it. She just wasn't sure how.

Vivian started out slowly on the treadmill. "It'll be good. You'll see. Everybody feels uncertain, but we're all coping in our way. Some better than others. You know that's how I met Nadia. I'm not supposed to talk about other people's problems, but since you know her, and about the miscarriages, I don't think I'm really breaking the news. Anyway, that's how we became friends. Everybody in the group is good people."

"I don't open up well," Elizabeth said, breathing hard. She could feel the exercise in her calves and chest and she almost wanted to crank up the speed some more. It felt good to burn through all the anxiety and worry.

"That's okay. You can listen. Most of us do at first. Bring Chloe over and we can go together."

"I can get a babysitter."

"But why? I'm sorry Lissa made that awful comment to Chloe, but they have fun together."

"Perfect." Vivian smiled.

Elizabeth pressed for more speed and their conversation stopped. Another group, she thought warily, then decided that maybe opening up and sharing her concerns would actually help her.

CHAPTER 19

It was a pisser being left at Rex's house waiting for her clothes to wash while he was off following a lead. Ravinia had argued with him, but he'd left her high and dry anyway, heading out while she was still wearing the woman's robe he'd found for her in one of his closets. She'd asked about it, but he'd mumbled something unintelligible, which had led her to believe the robe was a leftover from some woman with whom he'd once been involved.

It had all been a ploy, anyway. He'd waited till she was without her clothes and then taken off. Just like that. Honestly, she hadn't thought him wily enough to pull that on her, which had been a mistake. He was an investigator and he probably did things like that all the time in his job. She'd just thought . . . well . . . she'd trusted him more than she should. She wouldn't make that mistake again.

Barefoot, she wandered from the living room into one of the back bedrooms, neither of which possessed a bed. It looked like he lived in only three rooms, but it was a nice place. Particularly nice with rain pouring outside. She'd turned on the television and learned that the Californians were rejoicing in the deluge as they'd been in a long-term drought, although the freeways were choked with creeping traffic caused by numerous fender benders.

I've got to get a driver's license. And I need Rex's help.

Ravinia wasn't calculating by nature. She was too up front and generally annoyed by obstacles to approach them in any way other than head-on. It was something she'd always known about herself. However, she saw that she was going to have to find a new tact with Rex. She'd chosen him as her mentor, of sorts. She knew she could work with him, if he'd just let her, and he could help her get the things she needed. If he helped her, she could help him.

"What's that called?" she asked the room aloud. Ravinia had been home-schooled at Siren Song by Aunt Catherine and her older sisters, and she had a "broad and eclectic education" her eldest sister, Isadora, was wont to say. She hadn't been the most interested pupil; she'd fought her education all the way. But she'd absorbed more than she'd ever let any of them know, and then had passed her GED without a hitch, surprising everyone but herself.

She'd always known she would leave and had dreamed of grand adventures. Once she found Elizabeth and made sure she was all right and safe, maybe those future grand adventures could begin. . . .

She returned to where she'd started, to the warmth and rhythmic beating of the dryer in the laundry room. For a moment, the word escaped her, and then it hit her. "Symbiosis," she said. That's what she and Rex Kingston could have. A symbiotic relationship where he helped her and she helped him.

She just had to convince him of that.

The Brightside Apartments were a lesson in deferred maintenance. The paint was peeling along the edges of the eaves and one downspout had completely disengaged from the building, allowing rain to pour over the choked gutter in an unbroken arc of water. Cracked and uneven concrete made treading along the sidewalks hazardous, and yet the cars he saw in the parking lot were newer, higher end models. Rex made an immediate assumption that the people living here valued their vehicles more than their abodes, not that it took a genius to figure that one out. No one was taking care of the building, although the cost of living in the area was high enough that he suspected it wouldn't be long until some conglomerate bought the apartment buildings, upgraded them, and jacked up the rents.

He found the manager's apartment on the lower level at the end of the north building and knocked loudly. What had once been a darkly stained door was scratched, faded, and marred. It had a brand new lock on it, however, and the door handle was sturdy. He glanced down the row of units and realized it was one feature available for every renter. Made him wonder if there had been trouble with break-ins.

The door suddenly opened inward and a skinny woman in her twenties with thin brown hair stood in the aperture. She wore a bright green bra top and tight jeans that squeezed over her flared hip bones, but the waistband was loose around her waist. Her collarbones were so defined it looked as if she was a skeleton with stretched skin.

Anorexia, he decided, making a snap judgment. The hell of it was, he was rarely wrong. "Are you the manager?"

"My dad is, but he's not here. You want a room, you can put your name down and we'll do a credit check, but we're pretty full up."

"What's your father's name?"

"Ben Drommer." She tilted her head and gave him a good, hard look, apparently encouraged enough by what she saw to trust him a little. "I'm Erin."

"I'm Rex. Has your father been manager here for a while?"

"Ages. The whole time I was growing up, and I'm twenty-two now. Eons before that, too. After the divorce, Mom moved away, but Dad stayed." She shrugged. "You want a place or not?"

Rex pretended to think that over as he debated whether to play a game to get to the truth or just hit her straight on with what he wanted. He chose the latter. "A family lived here when their daughter was young. The daughter's in her mid-twenties now, so you might remember her?"

"Don't count on it. You know how many people have lived here?"

"The last name was Gaines. They had a daughter who's a few years older than you are."

Erin shrugged. "You could always ask Marlena, I guess. She's been here forever and that's no lie. She's in the other building, lower floor now. She used to be on the top, but Dad had to move her 'cause she couldn't do the stairs."

"Which unit?" Rex asked, turning to look at the building that ran perpendicular to the manager's.

The two structures created an L-shape with a path between them. The interior walkways were overgrown by various succulents and threaded through with weeds. A listing jacaranda grew from a center planter, and Rex imagined when it was in bloom, the purple flowers might jazz up the place . . . then again, maybe not.

Erin pointed to the interior unit next to the lower eastern corner. "Number thirteen. Marlena didn't care, but I'd never stay anywhere that had a thirteen in it."

"Yeah?"

"Too unlucky." She looked at him as if he were really slow.

"I know a guy whose address is 666," Rex said.

"He's alive?" Her eyes were huge.

"Last I checked. Like your dad, he's lived there most of his life."

She shuddered. "Some people just look for trouble." With that, she closed the door as if he'd suddenly become persona non grata.

He supposed he had and walked down the cracked concrete to the door she'd pointed out. The number thirteen was nailed to the side of the door in wrought-iron numerals, the one above the three. He knocked loudly once again, but it took a couple tries before he heard what sounded like something being dragged across the floor and scrabbling at what he assumed was the chain lock. Finally, a wrinkled face appeared through the opening in the door and one blue eye raked over him.

"Hello, Marlena? I'm Rex Kingston." He pointed toward the manager's office. "Ben Drommer's daughter Erin thought maybe you might be the right person for me to talk to."

"Whad about?" Her voice was dry and creaky as if there wasn't enough lubrication in her throat.

"A family that lived here fifteen or twenty years ago, maybe? Ralph and Joy Gaines and their daughter."

"Whad're ya sellin'?"

"Nothing. I'm just trying to find the Gaineses."

The blue eye stared for a moment, then he heard the chain lock being released. The door opened to reveal a woman bent over a walker that had wheels on the back two legs, rubber stoppers on the front two. When she flapped a hand at him, an invitation, and started back into the room, he realized she didn't lift the walker, just pushed it along even though the front legs had no wheels. He determined she must be stronger than she looked as she moved her bent form back toward a chair with an ergonomic cushion. She sank into it with a sigh, leaving Rex to shut the door.

"Sit down," she ordered.

He glanced around at the overstuffed furniture, which looked as if it needed the dust pounded out of it, and settled on a kitchen chair that was doing double duty in the living room. The shades were drawn and a strip of light, choked with dust motes, illuminated a row of brown paper sacks on the opposite side of the room like an accusing finger, pointing to the leftover newspapers she was apparently saving.

Rex caught a glimpse of several tabloids with screaming headlines. I HAD A GOBLIN BABY! was the easiest to read.

He turned to the old woman. "Do you remember them, the Gaineses?"

"Whad do you want 'em for?"

"So you do remember them."

"Mebbe." She squinted at him. "He do somethin' wrong? Gaines?"

"Not that I know of."

"He was always actin' like he was so hoity-toity with that insurance business. Talked about how he was gonna git hisself a real house. Like we wasn't good enough for him around here." She snorted. "Little big man. The wife was even worse. Puttin' on airs. Lookin' down her nose at everybody and everything. She finally hightailed it outta here and left him standing around like he didn't know what hit him. Stupid man. I coulda told him that it didn't matter how he thought of himself, she knew he wasn't good enough. Just took her a while to git up the gumption to go."

"To Colorado?" Rex asked, remembering what Beth Harper had said.

"Mebbe . . . mebbe not. Don't really know."

"They had a daughter . . ." he prompted.

"Uh, yeah. Her. Always worried, that one. Little white face with big eyes. She spooked the Henderson boy, but then he was a little touched anyway."

"What did she do?"

"Told him the world was gonna explode, or somethin'." Marlena cackled in amusement. "Hid hisself under his bed for a week."

"Did she mention a bridge coming down?"

Marlena pulled back and looked at him from the tops of her eyes, almost as if she were trying to peer over a pair of glasses. "You know about that? It was big talk around here for a while. Her mama wanted to call the police, but her daddy said no. It wasn't long after that, that they moved."

"Do you know where to?"

"They didn't tell me nothin' on account I was so lower class to their level of people," she said with a curl of her lip. Then with a shrug, she added, "Though I thought it might be south o' here somewhere."

"San Diego?"

She made a face. "Not that far. I don't rightly remember."

Rex asked her some more questions, but Marlena had started to wind down. He'd been in her apartment less than half an hour, but its darkness and a cloying scent of sour milk were getting to him. He thanked her and got up to leave.

"You come back again," she told him. "I'll tell you more."

He wasn't convinced she had more to tell, but he said, "I may do that," and headed out her door, closing it behind him. As he turned toward the parking lot and his car, he heard her thumping her way after him to the door, no doubt to turn the lock again.

To date, his research had turned up a lot of Ralph Gaineses in southern California. Apart from the one who'd resided in Costa Mesa, none had filled the bill to be the one he was searching for. Maybe Elizabeth's adopted father hadn't stayed in the state. Beth Harper had thought Colorado, so maybe he should turn his attention there.

Why do you care? he asked himself as he drove away. *This job isn't likely to be a moneymaker.* So far, there'd been no money at all, but that was his own fault. Still, he had to question his own motivation. *What's your end game, Rex?*

The perplexing answer was, he really didn't know. He'd signed on to help Ravinia, and he knew that, even after giving himself a good talking to, he wasn't going to change his mind.

Channing Renfro heard the rain pounding on the top of his convertible and it turned his black mood even blacker. Goddamn pansy-ass drivers didn't know how to fucking move in this stuff and when they did, they jagged from lane to lane and he was damn lucky he hadn't been clipped by that Fiesta. He'd laid on the horn for all he was worth and had yelled "Fuck you!" over and over again, but what had the middle-aged white woman in the Fiesta done? Nothing. Just kept on white-knuckling it down the road, eyes glued straight ahead, mouth probably open in fear and stupidity. Bitch never even looked back.

He was lucky he'd made it to the club without a scratch, although this goddamn rain wasn't doing his paint job any good. Oh, sure it was beading up on the hood of his BMW; he'd paid enough for the detailing that it goddamn better be, or he'd be in that asshole's face again, the one that had done the work and charged him a fucking ransom.

It was a short jog to the front doors, but he didn't feel like getting wet, so he sat in his car and fumed. There was an app on his phone, he recalled, something that skinny bitch, Delia, had suggested he get. She was gone, good riddance, but the app remained and he was pretty sure it was something to do with weather. Picking up his iPhone, he scrolled through several screens. Ah, yeah. Dark Sky. That was it. Clicking on it, he learned the rain was going to stop in his area in about ten minutes. Fine. Good. He'd wait.

Delia, Channing thought, now that his mind had touched on her. *What a goddamn bitch.* Moving out of their rental house . . . leaving him and John with the total rent. He oughtta sue her ass. Drag her into court. Make her pay. John didn't have any money. Maybe a few bucks from the valet job he had, but most of that went to entertaining the ladies. It was those ladies that had turned Delia into such a screaming witch. She was always thinking Channing was screwing one of 'em. Okay. Maybe he had, but it was just *one.* And that was because he was so stoned he didn't know who he was with. Well, he knew he wasn't with Delia, but he didn't care which of John's women he'd ended up with, and then old faithful had kinda let him down anyway, which concerned him, but he wasn't going to tell Delia that part.

He reached down and adjusted his balls through his sweat pants and thought gloomily about his sex drive. Something was a little bit off there. Delia had told him not to take all those natural supplements, but he'd kinda just wanted to slap her. Maybe they weren't helping, and well, the steroids . . . his skin had sure broken out in a bunch of big, red zits. "Fuckin' A," he muttered.

What he needed was a good workout. Glancing through the windshield through the dark, he saw several other cars circling the lot, their headlights washing over him. Everybody wanted to be close to the doors.

Maybe he should just run for it. *Fucking rain.*

Scratching at one of the zits on his left shoulder, he glanced at Dark Sky again and saw that the rain was almost over. He leaned back in the seat and closed his eyes and started counting. He got to thirty-four and stopped. It was boring to count.

He glanced through the windshield. Rain was pretty much over. He grabbed up his cell phone, stretching back and lifting his right hip so he could stick the phone into his pocket. He drummed his fingers on the steering wheel a few minutes then threw open the door, sick of waiting.

Stepping out of the BMW, he threw an angry look to the heavens. The rain had stopped, but that didn't make him any happier. Weather report said it was coming right back. He hated the rain.

Across the way, he saw a guy get out of a car, no hat, oblivious to the precipitation. Kinda pissed Channing off. He could practically hear his mother saying, "It is just rain, you little shit," or something to that effect. Made him miss her, though she'd been a worse bitch than Delia, in truth. Most of the time, he was glad she was gone.

He reached back inside for his gym bag, which was on the passenger seat. *Blam!* Something hit him alongside the head and the next thing he knew he was sprawled on the wet pavement. "Wha . . . wha . . . ?" He tried to get up but was hit again. *Blam!* He saw stars. And little cuckoo birds swimming around in a circle. Just like the fucking cartoons.

Dully, he heard noise, something funny . . . out of the ordinary. A *whoosh* . . . and heat and the smell . . . gasoline. . . .

His eyes opened. *My car!* Some fucker had hit it with a Molotov cocktail!

He got a knee underneath himself.

Bam!

Pain exploded against the back of his head.

He was slammed back down to the ground. He tried to catch his breath, to stay awake. He was rolled over forcefully, a heavy shoe turning him.

What the fuck?

Too weak to struggle, he squinted upward.

Above him a demon in a mask was pouring something down on him.

Water . . . ? No . . . gas! "Fuck," he tried to yell, but the bastard poured it into his mouth!

Spitting and twisting, Channing saw the lighter.

Then fire.

Great hellish flames cracking, burning.

His car. His beautiful convertible. "Ugh . . . ga . . . ga . . ." he sputtered, struggling to his feet.

He saw it as it happened—the red flash of flame that jumped from the car to him in a brilliant arc. It was almost beautiful. Blinding. Horrifying. He gasped. Too late as the gasoline rained upon his body ignited all over him. Burning. Scorching. Melting his face and his hair and his jogging suit.

Pain seemed to rip off his skin.

Running, yowling, a human torch, he raced around the lot as the fire consumed him. He screamed and screamed and screamed.

CHAPTER 20

"Symbiosis," Ravinia said for the second time when Rex ignored her. Seated at his small kitchen table, staring through the window to the rain drizzling from a leaden sky, she was getting damn tired of being ignored. "I help you, you help me."

"I'm already helping you," he said distractedly, his gaze on the laptop screen. He was seated across from her, a cup of coffee having cooled beside him. "Tomorrow we'll do the contract."

He'd been distracted from the moment he'd returned with the news that yes, Elizabeth's family had lived at the Brightside Apartments, and yes, the old woman who'd known them had thought Elizabeth was an odd child, and yes, they were on the right track. But that didn't mean they had another plan. Rex had gone into his den and pulled out his laptop and he'd all but shut Ravinia out, which pissed her off no end.

"I'm trying to make a point here," she said, crossing her arms over her chest.

"Go ahead and make it."

She wanted to slam the small computer shut on his fingers, but she figured that would fly in the face of her argument. Besides, he was working and that work was likely related to her search—at least she hoped it was—so she didn't want to do something counterproductive.

"I could work for you. I could stay here and use your address and get my driver's license. I have a birth certificate. I have my GED. I should be good, right?"

His fingers stilled and he eyed her over the top of the laptop. "Use my address?"

"I need an address," she pointed out.

"How is any of that symbiosis?" he asked, surprising her that he'd been listening.

She spread her hands. "I help you and you help me."

"I get the part about me helping you. Where does your help come in?"

"In the investigation. Tomorrow, the lady with the butt implants is meeting her lover, right? Kimberley Cochran."

"Wait a minute . . . how did you know?"

"I overheard you talking to the husband and I already know where. Casa del Mar. I looked around Google and a few other web sites," she shrugged, proud of herself.

"You used my computer."

"The laptop was open."

"Jesus, you can't go poking into people's private lives, you had no right—"

"See," she cut in, not wanting a lecture. She'd just taken a quick peek while he'd been in the shower and she hadn't seen anything sensitive. "I can be an investigator."

"It takes more than just Googling a name or two." He looked perturbed, his jaw hardening.

"But they don't know me—Kimberley Cochran or even her husband. No one. I'm just a girl. I can help you. I'll follow her, and she won't even notice me."

"You look like a street person."

She frowned. She was wearing her newly cleaned jeans and an army green T-shirt that she'd bought just before the trip south.

"You got lucky and got away with it at the Ivy . . . just . . . but it won't work again."

"I am a street person," she pointed out. "Sort of."

Rex gave a slight shake of his head, but at least most of his anger seemed to have dissolved as he returned his attention to the laptop. "I found a couple Ralph Gaineses I could call," he admitted, seeming to consider her suggestion.

"But you don't think they're the right ones."

"No. I don't know. Maybe." He closed the laptop and stared off into space while absently scratching the beard stubble on his chin.

"You want me to get some new clothes, I'll get some new clothes," she said as he took a sip of coffee, found it cold and made a face.

He scraped his chair back, then walked to the sink where he tossed what remained in his cup into the sink.

Lithely, she pushed herself onto the counter. "I want to go to the school—Wembley—and ask around about Elizabeth, but I'll need a ride. Are you taking me ?" Once again, she glanced through the window to the dark skies beyond as he rinsed his cup and left it on the counter. "Tomorrow, I mean. When school's in session."

"I haven't agreed to your plan."

"Got a better one?" She arched an eyebrow, silently daring him to come up with an alternate idea.

"Maybe." He gave her the once-over and she thought he was warming to the idea. "You do look like a high school student," he admitted, drying his hands on a nearby towel. "That could work. Maybe someone will talk to you." He sounded like he didn't give it much hope.

Ravinia wasn't about to give up. "So, I'll find the oldest teacher, just like you said, and strike up a conversation, tell her I'm Elizabeth's cousin. No . . . not good enough. Her half-sister. Yeah, that's better. I'm her half-sister and we've . . . um . . . we've lost touch. I have to find her because our father's dying." She was proud of herself for the tale she'd woven. It sounded foolproof.

"Her or him," Rex corrected.

"What?"

"The teacher who's been at the school the longest. It could be a man." He tossed the towel aside and sent her an intense look. "You're pretty quick with the sob stories, you know."

Was that a compliment? She didn't think so. "Yeah, well, what're you doing to find Elizabeth? It's not like we've got a lot of time." She thought about the sense she had, that evil was on its way. She couldn't help but worry that she might be the reason that Declan Jr., if the evil was him, had somehow connected to her and had followed her like a wraith to southern California. Ravinia had traveled all this distance to warn her cousin, to save Elizabeth. Was it possible that she'd read the signs wrong and was, in fact, doing just the opposite, bringing danger with her?

Either way, time was of the essence.

"We need to do something!" she said, her fingers curling over the edge of the counter as Rex opened one of the cupboards, rummaged around and pulled out a box of pasta. When he didn't respond to her demand, she thought she might have pissed him off. "Okay, sorry," she apologized as he set the box on the counter next to her. "You're working on things, I know. But why don't I go to the school and see if I can find anything out? Or better yet, I'll talk to the old lady—that Marlena? I want to know more about what she said about Elizabeth and that bridge collapsing."

"I don't think she knew any more than she told me." He was still searching the cabinet, but gave up and let the door close.

"All I'm saying is let me help. *Symbiosis*," Ravinia persisted. "Come on, Rex. What have you got to lose?"

"I don't know. . . ."

"Then let me follow the Cochran woman. You find Elizabeth."

He was considering it; she was certain. Thoughtfully, he took in all of her, including her T-shirt and jeans, once more.

"I'll get new clothes. I already said I would."

He thought about it a moment, his eyes narrowing, then as if he'd made a decision, glanced at his watch. "Okay, here's the deal. I'll take you to South Coast Plaza. Bound to be something there that'll work for you."

"So, you're going to let me help?" She could hardly believe he'd changed his mind.

"I gotta go to LA tomorrow anyway, so we'll see. Don't look so pleased with yourself," he said to her spreading smile, then motioned to the box of pasta resting on the counter. "I got nothing to go with this. So come on. We'll get something to eat at the mall."

Driving to Vivian's house, Elizabeth squinted against the dark sky and flooding rain. Five o'clock and it was pitch dark except for the headlights streaming at her from the cars heading the opposite direction and the tall sodium vapor streetlights that lined the highway. After leaving the office with a stack of paperwork and the knowledge that tomorrow she'd promised to meet Amy, Mazie's daughter, she'd picked up Chloe and shuttled her into the car. Elizabeth wasn't sure why Amy wanted to meet with her, what that was all about. Nothing good, as far as she could tell, but maybe she was being too pessimistic. She wished she'd never agreed to attend the group tonight.

She glanced at her daughter in the rearview mirror.

Propped in her car seat, Chloe seemed to be asleep. Her eyes were closed and she was exceedingly quiet for her. She had been for all of the ride.

"Hey, pumpkin. You okay?" Elizabeth asked her.

Chloe didn't immediately answer and Elizabeth's heart went to her throat. "Chloe?" she tried again, her voice more strident.

Her daughter's eyes opened slowly and she stared vaguely straight ahead. Elizabeth could tell she wasn't completely awake. Worried, she glanced around for a place to pull over. Something wasn't right.

"Where are we?" Chloe asked.

"We're almost halfway."

"To where . . . ?"

They'd gone over the fact they were going to Vivian's not fifteen minutes earlier.

Elizabeth couldn't see anywhere to pull over. "To Lissa's, remember? We talked about this." Had her daughter just gone to sleep or had she fainted? Was this one of the fainting episodes the teachers at school had called her about? The reason she'd kept Chloe home? "I'll turn around. Maybe we should just go home." *Or to the doctor.*

"No!" Chloe declared, blinking, her voice stronger. "I want to play with Lissa."

"Were you asleep?"

"You promised I could play with Lissa!"

"I know. Don't get upset. I'm just concerned that you're not well, like what happened before."

"I want to play with Lissa," she repeated, and even in the dark interior, Elizabeth thought she noticed tears forming in the corners of Chloe's eyes. "You promised," her daughter charged.

"Okay. Okay." Elizabeth braked for a stoplight. With one eye on the glowing taillights of the car in front of her, she said, "I just want to be sure you're all right."

"I just had my eyes closed," Chloe insisted, but Elizabeth suspected she was lying.

"Would you tell me if you didn't feel well?"

"Yes . . ." Chloe met Elizabeth's concerned eyes in the mirror, then glanced away, her face set in concentration.

Elizabeth's stomach knotted.

The light changed and she eased onto the gas, following the car while still glancing in the rearview to her daughter.

Chloe said almost inaudibly, "I thought I saw Daddy . . ."

"Daddy . . . ?" Elizabeth's throat tightened. "You mean you were dreaming?"

"He's mad because we killed him."

"*What?* Chloe, my God. We didn't kill him," she choked out nearly ramming into the back of the car she'd been following. Her Escape started to fishtail, then caught, staying miraculously in her lane. "That's not right, honey." Her conscience asked, *Didn't you? With your thoughts, didn't you wish him dead and somehow cause the accident that took his and Whitney Bellhard's lives?*

"I was mad at him," Chloe admitted in a small voice, tucking her chin into her neck. "I didn't like that woman touching him."

Elizabeth's mouth went dry. "What woman?" Her hands were suddenly slick with sweat on the steering wheel. What was this? Had her little girl somehow seen Court with Whitney Bellhard? Had Court *allowed* it? For the love of God! Or was this all in her daughter's mind? The product of a vivid imagination and all the gossip she might have heard?

"They were in Daddy's car. She had her hand on his leg. I yelled at her to let go, but she never heard me. I'm still mad at him," Chloe added, her voice dropping to a whisper.

When? When had Chloe been with Court and Whitney, if, indeed she was the woman? Was it true? Or a fantasy? What, if anything, did it have to do with Chloe's "spells" where she seemed out of it for minutes at a time? And the fainting spell, according to her teacher, the reason Elizabeth had kept her home from school.

Dread settled into her heart. What was wrong with her child? She had to find out. First from a medical doctor, then a child psychologist or—

"Damn," she whispered under her breath. Elizabeth was so rattled she nearly missed the turn-off to Vivian's neighborhood. Wrenching the wheel hard at the last minute, she made the corner, then told herself to calm down. She would deal with whatever was going on with Chloe.

Another glance in the rearview showed nothing out of the ordinary. As she drove upward past McMansions with wrought iron gates and manicured lawns, the street winding to the crest of a hill that housed the neighborhood park, Chloe was doodling on the condensation of the window, once again blithely unconcerned about anything.

Elizabeth nosed the car downward to the street leading to the Eachuses huge home with its sculpted landscaping and exterior lights burning bright in the night.

Pulling into the drive, she switched off the ignition and yanked on the emergency brake before swiveling in her seat to regard her daughter. Rain pounded onto the roof and she had to raise her voice to be heard. "Honey? When you fainted before, those other times? At school? Do you remember?"

"Uh-huh."

"Did you have dreams then, too?"

Chloe stared at Elizabeth through the darkness, then nodded slowly.

"What were they about?" Elizabeth could scarcely form the words, her throat was so dry. And her heart was pounding painfully in her chest.

"He said he loved you, but I think he did some bad things."

"Your . . . daddy?"

Chloe hiked her shoulders to her ears. "I don't want to talk about it anymore."

"I'm just worried that—"

"We're here!" she cut her mother off as she quickly unbuckled her seatbelt.

"Chloe, wait!"

"No," she declared, throwing open the door and running through the swirls of windblown rain across the wet grass toward the massive front door.

Elizabeth scrambled after her. She caught up with her daughter at the porch, but Chloe had already pounded on the bell seconds before Lissa opened the door.

"Wait!" Elizabeth said again.

Chloe shot inside like a bullet.

Elizabeth opened her mouth to call her daughter back, but the two girls were already pounding up the stairs as she entered the foyer, the shoulders of her jacket wet, her skirt actually dripping. The moment for a heart-to-heart with her daughter had passed, she realized. She'd have to continue the conversation later, when she and Chloe were alone again.

Vivian, dressed in one of her ubiquitous jogging suits, appeared from the direction of the kitchen. "Ready?" She stopped by the coat closet where she grabbed a longer jacket and umbrella. "God, it's nasty out there. I *hate* this weather."

"Me, too," Elizabeth admitted.

"We'll deal. Bye, Honey!" she sang up the stairs to her daughter, then toward the kitchen, "Bill, you're on! See you later." As she reached for the door knob, she said, to Elizabeth, "Let's go, before someone decides they need me."

Outside, Vivian and Elizabeth ducked their heads against the rain as, unlike Chloe, they took the sidewalk to Elizabeth's Escape.

"I'm going to have to make it a quick night," Elizabeth told her as Vivian buckled herself into the passenger seat. Starting the engine and pulling into the street, she explained about Chloe falling asleep in the car, omitting what she'd said about her dream. "The kid's just beat, so I'll need to get her home."

As she drove, she sensed that Vivian wanted to argue, but those protests died in her throat. Instead, she directed Elizabeth two exits south on the 405, then to a commercial building whose back offices had obviously been converted from storage to a community room for rent. Elizabeth found an empty parking spot and she and Vivian dashed through the rain and the parked cars.

Once inside the room with its tile floor and suspended fluorescent lights, Elizabeth took a seat in the semicircle of chairs, but felt dissociated from the other women. The group called themselves Sisterhood, though Vivian had explained it was a loose term without any registered name or number.

The meeting opened with a woman named Judy greeting them as a group. Tall and thin with a sprig of red hair, she wore little makeup, jeans, and a comfy sweatshirt. After the mass greeting, she launched into a humorous story about how, in the rain, a little girl in her neighborhood had been trying to sell lemonade from a stand in front of her house. Everyone chuckled, but Elizabeth's mind was on Chloe and the disturbing things she'd said. How had she known about Court and Whitney Bellhard? Or, was that just coincidence?

He's mad because we killed him. . . .

The mood in the room grew sober and one woman and then a second began talking about how they were coping with their problems from loss or misery or death—whatever reason had sent them to Sisterhood in the first place.

He said he loved you but I think he did some bad things. . . .

"I don't care. I just can't forgive him," the second woman—her name tag read STELLA—declared. She told the story of a cheating husband who'd been diagnosed with terminal cancer. She finished with, "I'm sorry. I'll say it. I wish he'd just die."

Elizabeth's attention returned with a bang. Her throat tightened and she felt suddenly hot. This woman could be echoing thoughts she'd had before Court actually died.

Judy soothed, "You wouldn't be the first woman to express those feelings, Stella." A soft chorus of agreement followed.

"I don't think it's my duty to take care of him now," Stella continued, her fists clenched, her voice shredded with tears. "Why should I get that job? Call me a bitch. Go ahead. I'm not spending the next few years of my life taking care of that loser!"

She still cares about him, Elizabeth realized her heart breaking a little for the woman's obvious pain. For a second, she looked inward. *Do I still care about Court?* When she thought about him, guilt was the most consuming emotion. Guilt for wishing him dead. Anger, too, still simmered in her heart; she was still furious about the way he'd left her and left his daughter. It had been wrong. Heartless. Of course she missed him and felt his loss, for certain, but was that just because she was feeling rudderless without him?

You're putting too fine a point on it. You're sorry he's gone. Accept that and stop trying to make yourself out to be some kind of monster. You wished him dead, but really you just wanted the pain he'd caused you to end.

She looked around and asked Vivian in a whisper, "How often does Nadia come?"

Vivian leaned in close. "She doesn't anymore. I think she felt kind of like a fraud because her grief was different, you know, with the miscarriages. They happened pretty early in the pregnancies, so she didn't have a child or husband or family member that she could name."

"Ah . . ."

The meeting went on and a woman named Char spoke about how long it had been since her son and husband had died in an automobile accident. Elizabeth's head started to pound as she realized the depth of pain experienced by the women at the meeting. Their feelings were raw, their despair and grief palpable, tears flowing in some cases. Words of consolation and understanding were whispered throughout the room.

Like Nadia, Elizabeth felt a bit of a fraud for being here when her own feelings were so conflicted.

The discussion went from one person to the next and when it was her turn, Elizabeth shook her head as she'd seen a number of the women do. She wasn't ready to open up to these strangers about her feelings or her family. Instead, her fingers curled over her skirt and she bit hard on her lip. It was a mistake coming here. She was more certain than ever.

Unlike Elizabeth, Vivian was eager to take the floor. She spoke about her Carrie, how difficult that first year had been after her death, and how, even though she had Lissa, Carrie was with her every day. The others nodded in commiseration, and Stella, the woman who'd wished her husband dead, wiped a few angry tears away as she was still lost in her own misery.

The meeting wrapped up about nine and Elizabeth slowly let out a breath, relieved that the evening was over. Grabbing her purse and foraging inside for her keys, she didn't know what she felt more, a need to get away from all this depression or the desire to see her daughter again and scoop her into her arms, make sure she was all right. The last few weeks had been terrible, but she still had Chloe and that was worth everything. *Everything.*

Gratefully, Vivian didn't want to linger.

When she dropped Vivian off at the Eachuses house and picked up Chloe, Elizabeth learned that Chloe and Lissa had been in yet another fight. The girls were watching television in separate rooms, Chloe in the family room with Bill, Lissa in the master bedroom.

A frazzled Bill made a face, spread his hands, and declared, "Babysitting's hard," to which Vivian rolled her eyes even while she told him he'd done fine. "And honey," she reminded him gently, "it's really not babysitting when it's your own child." Turning toward Elizabeth, Vivian mouthed, "Men!" as if she couldn't believe how clueless they, and Bill in particular, were.

"Thanks," Elizabeth told him and ushered her daughter to the car.

Elizabeth tried to talk to Chloe on the way home, but it was impossible. Chloe was tired, grumpy, and uncommunicative. When Elizabeth attempted to return to the conversation they'd begun in the car on the way to Vivian's, about the woman Chloe had claimed to have seen touching Court's leg in his BMW, Chloe shut down completely.

"I don't wanna talk!" she practically screamed, turning her face away from Elizabeth to stare out the window of the back seat.

Once home, Chloe went straight to bed without a complaint, even running a toothbrush over her teeth without having to be reminded.

Elizabeth was left alone with her thoughts and worries. She slipped out of her clothes and into a robe, then washed the makeup from her face and applied a cool, soothing cream, telling herself she needed to ignore the concerns crowding and scratching at her brain.

After ten, she picked up the remote and clicked on the television. There was still a little time before the local news and a crime drama she'd watched the previous season was being aired. Elizabeth half listened while shaking out her clothes and draping the jacket, skirt, and blouse over a bedside chair. Her thoughts turned toward the next day, work in general and her upcoming meeting with Mazie's daughter. Padding from the closet, she realized she'd switched off her phone's ringer at the meeting and never thought about it again. She found the phone in her purse and discovered a number of texts and a phone message. The texts were from the Moms Group, the ones who knew she was going to a grief meeting with Vivian and wanted to offer encouragement. Nadia's text simply said, **Call me when you're back,** but Elizabeth didn't want to rehash the experience, no matter how well intentioned Nadia's motives might be.

The voice mail froze her blood—a message from Detective Thronson.

"Hello, Elizabeth," the detective's voice sounded in her ear. "I want to catch you up on the investigation into your husband's death. Would tomorrow work for you? Let me know." She finished the message with her cell phone number.

Oh. God.

Elizabeth knew the police would contact her. She'd been expecting a call from Thronson or one of her colleagues, but still, hearing the somber tone of the detective's voice chilled her to the bone.

Telling herself she had nothing to fear, that she hadn't caused Court's demise, that she couldn't be a suspect in his death, she couldn't shake the cold that settled deep in her soul and caused goose pimples to rise on her skin. Rubbing her arms, she walked to the window, looked out to the night beyond and felt almost that someone or some*thing* was staring back.

"You're freaking yourself out," she said, but snapped the blinds shut. As much to clear her head as warm up, she suddenly decided to take a shower. She turned on the taps, stripped off her bathrobe, letting it pool on the floor, then stepped under the needle-sharp, hot spray. Dunking her head under the showerhead and letting the water pour over her, she imagined it washing away the problems crowding her mind. Slowly, she began to feel warm again, but even then a shiver ran beneath her skin, reminding her that nothing was right.

Ten minutes later, she was cinching the belt of her robe again, her wet hair starting to dry a little as she walked into the bedroom and glanced at the television where the crime drama was wrapping up the episode. She'd lost interest in the segment and ignored the program as she picked up her clothes and examined the jacket, wondering if it was time to take it and the skirt to the cleaners. She had some other outfits that needed to go as well, but she hesitated. It wasn't that she didn't have the money now, but every expense added up and she didn't want to find herself in a position where she couldn't afford the mortgage. Court may have given Whitney Bellhard the impression he had money, but in truth, he'd been a terrible spender. Sitting on the edge of the bed, she saw how many allowances she'd made for him. If she had it to do over again—

Her cell phone buzzed on her dresser, sounding almost angry as it vibrated across the wood top. Scooping the cell up, she glanced at the caller with trepidation but saw that it was Jade, not the detective. *Pretty late for her to call.* While Elizabeth weighed whether she wanted to hear more words of encouragement from her friends, the phone suddenly stopped ringing.

I'll call her back tomorrow.

Grabbing up the remote again, she walked toward the bed, turning toward the set. The late news was just beginning, so she switched to her favorite newscaster, then tossed the controller onto the bed just as her cell began ringing again.

Detective Thronson again? No, no. It was too late for the policewoman to call. Right?

Crossing the room, she swept up the phone and breathed a sigh of relief when she saw Jade's name and number.

Again.

"Hey," Elizabeth answered, bracing herself for more *that-a-girls.*

"Turn on the TV to the news! Oh, God. Oh, my God," Jade shrieked.

"I've got it on. What's wrong? What's happened?" Elizabeth demanded in quick succession, her gaze moving to the screen.

"What station are you on? Elizabeth, for the love of God!" But Jade didn't need to say anything else.

Elizabeth's heart turned to stone as she watched the local reporter, an older man whose calm demeanor and lack of sensationalism appealed to her, as she stood in the Fitness Now! parking lot. A strobe of red and blue police lights flickered behind him where a slash of crime scene tape had cordoned off some kind of smoking wreckage.

"An unidentified male is in critical condition after the attack around five-thirty this evening," the grave reporter said. "No one saw the arsonist who appeared to have attacked the victim and then poured gasoline over him and his car. The incident was in plain sight of the building, yet no one witnessed anything out of the ordinary until a member just leaving the club saw what he describes as a fireball at the back of the parking lot."

The camera zoomed in on the blackened, misting hulk that had once been a convertible.

Elizabeth dropped the phone from nerveless fingers.

"Authorities are hoping that someone saw something and can identify a suspect. Perhaps someone walking away with a bag or possibly a gas can? The police are on the scene but not identifying the victim pending notification of his family." The reporter rambled on, asking for the public's assistance while Elizabeth, her eyes transfixed, her pulse pounding, her mind silently screaming, *No. No. No!* stared at the screen.

"Oh, Jesus," she whispered, a hand coming to her mouth in horror.

There, centered in the frame of the camera's lens, the torched vehicle's license plate was visible.

GOODGUY.

CHAPTER 21

"Elizabeth? Elizabeth!" Jade's tinny voice sounded from the phone laying on the carpet.

Blinking, Elizabeth found herself on the bed where she'd slumped when her knees had given way. She couldn't think . . . just couldn't think.

GoodGuy in critical condition . . . burned by an attacker . . .

You wished him harm. You did. You wished him harm.

"Elizabeth!!"

Climbing to her feet, Elizabeth sank to her knees and crawled across the carpet to where the phone lay like a fallen soldier. Flopping down on her side, she placed the cell to her ear. "I'm . . . I'm here," she said, not recognizing her own voice.

"Oh, good. Oh, my God. I just saw that horrible image and couldn't believe it. I'm sorry to shock you. I just . . . couldn't believe it!" Jade sounded completely undone.

"It's my fault," Elizabeth said, for once ignoring the self-imposed lock on her tongue.

"It is not. Don't . . . say that."

"I was mad at him. I chased him down and wanted to ram his car."

"Well, you didn't pour gasoline on him."

"There's some connection. I don't know what it is, but there's some connection. I'm weird, Jade. You know I'm damn weird! I saw Little Nate in trouble before it happened. You were right. You've been right all along. It's my fault that . . . GoodGuy was attacked. I just know it."

"Don't talk like that. You're hysterical. I don't blame you. I feel damn weird myself. But you *didn't do this*," Jade said tautly. "So, don't say that you did. To anybody."

"He's not the only one, Jade. I wished Court dead, too. . . ."

"Stop it, Elizabeth. I'm coming over there."

"And Mazie Ferguson. She was my mentor. She really pissed me off and she died in another car accident and now . . . and now . . . I'm getting all her clients. *Benefitting!* And then, oh, God, Officer Unfriendly."

"Elizabeth, don't take this the wrong way but *shut up*. I'm getting my keys now and heading out."

"No." Elizabeth insisted. "Please. Don't come. I'm . . . okay."

"You're clearly not. I shouldn't have called you. I'll see you soon." Jade hung up.

Elizabeth dropped the phone and just lay on the carpet, staring across the bedroom floor. The television was blathering on, but it was just so much white noise.

With an effort, she pulled herself to her feet and padded barefoot into the kitchen. She washed her hands and didn't know why, then caught her ghostly reflection in the window, a haggard-looking woman with fear in her eyes. How could this have happened? How could GoodGuy, whoever the hell he was, have ended up in a horrific accident at Fitness Now!?

Not an accident. Someone tried to kill him. Probably did. The TV reporter said "critical condition," but who knew if he'd survive?

She started up the coffeemaker without really thinking about it, filling the reservoir with water, measuring decaf coffee into the filter, and as a million questions peppered her mind, watched the brown liquid fill the glass carafe.

Who would torch his car? Torch him?

What kind of sick mind . . . ?

You mean, like yours.

"No!" She pounded her fist on the counter and jarred herself out of her reverie. She would never have done or conjured up anything so insidiously evil as to pour gasoline . . . Oh, God. It was all too bizarre. Her entire life seemed to be spinning out of its normal rotation.

What the hell is going on?

How does it involve me?

As the coffee pot sputtered and hissed, she walked down the hall and pushed open the door to Chloe's room—just to make certain her daughter was okay. Peering in, she found Chloe was fast asleep, the covers on her bed having slid to the floor. By rote, Elizabeth slipped the quilt and sheet over her daughter again, then kissed her on the forehead. Tears welled in Elizabeth's eyes. Her sleeping child was so peaceful and serene . . . but what she'd said earlier about Court and the woman, presumably Whitney Bellhard, was disturbing. So were her fainting spells and quick temper.

"Oh, baby," Elizabeth whispered, sending up a prayer that whatever bizarre events were happening to her, they wouldn't touch her child, that Chloe would be safe. Then she slipped into the hallway again and shut the door softly behind her.

In the kitchen, she tried to shake off her case of anxiety, which of course was impossible, but she poured herself a cup of coffee. Though her fingers were still trembling slightly, she carried it into the living room. Before she could sit down, a soft knock sounded on the door.

Elizabeth opened it and Jade stood beneath the porch light. "I didn't want to wake Chloe."

"No problem. I just checked. She's asleep. Come in." Elizabeth held the door open. "How about a cup of coffee? Decaf?" She held up her cup. "Don't ask me why, but I made a fresh pot."

Jade stepped inside and lay a hand on the side of her bulging abdomen. "Abercrombie's bicycling. No, thanks, but go ahead. Are you okay?" Her dark eyes were filled with concern. "I probably shouldn't have called."

"No, no! You should have. I'm glad you did. The news was on anyway and I was going to see it. God, how awful." Elizabeth shuddered again as in her mind's eye, she pictured the burned wreckage that had appeared on the television screen. "So, it was good that I had someone to talk to." With her free hand, she started to pull the door closed behind Jade when she felt that chill again, the all-to-familiar sensation that raised the hairs on the back of her neck, the feeling that someone, somewhere in the dark night, was observing her. Her throat went dry as she closed the door and herded her friend into the living room. "You really don't want some?"

"No. Seriously. I'm good." Jade eyed her. "Are you sure you're okay?"

"Yes. No." Elizabeth lifted a shoulder and shook her head. "It's all too weird. I just"—she glanced around the room as if expecting to find an answer that didn't exist—"don't know what the hell's going on."

"Sit down." Jade took the cup from Elizabeth's fingers, set it on one of the magazines fanned across the coffee table, and guided Elizabeth to the couch. Sitting down next to her friend, Jade said, "First, let me say this isn't your fault. None of it is. That's not how the world works."

"How do you know?" Elizabeth asked on a short laugh.

"It just doesn't. I don't know how you knew about Little Nate, but you saved him. That's all that mattered. You saved him. That's who you are. You're not causing people to be hurt . . . or anything else."

Elizabeth closed her eyes. Tried to pull herself together. The truth was, she'd told Jade too much about herself already. Of all of Elizabeth's friends, Jade was the only one who knew about her strange ability to sometimes see things that were going to happen a second or two or a few minutes before they occurred.

All of her life, or at least for as long as she could remember, Elizabeth had told herself it was intuition. Some form of primal communication that arose when she was near a coming disaster. Nothing all that spectacular. No ESP or anything remotely psychic. God, no.

But . . .

Dark memories assailed her, one in particular.

"The bridge is falling!" She was a young girl, screaming those words. Fear engulfed her. She had a vision of cement decking buckling, girders twisting, the groan of metal as it was wrenched from its anchors.

It was all so vivid.

"Elizabeth?" Jade asked, snapping her back to the here and now. Jade's face was contorted in worry.

"I'm okay," she said.

"You're pale as death."

"It's nothing. Just something I remembered from when I was a kid." Sighing, she said, "Look"—she reached out a hand and clasped her friend's, squeezing tightly—"I know what happened to GoodGuy is not my fault. I mean, I was nowhere near the gym. But . . . it's all so . . . shocking . . . so terrible. . . ."

"I know." Jade linked her fingers with Elizabeth's.

"I'm okay."

"You say that—"

"No. I am." Elizabeth was firm. She meant it. The darkness in her mind had receded and she was in control again. At least more in control. "Jade, I love you for coming by, but I'm okay. Truly." She noticed her friend rubbing the side of her abdomen again. "Go home and take care of yourself and Little Nate and Byron. I'm perfectly fine."

"You're sure? You do look a little better," Jade said, still uncertain as she critically examined Elizabeth's face.

"I'm sure."

It took a bit more convincing, but Jade finally headed for the door. Once outside, she took a final glance over her shoulder, a line of worry furrowing her brows as if she were concerned that she'd been given the bum's rush.

"Bye," Elizabeth called after her. "Thanks."

"Anytime." Jade waved.

Elizabeth waved back, watching her friend climb into her car and drive away, taillights glowing in the night. The air was fresh. Damp from the recent rain. She gazed up and down the street, searching the shadows, but saw no one.

Once Jade's car disappeared around the corner, Elizabeth closed and locked the door and rested her forehead against the inner panels, her thoughts turning to GoodGuy again. *It is my fault,* she thought, now that she was alone. *If he dies, it is my fault.*

Snapping off the lights, she tried to dissuade herself of the notion that she was to blame but couldn't. Feeling lightheaded and weird, she went to bed. She hadn't wanted to lie to Jade, but she needed time to process everything that had happened.

In the morning she turned on the news again and learned the top story was the horrific death of a man at Fitness Now!; a member by the name of Channing Renfro. A man had been seen near the vehicle minutes before it exploded into flames, and the police were calling him a person of interest.

In the passenger seat of Rex Kingston's car, Ravinia tugged on the hem of the short black dress and wriggled her toes in shoes that felt a size too small though the woman in the shoe shop had haughtily told her that they were Italian leather and fit like a caress.

Okay. If that's what it was all about, that's what it was all about. The shoes were black "kitten heels" with a flat black bow on the toe.

Last night at the mall, she'd eyed an array of five-inch-heeled shoes and boots with a stirring of lust as she thought about the models she'd seen on television in such wear, but her overall pragmatism won out and she forewent them in a hurry, suspecting she would snap an ankle if she actually tried to walk around in something like that.

They were currently cruising through west LA in the late morning, heading toward Rex's office. He'd given her the choice to stay in Costa Mesa and work her way over to Wembley Grade School in her search for Elizabeth, but the new clothes were for the upcoming rendezvous Kimberley Cochran had planned with her lover. Ravinia had been torn. Yes, there was urgency to find Elizabeth. Even without Aunt Catherine's warnings, she could sense something going on, something coming. Was it Declan Jr., zeroed in on another one of them? Had he made his way south ahead of her? Or was she just being overly sensitive to her aunt's fears and worries?

In any event, she'd chosen to go with Rex and work on his other case. If she helped him, then he would help her. He'd promised to drive back to Costa Mesa after the rendezvous. She could go to the school tomorrow. *Symbiosis,* she thought, gritting her teeth and giving her skirt another tug. She just hadn't counted on helping him *first.*

"Pulling on it isn't going to make it any longer," he drawled.

She ignored that. "Where's Casa del Mar?"

"Santa Monica. Right on the beach south of the pier."

"The pier with the Ferris wheel?"

"Yup." He pulled into the parking lot behind his office. "This'll be quick."

"I know. The contract." She followed him in through the back door, aware that even the kitten heels were a balancing act. *Fine.* She could master it.

As Rex peeled off for his office, she heard from down the hall, "Joel? Is that you?"

Pain in the ass Bonnie. Ravinia smiled to herself, walking carefully. She'd never worn such a short skirt ever. The cool California air slipping up her thighs had made her feel half-naked, but she could see the possibilities of dressing up and looking good.

As long as she didn't trip and fall.

"Yeah, I'm just here for a minute," he called back to Bonnie.

Ravinia passed by his office door. She'd washed her hair and let it dry straight. One of Rex's mysterious female visitors had left some makeup scattered in a drawer so Ravinia had attempted to put some on. She'd smeared the eyeliner and had to wash it back off and had hit her eyeball with the mascara wand, but all in all, she thought she'd done okay.

Rex eyed her critically when she'd appeared in the kitchen, then stood in front of him, her hands on her hips. "You look like somebody else," he admitted.

"That's the point, right?"

"That's the point," he agreed.

She carefully strolled into the front of the office. Bonnie's back was to her as the girl was looking through the front windows. Sensing someone, she turned around, clearly expecting Rex. The way her mouth popped open and her jaw sagged was an image Ravinia would treasure for a long time.

"Wha . . . what are you doing?" she asked in a strangled voice.

"I'm on a job with Rex," Ravinia told her.

Rex came out of his office at that moment, holding some papers, frowning down at them. "Bonnie, would you print off a contract for me?"

"For who . . . her?" She looked stricken.

"Yes. Ravinia Rutledge, right?" He glanced at her.

"That's what's on my GED."

He checked his watch. "We'll pick up lunch then head over to the Cochrans. Kimberley's rendezvous at Casa del Mar could be a nooner. Don't want to miss it."

A nooner. Ravinia filed that away as Bonnie slowly sat down in her chair and pulled up something on her computer. She pressed a few buttons and Ravinia could hear a machine chunking away in another room.

"It's printing," Bonnie said dully.

"Thanks." Rex moved down the hall toward the sound.

"I should be the one going," Bonnie said in a voice so low Ravinia almost didn't hear it.

Ravinia thought up a number of retorts, but in the end, she just lifted her shoulders, spread her hands, and smiled. Pretty sure she was the victor in that skirmish, she went in search of Rex.

* * *

If Elizabeth hadn't already had the appointment with Mazie's daughter, she would have taken Chloe to school, driven home again, gone back to bed, and pulled the covers over her head. GoodGuy was dead. She didn't even bother to pretend it had nothing to do with her; she knew it did. She could think of no other explanation. Whoever had poured the gasoline on Channing Renfro had done so because they knew she'd thought he was a far cry from what his license plate had proclaimed.

But who was doing it? And to what purpose? The only people who knew about GoodGuy were her friends and whomever they'd told.

But they don't know about Mazie . . . and Officer Unfriendly . . . Or do they?

She shook her head as she walked up the steps to the front door of Suncrest Realty. None of her friends were *killers*. She wouldn't believe that. What did that leave? Some stalker? Something indefinable . . . supernatural . . . like her ability to sometimes see disaster right before it happened?

Pat was at the front desk and Elizabeth made a quick jog left toward Mazie's office where she was meeting Amy.

"I saw the news," Pat said loudly to Elizabeth's back as she tried to ease past. "That guy you were talking about with your friend. GoodGuy. That was his license plate on TV!"

Elizabeth stiffened. She'd forgotten that Pat had overheard her talking with Jade. "I didn't know him, but it's a tragedy."

"Really?" Pat said with a disbelieving look over rimless glasses. "I thought you didn't like him."

"We never met."

"Just on the road." A nasty glint surfaced in Pat's stare.

Elizabeth's pulse skyrocketed, but she wasn't going to be baited. She walked down the short hallway to Mazie's office and wanted to slam the door, but she didn't get the chance. Connie Berker breezed in behind her and did the honors by pulling the door shut behind her.

Connie's frosted blond hair had been freshly cut, the back of her neck shaved beneath stiff, product-laden strands that shone beneath the overhead lights.

"What's going on?" Elizabeth asked as she opened one of the drawers in Mazie's desk where she knew a stack of notepads was kept.

"I should be asking you that. You don't know this is my office now?"

"No . . . I didn't." Elizabeth closed the drawer.

"You're meeting with Amy Ferguson." It came out like an accusation and she could see that it was meant to be taken that way, too. "Right?"

"Yes. I thought I'd meet her in here as I forgot to tell her that my office is down the hall," Elizabeth explained. "I didn't know you'd moved." She glanced at the walls and desk. Nothing had changed.

If Connie were staking her claim, there was no proof. She hadn't hung a picture, or an award, or put anything on the desk, including her name plate.

"This is one of the best offices in the building," Connie went on, her head bobbing, blond hair unmoving. "You can see right out to reception." She motioned toward the glass door and Elizabeth followed her gaze, spying Pat at her circular desk, peering as always, over her shoulder.

Get a life, Elizabeth thought as the front door opened and Amy walked in. A tall, somewhat gawky young woman, she said a few words to Pat who nodded, a fake smile tacked onto her face.

Pat half-turned again. Reaching out, her fingers pointed to where Elizabeth stood in her mom's old office.

"I've known Amy for years," Connie said stiffly, her spine seeming to lengthen. "And yet suddenly she's your client. Just how did that happen?"

Elizabeth wasn't about to play office politics or get into an argument, so she didn't respond and moved toward the door, reaching for the handle. "I'll meet with Amy in the back."

Connie put out a hand and held the door closed. "Watch yourself. You're making enemies right and left around here. I'm telling you this as a friend."

Connie's advice didn't sound very friendly to Elizabeth, but she merely nodded and put her hand on the doorknob. "Noted," she told the angry Realtor then twisted the knob to open the door and walked down the hall where she met Amy. With every step, Elizabeth felt Connie's gaze like a hot knife between her shoulder blades.

For someone carrying on an extra-marital affair, Kimberley Cochran wasn't trying to be careful, secretive, or even discreet. She backed her silver-blue Mercedes out of the garage, then guided her car through the slowly opening gate, and hit the gas. Without a look in her rearview mirrors, she kept the Mercedes at maximum speed until she reached Ocean Avenue and the crawling traffic that forced her to slow.

Rex and Ravinia followed behind in the Nissan.

At the hotel, Kimberley valeted the car and stepped toward the front doors. In a silver dress with matching five-inch heels, she sashayed her butt like an open invitation, drawing stares from men and women alike.

"I'm dropping you off," Rex said.

"I know the plan," Ravinia retorted. She was already pushing open the door as Rex eased to a stop and let her out.

"Just try not to be obvious."

That was a joke. In her short skirt, she felt like a beacon, although she didn't get quite as many stares as Kimberley.

Ravinia walked up a short flight of sweeping stairs to the upper lobby where she caught a glimpse of Kimberley heading toward the restaurant that faced the ocean. Hurrying after her, Ravinia's right ankle wobbled a bit. She had to slow down to bring that under control and by the time she reached the maître d's stand, she was walking like she'd been in heels her whole life . . . pretty much. "Is there a table by the window?"

Kimberley, soul of discretion that she was, had already enthusiastically hugged her date, a young, buff man with longish brown hair, smoldering dark eyes, and an avaricious look about him.

Ravinia searched his heart as she cruised past to the next table, drawing a startled look to his face, but found only a modicum of interest in anything of the world outside himself.

Bad choice, Kim.

She was seated at the table next to them and when the waiter brought her a menu, she pretended to peruse it, nearly losing focus from Kimberley and her friend when she saw the prices.

She glanced over the top as she heard Kimberley telling him eagerly, "Putting together a reunion show. All of us that were modeling before are in one place, well, except for Donna, since she's gone on to other things. The men, of course, have their own rooms, but the new competitors are staying at another hotel."

Her date wore a dark gray T-shirt molded to his sculpted chest. He was leaning his bare forearms on the table and her fingers slid across to touch them. Her smile turned absolutely naughty as she trailed one hand possessively up his taut muscles toward his shoulders. "That's where you'll be," she assured him huskily.

"That's a solid?" His voice was surprisingly squeaky.

"Yes, Donovan. Yes."

His smile spread to a thin, wicked line. "Ya wanna fuck?"

"Yes, Donovan. Yes . . ."

Elizabeth walked Amy Ferguson, who was as nice as her mother was mean and suspicious, to the front door under Pat's watchful eye. Amy had her cell phone out and was looking at her calendar. "I'd like to meet before Saturday, but I don't know that I can. The rest of Mom's stuff is being picked up that morning. The house should be completely empty by the afternoon."

"Saturday's fine," Elizabeth said, annoyed at the way Pat hung on every word.

To make matters worse, Connie suddenly burst out of Mazie's old office and stalked their way.

Amy was saying, "I almost moved into it, but my job's taking me to Seattle. You never know, do you?" She pushed through the front doors to the outside where weak afternoon sun was fighting its way through a bank of gray clouds.

"No, you never do." Elizabeth tried to pull the doors shut behind her, but Connie yanked them open and rushed out.

"Oh, Amy, how're you doing, girl? Haven't seen you since the memorial service. It's Connie. Connie Berker," she said to Amy's blank look, thrusting out her hand and pumping Amy's for all she was worth. "Your mom was such a fantastic person. I learned everything from her. She just knew this business and everybody in it. A real dynamo."

"Thank you," Amy said, shooting a glance to Elizabeth.

Elizabeth stepped outside. "I'll see you Saturday."

"Amy, you need anything, you can call any one of us." With ill grace, Connie added, "I know Elizabeth was your mom's right hand woman. She took great care of all her clients." Something in her tone made it clear she didn't believe a word of it. From the palm of her hand, she suddenly produced a business card with the adroitness of a magician. "All of us at Suncrest feel like you're family, just like Mazie was." Her lips trembled and for a moment Elizabeth thought Connie might actually produce a tear. "I miss her so much."

Amy looked down at the card, opened her mouth as if to speak, then closed it again.

Burning with repressed anger, Elizabeth said tautly, "Let me walk you to your car."

As they headed away from Connie who seemed to want to follow them but couldn't figure out how without being a further buttinsky, Amy said, "Mom was a lot of things, but she wasn't well loved at work."

Elizabeth shook her head, glad for the honesty but aware that, no matter what she said, they were talking about Amy's mother. "She was a hard worker."

"What's the story with this other agent?" Amy held up the card.

Elizabeth decided to answer Amy's honesty with some of her own. "She's trying to poach you as a client."

"Mom trusted you. So do I."

Elizabeth's heart stuttered. *She shouldn't have trusted me*, she thought, but she smiled a good-bye at Amy then looked around to see what had happened to Connie. The agent was lingering by her white Lexus, probably calculating if there was some way to intercept Amy before she climbed into her Range Rover.

No chance, Elizabeth thought with a renewed spurt of anger. She felt guilty where Mazie was concerned, but she hadn't asked for her daughter to seek her out as the agent to sell Mazie's house.

As Amy pulled away and Connie followed her out of the parking lot, Elizabeth gazed after them. Though a glint of sun peered through the high clouds, she felt a sudden chill slip down her back, an icy finger skimming her spine. Again, as if hidden eyes were watching.

She spun around quickly, scanning the lot and the surrounding street.

"Who's there?" she said aloud, but the only answer was the sound of accelerating cars on the highway at the end of the block and the whisper of the wind through the trees in the lot.

There was no one.

Did you see, Elizabeth? Have you been watching? He got what he deserved and now he abides in whatever special hell is reserved for scum like Channing Renfro. I know there are others working against you. I've heard them, seen them, sensed them. But don't worry, we'll take them out together, one by one. I'm right behind you, love. Your savior, your soldier . . .

You don't see me yet, but you will when I'm ready.

All for you, my love. All for you.

CHAPTER 22

The drive back to Costa Mesa was a nightmare as Rex chose to fight the traffic rather than wait until it was late enough to make the trip with little or no delays. Ravinia reported what she'd seen and heard. Rex called Dorell Cochran and told him his wife was at Casa del Mar with someone whose first name was Donovan and that they'd taken the elevator to an upstairs hotel room.

"Donovan Spinelli, the eternal surfer boy," Dorell responded in a voice taut with anger.

"So, you know him," Rex said.

"Oh, yeah. Calls himself a model. Vacant between the ears, but knows how to sniff out money. *My* money." Dorell paused, then added, almost under his breath, "She was supposed to give him up."

"They're at the hotel right now if you need proof," Rex told him.

"Can you get a picture of 'em coming out of the hotel together?"

Rex considered. "I could, but I don't think that's going to net you what you want. This is an opportunity for you to . . . see for yourself."

"Jesus Christ. Sounds like you want me to confront them," Dorell raged, though Rex could tell he was mad at himself.

"Confrontation . . . no. But having the upper hand, and still acting like a gentleman will go a long way to getting what you want."

"Fuck that."

Rex inwardly sighed. "You hired me to follow her and find out if she was having an affair, and I believe that's what I've done."

"All right, all right. I'll go and nicely confront the bitch. And I'll send you a goddamn check." Dorell slammed down the phone.

Though Ravinia wasn't part of the call, she heard enough from the passenger seat to get the gist. "He's not happy."

"Didn't expect him to be."

"You don't look happy, either," she pointed out.

Rex shrugged. "Sometimes you just wish for something better." The words were out of his mouth before he realized how naive and hopeful he must sound. He'd followed a lot of cheaters and it was depressing how little love and caring went into most relationships. Not that he was any kind of romantic, but sometimes the job made him wonder if any good was left in people.

"What?" Ravinia asked.

He realized he'd made some kind of frustrated sound. "Never mind."

"We're not going to make it back in time to go to the school, are we?" Ravinia asked, peering out at the traffic.

"Unlikely."

"So, what are we going to do?"

"Go home. Get something to eat. Have a beer . . . well, I will. Make some calls that I've put off."

"I want to meet that older woman at the apartments. Brightside."

"Tomorrow," he told her firmly. The way he'd let Ravinia take over his life needed to be controlled.

Her expression clouded. "Maybe I should go by myself."

"Be my guest."

If he sounded snappy, he didn't care. He felt snappy. Though he was glad he didn't have to follow Kimberley Cochran around any longer, it felt like he'd tangled himself up in Ravinia Rutledge's affairs for no goddamn good reason.

"I've helped you. It's your turn," she stated stubbornly.

He cut her off. "Symbiosis. I know. But the way I see it, you want to be a part of this investigation, and you're angling for some kind of long term position that's not there. Understand? You're not a partner of mine. You're a kid, and as soon as we find your cousin or give up, we're going our separate ways."

"Testy," she said, affronted. "We are going to find her."

"Then it better be damn soon," he growled, hitting his brakes and the horn at the same time as a black Mazda suddenly jigged in front of him, narrowly missing his bumper.

"Pain in the ass," Ravinia said.

"Amen."

* * *

Elizabeth's cell sounded the default ringtone as she dropped her purse on the kitchen counter, kicked off her heels, and rubbed her right insole. She'd dead-bolted the front door behind her as soon as she'd entered the house. The sensation that someone was following her hadn't abated once she'd finished work and driven home. She planned to pick up Chloe from preschool by three thirty, but had wanted a moment to unwind and assess first.

Sweeping up the phone, she checked the number. Not one she knew, so she let it go to voice mail. She poured herself a glass of water and drank half of it down, staring through the window above the sink to the small patio beyond. It was a nice house, but she wouldn't miss it. Chloe, though, had known no other home and it would be one more huge life change in a series of huge life changes.

Maybe she could hang onto it. If she actually sold Mazie's house, the commission would be enough to keep her afloat awhile. And if the Sorensons would ever settle on a property . . . or any of Mazie's clients who'd called her and sworn they wanted Elizabeth and had decided to sell . . .

Her cell beeped, alerting her to a voice mail. Curious, she clicked on the number.

"Hello, Elizabeth. It's Gil Dyne. I was wondering if you'd like to have dinner tonight? Give me a call at this number and let me know. I'd love to see you again."

"No," she said to the empty room, hanging up.

She was in the process of putting on her coat before heading to the preschool—rain was in the forecast again—when her doorbell rang, startling her. She actually jumped at the sound, her heart thrumming. "Geez, Louise," she muttered, annoyed, then walked to the door and peered through the peephole.

Detective Thronson stood on her doorstep, head bent against the rain, her short gray hair glistening with moisture.

Elizabeth immediately froze. Her rate had slowed to normal, but it leaped in fear again. *Stop it,* she warned herself. *Stop it.*

She opened the door.

The detective gave her a fleeting smile. "I didn't hear from you, so I thought I'd just stop by."

Elizabeth looked past her, that sense of someone, or something, watching her washing over her again. A car drove past, a man at the wheel, but he didn't look her way. "Yes, uh, I've been busy. Come in."

She led the detective into the family room, then stood by the counter that separated the kitchen, leaning a hand on it for support. A lash of rain battered the sliding glass door.

"You'd never know it was southern California," Thronson observed. Her barrel-body was wrapped in a navy blue jacket. If she wore a gun, it was probably beneath that coat because it didn't appear to be at her hip or back.

"I have to pick up my daughter soon."

"I won't take much of your time. We're still looking for the woman who played tag with your husband on the freeway and the one that was at Tres Brisas when your husband and Mrs. Bellhard were there."

Elizabeth hung onto the counter. "Any luck?" She wanted to press her hands together and wring the hell out of them but managed to hold herself back. Just.

"Some," Thronson said. "Both women have been described by witnesses as blonde, slim, mid-twenties."

"So you said."

"We're running on the theory that it's the same woman." Her gaze was mild, but Elizabeth felt the scrutiny beneath it.

"Okay," she said slowly.

"I think it's someone who knew your husband or Whitney Bellhard or both, and also knew of their love nest at Tres Brisas. I think she followed them down the freeway and, rather than playing a game of tag, she was purposely harassing them. I think she forced them off the freeway, and I think she meant to do it."

Elizabeth could feel her knees begin to quiver and took one of the counter bar stools, half-falling into it.

"Do you know anyone who looks like that who would wish your husband and or Whitney Bellhard harm?"

Elizabeth hesitated. *Only practically every friend I have* . . . "I think what you're trying to say is that you think it's me, but I was not anywhere near San Diego that day. I can't prove my whereabouts, unless there's a camera somewhere that I didn't see, it but I was here, in Irvine. That's the truth."

"Would you consent to a polygraph test?"

Lie detector. "Yes!" Elizabeth said emphatically. "Yes, I would. Set it up."

The detective slowly nodded. Whether she found Elizabeth's enthusiasm surprising, she couldn't say.

"You told me that Peter Bellhard followed my husband and his wife to Tres Brisas," she reminded the detective.

"That's correct."

"But you're not looking at him as a . . . jealous spouse? It's just this blond woman who looks like me?"

"We haven't ruled anything out."

"That's not really an answer."

"We want to find this woman." The detective seemed to want to say something more, but she pressed her lips together and kept it to herself.

Suddenly, Elizabeth felt the urge to tell her everything. Pour it all out. Let the chips fall where they may. She hadn't been to Tres Brisas, nor had she been on the freeway to San Diego. But she had wished them all deadly harm.

"You have something to say?" Thronson asked, correctly interpreting what the look on Elizabeth's face was telling her.

But Elizabeth froze, knowing how it would come off if she did start blurting out all the thoughts and feelings jumbled inside her. "I really have to pick up my daughter," she said, moving toward the door, holding it open for the detective, letting in a mist of rain.

Thronson took her time following after Elizabeth. Clearly, she wasn't ready to go. "I'll get back to you on the polygraph."

Elizabeth was afraid to have her stay, afraid she would change her mind and say too much. She wanted nothing more than to push her out and slam the door shut behind her, but the detective lingered on the outside steps a moment, turning back at the last moment, unmindful of the rain dampening her hair. "I showed a picture of you to the Tres Brisas staff. Two of them identified you as the woman at the hotel."

Elizabeth heard a buzzing in her ears and felt light-headed. "It wasn't me," she choked out, then shut the door on the detective. She threw the dead bolt again and walked backwards away from the door. *Oh, God . . . oh, dear, God.*

She thinks I killed Court.

What if she finds out about GoodGuy?

"There's nothing to find out," Elizabeth whispered aloud.

You need to tell her about him. And Mazie. And Officer Un-friendly. You need to come clean. Now! Call her back!

"Jade told me not to . . ." Elizabeth whimpered.

She's right. I can't. Everyone would think I've lost my mind. And Chloe needs me. What if . . . what if I ended up under a doctor's care or in a mental hospital? What if they took her away from me?

No. She couldn't say anything. Nothing. She shouldn't have even told Jade.

Five minutes later, she dashed out into the rain and jumped into her Escape. *Chloe.* She needed to grab her daughter and hold her close.

"Let's go to Wembley Grade School," Ravinia said, looking at the clock on Rex's dash. "There's still time."

Rex followed her gaze. Three-thirty. "Might be too late to find someone who'll talk to you."

"You said school gets out at three-thirty."

"It's a guess. Three o'clock, maybe. And nobody sticks around unless they have to."

"Just take me there."

Rather than argue the point, Rex headed in the right direction. *What the hell.* If it was a waste of time, it was his time to waste.

The series of buildings that made up Wembley Grade School looked as if they could really use a facelift. They were painted concrete and the paint was faded, appearing as if it had been a few years since the last application of medium brown had been rolled on. The drinking fountains were circa 1965 and though the playground equipment still looked sturdy enough, Rex figured it had been erected enough decades ago to make him question its current safety compliance rating.

"You're overdressed," he told her, examining her short black dress.

She made a strangled sound, tugging on the hem. "Underdressed, overdressed. Who cares? I'll tell her I just came from work."

"I'll come with you."

"Yeah, what are you gonna be, my dad? I can handle this." And with that, she climbed out of the car and hurried somewhat awkwardly on her short heels.

Rex tapped his fingers on the steering wheel. He shouldn't let her just go on her own, but he also sensed she might have more success without him. A man showing up at a grade school without a student and asking questions was enough of an anomaly to raise questions. A young woman, barely more than a girl, looking for a relative might be more palatable. Not that he expected her to come back with any meaningful information. The best link they had to the Gaineses was Marlena from the Brightside Apartments, but he was pretty sure he'd tapped her out. Still, Ravinia wanted to meet her and maybe she should. *She isn't half bad at the job,* he thought grudgingly, which made him feel superfluous in a way that bothered him and made him feel far older than his thirty-six years.

Fifteen minutes passed. Then twenty. He was thinking about driving away and searching out food, figuring it would take her awhile. He could call her on her cell to let her know, but just as he was reaching for his phone, she suddenly appeared, hurrying as fast as her command of her shoes would let her.

At the car, she ripped the pumps off and flung them into the back-seat.

"She went to Van Buren High," Ravinia said in a rush as she settled herself in her seat. "Some teacher there named Bernice Kampfe—*K-A-M-P-F-E*—took an interest in her. That's what Mrs. Holcomb said, the lady I talked to. She said Bernice Kampfe knew Elizabeth Gaines well, so maybe she knows where she is now. Let's go to Van Buren. How far away is it?"

"How'd you get all that so fast?" he demanded.

"Holcomb was the oldest teacher I could find. I told her I was Elizabeth's cousin. You were right. They were all leaving. School was already out, but I caught up with this one who walked with a limp. She's retiring next year. I pretended that Elizabeth and I were close once, but her parents divorced and it was bad and I've lost touch with her. I looked into Mrs. Holcomb's heart and she's one of those really nice people who want to believe the best in everybody. So anyway, she remembered Elizabeth and said I should talk to Mrs. Kampfe."

Ravinia was flushed with success, and he could only sit back in reluctant admiration. He didn't believe in this looking into the heart thing much, but there was no accounting for Ravinia's ability to suss information out of people.

"Well," he said, accessing the GPS app on his cell phone. "I think Van Buren's the one about half a mile away."

"Good." She smiled broadly. "And then let's get food. Pizza."

"That works."

Her good mood was infectious, and though Rex sensed he should be a lot more worried about his "new partner" than he was, he drove her to Van Buren High School. She hurried inside again, but was back within ten minutes. "They've gone home for the day. Maybe you can look up Bernice Kampfe's address."

"Might be easier to find her at the school tomorrow. You never know how people will take it when you show up at their door unannounced."

"Doesn't sound like I have a choice," Ravinia groused. "When I get my license, though . . ." She made it sound like a threat.

"You can go into the private investigation business all on your own."

"Don't think I don't hear the sarcasm."

A smile crept across his lips and when she glared at him, he just couldn't help the little bark of laughter that followed.

CHAPTER 23

Tara caught up with Elizabeth at the preschool playground where their girls were chasing each other around the equipment in a game of tag that was being supervised by their teachers. The rain had abated and they were enjoying stomping in the shallow puddles as they ran after each other, their laughter filling the air.

"Hey, I was going to call you," Tara called as she came to where Elizabeth was leaning over the sign-out page to pick up Chloe. "Dave's out of town, so I wanted to know if you and Chloe want to join Bibi and me at that burger spot down the street from Uncle Vito's?"

Uncle Vito's was an Italian restaurant at the end of the strip mall that was close to Elizabeth's house. The mall also held a Ralph's grocery store, a coffee shop, a cleaners and a UPS store along with a several businesses that seemed to come and go with the economy. The burger spot was around the corner and down the street.

It was all Elizabeth could do to react normally. Thronson's comments and insinuations had made her feel almost physically ill, so her first inclination was to decline. But the thought of heading back to the house was equally unattractive. Besides, she didn't have a clue what she would serve for dinner. And the burger spot was cheap.

"Lots Of Beef," Elizabeth said, forcing a smile.

Tara snapped her fingers. "That's what it's called. I can never remember. I know it's early, but do you care?"

"Not at all. It'll be nearly five by the time we get there," Elizabeth said.

They collected Chloe and Bibi, although it was a bit of a wrangle as neither girl wanted to leave the playground. As they were leaving, Vivian came and picked up Lissa, and Jade got Little Nate, but though they invited them, neither could join them for dinner.

By the time Bibi was ensconced in Tara's car and Chloe in Elizabeth's, and they got the girls through their mopey meltdowns as they wanted to ride together and could barely stand it that they had be separated, it was five. By the time they reached the strip mall where both restaurants were located, it was closing on five-thirty and the early dinner crowd was filling up the lot.

Traffic was coming fast off the main street toward Uncle Vito's and the cars were circling around like a pack of hungry wolves. Elizabeth was lucky enough to find a parking spot, though it was a bit of a hike to Lots Of Beef. Even so, she and Chloe arrived first and grabbed a table, waiting for Tara and Bibi who finally blew in about ten minutes later. In that short interim Elizabeth had gone back inside her head, Thronson's words running around and around.

I showed a picture of you to the Tres Brisas staff. Two of them identified you as the woman at the hotel . . . I showed a picture of you to the Tres Brisas staff. Two of them identified you as the woman at the hotel. . . .

"Want me to order?" Tara asked, breaking into her reverie. "What do you both want?"

As Chloe declared for chicken strips and a strawberry milkshake and Bibi ordered the same, scooting into the booth beside her friend, Elizabeth looked up at Tara, the words dying on her tongue as she really looked at Tara's hair in its messy, blond bun, just like she wore hers.

I showed a picture of you to the Tres Brisas staff. Two of them identified you as the woman at the hotel. . . .

"Do they have salads?" Elizabeth asked, pulling herself together.

"Kind of a chicken Caesar," Tara answered, staring up at the menu, her face in profile.

"That sounds good." When Elizabeth reached for her purse, Tara waved her away.

"We'll settle up later," she told her.

Thronson was just trying to scare you. Maybe you should talk to her after all. Risk her thinking you're crazy as a loon.

Tara came back with their drinks and then waited at the designated pick up spot, returning a few moments later with Chloe and

Bibi's chicken strips. "Salads are still coming up," she said as she'd decided on the same thing as Elizabeth.

It wasn't me. Lots of people look like me. . . . The woman at the hotel could be totally innocent . . . a complete stranger to Court and Whitney Bellhard . . . She doesn't have to be the same one as the one on the freeway, if there even was one. What if . . .

Elizabeth's thoughts shut down. Were overridden. A terrible vision overtook her and she suddenly stood up, nearly knocking over her chair. Tara was just bringing up the rest of their food order and she looked at Elizabeth in surprise.

"I have to go," Elizabeth told her flatly.

"Go?" Tara looked at her in disbelief. "Go where? What do you mean?"

"Take care of Chloe. I'll be back."

And then she was running. Out of the burger joint and across the parking lot to Uncle Vito's, racing among the cars, and causing people to stare.

Oh, God . . . oh, God . . . oh, God . . .

She barreled into the Italian restaurant, nearly knocking over a woman walking toward the restrooms. The woman glared at her and stomped onward.

"Get away from the windows!" Elizabeth screamed at the couple seated in the waiting area directly in front of the windows that looked straight toward the street entrance into the strip mall.

As they gaped at her in surprise, she grabbed up the young boy about three years old who was standing in front of them and ran for the interior of the restaurant. Shrieking, the woman leaped to her feet and charged after her. Her husband damn near ran over his wife in his own attempt to reach Elizabeth.

"Stop!" he yelled

At the same moment, a car smashed through the window with a roar of engines and shattering glass. A collective gasp and shriek ran through the crowd. People clattered from their chairs, running to safety as a green Buick flew forward, humping over tables and chairs before smacking into a pillar. The building shook. The alarm blared. *Woowoowoowoo.* Steam hissed from the radiator.

The boy in Elizabeth's arms wriggled free and found his mother who was crying and gulping and shaking as if stricken with palsy. The father gazed at Elizabeth dully.

Elizabeth surfaced from the terrible scene in her mind, slowly focusing on reality—the elderly man slumped over the steering wheel of his car, the noise, the panic. She placed her hands over her ears and stepped toward the car.

"You knew," the husband said. "You knew. . . ."

"I-I saw it coming," she choked out. The truth.

People were gathering around the vehicle. Blood ran from a gash in the driver's head. Elizabeth saw a man press 911 on his cell and hold it to his ear.

It took several minutes, but blessedly, someone finally cut the alarm. The sudden silence was immediately replaced by the sound of an approaching siren.

"Oh, my God . . . oh, my God . . . oh, my God . . ." the mother was saying over and over again, cradling her son and rocking him in her arms.

Get out.

Elizabeth stepped toward the door next to the shattered window. A crowd had gathered outside under a sky fraught with dark clouds and softly falling rain. A police car jerked to a stop and an officer stepped out. A woman. Officer Maya.

She saw Elizabeth the same moment Elizabeth saw her. "You were here when this happened?" Maya asked, surprised.

Elizabeth looked for her partner, DeFazio, but the officer was alone.

"He just accelerated," a man nearby said, catching Maya's attention. "Goddamn. I think he hit the gas instead of the brake."

"Yeah, yeah," a young woman with short red hair agreed. "That's what he did."

A chorus of voices followed, echoing the sentiment. Elizabeth moved away.

Get out. Get away. Get to your daughter.

She slipped away and walked rapidly across the parking lot back to the burger spot. She would have broken into a run except that it would have called too much attention to her. She was still thirty feet away from Lots Of Beef when Chloe burst outside and ran to her, heedless of anything but her mother's arms.

Elizabeth scooped her up and Chloe pressed her face into her mother's neck.

"What happened? What happened?" Tara babbled. She'd come outside with Chloe and was standing with a growing number of other patrons who'd heard the crash and slowly worked their way outside. Bibi was clutched to her side.

"An accident. I heard it happening," Elizabeth said.

"*How?*" Tara asked, wide-eyed.

"They think this elderly man hit the accelerator instead of the brakes," she said, ignoring the question.

At that moment, an ambulance pulled up outside Uncle Vito's and two EMTs jumped out.

"My God," Tara said.

"I wanna go home," Chloe said on a gulp. Tears threatened.

Elizabeth said to Tara, "I owe you for dinner."

"God, no. Forget it." Tara suddenly reached over and hugged Elizabeth and Chloe. "I'm so glad you're safe. When you ran out like that . . . and then we heard the crash . . ."

"I know. I'm sorry. I was scared. I just saw what was happening, and I had to get there."

"I thought you heard it."

"I did. I heard it." Elizabeth clasped Chloe's hand. "Thank you. So scary. We've gotta go."

Tara nodded. "Yeah, yeah. Us, too."

"I'll call you." Elizabeth didn't have to tell Chloe to hurry as her daughter was practically dragging her away toward their car.

Chloe climbed into her seat and buckled herself in. "Mommy, I'm scared."

Elizabeth could feel herself trembling as she adjusted her own seatbelt and switched on the ignition. "We're okay."

"But that man in the car . . . he's going to die, isn't he?"

Elizabeth gazed at her sharply. "Not necessarily."

"He is," Chloe said, a hitch in her voice. "I saw it, Mommy. I saw it. . . ."

An hour and a half later, Elizabeth lay beside her daughter in Chloe's twin bed, her arms around her, her cheek resting on Chloe's blond crown as her daughter fell into a deep sleep. It was early, but Chloe had gone straight to bed, which said a lot about her frame of mind. Elizabeth stared through the soft darkness that was kept at bay by the night-light.

For years, she'd managed to stop the visions of pending danger by keeping a tight rein on her own emotions. At least, that's what she believed. She could get mad, but not too mad, scared but not too scared, frustrated, but not too frustrated. It was something she'd learned as a child, a way to combat the strange sensations that had overwhelmed and frightened her, and it had worked most of the time.

But when she'd seen the footbridge collapse, she hadn't yet learned to hide her ability. She hadn't realized how people would react. She hadn't known they didn't possess the same ability, so she'd shouted and shouted about it. No one listened until it actually fell, but when it did, her father and mother looked at her closely in a way that frightened her. She overheard them talking.

"Who are her parents?" her mother had demanded in a quivering voice. "We didn't ask enough questions."

"You're making too much of this," her father had answered, but Elizabeth heard the awe and concern in his voice.

Her father started questioning her, and then he wanted her to do it again . . . to predict something, anything. That had sent her mother over the edge and the fights between them escalated until her mother moved out and left them. She made a half-hearted attempt to take Elizabeth with her, but Elizabeth didn't want to leave her school and truthfully, Joy Gaines seemed just as happy to leave her.

Her father had wanted her with him, seeing some get-rich-quick scheme with his psychic daughter, but she never saw another vision, as far as he knew. He grew impatient with her. His money-making scheme had gone up in smoke and she'd sensed that he'd grown to resent her. Whether he knew that she'd purposely started hiding her reactions to such visions, she couldn't say, but he definitely lost interest in her as a person . . . if he'd ever really had any.

She'd stayed with him because she didn't know what else to do, and even through community college and the last two years at UC Irvine, she'd kept in touch with him. But after that they drifted apart. He didn't want her unless she was special, and she didn't want him.

Court wooing her with no knowledge of her past had been like throwing a lifeline to a drowning person. She'd loved him for it. Or at least thought she had. She wondered if it been more gratitude than love, but it didn't matter. Their union had produced Chloe and as soon as she was born, everything had been better. Court had wanted to meet her father, and though Elizabeth had been reluctant, she'd made the effort. But the two men hadn't liked each other.

Takes one to know one, she thought.

Elizabeth hadn't had a vision throughout most of her marriage and she'd begun to think she was cured of the ability. But then Little Nate had nearly fallen off the jungle gym and she hadn't been able to sit by and let that happen. Jade had known Elizabeth couldn't have seen Nate falling from her angle of vision, especially seconds before it happened, and had mentioned it in front of their friends. But Elizabeth had brushed it off and everyone thought Jade was making too much of it.

All was well again, but then the deaths started occurring. And now the car through the restaurant . . .

Slowly, Elizabeth removed her arm from beneath Chloe's sleeping form and eased herself from her bed. She tiptoed out of the room and paused in the doorway, looking at her for long moments.

But that man . . . he's going to die, isn't he? He is. I saw it, Mommy . . . I saw it. . . .

She sees things, too, Elizabeth thought, her arms prickling with gooseflesh.

Knock, knock, knock!

Elizabeth gasped and her heart lurched. The sharp staccato sound made her damn near jump a foot. It came from her front door. Someone was on her porch. A hand at her chest, she glanced at the kitchen clock and saw it was only a little after eight. God, it seemed like a year since the accident at the restaurant and she and Chloe had raced home.

She walked quickly toward the door before they could knock again and peered through the peephole. Her heart lurched in fear. Detective Thronson stood on her front porch again. For a moment, Elizabeth thought about not opening the door, but she had a feeling Thronson knew she was home. Being cowardly wasn't going to help. She would just be putting off the inevitable.

Drawing a deep breath and exhaling it slowly, she flipped on the outside light and opened the door a crack, blocking entry to her house with her body. No more playing nice with the police. She had Chloe to consider, and she didn't trust this detective or any of the police, for that matter. They were trying to force the facts to fit the supposed crime rather than the other way around.

"Yes?" Elizabeth said, schooling her expression though her pulse was pounding in her ears.

"You don't want me to come in." It was a statement rather than a question.

"My daughter's asleep. I want to keep her that way. Whatever you have to say, just say it."

"I talked with Officer Maya. You saw her at the restaurant accident this evening."

Elizabeth hung onto the edge of the door with a death grip. "That's what this is about?" she asked, hearing how squeaky her voice sounded. She'd suspected that it was. The people in the restaurant were bound to give her away and Officer Maya had recognized her. "Not the polygraph test?"

"No. Officer Maya interviewed a couple who say you saved their son and them from injury, maybe death, by your quick response."

"I just saw the car coming, that's all." She had to bite her tongue not to say more, some kind of explanation that would just backfire and incriminate her.

"Before anyone else saw it."

"I guess so."

"Before the car was in sight, according to a dozen eyewitnesses."

"I've heard eyewitnesses are the worst at recall." Elizabeth could feel hysterical laughter bubbling up and held it back with an effort.

"Sometimes they're incredibly accurate."

"Well, I don't know what to tell you. . . ."

"Why don't you start with the truth? You know something about all of this. I don't know what it could be, but I've been around a long time, and I know when people are lying or covering up, and I think you're doing a little bit of both."

"I just saw the car coming. I heard it."

The detective stared at her. "What happened to your husband?" she asked, changing direction.

"I didn't kill him. I wasn't on that freeway. . . ."

"You know something. Something you're not saying."

"No."

"Yes. Tell me what you know," the detective suddenly urged. "Get it off your chest."

"You wouldn't believe me," Elizabeth said on a half laugh. "You wouldn't." She could feel herself cracking apart, wanting to confess, needing to let it all out.

"Try me."

"I can't."

"Just say it."

"I wished them dead, okay? All of them. Court . . . and Mazie . . . and even that officer that gave me the speeding ticket. Daniels. I was angry at all of them, and I wished them dead. And now they're gone. They are dead."

Thronson was staring at her, her expression unreadable.

"And that's not all," Elizabeth whispered, her legs feeling like jelly. "GoodGuy. He cut me off in traffic and flipped me off and it infuriated me and . . . and I . . . wanted to kill him. Just drive him off the road."

"Good guy?" the detective asked carefully.

"His name is Channing Renfro. I didn't know it at the time. His license plate is GoodGuy."

A deep line grooved between Thronson's brows. "You're talking about the homicide at Fitness Now!? You're saying that was you?"

"God, no. *I just wished it!* All of it! Do you understand? I wish things, *and they happen!*"

Detective Thronson stood up straight and rested her hand on the butt of her gun. She stood frozen for several moments, apparently unsure quite how to proceed.

The hysteria that had been building inside Elizabeth finally spilled over and she bent forward and started to laugh. Great, sobbing, gulps of crazed mirth that she knew would dissolve into tears eventually. She was dizzy with exhaustion. She didn't give a damn what the detective thought, or Jade, or anyone else who knew the truth from here on out. She was glad she'd said it. Glad.

It took several minutes before she pulled herself together, and it was only the thought of Chloe and what she would think if she should awaken and find her lunatic mother losing it. Straightening, she heaved a deep sigh and faced the detective wearily. "So arrest me if you will, if wishful thinking is a crime."

"You're saying you did not cause your husband's death, but you—"

"Wished it. Yes. And Mazie's accident. And I didn't shoot Officer Daniels, but it wasn't long after our court date that he was shot and killed."

Thronson was clearly nonplused. "To be clear, you feel responsible for these deaths, but you didn't actually act on them. That's what you're saying."

"Yes."

"And you saw the car coming at the restaurant, or heard it, even though no one else did."

"Yes. I knew it was going to hit."

"You say your daughter is asleep?"

Elizabeth nodded.

"So, you're not going anywhere tonight."

"Detective Thronson, if you want to arrest me, you're just going to have to do it. Otherwise this conversation is over. I've told you the truth about what I know and what I feel, and I know it sounds crazy, but there it is. That's all. That's all there is. I'm sorry Court's dead. I'm sorry they're all dead. I don't know how it's my fault, but it kinda feels like it is, even though I did nothing to hurt them."

"Except wish them dead," the detective repeated slowly.

Elizabeth nodded. "That's right."

Thronson was clearly having a very tough time with everything Elizabeth had said, and why not? When she heard the words escape her lips she knew how crazy they sounded.

"I'm going to leave you," Thronson said. "I'd like to do that polygraph test soon. Maybe tomorrow. I'll put it together and call you."

Elizabeth lifted a hand and let it drop. She felt as tired as if she'd run a complete marathon.

"Don't go anywhere," the detective warned as if she thought Elizabeth was suddenly a flight risk. "Or, I'll find you and I will arrest you—on suspicion of homicide."

"I'm not leaving."

Thronson slowly turned away from the door, and then seemed to hesitate a moment, looking back, but she finally stepped down the porch stairs and crossed the road to her black Chevy Trailblazer.

Elizabeth closed the door and hesitated a moment herself, then she headed for the wine rack and a bottle of Chardonnay.

Dear Elizabeth, my love,

I watched you tonight. I saw what you can do! You are amazing and so beautiful. Are you receiving my mental messages? I'm sending them to you. Concentrating. I know you can hear me. Should I send this pile of missives so that you know how I feel? I love you so much I ache inside. We're connected, you and I. Almost like family except my emotions run so much deeper than that. Desire . . . yes. I'm consumed with it, but there's a spirituality between us, the kind that exists only through purest souls. Soon the unveiling will happen and we will be transcended.

My love . . . I don't deserve you and yet, there is no one like me for you. We have always belonged together . . . always.

CHAPTER 24

Rex and Ravinia headed back to the Brightside Apartments about ten the next morning. Ravinia had been up and ready to go at the crack of dawn, but Rex explained that ten was a more civilized time for making interviews, especially with little old ladies like Marlena, the one person who seemed to remember the elusive Ralph Gaines.

They were seated on a sagging floral couch, next to each other, the old lady across the room in her chair, a La-Z-Boy with worn arms and headrest that she must've owned since sometime in the previous century.

Though Rex had watched Ravinia in action following Kim Cochran at the Ivy and again at Casa del Mar, and he'd been impressed at how fast she'd found out the information from Mrs. Holcomb at Wembley Grade School, he couldn't bring himself to really think of her as an investigator. How could he? She was only nineteen and her experiences in the world were practically nil. Still, she hadn't been made yet. No one had found her out. And well, she got results.

He certainly wasn't planning on bringing her into his company. If he wanted a young woman as a sort of business partner, he already had Bonnie, which wasn't all that comforting a thought, the more he considered it.

As he observed Ravinia speaking with Marlena, he had to admit the kid had a knack for digging out information. People either didn't notice her—she could make herself blend into the surroundings—or if they did spy her, they didn't find her intimidating. Her refreshing directness coupled with her youth was somehow nonthreatening.

Ravinia handed Marlena a small red box of special truffles they'd purchased at a See's store on the way—her idea. The elderly woman accepted the unexpected gift of chocolates readily, sliding the slim box to a side table next to a lamp and a worn copy of the Bible. She made no indication that she planned to open the gift or share any of its contents.

Yep, the ploy was masterful.

Ravinia started in on her lie. "It's just that our family has become so splintered," she was saying, holding Marlena's attention in the airless room. In a long-sleeved T-shirt, jeans, and boots, without a speck of makeup, Ravinia appeared younger, fresher, and more ingenuous than she had in her tight dress and short heels when she'd followed Kim Cochran.

"It's a bad thing," the older woman was agreeing. "All these families splitting up the way they do nowadays." She reached to the table, her fingers touching the worn, leather-bound Bible. "A sin, if you ask me."

Ravinia nodded. Her blond braid moving gently between her shoulder blades, she leaned forward as if rapt. "That's why it's so important I find Elizabeth. For my family." She actually blinked as if she were on the verge of tearing up and Rex had to cough into his fist to hide a smile. "My mother is very upset by it. I don't know how many candles she's lit." Bald-faced lies tripped off her tongue so easily.

Marlena hitched her chin toward Ravinia, but spoke to Rex. "She's your client. Right?" This fact had already been established, but obviously the older woman didn't completely trust that Rex had been honest with her. "You shoulda brought her with you the other day."

"He shoulda," Ravinia agreed. "I came down from Oregon and hired Mr. Kingston to help me find Elizabeth."

"Huh." Marlena's eyes thinned as she looked from Ravinia to Rex and back again as if she suspected a little hanky-panky might be going on.

Ravinia soothed over the moment. "Mr. Kingston has been so helpful in helping me try to put my family back together. I can't really complain."

"Well, I can't tell you much more than I did the last time," Marlena told her.

"You said Elizabeth was an odd child," Rex prompted when Marlena seemed to have shut down.

"You woulda thought so, too, if you'd heard her go on about that bridge." She shook her head.

"Mr. Kingston told me about that," Ravinia said, sounding concerned. "I don't understand how she could have known that it collapsed . . . before it did."

Marlena pursed her lips. "Who's to say she really did. She was screechin' about a bridge and then one goes down and everybody thinks she can see into the future or somethin'. She was different. That's all. But her daddy sure thought she was a gold mine. Got the two of them squabblin', he and his wife, but then they were always at it. When she took off, though, Lendel got kinda quiet then."

Rex's head snapped up at the name. *Lendel? Weren't we talking about Ralph Gaines?*

He was just about to ask when Ravinia did it for him. "Lendel?" she queried.

"Isn't that why you're here?" Marlena asked, annoyed. "Lendel Gaines?"

Rex was about to step in again, when Ravinia looked thoughtful. "Well, um, Mom always called Elizabeth's father Ralph. . . ."

"Don't recall anyone calling him Ralph around here," Marlena said tartly as if pleased they'd gotten it wrong.

"But his daughter was Elizabeth and his wife was Joy?" Rex asked.

"That's what I said."

"Maybe he changed his name," Ravinia suggested. "It just sounds like I'm on the right track to reconnecting with my family."

Marlena frowned and glanced at the chocolates. "Y'know, I did see *R. Lendel* on something once, I think. The man was always puttin' on airs, tryin' to convince everyone he was somebody when he wasn't. Him usin' an initial like that? Seemed like the kinda thing he'd do. Tryin' to always get one up on everyone. Claimin' the best parkin' space, or that he had a right to more of the common area than the rest of us." She threw up a hand in disgust.

"I can't say I wasn't glad to see his backside, but I don't know where he went. I did feel sorry for the kid, though. Wasn't her fault those parents of hers didn't stick together and raise her right." Marlena placed her hand on the Bible. "Shoulda spent more time in church and payin' attention to the family instead of out runnin' around. That's what I think."

Ravinia tried to come at Marlena a couple different ways, hoping for more information, but apart from twisting her faded lips into a mask of disapproval, the older woman couldn't give them any further information. Rex sensed they'd definitely tapped her out, and he was glad to see that Ravinia, on his wavelength for once, thanked her and got to her feet.

Marlena slid a hungry glance at the box of candy, but made the effort to walk them to the door, her walker thumping along.

They stepped outside and immediately heard the familiar click of the dead bolt sliding into place.

They didn't speak as they headed back to the car, but as soon as the door was shut, Ravinia threw him a proud glance. "I did good," she said as he slid the Nissan into gear and drove to the edge of the lot.

"You did." He nodded as he melded into traffic.

"The candy was a good idea."

"Brilliant," he agreed, which put a smile on her face as she leaned back in the seat.

"So now you're going to find this *Lendel* Gaines?"

"Yep. I'm going to search on my laptop rather than my phone. And my iPad's dead." He hooked a thumb toward the back where the little-used device was tucked in the pocket behind the seat. He still preferred his laptop keyboard. "Charger's at the house."

"But that's where your laptop is, too."

"Well, that's why we gotta go back."

"What about Van Buren High?"

He checked the time. "A little early yet. You want to catch that teacher at lunch or after classes."

"It's almost lunch. Let's go to Van Buren, then back to your house."

"I thought you wanted to attack this with all speed," he reminded her.

Ravinia frowned, thinking hard, and he saw that she thought he might forego stopping at the high school. "I want to meet this Mrs. Kampfe and find out what she knows about Elizabeth."

"All right, then."

Ravinia relaxed a little and looked out the window. "That Mrs. Holcomb at the grade school kind of reminded me of Aunt Catherine, only older. She wore her hair in the same kind of bun."

"Hmmm," Rex said, and they lapsed into silence.

He wondered briefly about the mystical mother figure of Ravinia's aunt. He still hadn't figured out just how much of Ravinia's story was true. He'd done a little research on her when her back was turned, mainly through the Internet, then from a call he'd placed to a friend who lived in Quarry, an Oregon town about halfway to the coast from Portland. His friend often went fishing near Deception Bay and had heard not only of Siren Song but of the women who lived there in isolation. And yes, the friend had thought they'd worn century-old styled dresses.

"Kinda like the Amish out here in Oregon, except there's a little woo-woo that goes on with those gals," he'd said, at least sort of confirming Ravinia's bizarre tale. "And they're all female, leastwise that's what I've heard."

At the next light, Rex saw that his passenger was staring at him and he realized he'd missed a question. "What?"

"You told me earlier to act like a normal American kid when I meet up with Bernice Kampfe."

"So?"

A teenager plugged into his iPhone while riding a skate board flew by in a blur of tattoos, piercings, and baggy shorts, and Ravinia's eyes followed him. "Does that qualify?" she asked as the light changed.

"It's definitely in the spectrum," Rex said.

"What does that mean?"

"Yes. He's normal, and you look the part, too."

"Even if I'm not," she said with a slight smile.

"Even if you're not."

"I'm sure I saw a listing for a house that might be just perfect," Marg Sorenson was saying.

"Hmmm," Elizabeth said, though she was having trouble keeping her mind on the conversation. She was at her desk, cell phone pressed to her ear, but she couldn't think past last night—first the car flying through the restaurant window, then confessing everything to Detective Thronson and challenging the detective to arrest her, and Chloe saying she'd seen the elderly man's death. . . .

Elizabeth tried to focus as Marg rattled on. "I was just looking on Zillow and bingo! There it was. I can't believe you missed it. Four bedrooms, a pool, completely remodeled, and in our price range. I've convinced Buddy to see it, so maybe this afternoon . . . if you have time?"

Elizabeth glanced at her calendar. The afternoon was clear, but she didn't know if she was up for another round with Marg and Buddy. But then again, could she afford to lose them as clients? If she didn't step up, Connie Berker would be all over them like a bad smell. "Sure," she agreed, forcing herself to concentrate. "How about after lunch, maybe around two? Meet here at the office?"

Marg agreed and gave her the necessary information.

"I'll double check with the listing agent and if there's a problem, I'll call you back." Elizabeth hung up then rested her head on her arms on her desk. If she was lucky, the showing would go quickly, leaving plenty of time to pick up Chloe early from school again. All she wanted was to be with her daughter.

She'd planned to keep Chloe home, spend the day with her, and shut out the world, but Chloe, as capricious as ever, had insisted she wanted to go to school, no matter what. She'd argued with Elizabeth over a bowl of cereal, then had marched into her room, dressed herself, and announced, "I'm ready!" in that belligerent way she had that meant she wasn't going to listen to any ideas to the contrary.

Rather than upset her further, Elizabeth had acquiesced and once Chloe was dropped off and she was back home, she'd found she didn't want to be at the house without her. The vision, the crash, the aftermath, and Detective Thronson's probing questions kept circling her mind and circling yet again.

At work, she'd heard from all her friends. Tara told her that the media was asking about the woman who'd saved the little boy and his family and then walked away. She also told Deirdre and Jade about what had transpired, and Jade, of course, had asked probing questions that, once again, Elizabeth had to fob off. Vivian called, and Nadia, because they knew Elizabeth and Tara had planned to be at Lots Of Beef around the time of the accident.

It had almost been too much. Elizabeth had been a bit short with Vivian and even worse with Nadia. Short enough that she'd called them back and apologized, though the messages had gone to the women's respective voice mails.

Closing her eyes for a second, she took in a deep breath, told herself to stay calm, find some kind of inner peace. Serenity was elusive, however; guilt, anger, and fear kept right on clawing at her brain.

When her cell phone rang again, she lifted her head and reluctantly reached for it. Marg, again. She let it go to voice mail. From the corner of her eye, she saw Pat strolling past her cubicle, smiling as if at a private joke. She continued on toward the front of the office and Elizabeth felt anger bubbling up. *Nosy old bitch,* she fumed, then shut that thought down *toute suite. So Pat was grinning like a devil, so what?* She couldn't afford to think ill of her.

You're jumping at shadows. Getting paranoid and you can't afford to. Chloe needs you.

Throat thick, Elizabeth picked up a small framed picture of her daughter at age three. In the shot, Chloe's blond curls had been tamed into pigtails and her face was turned up to the camera. Apple cheeks, wide eyes, and a smile filled with pure mirth showing her baby teeth.

How long had it been since she'd seen such joy on her child's face?

He's sending me messages, but I think they're for you.

"Who, Chloe?" she whispered.

Deep in thought, she didn't hear the sound of footsteps coming down the hallway until they paused on the other side of her cubicle. She looked up just as a male voice asked, "Elizabeth?"

Gil Dyne.

Elizabeth felt herself tense and forced a smile to her lips as she greeted him. "Well, hi."

"I hope this isn't a bad time," he said as she righted the picture and set it back in its spot on her desk. "I was in the area and I'd thought, well, I'd hoped, maybe you'd gotten my message and were up for lunch?"

Not a chance. "I-I don't know. I'm—"

"Don't say no," he said, smiling charmingly.

Again, she caught a glimpse of Pat at the end of the hall, craning her neck to watch the exchange. Elizabeth wanted to throw something at her, but once again curbed the impulse.

"Lunch sounds great," she said, deciding she wanted nothing more than to get out of the office, away from the ringing phones, away from

Connie's avaricious interest in her listings, away from Pat's sharp ears and sidelong glances.

Gil was pleasantly surprised by her reaction as she pushed her chair back. "Well, that was easy. I was sure you were going to say no."

"It's got to be quick. I've got clients coming in."

"Ahh, I knew there was bound to be a catch."

"How about Sombrero's? It's just down the street about quarter of a mile. Er, I mean unless you had another place in mind?" She still needed to call the listing agent on the house Marg had found on Zillow. "And I just need a sec to finish up something."

"Sounds great," Gil said. "I love Mexican."

He waited while she made the call, left a message, and then listened to Marg's voice mail—just a confirmation of the two o'clock.

Elizabeth gathered her purse and together she and Gil walked past the reception desk to the outside where the weak rays of a winter sun were piercing the high clouds. Hallelujah, the rain seemed to be staying inside the clouds, for the moment. As she slid a pair of sunglasses onto her nose and into the passenger seat of Gil's Lexus, she saw Pat still watching her through the glass doors, not even bothering to hide her stare.

Her nosiness knew no bounds.

"I'm glad you could come," Gil said as they drove out of the lot and she directed him to take a left.

"Me, too," Elizabeth lied. But she couldn't stand being alone with her own thoughts. Pat's watchfulness and Connie's greed only exacerbated the problem.

"Your cousin, you say?" the school clerk asked from behind a glass partition near the front door of Van Buren High School.

"Yes." Ravinia offered up her most innocent smile. "We've lost contact with Elizabeth and her family and I need to get in touch with her. Family crisis."

"I'm sorry, but we don't give out information about students." The woman, gray-haired and stern, eyed her through huge glasses that gave her an owlish appearance. Her name plate read Mrs. Loreen Dixon.

A younger woman seated at a computer screen looked up in interest.

"You must help people, if . . . if it's a situation of life or death," Ravinia said to the clerk.

"Is that what this is?" Clearly, the woman didn't think so.

"It's a serious situation, believe me," Ravinia said soberly.

Mrs. Dixon's gaze scraped Ravinia up and down and in that moment she realized the clerk had seen it all, every scam that a kid had used, trying to get out of school. Ravinia took a second look into the woman's heart and saw that she was a lonely woman, dedicated and honest, but jaded. She wouldn't give an inch.

As if she felt some unfamiliar sensation race through her, perhaps an intrusion into her soul, the clerk's eyes widened more. Her lips parted and she stared at Ravinia, placing a fluttering hand over her chest at the same moment.

Before Ravinia could ask about Bernice Kampfe, a door opened behind the clerk and a woman in her sixties strode in to the office. Dressed in a long skirt and boots, gray hair clipped at her nape, she said to the girl at the computer, "I need to schedule time off. Next week, can you get me a sub for Thursday? From noon on. I've got a doctor's appointment and it can't be pushed back until after school."

Loreen Dixon's attention strayed. "Look on schedule B," she said a little distractedly to the younger woman, wiggling her finger at the computer monitor.

"Got it. No problem, Mrs. Kampfe. You're in"—she checked a computer screen—"room 226, right?"

Ravinia's attention zeroed in on the woman, the person she needed to talk to.

"Wait, no, not Thursday. I'm in the computer lab." Bernice Kampfe pulled a face as she mentioned that particular duty and slipped a pair of glasses onto her nose that had been resting in the neckline of her shirt. "Thirty years at this school and I still get assigned to the lab on my prep. Thanks very much, budget cuts."

The girl laughed a little nervously, her fingers flying over her keyboard as she made a note while Bernice Kampfe looked over her shoulder at the screen, presumably confirming her mission had been accomplished. Satisfied, she walked out the way she'd come in.

"I can't help you," the clerk was saying, eyeing Ravinia as if she were some exotic reptile. "I'll have to ask you to leave."

The girl at the computer stared, her mouth dropping open at

Dixon's rudeness, but Ravinia took it in stride. Occasionally, when she looked into a person's heart, she got this reaction, and besides she'd fallen into the information she needed.

Turning from the clerk to the girl at the computer with a *Can you believe this?* expression, she left through the glass doors by which she'd entered.

As soon as she was down the outside steps, she made as if she was leaving the campus, walking across the street to disappear around the block, then doubling back to skirt the high school campus where she spied a huge building with a domed ceiling, probably the gymnasium. Attached to the gym was a wide staircase walled in glass. A bell sounded and soon students filled the stairwell, a clamorous horde talking, laughing, and shoving as they poured through the doors on ground level in a heavy stream. Once outside, most of the older teens headed to a parking lot where their cars were parked.

Lunch.

Perfect.

Ravinia didn't hesitate. She slipped inside through the open doors and like a salmon swimming upstream, fought the current of kids flowing ever downward. On the second floor, she quickly assessed, taking a hallway that connected from the gym area to the classrooms. The locker-lined hallways had emptied, only a few straggling students slamming their locker doors. Eyeing the room numbers, she passed by a set of restrooms and a water fountain as she made her way to room 226.

At the open doorway, she peeked inside and spied the same teacher she'd seen in the office less than fifteen minutes earlier. "Mrs. Kampfe?"

"Yes?" Head bent over a stack of papers, Bernice glanced upward over the top of her reading glasses. Her graying eyebrows lifted and she stared at Ravinia as if she were trying to place her. "Can I help you?"

Ravinia stepped into the room and gently closed the door to the hallway. "I hope so. I need to ask you about my cousin, Elizabeth Gaines. She used to be a student here. I'm trying to locate her."

"Elizabeth Gaines." Mrs. Kampfe set down her pen slowly. "You're her cousin, you say?"

Ravinia nodded and Bernice seemed to search her features as if trying to find a resemblance. Whatever she saw seemed to satisfy her enough to say, "She kept in touch with me for a while after she left school. How did you know to ask for me?"

"I heard you were close to her."

"But from whom?"

"Mrs. Holcomb at Wembley Grade School. She said you were like her mentor." That was a stretch, but an easy guess, Ravinia felt.

"Well . . . Elizabeth was an interesting person." Bernice seemed to be weighing how much to say. "I got a couple Christmas cards from her after she graduated. I don't know if I can help you."

"She's adopted and her birth mother, my aunt, is very ill," Ravinia said, expanding on the lie. "I don't know if Elizabeth even wants to see her, but I'd like to give her the information."

That seemed to touch a chord. "Her family moved to Dana Point. I remember because the street, Del Toro, was familiar to me. I had a college friend from that area and we would take Del Toro to get to her house. Whether they're still there, though . . . it's been a few years."

"Thank you," Ravinia said.

A bell rang and Bernice glanced at her watch. "I'm sorry, is there anything else I can do for you?"

"No, there isn't."

"If you find her, say hi from me."

"I will."

Ravinia left using the staircase by the gym and hurrying down the empty stairs. Her footsteps echoed against the risers in a quick beat. At the first floor, she threw open the doors and pulled her cell phone from her pocket. Still enough minutes left.

At least I've found out where Elizabeth went after high school, Ravinia thought as she rounded the building again and walked along tree-lined streets.

She put in a call to Rex and relayed the information, to which he said, "Good work. I looked up as many R. L. Gaines and Lendel Gaines as I could find and there was an address in Dana Point on Del Toro. I could give a call now, but—"

"No way! We have to go there! It's better in person. You said that." Then, "Where's Dana Point?"

After a brief hesitation, it sounded like he muttered, "Might as well see this to the end."

"What?"

"Had to get gas. I'll be outside Van Buren again in ten minutes."

"Is Dana Point in California?"

"Yep. We can go today."

Ravinia hung up with a smile on her face. She was a definite help to Rex and it felt like she was destined to be his investigative partner. She just had to convince him of that.

CHAPTER 25

The afternoon with Marg and Buddy Sorenson was more of the same. Though Marg loved the house she'd found on Zillow, Buddy was more interested in pointing out everything wrong with it. Elizabeth's head was so full of other problems that their bickering barely registered. Eventually they all left and Marg sat in silence, fuming at her husband's need to "put everything down" and be a "horse's ass."

Elizabeth split with them at the Suncrest parking lot and dropped them from her thoughts, her mind touching on when Gil Dyne had brought her back after lunch. His last words had chilled her.

"Strangest thing happened to me last night. I got sideswiped by this SUV. I was just driving along, and it swerved at me and scraped the side of my car before taking off. This one's a rental."

"Weird," Elizabeth said.

"It was night, but the woman had sunglasses on. For a minute, I thought it was you."

Elizabeth's blood froze. "What color was the SUV?"

"A dark gray, almost black. Actually, I barely noticed. I was trying to see the driver." He shrugged. "It seemed significant at the time, but maybe she was just drunk or something. I was mad enough to chase her, but by the time I got turned around, she was gone."

"Do you know what make it was?"

"Ford Escape. That's why I thought it was you. Vivian said you have an Escape."

* * *

Elizabeth gathered up her purse and work from her desk, trying not to make too much of what he'd said. Was it a reach to think he was playing with her somehow? Making it up?

He said he loved you, but I think he did some bad things.

"Who is he, Chloe?" she asked aloud again, heading out the door and glad that for once, Pat was away from her desk and unable to see when she left.

"It's public record," Rex told Ravinia once she was back in his car. "Easy to find if you know what you're looking for. R. Lendel Gaines is still the owner on record at the Del Toro address."

"Let's just get there."

"Sure thing." He was half-amused by her lack of tact when it came to him, especially since she seemed to be quite the little actress when she was trying to weasel information out of people.

By the time they reached the townhouse on Del Toro, it was mid-afternoon, shafts of sunlight attempting to pierce through the low hanging clouds. They walked to the front door where a welcome mat in the shape of a cat covered the single step. Rex rang the bell. When no one answered, he rang it again. They heard nothing for a while, then finally the sound of heavy footsteps approaching. A second later the door was pulled open by a tall man who was in his late fifties or early sixties. A horseshoe of hair crowned his head, a few strands of red holding firm within the mostly gray mix. The bald part of his pate was as freckled as his suspicious face. Dark eyes peered at them over a hawkish nose. "Yes?"

"Ralph Lendel Gaines?" Rex asked.

"Who's asking?" the man wanted to know.

Rex introduced himself and Ravinia, then handed the man his card. "We're looking for Elizabeth Gaines."

The man scowled as he stared at the card. "What's she done now?"

Now? Rex ignored that and asked, "She is your daughter, right?"

"Can't see that it's any business of yours, but I have a daughter by that name."

"You and your ex-wife adopted her?"

"Who are you? What the hell is this?"

Sensing that he might get the door slammed in their faces, Rex said quickly, "Ravinia's traveled from Oregon and she believes your daughter is her biological half sister." That was a lie of course, but they had agreed that cousin wasn't a close enough relative for an adoptive father to care about.

Gaines glared at Ravinia as if she'd lost her mind. "Elizabeth never had a half sister." But there was a hesitation in his voice as he stared hard at Ravinia.

Rex wondered if he was seeing something in her, some form of recognition. "We'd like to come in and talk to you about her."

"People say I look like her," Ravinia piped up.

Gaines rubbed his chin, seemed about to say something, then to Rex's surprise, the man suddenly stepped to one side of the hallway and continued to hold the door open. Before they could make a move, however, he glanced again at the card Rex had shown him and asked, "You got ID?"

Rex slid his wallet from his back pocket and flipped it open.

The man leaned forward and stared hard at Rex's picture. After a few moments, he gave a short, sharp nod and said, "You can't be too careful, y'know. Come on in. But call me Lendel, would ya? I never much liked Ralph as a name."

Rex had never much liked *Joel,* either, but he saved that bit of information, not wanting to explain too much. The more questions they could ask and elicit information the better, but they didn't need Gaines asking too much in return.

A few minutes later, they were situated in the living room, each occupying one of the side chairs flanking a long leather couch positioned in front of the window. An underlying odor wafting through the rooms suggested the existence of coffee, bacon grease, and a cat or two. Actually, there were three felines that Rex noticed, two tabbies taking up residence and sunning themselves on a blanket thrown over the back of the couch and a shier black creature peering through the rails of the staircase leading to the second floor.

Who knew how many more could be hiding in the nooks and crannies of R. Lendel Gaines's home?

"I don't know what I can tell you," Gaines admitted, taking a spot on the couch where the cushions seemed permanently indented. He rubbed his hands over the knees of his khaki trousers and glanced at the flat screen mounted on the opposite wall. A talk show was airing, the sound muted.

"But you do have a daughter named Elizabeth?" Rex asked, noting that there wasn't one framed picture visible in the room. He'd scanned the bookcase, tables, mantel, and walls. Nothing.

"Elizabeth and I . . . we don't keep in touch much," Gaines admitted. "It's always been strained between us and these last few years—" Shaking his head, he added, "Ever since she married that shit of a husband of hers, it's been worse. Shouldn't speak ill of the dead, I suppose."

"Her husband died?" Rex asked, feeling that Ravinia wanted to jump in and hoping she would cool it for the moment.

"A week or so ago. Courtland Ellis. Thought awful high of himself, he did."

"Was there a funeral?" Ravinia asked.

"There was something. I didn't go. What's the point? I didn't like him. No reason to pay my respects and be a goddamned hypocrite. Besides, Elizabeth didn't want me there. Got one phone call from her. Pretty much told me all I needed to know."

"What happened to him?" Rex asked.

"Car accident on the 405. Papers said he was with some woman, not Elizabeth."

"Why don't you see each other anymore?" Ravinia asked.

"Oh, she thinks a lot of things that aren't right . . . about people," Gaines said, skirting the issue. "You know about her?"

"What do you mean?" Rex asked.

"About the bridge that collapsed?" Ravinia said at the same time.

Rex glanced her way, wanting to give her a warning frown, but Lendel Gaines was watching them too closely.

"Who you been talking to?" he asked, sounding merely curious.

"We went to the Brightside Apartments," Ravinia said, and Rex would have kicked her if he could.

Gaines responded with a snort. "Marlena. Old hag."

"She said your wife left you," Ravinia added for good measure, and Rex stopped trying to derail her as her tactics seemed to be working a hell of a lot better than he would have ever expected.

"That woman left us both. She made a half-hearted attempt to get Elizabeth to go to Denver and live with her, but Elizabeth balked. Can't say as I blame her. She was in high school at the time. Wanted to finish out around here. And the truth was that Joy—that's the bitch, my ex-wife, and don't you believe there was any joy in her at all—and the joker she married weren't all that thrilled to have a teenager come live with them." Gaines's face pulled in on itself. "Kids that age are a trial, mind you, but that man's a prick, no two ways about it. Got what he deserved when he married Joy."

"You ever talk to Joy?" Rex asked.

Lendel's mouth twisted. "Nope. She's dead; died a few years back. Cancer of some kind, I think." He waved a hand as if what kind of disease didn't matter. "You know what they say, 'what goes around, comes around.'"

Ravinia asked curiously, "You think the cancer was some kind of payback?"

He shrugged, glanced at the muted television again.

"So, Elizabeth stayed with you?" Ravinia asked, getting back to the purpose of the visit.

"She slept here. That was about it. Left soon after graduation and I never saw much of her afterward. Especially after she married Courtland. Jesus, what was she thinking? A lawyer." Gaines said the last word as if it made his point all too clearly. "She always blamed me for everything, but it wasn't my doing."

The vitriol the man had for his son-in-law was palpable. Even the cats seemed to feel it. The two on the back of the couch slid down to the floor and slunk out of the room while the black one on the stairs stared with unblinking eyes, his long tail twitching.

"Do you have an address for Elizabeth?" Rex asked.

Gaines nodded. "Long as she hasn't moved." He got up and walked, stooped over, into the kitchen where Rex could see him rifling through a small drawer near a sliding door. Perching a pair of reading glasses onto his nose, he sifted through a stack of papers until he found what he was looking for, then walked back to the living room, holding out a scrap of paper.

He turned over the handwritten scrap of paper to Ravinia, who had her hand out "Always meant to put it in my permanent file, but I know it anyway, so you can keep it. Phone number's there, too. You've got that same look as she does."

"Do I?" Ravinia asked, looking up from the address and folding the note into fourths. "What does she blame you for?"

"Wanting to make a better life for us. Trying to get her to try harder, get ahead in the world. Realize her potential." He was bitter. "Joy was always screaming at me and she listened to that bitch for too long. Shut her right down."

Then, as if he'd had enough of reviewing an unhappy past, he picked up the remote and pointed it at the television. "When you talk to her, don't believe everything she says. I loved that little girl. She just got everything turned all around." Music came on in a blast as the television came to life. "Ellen's on," Lendel Gaines added, and that pretty much took care of that.

"I didn't like him," Ravinia said on the drive up the coast, back toward Costa Mesa. It was getting dark, the headlights of other cars bright against the coming night. She was thinking over the events of the day, the people she'd met. Bernice Kampfe was nice, Gaines, a pain in the ass. But, she reminded herself, she was closer to finding Elizabeth.

Rex maneuvered around a slower vehicle, a white van of some kind and just nodded.

Ravinia leaned back into the seat. She should be gladder than she felt that she was close to finding her cousin, but she felt oddly anxious. Something was niggling at her and she couldn't figure out what it was. A memory, or a thought, or a voice in the back of her head. That was it. That described it. Something new she couldn't figure out. A twinge of the mind, almost as if she were receiving a message. The hairs on her arms lifted a bit. A voice . . . not clear, but faint and scratchy as if the words were dulled by static, was teasing at her brain. *Elizabeth?*

Closing her eyes, Ravinia tried to concentrate, to hear the words. Was Elizabeth aware that they were getting close? Was she trying to send her a mental message? Stranger things had happened.

Come on, come on, Ravinia thought, hoping that Rex just thought she was sleeping. The words in her mind remained garbled, however. Just out of reach. Was she trying too hard to understand? Expecting a sign of Elizabeth's gift? As a little girl Elizabeth had cried that the bridge was falling and then a pedestrian bridge had fallen. That was the kind of thing that happened to the women of Siren Song. Was it that farfetched to believe she was trying to contact Ravinia?

I'll see you soon, Ravinia sent back, hoping she could respond to the sender.

But though she stayed still and tried to empty her brain, she never received a clear response. *Who are you?* she asked silently, but Elizabeth or whoever was on the other end, didn't answer.

Elizabeth pushed the speed limit as she hurried to collect her daughter before six P.M. She'd meant to pick her up early but had gotten trapped at the office with a deluge of phone calls. Then she'd hurried to the grocery store for the making of another cheese quesadilla for Chloe, and a raft of salad greens, tomatoes, carrots, red and yellow peppers, scallions, avocados, and several boneless chicken breasts to put together a salad for herself. She wasn't eating enough, she knew. The lunch with Gil Dyne hadn't sparked her appetite, and what he'd said dropping her off had made her stomach clench in knots. And Peter Bellhard had called in the afternoon, trying to set up that coffee date, which made her want to clap her hands over her ears and yell, "Stop!"

She wanted nothing to do with either of them. All she wanted was to be with her daughter and feel safe. In fact, the way she was feeling about men in general, she was pretty convinced she would never want another one again. She couldn't trust them. Her father had only been truly interested in her when he'd discovered her extra abilities, and Court's love had been too narcissistic to count.

He said he loved you, but I think he did some bad things.

Chloe hadn't been talking about Court. Elizabeth was sure of it. She had to have a heart-to-heart with her daughter and get to the bottom of that statement, if Chloe would let her.

But when she collected Chloe from school, her daughter was in such a good mood that Elizabeth couldn't find the heart to bring her down with questions she wouldn't want to answer. Chloe skipped up the front steps, making straight for the television and her favorite animated program about the hive of bees that solved mysteries. Deciding to concentrate on dinner, Elizabeth pushed aside all the fear and static in her mind. She kept looking over at her daughter as she put together Chloe's quesadilla and began sautéing the chicken breasts and cutting up the peppers and scallions. She knew ways to broach subjects with Chloe, but it was tricky. She had to come at her sideways or risk raising her stubborn streak with too many questions.

The house phone rang as Elizabeth was taking the pit out of an avocado. Startled, she nearly cut herself with the knife. Swearing softly under her breath, she reached for the receiver. None of her friends called her on the land line so she worried that it was the detective, remembering as she examined Caller ID that Thronson had her cell number.

GAINES, LENDEL R was followed by her father's number.

Elizabeth paused a moment, half-inclined to send the call to voice mail. She hadn't spoken to her father since she'd called him to tell him about Court, and that had been a singularly uncomfortable conversation. Her father had awkwardly tried to comfort her even while both knew that he hadn't liked Court one bit. Add that to their own estrangement, and Elizabeth had been eager to get off the phone and was probably rude in the process. She'd been too upset to worry about her dad's feelings, and let's face it, he'd never really cared about hers.

"Hello, Dad," she answered. "What's up?"

"Hello, Elizabeth. How're you doing?"

She clenched her teeth, then forced herself to relax. "Fine. Better. Is that why you called?"

"I suppose it should be." He sounded kind of sad for him, but she knew better than to believe it. Her father had practically ignored her until he'd thought she was special, then he'd nearly driven her mad with the questions and ideas on how they could make a fortune. She'd done her best to keep from having another episode, however, purposely thwarting him and saving herself in the process. Whenever she'd had one of those crystalline moments that meant impending disaster, she'd shut herself down completely, even to the point of being sent home from school because her teacher thought she'd fallen into a coma.

Her gaze suddenly flew to her daughter and her stomach tightened. Chloe. Was that what was happening to her?

"I didn't quite believe her at first, but she looks a lot like you and that's what she says," her father was saying. "The guy was a private investigator, but it was the girl who wanted your address."

"What are you saying?" Elizabeth suddenly demanded.

"The girl . . . Raven something. I don't want to fight with you, Elizabeth, but if they're coming your way, I think you should know."

"Who is she?"

"I told you," he said, annoyed. "She says she's your half-sister."

Elizabeth froze. She knew nothing about her birth parents. "What are you saying? When did you see this girl?"

"Open your ears. She and the guy came to the house."

"A private investigator?"

"He had a card that said he was. Joel Rex Kingston."

"And her name's what? Raven?"

"I'll start again," her father said with forced patience. "This man and girl came to the house. He said he was a private investigator, name of Kingston, gave me his card, but the girl would hardly let him get a word in. She said she was your half sister and that she's been looking for you, and then she asked for your address."

Elizabeth's hand hurt, she was gripping the phone so hard. "Did you? Give her my address?"

"Well, in the end she convinced me."

"Dad!"

"It's all right."

"It's not all right! You don't know these people. You don't know what they're capable of! You can't just hand out my address. They could be anybody . . . they could be—"

"What the hell are you afraid of, girl? You don't like 'em, don't talk to 'em. All I'm saying is, I believed her. You meet her, I bet you believe her, too. And it's Ravinia. That's what it is."

"How is she my half sister? Who are her parents? Who were mine?" Elizabeth demanded, asking the questions she'd never had the courage to ask when she was younger.

"We adopted you from a lawyer in LA. You know that."

"But I was from Oregon. Mom said so."

"Yes . . ." Gaines sounded a little perturbed that she knew as much as she did, but then he bowled her over by adding, "This girl's from Oregon, too."

"You shouldn't have given them my address," she repeated. A private investigator. Oh, God, what did that mean? "Did you give them my phone number, too?" she challenged. His silence was answer enough. "Did you get their phone number?"

"I told you I got his card."

"What's the number?"

Her father rather reluctantly read off an office number and a mobile number.

"Joel Kingston, you said?" she asked tersely.

"That's what it says on the card."

"You shouldn't have given out my address," she told him again.

"Well, I'm sorry all over the place," he said tightly. "Guess I'll be talking to you later."

Much later. Elizabeth was upset enough not to trust herself to speak. If she did, she might start screaming at him. It was amazing how quickly she'd fallen back into old, bad patterns with him.

A few moments later, he heaved a put-upon sigh and clattered down the phone.

A private investigator? And a girl who *looked like her?* Good God . . . what if she was the one who'd played the game of deadly tag that had gone so wrong on the freeway with Court? What if she was the one who'd been seen at the hotel in Rosarito Beach, Tres Brisas? What if she was the one who'd sideswiped Gil Dyne's car and what if . . . what if . . . she was the reason all those people were dead?

What if all this was because of *her?*

CHAPTER 26

"Chloe," Elizabeth said aloud, but her daughter was still tuned into the television program, which had back to back episodes. "Chloe!"

Chloe jerked to attention and turned to frown at her mother. "What?"

"You said some things the other day. About the old man who drove through the restaurant."

"He died?" she asked, her eyes round.

"Not the last I heard, but I haven't turned on the news . . ." *Because I didn't want to see some media person speculating on the woman who'd predicted the crash.* "But you also said that you thought . . . we'd killed Daddy . . . and though that's *not true*, I want to know why you said it. And why you said, 'He said he loved you, but I think he did some bad things.' I thought you meant Daddy, but now I don't know." Elizabeth was rambling. Doing exactly what she'd warned herself not to do, asking question after question. Fear seemed to have a grip on her tongue, making it wag and wag and wag.

Chloe stared at her with that frown on her face that Elizabeth knew meant she was concentrating very hard. "It's not Daddy. He's somebody else that I sometimes hear."

Elizabeth expelled a pent-up breath. "Where do you hear him?" She felt chilled as she shot a fearful look down the hall toward the front door. She wanted to shut all the blinds, sweep Chloe up, run to the bedroom, and hide under the covers.

Solemnly, Chloe pointed to her head and Elizabeth didn't know whether to laugh or cry. She'd meant where as in what locality, like at school or at the house. "You hear him in your head?"

"I think he wants to talk to you." One of the bees found a clue to their missing friend and was buzzing in figure eights on the screen. Chloe's attention was divided and she went immediately back to watching the program.

It was all Elizabeth could do to keep from switching off the television and dragging Chloe's attention back, but she knew it wouldn't work. She didn't know what to make of what Chloe said, but she had other issues to worry about. A half-sister . . . or charlatan? Coming her way? She'd always known she was adopted, but she'd also gotten the impression from her mother that both of her birth parents were dead and there were no siblings. Whoever this Ravinia was, she was a fraud . . . or worse.

Ravinia could scarcely contain herself on the drive back from Dana Point, but the closer they got to Costa Mesa and Irvine, the slower Rex seemed to be driving. "What's the problem?" she demanded.

"What's your plan upon meeting your cousin? You're not going to call her your sister."

"I don't know. I want to be more important than a cousin so she'll listen to me."

"It's still a lie, and people don't like to be lied to. It doesn't exactly inspire trust, and you need her to trust you or she'll slam the door in your face."

"I'll just keep going back," Ravinia said stubbornly.

"Until she calls the police and you're arrested for stalking."

"Okay, I'll tell her I'm her cousin," Ravinia snapped.

"Let's think on this a bit."

"To hell with that. I want you to take me right to her house."

"When are you going to tell your Aunt Catherine that you've found her?"

"When I actually find her." Ravinia glared at him. "What's going on with you?"

He shook his head. Meeting Lendel Gaines and listening to the words beneath the words, he'd recognized there was a deep divide between him and his daughter, a chasm. He had a feeling if they just barged in on Elizabeth Gaines Ellis, their reception would be unwelcome to the extreme.

Chloe moved from the television to playing in her room. Hearing different voices from within, Elizabeth pressed an ear to the panels of the bedroom door but realized that Chloe was just playacting several parts.

Elizabeth returned to the kitchen and finished her salad, still thinking about how she wanted to approach her daughter when a call came through. Sweeping up her cell phone, she saw it was Tara. She tucked it against her shoulder, a precarious position as she rinsed off the end of the dishes and put them into the dishwasher. "Hello, there," Elizabeth answered.

"Elizabeth, don't freak out, but everyone wants to talk to you about what happened last night," Tara said.

"Oh, God. Please, don't make this a bigger deal than it is." She slammed the dishwasher door closed and switched it on.

"You *knew.* How did you know?"

"I can't really talk tonight."

"We want to see you. Please. We're all going out for drinks tonight and want you to join us."

"Tara . . . I'm in for the night. We just finished dinner and Chloe's beat."

"No, I'm not!" Chloe suddenly appeared in the kitchen, having burst out of her room when she heard Elizabeth's cell ringing. "Is Bibi there? Are we going somewhere?"

"No," Elizabeth told her. Into the phone, she said, "I've been out too many nights and it's time to stay home."

"Nooooo!" Chloe wailed.

"Chloe, go to your room," she told her daughter.

"How about we come to your house?" Tara said after a beat.

"No, no. Really." Elizabeth forced out a half-laugh. *Keep it light. Keep it light.*

"Have you seen the news?" Tara suddenly asked soberly.

Elizabeth tensed, sensing where this was going as Chloe trudged away on leaden feet. "Um . . . do I even want to?"

"They're talking about a woman who raced in and saved a little boy and his family from the car that smashed into Uncle Vito's. Everybody wants to know who you are."

Elizabeth gritted her teeth. She wanted to deny everything, but Tara had been there. Instead, she offered her same, lame excuse. "I just saw it happening."

"From Lots Of Beef?" Tara's tone said, *I don't think so.* "I talked to Jade. She's always said you knew Little Nate was going to fall, but you couldn't have seen it. I'm thinking you did see it, somehow, even though you couldn't have."

"Sounds like you all think I'm some kind of freak," Elizabeth said, her voice catching.

"Good God, no. We all love you, but *what the hell's going on?* GoodGuy . . . and . . . Court . . ."

"You think I had something to do with . . . that?" she finished as Chloe was still within earshot, moving away by degrees.

"*No.* None of us think that. God, no! You couldn't hurt a fly. But . . . something really weird is going on. You gotta admit that. Vivian was saying she really wants you to go to another meeting of that group, Sisterhood, and—"

"I'm not going back." Elizabeth cut her off. "It wasn't right for me."

"Okay. All right. Fine. Don't go. If it's not right, it's not right. But come out with us tonight. Talk to us. We're your friends. Vivian's got Deirdre's nanny all set up at her house. We won't be late, and it's just us girls. No husbands."

"Where's Bill? If Vivian's taking the kids . . ."

Hearing capitulation in her mother's voice, Chloe returned in a flash, gazing at her with pleading eyes and clapping her hands together as if praying.

"He's out of town on business or something."

"Why does it feel like you guys are setting me up for an intervention?" Elizabeth asked, only half-joking.

"No intervention. Just drinks and friendship. And if you want to talk . . . we're listening. Jade said you confided in her about a few things, but she didn't say what."

"Well, Jade told me to keep my thoughts to myself or people might think I'm crazy, in so many words."

"You're my best friend," Tara said. "Come out with us."

Chloe was practically hanging on Elizabeth's leg, trying to listen in. "Am I going to Bibi's?" she asked eagerly.

"Bibi's going to be at Lissa's," Elizabeth said reluctantly.

"Then I want to go there. Please, please, *please*!!!"

"One hour," Elizabeth said into the phone, caving.

"Meet at Vivian's and we'll go in my car," Tara said quickly as if she expected Elizabeth to change her mind.

"The last I heard, you don't even like Lissa," Elizabeth reminded her daughter once she was off the phone.

"Oh, she's okay," Chloe said brightly.

"I'll go," Elizabeth told her. "But then I want to talk to you about the voice you're hearing."

"I already told you everything," Chloe whined.

"Then tell it to me again. After Lissa's house." Seeing that Chloe wanted to get herself worked up again, Elizabeth said, "Deal?" She held out her hand.

After a moment, Chloe grudgingly shook it. "Deal."

Ravinia wasn't sure what to make of Rex's sudden reluctance to find Elizabeth. She was so close, and all of a sudden he was making excuses. Well, okay, maybe she could use a better plan, but they'd stopped at an In-N-Out and ordered burgers and Rex had spent the better part of the time on the phone to someone who wanted him to do some kind of background check on the woman who was marrying his son. Sounded like the guy had a lot of money and didn't trust the woman's motives.

Her cell phone rang in the midst of this and Ravinia was so surprised, she dragged the sleeve of her shirt through her teeny tub of catsup trying to pull it from her pocket. It had to be Aunt Catherine. "Hello?"

"Ravinia, it's Ophelia."

"Oh, hi. Is something wrong? Where's Aunt Catherine?"

"She's here. She wanted me to call you and find out how you're doing."

"Why isn't she talking to me?"

"She's making dinner with Isadora."

And she's a little uncomfortable with the cell phone. Ravinia glanced through the glass doors of the restaurant to the outside where Rex was pacing around, talking on his mobile phone. "I know where Elizabeth is." She then told her sister how she and Rex had found Ralph Lendel Gaines and had just come from interviewing him. She finished with, "I want to go there now, but Rex is on the phone and I don't know . . ."

"Rex is the private investigator?" Ophelia asked dubiously.

"Yes. Rex doesn't want to just barge in on her. Her husband died just a week or so ago." Hearing her own words ringing in her ears made Ravinia realize Rex was maybe right to think things through as Elizabeth might not be in any frame of mind to meet her cousin on the heels of his death.

"Her husband died?"

"In a car accident." *With another woman, apparently.*

"Aunt Catherine will be glad to know she's all right."

"So far. I haven't met her yet."

"Call when you have."

"Ophelia," Ravinia said, sensing her sister was about to hang up.

"Yes?" She sounded somewhat impatient.

"When Elizabeth was a little girl, she predicted a footbridge collapse. We've heard it a couple times, from several different people. Do you think . . . does it sound like she sees things maybe like Cassandra does?"

After a pause, Ophelia said maddeningly, "Anything's possible, I suppose."

"Do you think he knows about her? Declan Jr.? And I know this is going to sound weird, but I'm picking up something, too."

"What do you mean?" Ophelia asked sharply.

Ravinia thought back to the voice that seemed to be trying to reach her and a shiver slid down her back. "I don't know. It's just weird."

"You've got this cell number now, right? After you meet her, call me. I'll put Aunt Catherine on now."

"What if it's late?"

"We don't care."

"Okay." Ravinia talked with her aunt a few minutes, hanging up just as Rex appeared to be finishing his calls and coming back into the restaurant.

At the Barefoot Bar once again, Elizabeth's friends questioned her and questioned her, trying to make it all seem light and airy when their faces were full of worry and concern. Elizabeth understood. If she were in their shoes, and hadn't been the one experiencing these strange events, she would have probably felt the same. But no matter how many questions they asked her, she had no answers for them.

She didn't understand her ability, either. It just was, and though she'd fought it down for years with her own iron will, it never went away, evidenced by what had occurred at Uncle Vito's.

They were all there—Tara, Vivian, Deirdre, Jade and Nadia. Tara was the one who initiated most of the queries. Jade, knowing how reluctant Elizabeth was in even admitting anything unusual had happened with Little Nate, ran a little bit of interference for her. Deirdre boldly asked her if she really wanted them to believe she was clairvoyant, making it clear she, of all of them, thought the whole thing was a crock. Vivian tried to change the subject, patently uncomfortable with the idea. Nadia seemed to be reserving judgment, though she did show Elizabeth a news item that ran on one of the more salacious local television stations where the reporter pleaded with the mystery savior to show herself and let the world thank her for her heroic efforts.

Elizabeth realized two things from the evening. One, her friends were not going to be able to keep her secret for long, if they hadn't given it away already, and two, their friendship with her had taken an unexpected turn, maybe not for the better.

With exhaustion coming on like a drowning wave, Elizabeth finally had enough and asked Tara to drive her back to Vivian's to pick up her car and Chloe. Deirdre tried to talk everyone into staying, but no one really wanted to.

When they got back to Vivian's house, Lissa and Bibi seemed to have ganged up on Chloe who was near tears but wouldn't let them fall until she was in the car on the way home. "I hate Lissa," she said again, brushing aside angry tears.

"We don't hate anyone," Elizabeth answered, tired.

"Yes, we do." Chloe sounded so positive Elizabeth wondered if something more was behind her words, then decided she was chasing ghosts. Chloe was a child who loved and hated all at the same time.

Back at the house, Elizabeth indulged her with a Popsicle then read her two stories at bedtime. Closing her door, she walked to her bedroom, kicked off her shoes, and changed into a pair of pajamas. She'd had one glass of wine at the bar and wondered if she should indulge in another, but a headache was knocking at the back of her brain, so she let it go.

She was in bed, reading and rereading the same page of a book Nadia had recommended to her that she just couldn't get into, when her doorbell rang. Her first reaction was to burrow under the covers and hold back whatever was coming her way.

The half-sister.

Immediately, she was angry with her father again. He should have asked her before he just handed out her address. "What was he thinking?"

Throwing off the covers, she hurried to the door, not bothering with a robe. She wanted to catch her visitor before she rang the bell again and risked waking Chloe. She would get rid of her, and the private detective, too, if he was still with her.

Peering through the peephole, Elizabeth felt a distinct shock. Not a supposed relative. Officer Maya. *What's she doing here? Did Detective Thronson tell her what I said?*

Cautiously, Elizabeth turned on the outside light and opened the door. "Officer Maya," she said, her tone purposely neutral.

"I'm sorry to bother you again, Mrs. Ellis, but I have some disturbing news."

The restaurant crash. "Did he die? The man in the car?"

Officer Maya hesitated, then said, "Yes, unfortunately, but that's not why I'm here. I'm here because Detective Bette Thronson was killed last night. Shot in her own home. And we believe you may have been one of the last people to see her alive."

CHAPTER 27

"*What?* Shot? No!" Elizabeth stumbled backward away from the doorway. "She can't be dead. She can't!" But even as she said the words, she could read the truth in Maya's sober and stunned face. "Oh, God . . ."

We think you may have been the last person to see her alive. . . .

Crumpling into a chair in the living room, Elizabeth buried her face in her hands. *How can this be happening?*

Her world had tumbled off its axis, tragedies befalling people she knew, people who'd touched her life. Her hands were wet with tears and she felt darkness squeeze in on her.

"Mrs. Ellis?" Maya's voice. From a distance. As if the officer were on the far side of a long tunnel. "Mrs. Ellis!"

In her shock, Elizabeth had left Officer Maya standing on the porch, but she'd come into the house anyway and was leaning over her. With an effort, Elizabeth pulled back from the seductive embrace of oblivion. She needed to keep from fainting. She needed to be present.

She dropped her hands. "I'm . . . I'm okay," she said, though of course, that was a lie. She was far from being anything close to okay. "I don't understand. What happened?"

"There was an intruder in her home. No forced entry. Looks like he or she followed Bette home and pushed their way inside." Maya was having difficulty keeping the emotion out of her voice. "My partner's on the scene with the techs."

Elizabeth gazed dispiritedly at the officer. Her heart pounded erratically. *Dead because you had a problem with her. Dead because you argued with her, baited her, in so many words told her to go ahead and arrest you.* "Do you . . . Do you know who did it?"

"Not yet," Maya said, her dark eyes somber. "But we will."

Something in her tone alerted Elizabeth to the realization that Maya thought she had something to do with Thronson's death, just as Thronson suspected she was involved with the others.

You can't wish someone dead.

Thronson's claim came back to her, but her stomach twisted because it was a lie. She had wished them dead, and they'd died. "Didn't anyone see anything?" she forced out. "Someone walking by? A car out of place or . . . ?"

"The investigation's just starting. Why don't you tell me what you and Detective Thronson discussed. Give me a replay of what you said to each other."

Elizabeth nodded. Their conversation was still so fresh that she could relate it practically verbatim, but she only told Maya about wishing Court and Mazie dead, not Officer Daniels or GoodGuy; she could see Maya thought she was crazy enough as it was. She also left out her challenge to Thronson to go ahead and arrest her. It just seemed prudent. She finished with, ". . . and after that, she left. That was it. I didn't hear from her again."

"Detective Thronson was scheduling you for a polygraph."

Elizabeth could easily read between the lines on that. She'd just told Maya that she'd wished people dead, and though she hadn't elaborated on her statement, it was the kind of comment reserved for crackpots, she was certain. A lie detector test was a good start to separate truth and fiction, at least about what someone truly believed. "I still want to go through with it," she assured the officer.

"Mind if I sit down?" She was already perching uneasily on the ottoman directly in front of Elizabeth.

"My daughter's sleeping and I don't want to wake her."

Maya nodded and said quietly but with an edge, "The crash at the restaurant. How did you know it was coming?"

She'd explained already, but Maya, like Thronson, wanted answers. "Like I told Detective Thronson, I heard it coming. I saw the car speeding out of control, aimed straight for the restaurant."

"No," Maya disagreed. "You were in the car's path at least half a minute before the car plowed through the glass. You saved that kid's life because you knew the crash was going to happen."

"I just reacted," Elizabeth insisted, her head beginning to pound.

"Well, see, that's the problem. I think you acted. Not reacted. It was impossible for you to see that car coming."

Elizabeth's back stiffened. "Did you come here to tell me about Detective Thronson or was that just an excuse to badger me? I reacted to a situation, a calamity I saw coming, and that boy and his family are alive because of it. I'm not going to feel bad about doing what anyone would have."

"People are asking who you are. They know I spoke with you at the site. I haven't given them your name."

"Media people?"

Maya nodded slowly.

"I appreciate that," Elizabeth said shortly.

"I don't want this turning into a circus any more than I imagine you do, but I intend to get to the bottom of it. And I intend to find out who killed Detective Thronson."

"I wish you the best of luck in that."

Maya studied Elizabeth's face, looking for signs of guilt, she suspected. "If there's anything you've left out, something you remember later, call me." Maya pressed a card into Elizabeth's hand.

"I'll do that." Elizabeth got to her feet and ushered the officer outside. Once she closed the door behind Maya, Elizabeth threw the dead bolt, exhaled a long breath and leaned against the panels.

Detective Thronson's image swam before her eyes and she swallowed hard. From fear. From grief. From not understanding what kind of vortex had caught her in its deadly swirl, trapping her. People around her were dying ugly, tragic deaths. Some of those deaths were presumed to be accidents. Mazie's single-car crash. Court losing control due to road rage. Others were not. Someone had definitely shot Detective Thronson, like Officer Daniels had been shot. Yes, Thronson's and Daniels' homicides could have been brought on by someone not connected to Elizabeth. They were both police officers, and Thronson was a homicide detective, investigating murders. Her line of work was dangerous. But the timing of her murder was directly after she left Elizabeth, if Maya could be believed. Elizabeth didn't think the officer would get it wrong. It seemed more than coincidence. A lot more. Elizabeth felt sick inside. And someone had definitely gone out of their way to kill Channing Renfro, GoodGuy, dousing him with gasoline and setting him ablaze. That took a certain amount of planning.

As she leaned against the door, she saw them all . . . the victims, each face appearing in her mind's eye, distorted and pained, eyes accusing. One image replaced by another, those victims included Detective Bette Thronson. Would there be no end?

Not as long as you keep becoming enraged with people.

Elizabeth felt a serious lurch of her stomach. She ran to the kitchen sink where she heaved up most of the little she'd eaten during the day. Clutching the edge of the counter, leaning over the sink, her nostrils and mouth smelling of bile she dry-heaved a second time.

Rinsing out her mouth, she splashed water over her face and told herself to calm down, to think rationally as she cleaned the sink. No such luck. The shaking started in her fingers, but soon involved her hands and arms, crawling up her body until her teeth started chattering and she wondered if she was literally falling apart, not only mentally, but physically, as well. She slid down the cabinetry to puddle on the floor and dropped her face into her hands. What was happening to her? Tears burned in her eyes and it was all she could do to keep from breaking into full-fledged sobs.

Don't do this.

Pull yourself together.

You can't let whatever's happening steal your sanity. You can't fall apart. What would Chloe do without you? Get a damned grip! Do it. Your daughter needs a strong, sane mother, not some sniveling weakling who's confused and feeling sorry for herself. Get the fuck up!

"Oh, for the love of God," she whispered, swiping at her eyes with the back of her hand. Setting her jaw, she stood up and forced her knees to hold her. She stalked to the front door and looked out the peephole to make certain Officer Maya had left.

Sure enough, the cop and her car were no longer in view, but she didn't breathe a sigh of relief just yet as through the fish-eye lens she saw a man and a woman walking up to the porch!

"Oh, God." The supposed half-sister and the investigator her father had warned her about. She thought about not answering, but as before, she knew she would just be putting off the inevitable. But that didn't mean she would be buying the girl's tale. The world was rife with predators who, upon learning of a family member's death, would come out of the woodwork to take advantage of those left behind. Often times claims were filed against an estate by long-lost family members who felt they were entitled to their due. Maybe that was what was happening. Maybe this girl thought there was money to be had, that Court, a lawyer, had been wealthy when he died. . . .

Except that, according to dear old dad, this girl's claiming to be your sister, so she can't really lay claim to Court's estate.

But why else would she suddenly appear, so close to his death? For a fleeting second, Elizabeth wondered if her father was actually behind this total fabrication. Along with a lot of people, he believed that because Court was a lawyer and drove a BMW, he was wealthy. And yet, for all her father's faults and his desire to use her "ability" for profit, she didn't think he would try to steal from her.

Before they could ring the door and wake Chloe, Elizabeth slid the chain lock free and opened the door a crack, just enough so that she could see her visitors.

The man stopped short. He was tall, around six-feet, with deep-set eyes and dark, almost black hair that shone under the porch lamp. The look on his face was intense.

Great. Just what she needed.

The woman next to him, barely out of her teens, was staring hard at Elizabeth as if memorizing every plane of her face. Dressed almost like a boy, or street kid, she was a honey-blond, her hair pulled away from a face devoid of makeup, her features even.

With an inner jolt, Elizabeth recognized a resemblance between them. Her father hadn't been wrong about that.

But whatever story they were peddling, she wasn't interested.

"Elizabeth Gaines?" the man asked.

"My name is Elizabeth Ellis," she said, her pulse elevating again. God, she was wrung out; she shouldn't even be talking to these people.

"But it was Gaines," the girl insisted. "You're Elizabeth Gaines who went to Van Buren High."

The guy sent his companion a look meant to silence her.

"Rex Kingston," he introduced himself, focusing on Elizabeth's face, or what he could see of it in the crack of the door. "Kingston Investigations." He pulled out a card and moved up the steps to reach it toward her.

Reluctantly, Elizabeth took it from his fingers, then scanned it in the illumination from the porch light. *Rex* wasn't the name her father had told her, but there it was on the business card. Joel "Rex" Kingston.

"And this is Ravinia Rutledge, my client."

"I'm actually your cousin," the girl cut in again.

"Cousin?" Elizabeth repeated. "I thought you were claiming to be my half-sister."

"You spoke to your father?" Ravinia asked.

"I . . . yes." Elizabeth gazed at Ravinia who kept on studying her as if searching for something she couldn't quite find. In those moments, Elizabeth felt something move through her, something she couldn't name, but it stilled the breath in her lungs and for a second her body was suffused with heat. And then as quickly as it came on, it dissipated.

What the hell?

She turned back to Kingston, unnerved by the girl. "Why did she claim to be my half-sister if she's my cousin?"

His eyes also seemed to be searching her face, and his lips parted as if he were going to answer, but it was Ravinia who spoke up first.

"I wanted to find you. I thought your father wouldn't believe a cousin as much as a sister. But I am who I say I am."

"Well, that's fine, but I don't want to talk to either of you."

"Wait!" Ravinia called as Elizabeth started to shut the door.

"Think about it," the investigator said. "You've got my card. She has some information for you that you might like to hear. Call, if you change your mind."

Ravinia looked at him as if he'd lost his senses. "I'm not leaving."

"You're leaving if she says you're leaving. This is her property, and you're a trespasser."

"I'm her cousin!"

"She doesn't think so," he pointed out, and Elizabeth got the feeling that this kind of conversation went on between them more often than not.

"Are you related?" she asked him, indicating Ravinia.

"No." He was definite on that. When she didn't immediately shut the door, he pulled out his wallet and took out several pieces of identification, his California driver's license and a PI license, both of which could be bought on the streets of LA. You just had to have enough cash and the right connections. "Ravinia showed up in my office and asked me to locate you. That's how we met. That's how we ended up here," he said.

"It's important I talk to you," Ravinia insisted, throwing Kingston a look that said, *you're not helping.*

But he was helping, she realized. He'd disarmed Elizabeth with his honesty. If it was a ploy, it had certainly worked because she turned her attention to him again.

He spread his hands. "As I said, you might want to hear what she has to say."

Elizabeth hesitated. More out of curiosity than anything else, she almost let them in. But she had enough to deal with. More than enough. "Sorry." With that she shut the door. She didn't have the time nor the energy for this. Her life was enough of a shambles as it was.

Bam! Bam! Bam!

The knocking was so loud, Elizabeth whirled to face the door again just as the bell chimed. Oh, for the love of God! They were going to wake Chloe and she—

"Mommy?"

Elizabeth gritted her teeth. *Damn it. Too late.*

Rubbing her eyes, and gripping on to her favorite blanket, Chloe stood in the hallway. Her hair was tousled, sticking up in all directions, the line between her brows etched deep.

The damn bell rang again. "Elizabeth! Open up!" Ravinia called, her voice muffled through the door panels. "We *are* related! I'm just trying to help, and I need to tell you things." She sounded frantic, almost hyped up.

Elizabeth hadn't gotten the hit that either one of them was on any kind of drug. Nor, after the brief conversation did she think they were running some kind of obvious scam. *Because they're good at it. Ignore them.*

"I'm one of your cousins."

There are more?

"I've come from Siren Song. It's a place near Deception Bay. In Oregon. I . . . Your mother is my aunt."

Oh, good Lord.

"Who is that?" Chloe demanded and pointed her free hand toward the front door.

"No one."

"It's someone," she said in a tone that said Elizabeth was lying to her.

"No one I know," Elizabeth corrected. "I'm sorry for the racket." Refusing to answer the door again, she shepherded her child back toward her bedroom, guiding her daughter in the glow of a night-light. "I didn't mean to wake you. Just go back to bed and—"

"No!" Chloe balked, digging her heels into the carpet.

"Chloe, it's late. I'm sorry that you woke up, but it's time to sleep." Elizabeth was growing angry with the girl on her doorstep. Worse yet, the pounding continued only to be interrupted by the peal of the doorbell again. If she weren't already in trouble with the damn police, she would have dialed 9-1-1 in a heartbeat and have the cops remove Kingston and Ravinia from her property. Maybe she would, anyway.

"Not going to bed," Chloe insisted and to prove her point, dropped to the floor and wrapped her blanket around her as if it were some protective shield.

"Of course you're going to bed. Me, too. Real soon."

"Who's out there?" Chloe demanded.

"I told you, I don't know them. They're strangers."

"They're loud!"

"They sure are."

"Why don't you let them in?"

"Because they're strangers."

"She said she was your cousin."

"Yeah, well, she lied." Elizabeth leaned over Chloe's bed and straightened the cover.

"Why would she lie?"

"Beats me."

"I want to meet her!"

"Don't be silly, we don't even know her."

"Lissa has cousins. Lots of 'em and so does Bibi," Chloe argued.

"Well, great. Lucky for them." When Chloe remained obstinate, Elizabeth added, "I don't know that she's my cousin. Just because she says she is, doesn't make it true. This could all be a ruse."

Chloe scowled up at her. "What's a rube?"

"A ruse," Elizabeth corrected. "It's like a fake."

"Why would anyone say they were a fake cousin?"

"Chloe . . ."

"You don't want to have a cousin," Chloe wailed, scooting away when Elizabeth reached for her. She tossed her blanket aside and sprinted to the front door.

"Wait!" Elizabeth yelled. She charged forward but caught a foot in the blanket and nearly fell over.

Just that moment's delay was enough and suddenly Chloe was unlocking the door and throwing it open. "Hi," she yelled. "Come back!"

"Chloe!" Elizabeth caught up with her and saw Kingston and Ravinia had started off the porch. But the girl was lightning fast, and she swept back before Elizabeth could get Chloe out of the way.

"Hey," Ravinia said to Chloe.

"Are you my cousin, too?"

"I'm sorry," Elizabeth said at the same time. "My daughter should never have opened the door."

"Why?" her daughter demanded.

"If you don't leave, I'll . . . call the police," Elizabeth said.

"Good idea," Kingston said, coming up behind Ravinia. "Give them my name. I used to work on the force." His gaze was level and she believed him. Something about him suggested he'd been a cop, maybe his stance or forcefulness. "Call Barney O'Callaghan or Mike Tatum. Detectives."

The last thing she needed was to get involved with any more detectives. He'd called her bluff.

"You want to come in?" Chloe invited.

"Only if your mom says it's okay," Kingston told her.

"It's not okay," Elizabeth said, but she heard the weakening in her own voice.

"How about you talk to Ravinia," Kingston suggested. "I'll stay outside."

Ravinia shot him a look, and he held up his hands. "I've done the job you hired me for. To find Elizabeth Gaines."

She looked from Chloe to Elizabeth. "I know about the bridge falling down. And I might be able to help explain why you knew about it. . . ."

Elizabeth held tight to Chloe, then slowly opened the door.

CHAPTER 28

Ravinia looked into Elizabeth's heart. Yes, she was the right person, and yes, she was a good person. Also, she was scared as hell.

"You can come in," Elizabeth said. "Only you. Before I let you into my house, though, you won't mind proving to me that you don't have a gun or a knife or any other kind of weapon. Right? And, just so we're clear, until I'm certain you're not here to sell me a bill of goods or something worse, I'll keep my phone in my hand, 9-1-1 keyed up and ready to go should I need to call for help."

"Okay." Ravinia was there to warn Elizabeth, to help her, not to harm her. It kind of pissed Ravinia off that Elizabeth couldn't figure that out or sense it some way, but whatever it took to get through the door. Turning her pockets inside out, she cocked her head at an angle and silently asked Elizabeth if that was enough.

For her part, Elizabeth seemed somewhat mollified, if not convinced, and moved out of the way. She glanced back toward Rex for a moment, then closed the door and locked it once Ravinia was inside.

"Come see my room!" Chloe insisted.

"No, honey," Elizabeth countered. "This lady is here on business."

Lady . . . Ravinia felt her lips twitch. Never in her life had she considered herself a "lady," though Aunt Catherine had certainly tried her hardest in that regard.

"Nooo," Chloe wailed and grabbed Ravinia's hand, pulling her down a short hall as Elizabeth muttered something like, "Give me strength," under her breath.

Ravinia restrained herself from looking into the little girl's heart; she didn't want to scare Chloe, who was an ally. With Elizabeth half a step behind, Ravinia allowed herself to be dragged along. Chloe took her into a room decorated in bright tropical colors. Toys were overflowing from a basket, blocks and books were stacked in a corner, a few dolls were scattered across the floor, and stuffed animals spilled off the small bed. The white furniture all matched—a dresser, bookcase, and twin bed.

A perfect little girl's room . . . glaringly different from the home in which Ravinia had been raised. She couldn't remember a time she hadn't shared a bedroom with at least one of her sisters on the upper floors of the lodge. There had been few toys, and the books they'd read had come from the Deception Bay library, courtesy of Aunt Catherine. Handmade curtains and a patchwork quilt that Ravinia's aunt had pieced from calico and gingham scraps left over from the dresses she'd sewn adorned the windows and beds.

"Are you really Mommy's cousin?" Chloe asked.

"Yes, I am."

"Do you like *Busy Bees and Friends*?" she asked as she showed off her most prized possessions, a doll that looked like a pirate and a once-white, stuffed, lop-eared bunny that was missing an eye.

"I don't know them," Ravinia said, aware that Elizabeth was watching carefully from the doorway.

"Her favorite television show," Elizabeth explained. Then to her daughter, "Okay, back to bed."

"No," Chloe said.

But Elizabeth was firm. "It's late. Ravinia came here to talk to me."

"Will she be here when I wake up?" Chloe demanded, scowling over a yawn.

"We'll see," Elizabeth said, walking into the room. "Come on. Take Henry and Clover with you."

Reluctantly Chloe climbed into the bed with her favorite toys. "That means no," she revealed as she snuggled under the covers. "Just like when you tell me we'll see about a dog."

"If I'm not here, I'll come back," Ravinia told her and felt the weight of Elizabeth's stare. *If I'm allowed by your mother and if it's still safe,* she silently added.

"Promise?"

"Yes," Ravinia said.

Though Chloe still seemed doubtful, she was just too tired to argue and allowed Elizabeth to tuck her in and leave a night-light on before ushering Ravinia out of the room, shutting the door behind them.

"Just let me get my robe," Elizabeth said and was through another door and back again in fifteen seconds as if she were certain Ravinia might rob her or try to kidnap her child if she weren't watching her like a hawk. "Okay, this way." Elizabeth shrugged into a thin robe and cinched the belt as she led the way. Once they were in the kitchen area, she leveled her gaze at Ravinia again. "What do you know about the falling bridge?"

Rex sat in the Nissan and gazed at the house where Elizabeth Gaines lived with her daughter. His job was finished, but he didn't want to leave. His mind was on the elusive, harried woman he'd seen for a few brief moments. *She was tough,* he thought, *or tried to be, protective of her daughter, but mostly she was scared out of her mind.* It didn't take Ravinia's "gift" to see that.

Something was making Elizabeth very, very afraid though she was trying like hell to hide it.

What?

He was certain she was Ravinia's long-lost relative. The family resemblance was strong. High cheekbones, arched eyebrows, blond hair, and pointed chin. Elizabeth's eyes appeared to be blue, though, he suspected they might change with the light. Similar to Ravinia's. Something else seemed to connect them, too. Something beyond the physical.

Shit, Kingston, now you're sounding as crazy as Ravinia.

Not that it mattered why Elizabeth was scared. His part in the bizarre escapade was over. He could probably go home and leave Ravinia to her own devices, but still he sat in his car, parked a block and a half down from the Ellis house. He'd chosen the area because it was in the shadows, away from the vaporous illumination cast by street lamps.

When he and Ravinia had first arrived, they'd found that Elizabeth wasn't home. Ravinia had insisted on waiting and he'd gone along with it, telling himself that it was just best to get this investigation behind him. While they'd waited, a police cruiser had come by several times and he'd realized he wasn't the only one watching the Ellis home. A female officer had stepped out and knocked, then when no one answered, she'd gotten back in her cruiser and circled the block.

Rex had been forced to move his car, regardless of how much Ravinia squawked; he didn't want to be questioned unnecessarily. Then Elizabeth had returned and the woman cop had gone to her door and inside. Rex had wanted to ask Elizabeth what that was all about, but she was too skittish. He was surprised, really, that Ravinia had found her way past the door at all.

His natural curiosity was aroused by all of it, and though he should just drop the whole thing from his head, collect his fee, and move on, he couldn't quite make himself. Seeing Elizabeth Gaines Ellis in the flesh had also woken something inside him. He could feel it, and it kind of pissed him off. What the hell was that about?

God help him, he couldn't be interested in her.

"Christ," he muttered, frustrated. Still, while Ravinia was inside the house and probably telling Elizabeth her fantastical story—and how was Elizabeth going to react to the tale of young women dressed as if they belonged to a previous century by a loving but frightened matriarch who suppressed their natural gifts of ESP and kept them safe from the outside world and maniacal half-brothers?— he reached for his iPad, glad he'd taken the time to charge it, and did some research on Elizabeth, looking into her life, her job at Suncrest Realty and as much as he could learn about her late husband, Courtland Ellis.

Elizabeth braced herself and listened in silence to the story that unfolded from the girl.

Ravinia began with, "You probably have an ability to see things before they happen. You saw the bridge collapse."

"How do you know about that?"

"I've met some people from your past, Beth Harper and Bernice Kampfe. They wanted me to let them know how you're doing. I think they were worried about you, too."

Beth Harper and Bernice Kampfe . . . Elizabeth felt unexpected tears suddenly burn behind her eyes. People who were always nice to her. There had been so few when she was growing up.

"My Aunt Catherine is your mother," Ravinia went on. "She gave you away when you were a baby because . . . well, it's a really long story, but she didn't think you'd be safe if she didn't give you up."

Elizabeth folded her hands, her pulse running fast. Her biological mother. The thought pulled at her heartstrings and she reminded herself that she was vulnerable, that she had to tread carefully in these dangerous emotional waters. *Don't believe this. It's a ploy, and a damn good one.*

Ravinia went on, telling her of the lodge where she'd grown up with her sisters, Elizabeth's cousins, of which there were many, apparently. When she got to the gifts each of them possessed, Elizabeth felt herself pull back. No. She didn't want to hear this. She didn't.

But she did. Breaking her silence, she asked, "What's your gift?"

Dead serious, Ravinia answered, "I can look into a person's heart and see if they're good or bad."

"Really."

"You don't believe me, but I looked into your heart at the door. You're a good person. Just scared."

Elizabeth opened her mouth to say that what Ravinia was suggesting was impossible, but she remembered the heat that had suffused her, the sense that something had gone through her.

She was starting to believe there was something . . . a connection to the lodge called Siren Song, a link that sent a cold sliver of fear through her.

"You don't need to be scared of me," Ravinia said, reading her.

"I'm not." But it was a lie, and they both knew it. Elizabeth, nerves shot, grabbed a glass from a cabinet, filled it with water from the tap and glanced over her shoulder at Ravinia. "Would you like a drink?"

"No, thanks."

Fair enough. Elizabeth took a long swallow, thinking she could really use a glass of wine, firmly convinced that would be a really bad idea about now. She needed her wits about her. Silently counting to ten, she said, "Can you start at the beginning? I feel like I've just walked into the third act."

"Sure." Ravinia started again, launching into a tale that was as outlandish as it was intriguing about her promiscuous mother, Mary, and the woman's dedicated, and strict but loving, sister Catherine who had taken over the brood of women who inhabited the gated compound called Siren Song. The children were raised away from the world, locked away from modern civilization. Catherine eventually banished Ravinia's mother to a solitary island because her liaisons with all kinds of men brought danger to her children.

A last, and current, deadly threat had caused Catherine to send Ravinia to find Elizabeth and warn her of the danger.

"That's why I'm here," Ravinia finished simply. "To warn you."

"What danger is it, that I should look out for?" Elizabeth asked cautiously. She didn't know how much she believed of the tale, but there was no denying strange things were going on in her life.

"Declan Jr., for one." For the first time Ravinia sounded unsure. "He could be looking for you, if he knows about you yet."

He said he loved you, but I think he's done bad things.

"He's another of my cousins."

Elizabeth finished her water and set the empty glass in the sink. Her headache was still there, but had receded to a dull ache in the back of her head. A part of her wanted to trust Ravinia, to find an explanation, even a partial explanation, for the horrendously weird happenings that surrounded her, especially the deaths that had occurred. Maybe there was a connection . . . but then again, really? And if she bought into part of the girl's story, wouldn't she have to swallow the entire unbelievable tale?

"I honestly don't know what to say."

"Have you seen other things? Besides the bridge?" Ravinia asked her.

Elizabeth half-laughed. "Do you watch the news?"

"No. Why?"

"Never mind. I . . . thank you. For warning me—"

"You don't believe me." Ravinia cut her off, affronted.

"I see that you believe it, and I'm not saying you're lying, but I can't— I have a life here. A suburban life." Elizabeth spread her arms. "I'm a normal person, and Chloe and I have just been going through some bad times."

"You're lying."

She shook her head, though she felt her pulse pounding a bit, adrenalin flowing through her blood, a new fear darkening her heart. "Let's leave it at I don't disbelieve you."

"Something's happened," Ravinia suddenly guessed. "That's why you're afraid. What is it? I can help."

"Nope, nope. I'm fine. Why don't you leave me . . . Catherine's number . . . and I'll call her."

"It's really Ophelia's number. She has a cell," Ravinia said, her lips turning downward. "There isn't a phone at the lodge."

Elizabeth remembered that Ophelia was one of the cousins Ravinia had named. "Fine. I'll try calling her, later."

"Do you have paper and pen?"

Elizabeth searched through her junk drawer and discovered both, handing them to Ravinia who scribbled down a number. Then, she added a second number and wrote down her name. Ravinia Rutledge. "My cell," she said. "In case you need me or want to talk. I'm going to buy some more minutes, so if you call and can't get through, just try again." She started to hand the slip of paper to Elizabeth, then pulled it back and added another number. "This is the number of the Tillamook County Sheriff's Department. Ask for Detective Savannah Dunbar. She can verify everything I've told you." Ravinia handed the slip of paper over and said again, "You do need to call me."

Elizabeth just nodded, too tired to come up with some clever remark about Ravinia not really needing a phone since she could probably "sense" when someone wanted to talk to her, but she kept that to herself.

It felt like she had to finesse the girl out the door and onto the porch. Just as she was about to shut it, Chloe came bouncing out of her room.

"What are you doing up?" Elizabeth asked her sharply.

Chloe ignored her as she waved to Ravinia, then asked, "Is that your dog?"

Elizabeth looked outside as a shadow passed across Ravinia and a gust of wind rattled the leaves in the trees at the edge of the lawn.

Standing in the doorway, one arm wrapped around Elizabeth's leg, Chloe pointed with her free hand, her index finger aimed at a copse of trees on the far side of the house across the street. "The big one. With the shaggy fur and yellow eyes."

Ravinia whipped around to see where she was pointing and Elizabeth said, "There's no dog."

"Yes, there is. He was right there!" Chloe insisted, frowning as she eyed Ravinia. "Right there. And you saw him, too."

CHAPTER 29

The door to the house shut firmly behind her and Ravinia immediately turned to watch the wolf slinking through the shadows,
hiding between two houses in the middle of suburban southern California. "What are you doing here?" she whispered. This was no place
for him. There were too many people, too many lights, too many
cameras, phones, and too much danger. If a neighbor saw him and
called the police, he could be shot or trapped or God only knew
what.

*If he's even real. Slow down. He could be a figment of your imag-
ination.*

But the little girl, Chloe, saw him, and she knew you did, too.

*Unless it was a neighborhood dog. She called him a dog, but she's
only four or five or so . . .*

*Or maybe she has her own gift . . . she is Elizabeth's daughter . . .
and that could mean anything.* "Genetic anomaly," *Aunt Catherine
called it.*

As the wolf's eyes glowed in the night, Elizabeth's porch light
clicked off and all illumination for the grounds faded quickly. Ravinia
glanced over her shoulder and noticed that each and every blind facing the street in Elizabeth's home was snapped tightly shut as if in so
doing she could cut her daughter and herself off from the world.

Just like Siren Song, Ravinia thought. *But it doesn't work. He can
still find you. Still get to you. You're not safe, Elizabeth. Not safe. Do
you hear me?*

She tried hard to send a message, but of course it didn't work.

She'd never been one who could send and receive mental transmissions. That was a singular gift bestowed upon only a very few, a line of mental communication between some of Mary's children or relatives, but one Elizabeth apparently didn't possess—which was a damn shame.

Ravinia thought of the message she'd thought she'd heard, that almost fuzzy sound. *Maybe you just wanted it so badly,* she scolded herself. She couldn't help feeling that if she were going to look as if she were a freak, she would really like to have something better than "soul searching."

Frustrated, she jogged back to Rex's car, which was parked around the corner, away from the cruising police car and the woman who'd knocked on Elizabeth's door directly before them. Ravinia had wanted to ask Elizabeth about her, but she'd barely gotten out her somewhat rambling explanation of her own half-sisters and Elizabeth's mother, Aunt Catherine. She wasn't even sure if Elizabeth had been listening closely. She'd seemed distracted and well, fearful, and anxious to boot her out the door.

The first meeting hadn't gone as well as Ravinia had hoped, and it kind of pissed her off that Rex had predicted as much. As she hurried to the Nissan, she heard the sound of a night bird calling and the whir of bats' wings, smelled the leftover smoke from a backyard barbecue, even heard the rush of traffic on a nearby highway. The neighborhood seemed idyllic, an American dream.

All that would change if Declan Jr. decided to take up his reign of terror on this serene street. Ravinia couldn't let that happen. She had to find a way to make Elizabeth believe her.

As soon as Rex caught sight of her approach, he switched on the engine and his headlights illuminated the vehicles parked in front of the Nissan and on either side of the neighborhood street. From the corner of her eye, she thought she saw the wolf, staying near the shadows, running in tandem with her, carefully skirting the twin beams of light.

"If you're real, you've got to leave," she warned, and the wolf turned its head to look at her again, golden eyes shimmering eerily for a second. "I mean it. Go away. Please . . ." The wolf held her gaze, then melted into the surrounding umbra and disappeared. "Thank you," she said heavily. Reaching the car, she opened the passenger door, flung herself into the seat, then slammed the door behind her. "Let's go."

"Who were you talking to?" Rex was reaching for the gear shift lever, but paused to stare at her as the interior light faded.

"What?"

He nodded to the passenger window. "You were talking to someone just now."

"Just myself." She scowled out the window and didn't think she was actually lying because she still wasn't convinced the wolf was real as opposed to something she'd just dreamed up . . . though Chloe had seen him. . . .

"I take it things didn't go well with Elizabeth."

Ravinia folded her arms over her chest as the damn seat belt alarm started beeping. Snapping it in place, she muttered, "You could say that." She shot a glance at Rex who was checking the mirror as he made a quick U-turn in the middle of the street. "She didn't believe me."

"Imagine that."

"She has to listen to me."

"You can't make her."

"Yes, I can. I have to. Something's going on with her. She wanted to believe me. She just . . ."

"It's a lot to swallow, and it's up to her now." He drove to the end of Elizabeth's street and turned on his blinker.

"Maybe she'll call me."

"Maybe."

Ravinia could tell he didn't believe her. Just one more person who wanted to think she was a crackpot. Well, fine. She'd go back to Elizabeth's tomorrow with or without his help and she'd find a way to get her to open up. If she would just trust in her a little bit, but then Ravinia hadn't really trusted in anyone, either. She threw a dark glance Rex's direction. She'd expected so much from him . . . had really thought this was her destiny and yet he didn't seem to care about her quest except for the payment she owed him.

Perturbed, she stared out the side window to the manicured lawns, trimmed hedges, and outdoor lights that set off the foliage. Well, Rex was right about one thing. It was up to Elizabeth now. Ravinia's mission had been to warn her and she had, but it felt like she'd fallen down on the job, that she should have convinced her of the danger or, better yet, stuck around to help her.

Whether Elizabeth believed her or not, Declan Jr. was probably on his way. If not already, sometime. She didn't know much about him, other than he was relentless. That, in itself, was why Elizabeth needed to listen to her.

Elizabeth peered through the blinds, holding one of the slits open with her fingers for a few seconds as she watched Ravinia jog down the street. Then she pulled her hand back and let the blinds snap into place. She felt a stirring within her, a reluctant acceptance of the fact that, at least partially, she believed the girl was telling the truth. Plenty of fantasy filled Ravinia's tale, too, she didn't doubt, but the bits of truth woven into her yarn were compelling. A part of Elizabeth wanted to step onto the porch and call Ravinia back, ask some probing questions, get answers, find out more about Siren Song, the women who lived there and their gifts. Especially their gifts.

Ravinia seemed to believe Elizabeth's foreshadowing was one of those gifts.

"Come on," she said, leading Chloe to bed once more.

"I really want a dog," the little girl said, stomping her feet.

"I know."

"And you won't get me one!" She climbed into bed and buried her face in her pillow. Elizabeth rubbed her back, but she wouldn't turn around. It was only a few minutes before her breathing deepened and she was asleep once more.

Elizabeth walked back to the kitchen and pulled out a bottle of Chardonnay and a wine glass, pouring herself half a glass. Eyeing the liquid, she knew it wouldn't be enough to get her to sleep. Detective Thronson was dead, Ravinia Rutledge claimed she and Elizabeth were related, and Elizabeth's ability to predict disaster moments before they occurred was a gift shared by her entire family. It sounded like a joke, put like that. It was a joke. *She* was a joke. She wanted to drug herself senseless. Drink herself into oblivion and damn the consequences. But she couldn't. Not with Chloe depending on her.

What do you believe?

"I don't know," she whispered aloud.

She did want to know more about her birth parents and her family, and Ravinia acted like she had the answers. Did she? Or, was this a really elaborate scam perpetrated by an accomplished con artist?

She'd named Catherine Rutledge as Elizabeth's mother . . . was that true? If so, why had she given her up? What sort of danger was so great that she'd abandoned her as a baby? And what about her father? Who was he? Was he still alive? Where was he? How did he figure into this? Did he care, or even know, that she existed?

If what Ravinia had told her was the truth, did she have any siblings? It sounded like she had cousins galore, ones who'd been sired by any number of men who'd come in and out of Mary Rutledge's life.

Elizabeth considered calling Catherine, through the number for Ophelia's cell phone, but did she really want to? What would she say? *I think I possess one of your gifts—or maybe two! It looks like I can save people, but I can kill them, too. . . .*

Her headache had ramped up again and started to throb. She needed sleep, about three days' worth, but she'd settle for seven, or even six hours, would that her mind could rest enough to allow it.

She tucked Joel "Rex" Kingston's card into a drawer in the kitchen and, after double-checking the locks on the doors and the latches on the windows, and one last peek in on Chloe who was resting comfortably, her cheek lying on the pillow instead of her face pressed down into it, Elizabeth unbelted her robe and walked to her room where she tossed the robe onto a nearby chair, then washed her face and finally sank gratefully onto her bed.

For a second, she stared at the far side of the mattress where Court had slept. She placed a hand in the spot he'd occupied and felt the emptiness, the sheets stretched over the mattress pad. He'd been her husband, Chloe's father. But whatever love she'd once felt for him was long gone. She was sorry he was dead. Really sorry. He should never have died, nor should have Whitney Bellhard.

Elizabeth closed her eyes and exhaled slowly, feeling the air go out of her lungs. For some inexplicable reason, she saw Rex Kingston's face in her mind's eye. She'd hardly gotten more than a glimpse of him, but somehow his image lingered. *A pleasant face, a mouth made for kissing,* she thought drowsily.

Her eyes flew open in shock. A mouth made for *smiling*. That's what she'd been thinking. He seemed like a nice man, the kind that would help you if you were stranded beside the road with car trouble, the kind who would help a friend put in a patio, or teach a child like Chloe how to ride a bike.

"God . . ." *You really are losing it, Elizabeth. With everything that's happened, this is what you think about? This is the vacation from your thoughts you've chosen?*

She was so annoyed with herself that she was suddenly wide awake. Punching her pillow, she flopped down on her back and tried to drift off again but her thoughts kept churning over and over. *Detective Bette Thronson's dead and Officer Maya seems to think you had something to do with it. The media's gotten hold of your save at the restaurant and your friends know it was you. You wished them dead . . . you wished them all dead . . . Chloe said he loves you, but he did some bad things. . . .*

Though Elizabeth dozed off and on, she always awoke with a start, fear breaking through her subconscious, only to realize she and Chloe were home and safe, then drifting away only to wake again and check the digital readout of her clock throughout the night. Some time after four AM she fell into a deep sleep only to drag herself awake at the sound of Chloe's bare feet scurrying along the hallway. Frightened, her eyes popped open and she eyed the clock again. Six thirty-seven. Morning.

"Ugh." she said wanting to burrow back into the blankets and sheets. No time for that. Throwing off her covers, she told herself to face the world even though she was sure there wasn't enough coffee in the universe to kick start her after that miserable night. But she needed something, *anything* to get her through the day.

Chloe had already climbed onto a bar stool and was waiting for her breakfast when Elizabeth entered the kitchen. She looked no worse for wear after being woken up by Ravinia and Rex Kingston. Her mind touched on him again and she felt heat suffuse her cheeks. She instantly wanted to turn away in embarrassment, more at herself than anything her young daughter would notice.

"Hungry?" she asked with forced brightness.

"Uh-huh."

"Let's do something about that." Intent on heating leftover coffee in the microwave, she poured a cup from the half full pot before catching herself. Wait. Just how long had the sludge been sitting on the kitchen counter? One day? Two? Longer? Didn't matter. She tossed the murky dregs into the sink, washed the carafe and started over with fresh grounds and clean water.

As the coffeemaker gurgled to life, she pulled a box of cereal from the pantry, poured her daughter a bowl, added milk, and set it in front of her.

Chloe looked at her with solemn eyes. "You want to talk now?"

"Are you ready?" So much had happened, Elizabeth had thought Chloe had forgotten their deal.

"Can I eat first?"

"You bet. I've got to get ready anyway."

Elizabeth quickly went through her morning routine, starting with a quick shower. Normally, she cranked up the hot water to just below uncomfortable, but today she threw the taps to cold and dunked her head under the spray. Frigid water blasted her and she gasped in shock. She shampooed her hair in record time. Good . . . great . . . she needed to wake the hell up and push aside all her fears. And she also needed to freeze out crazy thoughts of Rex Kingston's mouth.

A few moments later, she switched off the taps, briskly toweled off, then grabbed up her robe, cinching it around her waist. *Brrr . . .* But it felt good, too.

She returned to the kitchen and found the coffee maker had hissed to a stop. Pouring herself a cup, she watched Chloe slide her bowl across the counter. Elizabeth caught it just before it plunged over the edge to crash on the floor.

"More cereal," her daughter demanded.

"More cereal what?"

"More cereal . . . please?"

"You know you're a carb-freak, right?"

Chloe's little eyebrows knitted. "Not a freak."

"Poor choice of words," Elizabeth agreed but didn't add that she, with her visions, was certainly the freak in the house. She found the carton of milk in the fridge and topped off Chloe's small bowl so that the Cheerios were swimming again. "Do you know who this man is who did some bad things?"

"You mean, the one who loves you?"

"I guess so, yes."

Chloe shook her head.

"You don't . . . um . . . see him in your mind?"

"Uh-uh. He just says how much he loves you, and you're going to find out pretty soon." She moved her spoon around in her bowl but had lost all interest in her cereal.

"I'm making you uncomfortable."

"I don't like him very much."

In a terrible moment, Elizabeth's coffee cup halfway to her lips, it occurred to her that her own sudden interest in Rex Kingston was an aberration. Was he the man Chloe seemed to be sensing? "It . . . um, he wasn't the man who came to the door last night, was he?"

"What man?"

"The one with Ravinia?"

"No," Chloe said, looking at Elizabeth as if she were way off base. "Was that his dog?"

"I don't . . . think so." She was relieved that Chloe had been so positive about Rex.

"Are we done with the deal now?" she asked anxiously.

Elizabeth nodded, then left to work on the tangle of her hair and to get dressed. She dried the still wet strands, twisted them up into her ubiquitous messy bun, then brushed on enough makeup to disguise the dark circles under her eyes. When she noticed that the bedside clock that had been her tormentor during the night was registering eight-fifteen, she found her cell and, though it was low on battery life, put in a call to one of the numbers Ravinia had given her. The Tillamook County Sheriff's Department.

"Could I speak to Detective Savannah Dunbar?" she asked when the phone was answered.

To her surprise, she was immediately connected.

"Detective Dunbar," a woman's voice answered evenly.

"Oh, hi. Uh, my name is Elizabeth Ellis. I live in southern California and I got your number from Ravinia Rutledge."

"She called you?" The woman sounded dubious.

"No, I met her."

"In California?" She sounded surprised.

"Yes."

"Huh."

"So, you do know her, then?"

"Yes, I know Ravinia."

So far, so good. "She's down here because she claims she and I might be related and, well, she had a lot to tell me about Siren Song and the women there. You've heard of it?"

"I've been there, and I've met with Catherine Rutledge a number of times. She's the matriarch, I guess you would say."

"And she's Ravinia's aunt?"

"Yes. Do you mind me asking you how you're related?"

"I can only tell you what Ravinia told me." Elizabeth then relayed the highlights of Ravinia's story.

Detective Dunbar confirmed that Ravinia's tale was both fact and lore. "I can't explain everything. I've seen some things that would make me . . . want to know more, if I thought I were related. You understand?"

"You're talking about the gifts, as Ravinia called them?"

"I don't know what to call them, but I guarantee you, the women of Siren Song are unique. If you're one of them, you should make the effort to meet them. They don't have a phone, but it's worth—"

"I have a number for a cell phone. Ophelia's, I believe."

"Oh, well, good." The detective hesitated. "Any chance you could meet them in person? If I had any advice for you, that would be it."

"Yeah, I hope to," Elizabeth murmured. Swallowing, she screwed up her courage and asked, "Can any of them predict the future, or . . . or sense something dreadful happening before it occurs? I know that sounds ridiculous, but Ravinia alluded to a few things. I didn't want to just call. I just . . ." *Didn't want to sound like a lunatic or find myself talking to a bunch of lunatics.*

After a moment of dead air space, the detective said, "Ravinia would probably know. Well, or maybe Catherine."

Catherine. My mother . . . "What about wishing a person dead?"

"How do you mean?"

"I mean, like if one of them hated someone, or were enraged by them. Could that woman from Siren Song, say . . . could she get angry enough to literally cause their death?"

"No."

"What about any of them causing bodily harm to someone?"

"No. Excuse me, how did Ravinia find you, Ms. Ellis?"

"Do they have a brother?" Elizabeth blurted out. "Maybe a half-brother, someone who's . . . dangerous. Really dangerous?"

"Ravinia told you about Declan Jr."

It was like a second dousing of cold water. *It was true . . . oh, dear God, it was true!* "Who was he? She hasn't been specific."

"He's a fugitive from the law. He threatened a number of people, and he killed my sister."

"Oh, I'm so sorry." Elizabeth was shocked. Ravinia hadn't told her that.

"I believe he's dead as well, but his body was never discovered, so his death was never confirmed. He's listed as missing."

Cold fear filled Elizabeth's heart. Was it possible that everything Ravinia had said, including her dire warning about imminent danger to Elizabeth and Chloe, was the truth?

Elizabeth glanced out the window over the sink to the backyard where a bit of sun was peeking through the wintry clouds. Could unseen eyes, even now, be staring at her from some hiding place?

"Declan Jr.," Elizabeth repeated, her fingers surrounding her cell phone in a death grip, panic causing her lungs to constrict as she repeated the name Ravinia had given her.

"Ravinia warned you about him. She still thinks he's alive."

Insides shredding, phone pressed to her ear, Elizabeth looked at her daughter who'd lost interest in her Cheerios and was twisted around, fumbling with the remote, trying to turn on her TV shows. Normally, Elizabeth refused to let her watch in the morning as it was such a rush to get her out of the door to preschool.

"If there's any chance she's right," the detective said, "I'd advise you to avoid him and if you do see him, call nine-one-one immediately."

"Yes. Thank you. I will."

"Can you tell me what this is all about?"

"No, it's nothing. Nothing specific. I just wanted to see how much I could believe of what Ravinia was saying. It was so outlandish, that I didn't know what to think."

"She can tell a tall tale now and again," the detective said slowly. "But in the main, I think she believes what she's telling you. Again, I would meet the women of Siren Song, if I were you."

"Thank you . . . thank you for your time." Elizabeth hung up. Quickly. Aware that she had really gotten more questions than answers.

282 Lisa Jackson and Nancy Bush

Chloe had slid off her stool and was standing in front of the television, trying to find her channel. Sometimes she was capable, sometimes not.

"Chloe, brush your teeth and get dressed. I'll help."

"I can do it myself," she insisted, dropping the remote onto the couch and running toward the bedroom wing.

Elizabeth heard drawers being opened and shut as she tasted the remains of her cold coffee. Making a face, she poured the rest down the sink, then looked over at her cell phone where she laid it on the counter. Slowly, she picked it up again. With Detective Dunbar's confirmation about Siren Song, she was tempted to call Ravinia and get more information. Maybe even admit that she had her own gift, the foreshadowing of horrific events. Or, she could call Rex Kingston . . .

Nope. No. She set the phone back down on the counter and took a step back from it as if it were poisonous. Rattled, she picked up her empty cup and was pouring fresh coffee when the doorbell rang, startling her and causing her to slop hot coffee onto her hand. "Ouch!" She dropped the cup onto the counter, where it rolled drunkenly, spewing coffee in a spreading brown pool, over the edge of the counter and down her cabinet fronts. She grabbed up a dishtowel to mop up the mess as Chloe sang out, "I'll get it," and ran toward the door.

Elizabeth dropped the towel and saw Chloe streak by, naked except for her underpants.

"Oh, no you don't!" She was able to grab one little arm with her free hand before Chloe reached the doorknob. "You don't know who that is. We don't answer the door until we know who it is, and we always wear our clothes."

"You had your jammies on last night," Chloe argued, jerking her arm free.

"Better than just undies. Now, go on. Scoot. Wear the red dress and tights."

"I *hate* that dress," Chloe said, throwing her mother an angry glare as she stomped back to her room.

Her hand still smarting where the coffee had burned it, Elizabeth peered through the peephole mounted into her front door. Shifting from one foot to the other, once again was Officer Maya. And she wasn't alone, but the man with her wasn't DeFazio, her original part-ner. This man was dressed in a rumpled suit and tie and his heavy face was grim and sober.

A detective, Elizabeth thought, and as she opened the door, she braced herself for what was clearly going to be a continuation of what had started out as a very bad day.

CHAPTER 30

It was obvious that Detective Maya thought Elizabeth had something to do with Detective Thronson's death. And Maya wasn't alone in her theory. Detective Driscoll, the middle-aged, grim-faced man with her, seemed in complete concurrence with the other officer.

Driscoll was starting to go bald and had a bit of a paunch, but, she suspected, he was still tough as nails. He didn't bother combing what was left of his graying hair, and behind rimless glasses his light brown eyes had that *I've seen it all look* that said nothing she would say would shock him.

Elizabeth told herself she probably shouldn't have let the cops in, but she hoped being forthcoming would convince them that she was totally innocent and that she had been nowhere near Bette Thronson's home at the time of her murder. For God's sake, she had no idea even where the woman lived, and she said as much to Driscoll and Maya as she led them to her kitchen, adding, "I've got to leave to take my daughter to school in twenty minutes."

"This won't take long," Driscoll assured her.

From that point on, the interview was all business and, whether they'd said as much or not, she knew she was a person of interest. Driscoll took notes on a small spiral pad while Maya set a tape recorder on the middle of the table. She advised Elizabeth that the conversation was being recorded, then pressed a button so that the recorder's tiny light glowed red, indicating that it was functioning and recording every word she would utter, the kind of thing that could be used as evidence against her should they find her guilty.

She felt her hands start to sweat, but nodded, waiting for the interrogations.

After Driscoll explained where they were and who was in the room, he started asking questions. "Where were you on Tuesday night?"

"Home. I never left after Detective Thronson was here."

"Can anyone verify that?"

"Not really."

Driscoll then asked a number of innocuous questions, and finally circled around to Court's death. Once again, she was queried about the same things Thronson had asked her and once again she could only say she wasn't on the highway outside San Diego, and that she'd never been to Tres Brisas Hotel in Rosarito Beach.

Chloe came out of her room and stared at them suspiciously.

"Go get your shoes on," Elizabeth said, shooing her from the room. She checked the time, feeling anxious. It was clear that Thronson hadn't revealed what Elizabeth had told her that she'd wished Mazie, Officer Daniels, Court, and Channing Renfro dead . . . and that they'd all died. And Maya must not have considered her claim of wishing Court and Mazie dead worth even mentioning.

Driscoll asked, "Did you know that Detective Thronson considered you dangerous?"

"That's ridiculous. I'm a suburban mother. A recent widow. Do I look dangerous to you?" Elizabeth demanded.

He scratched behind his ear. "Not really." His tone suggested that her appearance was of little significance. "She also thought you were connected to some of the murders we're looking into."

Elizabeth's breath caught. "What murders?"

"Well, your husband and Mrs. Bellhard."

"I just told you I was nowhere near his car when it crashed." She pointed to the tape.

"Your boss at Suncrest Realty, Mazie Ferguson, was in a fatal accident a number of months ago."

Elizabeth glanced at Maya, who didn't react. Maybe either she or Thronson had revealed what she'd said. Should she admit again about wishing so many people dead? She'd been immediately sorry she'd blurted out the truth to Thronson and then . . . later that night, apparently, someone had killed her. "I've been straight with you. Over and over, but you're never satisfied. I didn't kill Court. I swear it. He was my husband and I don't have it in me. Mazie's death was an accident. There's nothing more to say." The last words nearly choked her and she saw the red recording light, burning bright. "You know, I think we're done here. I don't think I should talk to you, or anyone from the police department, without my lawyer present."

"If you've got nothing to hide—" he started, but Elizabeth held up a hand.

"I've got to go. I've tried to cooperate and help you. God knows if there's a killer on the loose I want him behind bars. But the more you ask me questions, the more I get the feeling that you're hoping I'll confess to something. I had nothing to do with Detective Thronson's death or Mazie's or Court's." She half-expected Maya to call her out, but she didn't. "And I have my own private detective on my husband's case, since I'm losing faith in the police," she blurted out at the end.

"Who's that?" Driscoll asked.

She hesitated and behind his glasses, Driscoll's eyes glittered. "Rex Kingston. Kingston Investigations." Driscoll blinked at the name, but Elizabeth rolled on tautly, "So, we're done here. " She stood and escorted the cops outside.

As soon as they were off her property, she gathered up Chloe who'd been standing in the hall outside her bedroom, watching them, shoes on her feet. Before she entered the garage, Elizabeth walked into the kitchen again and found the business card for Rex Kingston she'd tucked into the drawer the night before. Fingering it, she wondered if she should call, make good on her empty threat in case Driscoll followed up, which she suspected he would do. It felt like she had to do something or she would slowly drown in a sea of false allegations.

You're not charged with anything, Elizabeth. Slow down. Don't panic. And how would you afford to pay him?

That part she would figure out, she decided. But she certainly wouldn't be able to raise her daughter from jail if she were actually arrested. Good Lord, could that really happen? Even if proven innocent, it would take a while and there would be those who blamed her, anyway. Her reputation would take a beating and she might not recover professionally. Even worse, her life would become an open book. She was already having trouble explaining to her friends what had happened at the restaurant. What if everything came out? She thought of Ravinia, what she'd said of the women of Siren Song and all their oddities. If that were true, and she was that way, her connection to the cult-like family would be exposed. And Chloe . . . what about her? Where would she go if her mother were incarcerated for even *a day*?

Yes, she had to call someone and Rex Kingston, stranger that he was, a private investigator who had once been with the police force, was her first choice. She could go into the office, finish up a little paperwork, then meet him somewhere. Would he think she was crazy? No, probably not, as he'd been with Ravinia and apparently bought into her wild tale.

"You like him," Chloe said.

Elizabeth turned to find her child had followed her back inside when she'd come back for her purse. "What?"

"You like him. You thought he was the one talking to me, but he's not and that makes you happy."

Elizabeth shook her head and slid the card into a side pocket of her purse. "Come on, let's get into the car."

"You don't want anyone to know you like him," Chloe said.

"Where're you getting this? I don't even know the man." Elizabeth stepped into the garage and opened the back door of her Escape. Her daughter's comments bothered her, not just the content, but the perception.

Chloe climbed in and buckled herself into her car seat.

Not for the first time, Elizabeth wondered if her daughter had a little bit of precognition, too. Some kind of ESP or "gift" as Ravinia had called it. "Please, God, no," she muttered, thinking of her own trials growing up with a sixth sense. A curse, she decided and toyed with the idea, as she had all night, of calling the cell phone number on Ravinia's list and asking for Catherine.

What she really wanted was just to forget everything, for a little while, but with Detectives Maya and Driscoll breathing down her neck, that wasn't going to happen. No, Catherine of Siren Song would just have to stand in line.

"You will," Chloe predicted, her little chin set as Elizabeth backed out of the garage.

She would call Rex as soon as she got to the office. "I will what?" she asked but had lost the thread of her conversation as she moved into traffic. In the shafts of morning light bathing the interior of the car, she glanced in the rearview mirror and saw her daughter's serene face.

"You will know him," her daughter predicted. "Rex."

"What makes you say that?"

"When people love each other, they stop at nothing."

A chill went down Elizabeth's spine. "Where did you hear that?" she asked sharply. It was not the kind of phrase in her daughter's lexicon.

Sensing she'd given something away, Chloe just shrugged, and no matter how Elizabeth prodded she wouldn't say anything more.

The call from Elizabeth came into Rex's cell around midday. He'd been watching a client's bookkeeper, another surveillance job, keeping tabs on a woman the client suspected of embezzlement. Money was missing from the candy and card shop owner's personal account and he'd thought his bookkeeper had been cooking the books, but so far, following Louise Mendez had only proved that the extra time she spent on her lunch hour was to visit her mother at Resting Hills Retirement Home.

She was back at work, so Rex dropped the surveillance and was driving to the office. His cell rang when he was nearly there and he recognized the phone number as belonging to Elizabeth Ellis, information he'd gathered last night after Ravinia had gone to her room and closed the door. He'd stayed up until one AM learning everything he could on Elizabeth Gaines Ellis. It turned out she was a lot more interesting than he'd first thought, and he even had a call into Mike Tatum, a friend who'd worked with him in LA and now was with the Irvine PD, a cop who occasionally assisted him with information not available to the general public, but only when he felt it was warranted.

Elizabeth was calling. He felt his spirits lift as he wheeled into the office parking lot and answered. "Kingston."

"Hi, this is Elizabeth Ellis," she said as he cut the engine. "I think I might need your help."

He checked the time. "Okay. With what?"

"It's the police," she admitted. "They keep coming around. They even came by this morning and taped me. They haven't said it in so many words, but I get the feeling that I'm their number one suspect in my husband's death, maybe a couple others, including Detective

Bette Thronson's who was apparently shot in her home sometime Tuesday night."

"It just hit the news," he told her. "When she didn't report in, they gave her a few calls, but they didn't find the body for nearly twenty-four hours."

"He didn't say any of that."

"They try to give you as little as possible, hoping you'll hang yourself with inaccuracies in your testimony. What do they have as evidence against you?"

"I don't know. I don't have an alibi for the window of time when the murder occurred, but there's nothing else." Her words were coming faster and faster, as if she wanted to get them out rapidly, as if she were scared suddenly. "I was home the night she was killed and . . . and well, the police think I'm lying. Well, that's what I think. Look, I didn't know where she lived. I couldn't have . . . I didn't . . . I didn't even wish her dead!" She sounded frantic.

"Whoa. Slow down. Where are you?"

"At Suncrest Realty, where I work. But could I meet you? Maybe at the house?"

He remembered her not letting him inside the night before. Things must've changed drastically. "When?" he asked, climbing out of the car and slamming the door shut behind him. It would take awhile even if he turned around right now.

"How about two-thirty or three?" she suggested.

He checked his watch as he crossed the parking lot, the warmth of winter sun against his back. "I could be there around three. That'll work."

"Good," she said on a heartfelt sigh, then she said good-bye and hung up quickly, almost as if she were afraid she might change her mind, or maybe that she could be overheard.

He sensed something was bothering her, something she was holding back, but then clients did that all the time. He just hoped she'd be forthcoming when they met again.

When they met again . . .

He pictured her as he'd seen her standing in the doorway, vulnerable and determined at the same time. She'd gotten to him so quickly it made him want to hide in his office until this madness dissipated.

He'd learned a lot about her over the past eighteen hours, but she was still a mystery, a beautiful woman with a secret or two. Fascinating. Tempting. Emotional trouble, at least for him. He knew better, though he'd never been hit by Cupid's arrow so fast. It was downright embarrassing. On the other hand, when he'd tried to settle for an uncomplicated woman, one with her heart on her sleeve, like Pamela, he'd been bored to tears and anxious to move on. He'd left her wondering what she'd done wrong and the simple answer was nothing. He was looking for something more.

He already knew with a woman like Elizabeth, that something more was there. He'd felt it in those few minutes he'd met her. Crazy stuff. He had to get over it. She was a potential client, the subject of another client's search. Nothing more. And he barely knew her.

Shaking his head at himself, he walked down the back hallway to his office mentally kicking himself.

Get real, he told himself.

Bonnie, vigilant as ever, yelled from the reception area, "You've had a couple calls."

As he was dropping into his desk chair, she appeared in the doorway, holding a glass of some protein or diet concoction she was always blending in the small kitchenette and copy room. "Dorell Cochran. He wants you to do another tail on the Mrs."

Cochran already knew as much as he needed. Rex snorted. But who was he to turn down business. He was staring to think it was some kind of dysfunctional game the Cochrans played with each other. *Maybe they have fabulous makeup sex,* he thought and his mind drifted to Elizabeth Ellis before he shut it down and said harshly, "I'll call him."

"And a detective from the police department phoned, too. Driscoll. But he didn't leave a number. Said he'd call back."

"Did he say what he wanted?" Driscoll, if Rex remembered right, worked in homicide at Irvine PD. He'd have to ask Tatum about him when he called back. *Does this have to do with Elizabeth? Why would Driscoll be calling me about her already?*

"No. And I wouldn't give him your cell."

"Good thinking." Rex was distracted.

"So . . . where's your little friend?" Bonnie was leaning against the open door to the reception area and sipping the green goop from her glass.

"Um . . . you mean Ravinia?"

"You two have been like joined at the hip lately."

"That case is closed," he said, though that was a bit of a lie. It had morphed into something else with Elizabeth. "I'll work up a bill. Give you my hours." If he was going to get to Irvine in time for his meeting with Elizabeth he was going to have leave soon to avoid traffic.

"She got an address where I can send it?" Bonnie asked dubiously.

"Let me worry about that." Actually he was thinking that Ravinia might want to work off more of the bill by checking out Kimberley Cochran again, but he didn't admit as much to Bonnie.

The phone rang again and Bonnie scooted out of the doorway, presumably back to the reception desk.

"If it's for me, I'm not in," he shouted. "I'm outta here in fifteen."

She didn't respond to him, just said sweetly, "Kingston Investigations," as she took the call.

Pushing his chair back, Rex walked to the open door and closed it. Returning to the desk, he put in another call to Mike Tatum.

His ex-partner picked up. "I was just about to call you," Mike said obviously recognizing Rex's number, "but I haven't had a minute. We're swamped down here, more homicides in a few weeks than we've had in months." He paused for a second. "And that woman you asked me about? Elizabeth Ellis? Turns out she's right in the thick of it."

CHAPTER 31

"Where're you going in such a hurry?" Pat asked as Elizabeth breezed past Suncrest Realty's circular reception desk.

"Home. I'll be out for the day."

"Don't you have some appointments?" Pat questioned.

"Everything's rescheduled."

"But—"

"Really, Pat," she said, sensing the other woman's disapproval. "I've got my appointments covered. You don't have to worry."

Pat's back stiffened and she narrowed her eyes suspiciously. "I keep things organized around here. Running smoothly. It's my job."

"And we all appreciate it," Elizabeth snapped back as she shouldered her way out of the office. She could feel Pat's angry gaze boring into her back. *Too bad.* She couldn't worry about hurting the receptionist's feelings and truthfully, she was tired of treading lightly around the woman who seemed to make everyone else's business her own. It was definitely time for a change. Maybe, not only would she sell her house, but she could switch offices, or find a rival realty company where she didn't feel her personal life was being dissected through lunchroom gossip or over glasses of wine at happy hour in nearby restaurants.

Tossing her briefcase into the passenger seat, she settled behind the wheel. Despite the time of year, the interior of the car had warmed up as if it were at the equator, so she rolled down the windows and thought about her upcoming meeting with Kingston. How much could she reveal to him? How far should she bare her soul?

You have to tell him everything. Otherwise he won't be able to help you. You've already confided in your friends, so this won't be so hard. He's a professional. He'll help you.

"I hope so," she said, her hands gripping the wheel as she drove out of the lot and picked up speed, a soft California breeze tangling her hair. "God, I hope so."

On the way to Elizabeth's, Rex pieced together what he'd learned from Mike Tatum, which was supposed to be on the QT as Tatum had probably given out more information than the department may have wanted, and from Detective Vern Driscoll, whom he'd called back after talking to Tatum. Both men had said much the same thing about the Courtland Ellis case, which was why Rex had called Tatum, and why Driscoll had phoned Rex. The scuttlebutt around the department was that the widow was up to her eyeballs in her husband's death.

Bull. Shit. From what he could tell, the police didn't have a pot to piss in when it came to facts. He got that emotion was running high because one of their own had been killed, but it was early days in an investigation that hadn't gotten much past the theory stage. Thronson had been running on hunches as far as Elizabeth was concerned. So, a woman who may have looked like her had been seen on the freeway, possibly goading Ellis into a dangerous game, and another woman had been seen around the Tres Brisas hotel. Rex heard from Tatum about the positive ID on a picture of Elizabeth by several of the hotel's employees, but even Tatum had sounded skeptical. "Ask the right questions of someone who wants to please and you get the right answer. You know."

Yeah, Rex knew. Sometimes it was too easy to coerce a witness. They could be influenced by a few carefully chosen words. He also knew that he could be just as swayed if he wasn't careful. Look how he'd reacted to Elizabeth after meeting her once.

As he drove, he thought back to the conversation with Driscoll.

Driscoll asked pointed questions about how Rex knew Elizabeth Ellis. He kept his tone neutral and his answers circumspect. And what was there to tell anyway? He'd met her the night before. A client of his had been searching for her.

Who? Driscoll wanted to know, his tone sharp.

"Her cousin, Ravinia Rutledge, who had never met her until last night, either," Rex answered.

"So, you find her for her cousin and then Ellis hires you right on the spot?" Driscoll asked.

Rex discerned that it was Driscoll who'd scared Elizabeth into phoning for his help, so rather than lie, he shrugged and smiled. "Guess my reputation preceded me."

Driscoll went on to demand Ravinia's phone number or address, but Rex wasn't interested in revealing how involved he'd become with her life, so he said, "She's from a town in Oregon, on the coast, Deception Bay. I don't have an exact address."

"Why don't you?"

"I think it would be fair to say that she's between residences right now."

"Then give me the motel she's at." Driscoll started to sound belligerent.

"When you tell me why it's so important you talk to her," was Rex's answer.

"I don't have to tell you anything," the cop blustered. "But if I find out they're in collusion together, you don't want to be the guy who was in the way."

"They're not in collusion together."

"This is a homicide investigation," he reminded tightly.

"I can give you her cell number," Rex finally conceded, knowing Ravinia wouldn't answer if she didn't recognize the number calling in. He wanted to talk to her first, warn her about the police interest in Elizabeth.

The conversation with the detective went downhill after that. Driscoll pushed for Ravinia's address, where he could find her in the Irvine area, but Rex didn't cave. He asked his own questions about the Ellis investigation, chiefly, wasn't there any other person of interest?

Driscoll hadn't liked that question much, so Rex took that as a no.

"Thronson believed Courtland Ellis's death was a homicide," Driscoll told him flatly. "She was a thorough investigator. She spoke with Elizabeth Ellis several times and was killed shortly after that last interview."

"So she goes to Thronson's house and shoots her. Just leaves her *kid at home alone, somehow gets her hands on a gun, and drives over to the detective's house and takes her out."*

"She's connected, Kingston. You were a cop. You know how it works. The spouse and family are first at bat and it turns out Elizabeth Ellis didn't much like her husband. Can't say as I blame her. He was a cheating, bastard lawyer, but there it is."

"And so, Thronson learned something incriminating? And Elizabeth felt threatened and decided to kill her?"

"Thronson was on to something."

Rex scoffed. "Come on, Driscoll. This is thin and you know it."

But Driscoll seemed to dig his toes in deeper. Rex argued with him, but the detective was bullishly focused on Elizabeth. Rex had known other officers of the law who became single-sighted when their emotions got twisted into the mix. Driscoll wanted Thronson's killer bad, and Elizabeth was in his crosshairs.

Pushing the speed limit down the freeway, Rex felt a new sense of urgency. He'd left Ravinia at his house and now speed dialed her on Bluetooth.

"What?" she answered. "I'm down to my last minutes."

"Goddammit, go get some. The police will be calling you," he advised.

"Why?"

"They appear to be zeroing in on Elizabeth, thinking she might have had something to do with her husband's homicide."

"What?"

"I'm meeting with her now. When they call, be careful. It would probably be best if you avoided talking to Driscoll or Maya or anyone else until we can sort this all out."

"We're working a case for Elizabeth?"

"*I'm* working a case for Elizabeth," he stressed.

"Hey, I'm included in this, and I need to be there."

"I'll handle this and keep you informed."

"Like hell. She's my cousin. I brought you into this."

"This is a homicide investigation, and that takes things to a new level. You don't have the experience."

"I know things," Ravinia snapped. "Elizabeth asked me if I've been watching the news, so I've been watching the news."

"Ravinia—"

"She asked me that after I questioned her about how she knew about the bridge falling down when she was a kid. So, that's what I've been doing all morning. Watching the news. You know about the old guy who ran his car into that restaurant around here? The one who died?"

"I heard about it, but that doesn't—"

"Would you just shut up and listen? A woman was there when it happened. Ran in and saved this kid and his parents who were sitting right in front of the window. Swept up the kid seconds before this car slams right through the window. Woulda killed them all if she hadn't grabbed the boy. But everyone says there's no way she could have seen the car coming, like she claimed. She was there too soon. Ahead of the accident. But before she could be interviewed, she disappeared into the crowd. That's what Elizabeth was trying to tell me last night. She was that woman, and she understands she has a gift whether she wants to admit it or not."

"What I know is that Detective Vern Driscoll is determined to prove that Elizabeth was involved with his partner's recent murder."

"I'm coming. You need me."

"I'm meeting Elizabeth now. I'm not picking you up."

"Then you tell her I know about the restaurant. You tell her it's her gift! You—"

The phone went dead in his hand. "Ravinia?"

She'd finally run out of minutes.

He's here.

Peeking through the shuttered blinds, Elizabeth watched the Nissan whip into her driveway and lurch to a stop just short of the garage, Rex behind the wheel. In aviator sunglasses, a day's growth of beard shadowing his chin, and his lips compressed into a blade thin line, he climbed out of the car and half-ran up her walk.

It's now or never. You have to tell him everything.

Heart in her throat, Elizabeth opened the door and resisted an unlikely urge to throw herself into his arms. He was a PI, for God's sake, little more than a stranger. He wasn't her savior.

She moved aside just as he reached the door and stood back. He didn't hesitate, just stalked inside.

"Thank you for coming," she said, her heart beating faster than it should. She shut the door behind him, then, for good measure threw the dead bolt.

"Tell me about the police," he said as he surveyed the inside of the house, almost like a burglar casing the joint. "Why do they think you're a suspect in your husband's murder? I want to hear it from you."

"They think I look like this woman who was on the freeway . . . and at a hotel in Rosarito Beach where my husband stayed with . . . Whitney Bellhard."

"I know all that. What else?"

"I don't know. There isn't anything else."

To her shock, he placed his hands on her shoulders and looked directly into her eyes. She could see the striations of cobalt and royal blue in the gray depths of his. Her heart beat hard and deep. Her mouth was dust.

Tell him. Tell him now.

Elizabeth took a deep breath. "Ravinia said that some people, especially people associated with her family, sometimes have unique abilities."

"Yes, she's told me that."

"And you know she thinks I'm her cousin. That my mother is her Aunt Catherine who gave me up for adoption." She licked her lips, drawing his eyes briefly before they returned to stare into hers. "Ravinia said a lot of things last night and I was listening, but I didn't hear it all. It doesn't matter. I kind of knew where she was going."

"Because you predicted the pedestrian bridge falling before it happened."

Elizabeth nodded, feeling her knees sag a bit. "I may need to sit down."

In truth, she was relieved when he released her, and she walked on rubbery legs to the couch. He followed her, but stood against the kitchen bar, arms crossed over his chest.

"But that's not all I can do, apparently," she said, clenching and unclenching her fists. "I can see danger before it happens, but I can also wish people dead. Don't think Ravinia knows about that one," she added on a short laugh.

"You're going to have to explain," he said after a beat.

"If I get angry enough at someone, furious to the point of seeing red, they suddenly befall some horrid fate and die. At least, that's what's been happening recently."

For a moment, silence filled the room, then he broke down and laughed. "You're putting me on."

"I know what it sounds like."

"No, seriously. What is this?"

"I told this very thing to Detective Thronson the night that she was shot."

"You were mad at her? What'd she do that made you so mad?"

Elizabeth opened her mouth, then shut it again. He was making fun of her, but he'd inadvertently made a point. "No . . . I wasn't. Not mad. I was scared, though."

"Well, it's impossible to wish someone dead," he said, controlling his mirth when he realized she was being serious.

"Is it? You've spoken to Ravinia, heard what she has to say about her family who all live in that lodge, Siren Song. And I know you won't believe me, but I sometimes feel danger when it's coming near me."

"You were at the restaurant the other night."

"Yes! How did you know?"

"You told Ravinia to watch the news and she did, and she put two and two together."

"So, you believe, a little, that I do have this ability?"

"I believe that sometimes the unexplainable occurs. Most of the time, however, there's a helluva lot more logical reason than ESP, or whatever you're talking about. And I don't believe you can wish someone dead. Killing someone takes action. Forethought. Execution of the plan. If you could really wish someone dead, there wouldn't be anyone left on the planet."

"Four people that I wished harm are dead. Four." She then told him about Mazie, Officer Daniels, Court, and Channing Renfro. "I had interactions with all of them and one time or another they really pissed me off. Then boom. They were gone."

"Okay, then, try this. Have you wished anyone harm who's still living?"

"Well, I'm sure I probably have . . ."

"Recently. These deaths were recent, so have you wished someone dead recently."

Barb. "My sister-in-law really got under my skin when she was here after Court died."

"She still alive?"

"Yeah, as far as I know. She lives in Buffalo."

"Call her. See if she's okay."

"I'm sure she is," Elizabeth said, but she dutifully placed the call.

Barb answered on the fourth ring, sounding harried. When Elizabeth said she was just calling to see how she was, Barb snorted. "I'm fine. Just busy."

"I won't keep you," Elizabeth said and hurriedly hung up.

"So, she's okay," Rex pointed out.

Elizabeth made a face. "Barb's never really okay."

"A joke. Oho! So, you can lighten up a little."

She blushed a little, liking this side of him. It took all her energy not to stare at his mouth and wonder what it would feel like pressed to her lips.

"Couldn't it be coincidence, sheer unluckiness, that you're linked to their deaths?"

She shook her head, then said slowly, "I'd like to think so, but I don't believe it. Something is there."

"Then what is it?" He was pushing her to think more rationally, but it wasn't rational.

"Maybe . . . I'm being set up," she said, voicing a theory that had crystalized just recently in her mind, one she'd rejected at first pass. But with Rex's probing questions, she considered it again. "Maybe someone knows that I've had a problem with these people and he's killing them and framing me."

"Why would anyone go to all that trouble?" Rex asked.

"I don't know."

"How could he know who to target? The murders, and I use the term loosely as a couple were accidents, occurred not long after you had nasty thoughts about the victims. Right?"

"Yes . . ."

"Well, who could know all of that?"

She shook her head again.

"Any one person you confided in? Told how you felt about every one of the victims?"

"I talk to my friends, and I could have been overheard, like at the gym or in a restaurant or at work or on the phone, I guess. A lot of people might have heard me grumble about GoodGuy or Court or

Mazie . . . but . . . I never told the same person all of it, until I told Detective Thronson."

"It doesn't read right," he told her. "What would be the motivation?"

He said he loved you, but I think he did some bad things. Chloe's words. And then there was Ravinia's warning. *Declan Jr. He could be looking for you, if he knows about you . . .*

Rex said, "I want to hook you up with a friend of mine. Miles Cunningham. He's a defense lawyer."

She turned her face up to his and asked anxiously, "You think I'm going to be charged?"

He frowned as if wrestling with a decision, then said bluntly, "I think you could be, so you need to be prepared. They have no case, but you need to be proactive. The first thing you need to do is find a place for Chloe."

Elizabeth jumped to her feet. "I'm not sending Chloe anywhere. What the hell are you talking about?"

"I think any case the police are building against you won't hold water, but we need to be ready. You're the one who thinks you're being framed," he reminded her.

"Railroaded. That's what I think."

"Whatever. You need to be ready."

Things were bad enough, but from the look in Rex's eyes, he expected them to get worse. A lot worse.

"Okay," she said in a strangled voice. But who could she even think about taking care of Chloe for an indeterminate time? No one! Not her father, certainly. Barbara lived across the country. She was too far away physically and too emotionally distant. That left her friends in the Moms Group. She thought seriously about Tara and Jade, but couldn't imagine having to rely on either of them.

"I'd better get going," Rex said. "I'll call Miles and tell him you'll probably contact him."

"Okay."

"And find a place for Chloe."

"I will," she promised, hating to see him leave. It wasn't because he was handsome, though he was, and it wasn't because she felt like she had to have a man to protect her—oh, God no—not after her marriage to Court. But something about Rex Kingston touched her down deep. Silly as that sounded and as scared as she was, she couldn't help thinking what it would be like to lose herself in him. Have him hold her. Caress her. Assure her that things would be okay. Sleep next to him, make love to him. . . .

With an almost physical effort, she pushed those thoughts aside. Still, as she stood on the front porch and watched his car drive away she felt more alone than she had in a long, long while. A tug on her heart warned her to be careful, that she could make another mistake. She knew nothing about him, though she had noted he didn't wear a wedding ring.

"You are crazy," she admonished after his car disappeared around the corner at the end of the street. She went back inside, locked the door, then pushed her hair from her face. What the hell was she going to do? She couldn't remain passive and just hope that Rex could help her. He'd told her to be proactive where Chloe was concerned.

She caught her reflection in the foyer mirror. Fear shone in her eyes, and frustration dragged her eyebrows into a fussy line. "Stop it," she told her image. "Figure this out. Rex may help you, but this is your problem. *Do something* about it. For you and for Chloe."

My hand presses onto the vellum, ink flowing as I write, telling Elizabeth all my hopes and fears, expressing that love has two sides, one light and uplifting, the flirty side of affection. But as night is to day, there is also a serious side to love, a deadly side, if you will. Some may call this need and obsession, but I know it's just another expression of the true soul, that which lies in the darkest chambers of one's heart. I've felt it. I've acted upon it. I've sacrificed for it and I would again, in a heartbeat, for you, lovely Elizabeth, for you are, without a doubt, my true soul mate.

But as I put my words to paper, I sense another presence, and I feel you wavering. What is this unforeseen attraction you have to that investigator? He may call himself Rex, but he's no king. He's common and unworthy of you. And you want him. My blood boils with outrage. How could you betray our pure love?

How can you desire him? Lust for him, in its basest of forms?

Yes, that's what it is, lust and need, a dependence on this man you've barely met. I feel your filthy yearning and it comes upon me in sickening waves of disgust.

Elizabeth, you are mine. Do you hear me? Mine.

You cannot give yourself to another, nor can you have the slightest want for someone else.

Rage envelops me and I close my eyes and send you a mental message. Hear me. I am yours. Totally. And you are mine. Without doubt. Without regret. *Ours is a love forged in the stars, a love that knows no bounds, with no beginning and no end.*

You cannot care for another.

You cannot feel a breath of desire for anyone else.

If you do . . . if you cannot be true, if you cannot share my soul, then yours is mine to take.

I send this message, loud and clear. Hear me, Elizabeth. You are mine.

As I fling my mental missive, my physical body, zapped of strength, crumples and I knock the stack of letters I've written onto the floor. We fall together and the envelopes scatter around my weak, corporeal self.

I have to gather my strength. Slowly, with determination, my body responds again, regains its strength, and I sweep the letters into a pile and carefully stack them all. Now is the time for us. No more waiting.

Get ready, Elizabeth. I'm coming for you.

CHAPTER 32

Elizabeth suffered through another sleepless night. More nightmares plagued her. The victims who had died that she'd known, all came to her throughout the night. Their faces ran together and she was talking to them. Court in his BMW, Mazie at the office, even Channing Renfro at what appeared to be the gates of hell as flames were drawing nearer, ever nearer. As if in a movie, their faces melted before her eyes.

She tossed and turned, throwing off the covers only to draw them up again, glancing at the clock as she awakened. In the middle of the night, she was caught in yet another dream, but it was different, so real and visceral. She was lying in her bed not alone, but with a naked man whose long sinewy body was stretched over hers. Strong arms held her, warm breath teased the whisper of hair at her temple, and a wet, wicked tongue played at her ear, then slid along her neck and down her breastbone, touching, flicking, tasting and dipping lower as need pulsed within her.

Her blood heating, she was eager to love him, anxious to feel all of him, her skin flushed with perspiration as he toyed with her, causing the blood to rush through her veins, heat and desire swirling inside her. Her toes curled as he touched her, fingers skimming, gooseflesh rising, nipples tightening.

God, how she wanted him, though he was but a stranger, a man she'd just met and whom she already relied upon.

Rex, she realized. All she wanted was to make love to him.

Eyes closed, she writhed on the bed sheets. Her entire world centered on what he could give her. "Please," she moaned as he slid up her body, but then he stopped abruptly. His warm fingers turned to ice. Desire, so recently white hot, chilled.

As he dragged himself upward, his breath turned foul, his fingers skimming her ribs hard and bony, his hands burned and scaly. In the darkness, she saw his face, mangled and bloody, shards of bone poking through flesh where skin had melted off.

She woke on a shriek that echoed in her ears, heart galloping, sweat standing on her skin, another scream dying in her throat. The nightmare had been so real, so terrifying that she could have sworn the monster had been in bed with her. In the dark of her bedroom she waited, listening, willing her pulse to slow. Had she woken Chloe with her screams?

Half-expecting to hear frantic little footsteps charging her way, she let out her breath slowly. The house was silent as a tomb, until the soft rumble of the furnace blowing air throughout the ducts started up, a homey sound. Rolling over, she looked at the bedside clock glowing brightly, affirming the fact that it was three fifty-seven in the morning.

Ugh. Too early to get up, she thought, but climbed out of bed anyway to use the toilet and rinse her hot face with cool water. Grabbing onto her courage, she walked through the house but found nothing out of the ordinary. *Thank God.*

Before returning to bed, she slipped into Chloe's room to check on her and found her daughter sleeping soundly, her face down on the mattress, covers pooling onto the floor, pillow pushed aside, one arm flung down the side of the bed. Out of habit, Elizabeth pulled the bedclothes back into position and tucked them around her daughter.

With a sleepy moan, Chloe rolled over and opened an eye. "Mommy?" she said groggily.

"Yes, sweetie, it's just me. Go back to sleep."

"I don't want to die."

Elizabeth shivered. "You're not going to die. I'm here."

Around a yawn, her daughter said, "But I don't want you to die, either."

"Of course not." She patted her daughter's little shoulder. "I'll try not to. I think you've had a bad dream." She knew all about bad dreams.

Chloe drifted off to sleep.

Elizabeth took another round through the house, snapping on light after light, opening closet doors, double-checking locks and latches until she was convinced she and Chloe were locked safely away from whatever terrors lived in the rest of the world.

But even as she told herself that they were safe, that nothing could harm them in their home, she experienced a frisson of fear slip down her spine. All that she'd known and trusted had been shattered in the past few weeks and she sensed the horror wasn't over.

She walked to the living room window and peeked through the blinds. The neighborhood appeared serene and dark, bluish in the filmy glow from the street lamp. Elizabeth's gaze scraped over the neatly trimmed shrubs, the few cars parked on the street. Her heart lurched painfully when she caught sight of movement, a black shadow in the night, then realized it was only a cat, scurrying across a neighbor's lawn to disappear into the shrubbery.

"Get over yourself," she whispered but experienced another little zinging feeling, as if there were a disturbance in the atmosphere, as if someone, hidden in the shadows, was staring back at her. She let go of the blinds with a snap, chiding herself for her fears.

And yet, though the blinds and shades were drawn, the doors shut and locked, she sensed that someone was silently observing her, almost close enough to reach out and touch.

The hairs on the back of her neck lifted and a tremor swept through. She forced herself to open the door that led from the kitchen to the garage and peer inside. Nothing. Her Escape was just where she'd parked it, the garage door down, the room empty.

For the love of God, Elizabeth . . .

In her bedroom again, she left the door ajar so she could hear Chloe should her daughter wake with some other bizarre statement. Figuring there was no way she'd ever fall asleep again, she found a paperback she'd started a couple months ago and nearly forgotten. She found the spot she'd left off, remembered the thread of the mystery and read for twenty minutes, before the book became as heavy as her eyelids. She finally snapped off the bedside lamp and drew the covers close to her neck. Within minutes, she fell into a dreamless sleep and didn't wake until nearly seven o'clock.

Chloe, too, slept in, so Elizabeth took advantage of the quiet time to make a fresh pot of coffee, run through the shower, and get dressed. With the dawn came a fresh perspective, and surprisingly she felt herself ready to tackle the day. The worries of the night before faded. *Thank you, God*. It felt like she was out of time, and maybe she was. She wanted to get everything taken care of in case the worst case scenario happened and Driscoll found a solid reason to arrest her.

She considered what to do at work. She needed to double-check with Amy Ferguson about meeting with her tomorrow at Mazie's house. She also needed to deal with the Sorensons, and a few others who had called, and check on the Staffords' home as they were still on their month long tour of Europe.

Through the window she saw shafts of sunlight splintering through a thin layer of clouds while the palm trees in the back yard moved gently in the breeze.

Another beautiful day in southern California. Her throat caught as she imagined herself behind bars, unable to see it. *No. That isn't going to happen. It can't.*

Drawing a breath, she set her jaw. She would call the attorney Rex had told her about, and then, depending upon his advice, probably come clean with the cops about her sense of foreshadowing and her connection to Officer Unfriendly and GoodGuy. It was what it was. They could do with the information what they wanted.

Would they believe her? Well, probably not, but maybe it was time to lay all her cards on the table.

At least she had Rex on her side and at the thought of him, the sexual dream came to her and she felt herself blush. Yes, it had turned into a nightmare, but before that it had been really hot. Mentally reviewing it, she felt a throb of desire in her nether regions that had her shaking her head in disbelief.

After downing the first cup of coffee, she left the cup near the coffeemaker, and headed down the hall to Chloe's room where she found her daughter rousing.

"Don't want to get up," the little girl grumbled.

"Sure you do." Elizabeth sat on the edge of her daughter's bed and rumpled her curls. "We have a big day today."

"Is Ravinia coming back?"

"I don't think so. I was talking about school."

"Oh." Chloe wrinkled her little nose. "Don't want to go."

"It's Friday. The last day of school for the week."

"Don't care."

"Tell ya what. Why don't you take a quick bath? We missed it last night and, oops, the night before. I'll help."

The bath, washing of hair, and brushing of teeth didn't go all that easily, but a little over half an hour later Chloe was clean and dressed and plopped in front of a plate of peanut butter toast and sliced bananas. After a few bites, her sunny disposition returned.

"I'll get the paper," Elizabeth announced as she carried a second cup of coffee to the front door. She was determined to keep a smile on her face in front of Chloe no matter what her frame of mind truly was.

She stepped onto the porch and scattered a pile of envelopes left on the mat, then spent the next few minutes gathering them up. They were all addressed to her, just her name, *Elizabeth,* written in longhand on each one. *Huh.* Looking up and down the street, she cautiously opened the last one she'd picked up.

> *Elizabeth,*
>
> *It's all for you. Do you understand yet? I've been hiding my feelings for so long, but now finally, I can let you know. I'm sick, you see. Sick with love for you. Heartsick. Soul sick. I'm going to give you everything you desire. I am your slave, your genie in a bottle. Command me, and I will deliver. I grow stronger because of you. You don't see me yet. I'm just a flicker in the corner of your eye. But you'll see me soon, my love. Very, very soon . . .*

She dropped the sheet of paper as if it had burned her. It fluttered off the porch and landed softly on the rolled up newspaper. She backed away, hand to her mouth, her eyes jerking back and forth, searching the quiet neighborhood.

"Mommy?"

Chloe's voice made her gasp, and she stepped inside and slammed the door behind her. Her daughter was still sitting at the kitchen bar, leaning back and looking down the hall, trying to see her.

"Just a second, honey," she called in voice pitched several notes higher than her usual tone.

Were they all love letters? Sick, strange love letters?

Cautiously, she reopened the door. Darting glances all around, she stepped out and grabbed up the pile of envelopes, then ventured down the steps to where the newspaper and the first letter lay, snatching them up as well. She scurried back into the house, shut and locked the door, and stalked quickly down the hall to her bedroom. Chloe couldn't read yet, but she sure as hell would see how shaken Elizabeth was. She needed to pull herself together.

"Mommy?" Chloe called again.

"I'll be right there," Elizabeth yelled back. She opened another envelope at random and read another message. The same, only darker . . . more obsessive. Her pulse elevated. *Who did this? Why?* Panic rose within her and she tried to tamp it down, keep hold of herself. Her dream flitted across her memory, and the uneasy feeling that she was being observed.

Something evil was going on. Something she didn't understand.

Why? *Who?*

Hearing the thump of her daughter's feet hitting the floor, Elizabeth straightened her spine and went back down the hall to meet her.

"Mommy? Where are you?"

"Right here, honey." She put a smile on her face. Seeing Chloe standing by the front door, she said, "Hey, are you finished? We'd better get your shoes on and pick up your lunch pail. Today we take home your preschool blankets and wash them. Gotta get ready for next week."

Chloe stared at her. "What's wrong?"

"Nothing. I'm just . . . lots to do, and I'm making lists in my head. Let's get those shoes on and head to school. We're late."

"Again?"

"Yep." She turned Chloe around and down the hall to search out her shoes, then racewalked back to her own bedroom, gathered up the envelopes, and shoved them in her purse.

In the kitchen, she snagged Chloe's lunch box and was standing by the door to the garage when her daughter appeared, her shoes on the wrong feet. Quickly, Elizabeth exchanged them and then said, "Let's go," much too brightly.

Chloe frowned at her, but didn't make a comment as she buckled herself into her seat.

Driving through the familiar streets, Elizabeth kept checking her rearview mirror, her thoughts whirling in her head. *Who left those notes on the doorstep? Who would be so bold? And who wrote them?*

Someone who said they were in love with me, but what kind of love was that?

Who?

"Chloe, that man you heard in your head who said he loved me? The one who did bad things? Do you know what he looked like, by any chance?"

"I don't see him."

"Okay." It was stupid to question her daughter. She was grasping at straws.

Hands slick on the wheel, she thought about Gil Dyne whose wife had maybe committed suicide and who'd taken a real interest in her. And Peter Bellhard. He still was calling and trying to connect with her. She'd hoped he would give up, but apparently he wasn't a man to take no for an answer.

When people love each other, they stop at nothing.

That was the tone of the letters, she realized, shooting a glance in the rearview mirror at her daughter. Just exactly like the words that had come out of Chloe's mouth.

She dropped Chloe off at school and checked her in. They were late enough that she didn't see any of her friends. After handing her off to the preschool teacher, Elizabeth said, "I'll pick you up later," and then hurried away, her purse feeling inordinately heavy with the notes inside. She realized she'd left her briefcase at home, but didn't care.

At the office, Elizabeth shoved her purse under her desk then called Rex on her cell. As the call connected, she again thought of the sexy dream where Rex was her lover. When he suddenly picked up, she felt a thrill race through her.

"Hey, Elizabeth," he said, obviously recognizing her number.

She damn near fell apart at the sound of his voice, but she held herself together. "Something's happened," she said quietly, just in case Pat or Connie or someone else decided to cruise by. "I'd like to meet with you again. The sooner the better."

"What is it?" he demanded, his voice was sober.

She swept her gaze to where she'd stuffed her purse. "I got some letters. Left on my front porch. I want you to see them."

"Who are they from?"

"Anonymous."

"Left on your porch?"

"In the middle of the night. I stepped on them this morning. They're . . . disturbing."

"I'm working from home today. You mind coming over here? It's private. Ravinia's out trying to re-up her minutes."

"What's your address?" Realizing she might be overstepping her bounds, she added, "I mean, if you have time."

"I'll make it." He rattled off an address in Costa Mesa. "You okay?"

"I think so. Yes."

"You want me to come to you?"

"No, no, I'm fine."

"Where are you?"

"At the office. Chloe's at preschool."

"You want to drive over now?"

"Yes." With that she grabbed up her purse again and hurried back to her car.

Rex met Elizabeth at the door and was reminded once again how beautiful she was, but he ignored it as he led her to the kitchen. She spread the letters on the table. He avoided touching the missives, all written in a clean, sharp hand, and all with messages of a twisted, one-sided, obsessive love. Dangerous love. Possessive love. One even going so far as to explain the "dark side" of love.

Whoever wrote them was one sick fuck.

And obviously involved in the recent killings.

He read the words over again.

I watched you tonight. Are you receiving my mental messages . . . we will both be transcended . . . soon the unveiling will happen . . . It's just us against the world.

Rex's guts clenched. Whoever wrote these was stalker-esque and obsessive. "You have no idea who sent these or dropped them off?" he asked and noticed how pale she was, how worried.

"None." She took a seat at the table, her back to the sliding glass door. She glanced outside and said dully, "You have a nice house. I like the backyard."

"I'm thinking of selling. Know any good real estate agents?"

She blinked at him, clearly deep inside her own head, processing. She could scarcely get past her fear and he didn't blame her.

"Anyone you know who could have written them?" he asked, spreading his hands above the scattered pile.

"No," but after a moment she reluctantly named two possible candidates. Gil Dyne and Peter Bellhard. "The tone of the letters doesn't really sound like either one of them."

Rex made a note to check them out. "What about people you meet who aren't friends, in other social or professional settings?"

"I have my Moms Group of friends and their husbands. That's where I met Gil. I have some clients, none of whom come to mind. Oh, and I recently went to a grief group, but that's all women."

"What about someone from your past? Old boyfriends? Lovers?"

"There really wasn't anyone but Court," she said, shaking her head.

Rex tried to explore that angle some more, but Elizabeth had nothing much to add. He was scheduled for surveillance again today, and going into the office later, but he'd cleared his schedule after she called. Nothing he was doing trumped her safety, and from the looks of these notes, she wasn't safe. "You'll have to hand these over to the police."

"You think that's a good idea?" she asked anxiously.

"It shows there's another player, and maybe that player left some of his DNA around."

"What if there is no DNA? What if the police think I sent them to myself?" Her voice was rising.

Rex said soothingly, "Let's not borrow trouble."

"I don't think the police are on my side. They could twist this around on me."

"You've got to trust someone."

She looked at him through moist, blue eyes. "I trust you."

That look got to him. He could feel every protective fiber in his body come alive. "I'll call Tatum. No, I should call Driscoll. Don't want to antagonize the man any further by going around him."

"Why did he send them? What does it mean? And why write so many?"

"Whoever it is, is making their play. You've got a stalker, Elizabeth, and that person is ratcheting up, growing bolder. More dangerous."

Her bones seemed to melt as she sank farther into the chair. "You think he killed all those people? Officer Unfriendly and GoodGuy and maybe Court? Mazie? I don't know."

"This guy's MO reminds me of John Hinckley Jr. The nut case who shot President Reagan to impress Jodie Foster."

Her face turned ashen. "Oh, God. No . . . no . . . he killed Detective Thronson, too. It doesn't make any sense!"

"Who says it has to make sense? You're talking about a psycho. And this note . . . where is it? Here we go." He read, *"Did you see, Elizabeth? Have you been watching? He got what he deserved and now he abides in whatever special hell is reserved for scum like Channing Renfro. I know there are others working against you. I've heard them, seen them, sensed them. But don't worry, we'll take them out together, one by one. I'm right behind you, love. Your savior, your soldier.*

"You don't see me yet, but you will when I'm ready.

"All for you, my love . . . all for you."

Rex stopped reading and said, "This is a confession. Whoever wrote these notes is behind the deaths. We have to go to the police."

Elizabeth seemed about to acquiesce when his doorbell rang. She started.

"Stay here," he ordered, then walked to the front door and peered through the window for a view of the front porch.

Staring back at him was Ravinia.

Dressed in her uniform of dark jeans and a long sleeved T-shirt, a jacket and backpack slung over her shoulder, she motioned that she didn't have her key. She'd taken off on foot this morning to re-up her minutes, but it looked as if that hadn't worked.

Rex hesitated. Did he really want her to see the letters? Did he want her involved in Elizabeth's case?

She glared at him. Her expression said it without words. *Well, are you going to let me in or what?*

CHAPTER 33

Ravinia sent Rex a speaking look as she walked past him into the kitchen. She knew he was trying to freeze her out in the homicide investigation surrounding Elizabeth and it irked her. Add to that, she'd failed to find a place near Rex's house in order to get her phone up and running again. And she'd realized he'd set up a rendezvous with Elizabeth while she was gone.

She would have gone on being piqued if Elizabeth hadn't given her a watery smile, turned her palm to the pile of envelopes on the counter, and said, "Looks like I have a stalker."

Ravinia dropped her backpack with a thunk and reached for one of the letters.

"Be careful. We're turning them over to the police, see if we can find any DNA that isn't ours after we manhandled them," Rex said.

Her hand froze midair and instead she leaned over one of the nearest letters. They were all laid out, so she could see them without touching them. She read them one by one, and felt the hair lift on her arms at their fervent tone. She read them a second time and frowned. Something about them struck a chord in her. What was it? Something she should recognize, something just out of reach. "They're weird."

"Obsessive," Rex said.

The phrases burned in her brain. "This person feels they can communicate with you mentally. Can they?" She gave Elizabeth a look, wondering if she'd been holding back on her.

"No," Elizabeth assured her.

"You sure?" Ravinia asked.

314 Lisa Jackson and Nancy Bush

"I'm positive. I know these notes say that the writer's sending messages, but I'm not getting them. Maybe it's all a lie anyway, designed to make me feel like I'm going crazy. If so, they're succeeding."

"Have you felt anything at all? Like maybe there's just something in the wrong frequency?" She could speak from experience on that one.

"No," Elizabeth insisted. "Nothing."

Ravinia gave up and glanced down at the cards. "These seem off."

"Ya think?" Rex said.

"They sound wrong for Declan Jr. and he's the one out there you need to worry about." She suddenly had a thought. "Detective Dunbar's the one you should talk to. She dealt with Declan Jr., and I bet she would help."

"Who's Detective Dunbar?" Rex asked.

"I called her last after you left," Elizabeth said at the same time.

"She knows Declan," Ravinia said, ignoring Rex who clearly didn't like being left out of the conversation. "She knows him too well. He tried to kill her."

"He tried to kill a police officer?" Elizabeth asked, looking to Rex in alarm.

"He wants us all dead," Ravinia told her. "All of us connected to Siren Song. All of us who are related. That's what I'm trying to tell you. He's the reason I came to find you. To make sure you're safe. That's what Aunt Catherine wants. *To make sure you're safe.* But you're not safe. This . . ." She waved a hand to the letters. "Maybe it's him. I don't know. But you should really get away from here as soon as possible." She snapped her fingers. "Go to Siren Song. Meet Aunt Catherine, and you can talk to Detective Dunbar in person. She's with the Tillamook County Sheriff's Department which is right there," she added for Rex's benefit.

"You just said this Declan is a killer," Rex stated flatly.

"But he's not there anymore. He's somewhere else. That's why Aunt Catherine was worried about you," Ravinia repeated, exasperated. "With everything that's happened to you, he's probably *here*."

"I can't just go," Elizabeth said, though her tone suggested that she was rolling the idea around. "I've got Chloe to think of. And Detective Driscoll would take it as a sign of guilt."

"Chloe can go with you." Ravinia was firm. "I don't care what that detective thinks. It's not true."

"She's right," Rex said, shocking Ravinia and making Elizabeth's head turn. "This killer's making his move. You need to go somewhere safe."

Elizabeth shook her head slowly. "I can't just drop everything and go to Oregon. For how long? Driscoll will come after me and lock me up, and who's going to take care of Chloe? I can't be away from her. I can't."

Ravinia stared down at the handwritten notes. They were giving her a headache, messing with her mind. She walked to the sink and stared outside to Rex's back yard. "Siren Song is a safe place and it's far away. Aunt Catherine has made it like a fortress. She's in charge. And she's your mother."

"We're not sure about that," Elizabeth said.

"*You're* not sure about it. I am. Besides, Aunt Catherine's a strong woman. Not afraid of looking evil right in the eye and doing whatever she has to, to protect us. All of us." Ravinia dragged her gaze away from the window and stared at Elizabeth. "The same goes for you. Maybe even more so."

"Why don't we shift you to a hotel for the time being," Rex said. "Think about what you want to do, but get out of your house. I want you to talk to Cunningham, get your defense started."

"I have a job . . ." Elizabeth said. "And I can't afford a hotel."

"We'll work that out. You just need to be safe," Rex said.

"But if I call Driscoll with these letters . . . maybe he'll realize someone else is out there and go after him. Driscoll seems entirely capable."

"But what about you?" Ravinia demanded. "And Chloe?"

"I can't think," Elizabeth muttered, climbing to her feet. "I have to go to the office."

"I'll go with you," Rex said.

She held up her hands. "I'd rather have you take the notes to Driscoll. I don't want to see him or talk to him. I have appointments at work. Thanks for the offer, but I can't afford a hotel and I'm not letting you pay for one."

"I'll go with you, then," Ravinia said, echoing Rex.

"No. Thank you."

Ravinia saw the way Elizabeth looked away from her and realized

316 Lisa Jackson and Nancy Bush

that, though she seemed to trust Rex, she didn't share that feeling about her. Elizabeth hadn't completely accepted Ravinia's tale of their family. It was damn frustrating.

"Call me every hour," Rex told her, which pissed Ravinia off all the more.

She didn't have a working cell, and she had a feeling Rex would try to shake her loose from him. Well, she was going to be like a burr, she determined, as Rex walked Elizabeth to the door. She saw the way he touched her arm and that kind of pissed her off, too. They were bonding in all kinds of ways, and yet Elizabeth treated her with extreme caution.

She's wavering. I can feel it. Not only has Elizabeth fallen for that stupid private detective, but she's actually considering leaving the area, leaving me. I can't let that happen. What's wrong with her? Didn't she read the notes I penned for her? Doesn't she understand the depth of my love? That we're destined to be together? That I would do any damn thing to be with her.

My fists curl in frustration and a headache pounds behind my eyes. I can no longer suffer this loneliness. I have to stop her.

Feeling sick, I lean against the freezer, my hands braced against the top of the big chest. I need to stop her. I can't believe that she won't wait for me, or come to me. She must've gotten my messages . . . I thought she would respond in kind but so far . . . nothing.

My heart is breaking.

My soul is shredding.

She can't leave me. Not now. Not ever.

I force myself to take several deep breaths as I conjure up my beloved's face. I long to touch her. To kiss her. To seal our love . . . our special love.

I can wait no longer. I head upstairs to the kitchen to find my keys and slip the ring into my pocket.

Today, I will go to her. I know where she'll be.

Today is the first day of our forever.

The day crept by. As she called Rex every hour on the hour, Elizabeth began to feel foolish. He had taken the letters to Driscoll who'd been noncommittal about his thoughts, but it made her feel better to know they were in the rumpled detective's hands. While she'd talked with Amy Ferguson and, of course, Marg and Buddy, who wanted to see yet more houses—a plan she'd put off until next week—Rex had been following up on Gil Dyne and Peter Bellhard. He'd interviewed both men and had struck out. Though he was leaving the door open, Elizabeth could tell he didn't feel either man was capable of writing such heartsick notes, and well, she felt the same.

She was meeting Detective Driscoll at Rex's place as soon as she picked up her daughter. Ravinia had gotten on Rex's phone once, re-iterating that she felt Elizabeth should go to Siren Song ASAP. Well, maybe, but first the detective.

She was late, as ever. If she didn't get to the preschool by six PM she was charged an exorbitant rate every fifteen minutes past the hour. She understood, but it didn't mean she didn't push the limit sometimes. It was two minutes to six when she finally wheeled into the lot.

Vivian was just leaving. She waved at Elizabeth and called, "What are you doing this weekend?"

"Working," Elizabeth called back.

"Not every minute. Let's go to the gym."

"Can Chloe come over?" Lissa yelled.

"Not tonight," Elizabeth told her.

"We'll talk," Vivian said, and drove out of the lot, her blond poof of hair visible through the back window.

Chloe was standing on one foot and then the other, the only child left in the room. She ran to Elizabeth and hugged her tightly.

"Sorry," Elizabeth said to the teacher as she gathered up Chloe's things. "Traffic was a nightmare."

"It's getting awful, isn't it?"

"Yessiree."

Chloe held Elizabeth's hand as they walked out, something she rarely did.

"You okay?" Elizabeth asked.

"Yeah . . ."

She slid Chloe a look and a cold feeling stole over her as she re-called Ravinia's words from the morning.

Have you felt anything at all? Like maybe there's just something in the wrong frequency?

"Chloe, have you been getting mental messages from someone? More than what you've told me?"

"What are mental messages?" Chloe was walking toward their car, but looked back at Elizabeth.

"Like in your head. You said the man loves me, but you can't see him."

She nodded soberly.

"Does he say other things?"

"He says lots of things. He's kinda mad now." And with that she ran for the car.

"Chloe!" Elizabeth hurried after her. "That's the wrong car!" she called as she realized her daughter had run to another vehicle that looked a lot like hers, only it was two spots away, closer to the exits and faced out.

Chloe had her hand on the door handle. "What?"

"That's not our car," Elizabeth said, pointing to her own Ford Escape.

At that moment, a woman slid around the side of the vehicle in question and moved toward Chloe.

Elizabeth looked at her blankly, then at the vehicle, a dark Ford Escape, and then to the gun in her hand that was leveled at Chloe's temple. "Nadia?"

"This is odd," Rex admitted to Ravinia. He'd spent most of the day tracking down Elizabeth's friends, the women from the circle she called the Moms Group and their husbands, though one of the women wasn't a mother. He'd also contacted the Sisterhood group who were singularly unhelpful.

He thought back to the conversations.

Because Elizabeth didn't want her friends to know she'd hired a private detective he told them he was with the police. He just asked them general questions, letting them think he was checking up on Elizabeth's story.

Jade Rivers told him flatly that she had nothing to say and neither did her husband, Byron. Looking at the list Elizabeth had supplied with all their names, their husband's names, and their places of work, Rex called Byron at work, but he wasn't much more forthcoming than his wife.

Deirdre Czursky admitted that Elizabeth and her husband were having problems, but she staunchly insisted that the police were pretty much all pigs and that she knew he was just trying to railroad her. She told him he should call up her husband Les. "In fact, I'll give you the number right now!"

When Rex put through the call, Les greeted him coldly, having been warned by his wife. He, too, told Rex he was barking up the wrong tree.

Tara Hofstetter said she was going to call Elizabeth up immediately after she got off the phone and tell her that the police were asking about her. And then she'd added, "She saved that family, you know. All of them. They would be dead if it wasn't for her, so you just leave her the hell alone!" Her husband Dave was actually taking a workday at home and said that Elizabeth should be considered a savior, and it was just like the police, and in the larger sense, the government, to get everything back-ass-ward.

Rex couldn't get hold of Vivian Eachus. Her husband, Bill, asked more questions than he answered but sung Elizabeth's praises as well.

"What's odd?" Ravinia asked, interrupting Rex's thoughts.

"Nadia Vandell hasn't answered her cell phone all day, so I finally decided to call her husband, Karl. He's an investment banker, and though Elizabeth didn't have a number for him, she knew where he worked. I just called his office, hoping he hadn't gone home yet."

"He wasn't there?"

"He wasn't there, but his boss still was. Looks like Karl hasn't been there for six weeks. His wife called his boss and said he'd up and left her and that she hasn't seen him since."

Ravinia stared at him hard. She was so still for so long that Rex's brows lifted.

"You okay?" he asked as he picked up his own cell and hit speed dial to Elizabeth.

When she didn't answer, he returned Ravinia's stare as he counted the rings for Elizabeth, staying on until the call went to voice mail.

"It's him," Ravinia said.

"Karl Vandell?" Rex's pulse leaped and he was on his feet. "How do you know?"

"I can hear him. No . . . I can hear *Chloe*. . . ."

"What the hell are you talking about?" Rex rasped.

"He's got Chloe and Elizabeth in the car!" Ravinia held her hands over her eyes and then suddenly yanked them away, her sea-green eyes distended wide with shock. "It's not him. It's *her*. Nadia Vandell!"

CHAPTER 34

In the backseat, Chloe had gone silent and Elizabeth tried to see her in the rearview mirror.

"Keep your eyes on the road," Nadia demanded, the barrel of the gun pressed tightly into the side of Elizabeth's rib cage.

"Chloe, you okay?" Elizabeth asked.

They'd been driving for about five minutes, heading west. Nadia seemed to have a destination in mind, but she wasn't sharing it with Elizabeth. She just wanted her to drive.

Chloe's eyes met hers and she shook her head slowly. "Where are we going?" she asked in a small voice.

Nadia glanced back for a brief instant. "Oh, it's somewhere your mom knows, back when our souls were still joined."

Elizabeth said carefully, "I don't remember it."

"That's because you broke everything," Nadia suddenly hissed at her, her face contorted. "Why did you do that? *Why?*"

Elizabeth stayed quiet, hoping Nadia wouldn't scare Chloe any worse than she already had, and it was no good trying to reason with her. She was past reasoning. When her cell phone had rung, Nadia had snatched it out of Elizabeth's purse, read the name, and shrieked in fury before tossing it out the window.

Elizabeth answered her in a voice infused with fear. "I shouldn't have broken it." She hoped she sounded regretful.

"You got that right, bitch." Nadia glowered, unappeased. "Your friends the Sorensons? You showed them all kinds of houses, but there was only one on the ocean with a spectacular view."

Staffordshire. "The house in Corona del Mar."

"Still for sale. Your *friends* couldn't afford it, but it's the best of what you showed them. The best. You remember the best, Elizabeth?" Nadia twisted the barrel into Elizabeth's side.

"I can't drive straight when you do that," Elizabeth said, and it was true.

"Well, fucking figure it out!" Nadia yelled.

They drove in silence for a while, then she said, "You don't remember me."

Is this a trick? "Um . . . no . . ."

"Good old Van Buren High. I was in the class below you."

Elizabeth couldn't think, didn't know how to answer her. A line of sweat was running down her back.

"I could feel you even then. I thought you felt me, too."

Elizabeth had no good answer to that. No, she hadn't felt Nadia, nor did she remember her as a school classmate, but she sensed if she admitted as much that it wouldn't go over too well.

"You think this is all coincidence? That I happened to join the Sisterhood, happened to become part of your Moms Group even though I don't have a child? I've followed you, Elizabeth. With my heart and soul. We're the same, you and I. We have abilities. You're amazing." There was awe in her voice. "But I had to find a reason to get close to you. Vivian's such a sap. She wanted to help me get over my miscarriages and begged me to join the Moms group."

Elizabeth shot another glance back to Chloe, who'd closed her eyes and appeared to be in a trance.

"Don't look at her," Nadia snapped, and Elizabeth focused her eyes on the road ahead of her. They'd reached the street that led to the Staffords' house . . . the Staffords couldn't help her as they were still outside the U.S.

"I've loved you a long time, but you don't love me." Nadia said it almost conversationally, as if she were really just rolling that idea around. "I wanted us to go to Mexico together. I like it there, particularly Rosarito Beach."

Elizabeth swallowed. "You were at the Tres Brisas Hotel."

"I saw Court with Whitney Bellhard. He was such a bastard to you. Why did you marry him?"

I thought I loved him. "I don't know," Elizabeth murmured.

They pulled into the drive and around the semicircle that led up to the house. Elizabeth tried to park under the portico, but Nadia said, "Drive onto the yard, toward the beach."

Elizabeth's pulse was pounding hard as she did as she was told. The house was one of the many she'd shown to Marg and Buddy, the only one directly above the ocean. Not much of a beach was below; rocks, dirt, and scraggly tree roots jutted from the cliff's edge. A low, wrought iron fence ran along the perimeter about ten feet from the cliff face, more for looks than safety. Directly in front of her was the Hobbit and Tolkien creature filled crèche and she swerved to avoid it.

"Stop here," Nadia ordered, then jumped out of the car and yanked open the back door, grabbing Chloe's arm and barely waiting for the little girl to unbuckle herself before dragging her onto the lawn, the gun trained at her head.

Sick with fear, Elizabeth climbed out of the driver's seat and held up her hands. "Please take the gun away from her. Put it on me," she said, her mouth dry. "Please."

"Please, please, please. Is that what you say to *Rex*?" Nadia snarled.

She knew about Rex? Of course, she knew about Rex. She knew everything.

Keep her talking, Elizabeth. Give yourself some time. Plan an escape.

"Rex Kingston was hired by my cousin to find me," she said.

"I know."

"I only met him a couple days ago. I barely know him."

"But you love him, don't you? *You. Love. Him.* Don't lie. You think I can't feel it?" Nadia dragged Chloe by one arm past the Hobbits, toward the backyard.

"Wait! Wait!" Elizabeth cried, her hands outstretched as they neared the barrier fence, which had Mondo grass growing on either side. Beyond was the ocean, a long, long way down.

So help her God, she would grab Chloe and save her daughter if it was the last thing she ever did.

Nadia stopped at the fence, breathing hard, as if she'd just run a marathon. Her icy blue eyes were wild, her blond hair tossed by the wind. "And what about Gil? On purpose, I spread the rumor that his wife killed herself, and you still didn't care! I tried to overlook it, but you kept on seeing him. You're too good to whore yourself out for money."

"I barely know Gil! I never wanted his money."

"I had to do something, but I got a bad angle on his car, and it smashed up Karl's." Her face grew brick red with anger at the memory. "So, I had to go back to mine."

"You sideswiped Gil . . ." Elizabeth realized the black Escape was Karl's car. Nadia's SUV was a dark blue Acura.

"All the things I've done for you, the sacrifices I've made, just so that you would have a perfect life, to ease the way into our melded future."

"What do you mean?" Elizabeth asked, though she already knew where this was going. *Keep her talking!*

Nadia moved the barrel from Chloe's temple and aimed it at Elizabeth's heart. "Mazie Ferguson. You wanted her dead, so you could have her job."

"No." Elizabeth shook her head.

"It was easy to convince her that I had money to buy whatever fucking mansion I wanted. Karl had enough money at first, before the stock market took it. Investment banker, my ass. He was too weak, and I couldn't afford to have him around anymore. But Mazie . . . she liked her wine as much as you do. I had to put a little something extra in her drink before I sent her on her way, but it worked. Kind of a shame she didn't take out another driver with her when she flew off the freeway. You know, California could really stand to lose a few motorists."

Sweating bullets in the cool air, Elizabeth's gaze shifted back to Chloe whose stillness was alarming.

"And then that police officer you told us all about?" Nadia went on. "The one that gave you the ticket? Officer Unfriendly? What a self-righteous prick. I took Karl's handgun, put stolen plates on my car, and sped by his police car on the freeway. Had to do it twice before the lazy ass finally decided to chase me. I drew him onto side streets to a place with big hedges that I'd planned out earlier, but it took awhile to get him there and he was *really* pissed when I finally stopped. Started screaming at me before he even got a foot out of his car. He charged up to my window and I just shot him. Two times."

Chloe finally opened her eyes and looked up at Nadia who had her left arm locked around the little girl's neck. Chloe gazed at her in shock and dawning comprehension. "You sent the messages. It was you. I thought it was a man."

"Yeah? You're not too smart, are ya?"

"Leave Chloe alone," Elizabeth ground out, her temper rising.

Nadia inhaled, almost in ecstasy. "That's it. That's the passion . . . oh . . ." She squeezed Chloe's head harder and pointed the gun back at her temple.

"Stop . . . stop! " Immediately, Elizabeth sought to quell her emotion. No . . . no . . . *Keep her talking!* "You were on the freeway with Court and Whitney Bellhard."

"I always knew you didn't love him. But then he started that affair with that bitch and all of a sudden you did care. You cared a lot. I could feel it. I knew it was time to show you I loved you."

"And Channing Renfro?"

"GoodGuy." Nadia snorted in disbelief. "Karl had everything in our basement. If he'd only just let things be, I wouldn't have had to . . ." She shook her head dolefully. "Everything would have been a lot simpler. But when he found out I loved you, when he saw the first notes . . ." She trailed off. "I used his Escape. Took one of the Molotov cocktails he'd made for me. Karl was really good at that stuff. And the gasoline can with the hose and nozzle. Threw the cocktail at GoodGuy's convertible, then aimed the nozzle at the bastard and sprayed him down. Such a fireball. I damn near got caught! But I didn't . . . because it's all meant to be. *All for you, Elizabeth . . . my love. . . .*"

"Stay in the car," Rex told Ravinia and she immediately started to protest. "You're not coming in with me, you understand?"

A hesitation, then, "Yes."

He checked his Glock. The safety was still on, and he intended to keep it that way unless he sensed trouble. Holding it down at his side, he moved to the Vandells' front door. No one answered his knock. He didn't wait, but walked around to the rear of the house and the back door. It was locked, but three good kicks and the wood splintered.

He didn't give a damn that he was breaking and entering. If Elizabeth and Chloe were inside . . . held captive . . .

The Vandells' house smelled of chemicals. Something sharp wafted through the air. He held the Glock in front of him and quickly recognized the smell was coming from an open door that led to a basement. He peered down into the gloom, then flipped on the light switch, waiting to see if something happened. No sound. Moving fast, he stepped lightly down the creaking wooden steps.

The smell of gasoline was strong. He traced it to a portable can tucked onto a shelf at the end of the room, a hose and nozzle attached. There didn't appear to be any gas leak or spill as he'd first feared. He saw two cans with wicks, and when he lifted one, it sloshed, heavy with fluid. *Molotov cocktails?*

Channing Renfro . . . GoodGuy, Elizabeth had called him.

Rex backed away, aware he'd left his own fingerprints on the can. No way to explain the B and E, but too damn bad. All he cared about was finding Elizabeth and Chloe.

"Rex?"

He whipped around, gun in hand, furious to find Ravinia at the top of the basement steps. "God damn it!"

"They're at the ocean," she said, talking fast. "Big house with lots of yard. Some kind of puppet scene in the yard. Short black fence and . . . a long way down."

"What do you mean? Elizabeth and Chloe? How do you know?"

"Do you know a place like that?" she demanded.

"I . . . no . . ." He felt his heart begin a hard, long beat. Ravinia's fear was infectious. "Puppet scene?" And then he knew which property. He'd seen it during his iPad search of the Ellises. "Corona del Mar," he said, scrambling through his brain for the address. "Get the iPad. It's in the car. Find Elizabeth's listings."

Ravinia was gone in a heartbeat as he stumbled for the stairs. He didn't know where she was getting her information and he damn well didn't care. ESP, alien transmissions, gifts from a divine source . . . she believed. And so he believed.

And he also believed Nadia Vandell was the danger.

He was halfway up the stairs, his gaze through the open stairway steps to the basement below when he saw the low freezer tucked in the corner. He almost left it, though it seemed to loom in front of his face like a beacon. Something about it.

Running on instinct, he jumped back down to the basement floor and in three steps was around the stairs, his hands on the freezer latch. Throwing the lid upward, he gazed down into the interior. A scattered array of Sara Lee pastry boxes, Texas Toast, and frozen steaks filled the space. He shoved them around. And four fingers suddenly jutted up, one with a wedding ring.

Furiously, he tossed the frozen goods out of the ice box and onto the basement floor, his breath coming fast.

Beneath was a gray face. Brown eyes open. Crystals on the lashes and across the forehead and receding hairline.

Karl Vandell, he guessed, and then he was running up the steps, two at a time.

"And Detective Thronson?" Elizabeth asked. "What about her?"

"I heard you on the porch with her. I heard you tell her all the people you wished dead. She wasn't going to give up. She thought I was you."

"She had a picture of me . . . and she showed it to the staff at Tres Brisas. They said it was me."

"That was a mistake," Nadia said. "I wasn't trying to get you in trouble."

The gun had slipped a little and was aimed toward Chloe's shoulder. Elizabeth swallowed against a dry throat. "Yeah? Well, you wore your hair like me. Must've been a reason."

"How many times do I have to tell you? *I love you.* I don't want to hurt you, but you're making me do this. I wanted to go to Mexico with you!"

"Then let's go. Right now. We can leave right now," Elizabeth said urgently.

"I'm not a fool. I know you don't love me, and that you're just trying to find a way to get rid of me. But that's not going to happen. Now, come on," Nadia muttered, jerking Chloe toward the barrier fence and the gray ocean beyond.

"Don't!" Elizabeth cried. "I will go with you. Maybe I don't love you yet, but I could. I never loved Court the way I should have. Maybe I'm meant to be with you from now on. Just don't hurt Chloe. I'll do anything you want, but don't hurt Chloe."

"You love her, but you don't love me."

"Please . . . Nadia . . ." Tears formed and ran down Elizabeth's cheeks. "Don't take her over the fence."

Chloe's eyes were locked onto Elizabeth's while Nadia glared at her with a mixture of frustration and yearning.

"You should have agreed to go with me," she said. "We could be in Mexico already . . . Rosarito Beach . . . or Acapulco . . . or Puerto Vallarta. I don't care! Have you been there? To the beaches?"

"Yes, they're lovely. I want to go with you."

"Liar! Why do you have to spoil everything!"

Elizabeth shook her head. She didn't know what to say. Chloe had closed her eyes again, back into her self-induced coma of sorts.

"It's his fault. *Rex!*" Nadia bared her teeth. "He's the one you want to be with."

"No, no . . . not Rex."

"You keep thinking you can lie to me. You think I don't know what love is? I cared about Karl, but I never loved him. I loved *you*. But I did care about him, and I'm sorry I had to let him go."

"What do you mean?"

She sighed. "I know you don't really care. You're just trying to stall."

"Tell me about Karl," Elizabeth stated firmly. "I want to know."

Nadia shrugged. "First I tried to reason with him, but he wouldn't listen, so I had to tie him up and gag him. He said *I* needed help." She laughed. "The whole fucking world needs help. So what? I believe in love, deep love. That's what I believe in, and I told him that. But what did he do? Just like you, he was trying to stall. He did work a hand free and get it around the base of a bedroom lamp. Stupid man thought he could surprise me, but I'm the one with surprises."

Elizabeth prayed Chloe was all right. The late afternoon sun was surprisingly hot. She could feel it digging into her scalp. *Stay calm . . . relax . . . be careful.* "What did you do to Karl?"

"I didn't do anything. He did it to himself."

"Where is he?"

"Oh, he's at home, but don't think he's coming to your rescue, 'cause he's not."

"How much farther?" Ravinia asked as Rex tore west toward Corona del Mar. He was passing cars and driving like a maniac and hoped to God he would pick up a traffic cop so that he could lead him to the house.

"Too far." He'd called the police, given them his name and number, and asked for a BOLO to put out on Nadia Vandell's car, just in case Ravinia's information was wrong. The dispatcher had sounded suspicious of him, saying he needed to talk to an officer. Rex snapped back, "The name's Vandell. Just like it sounds. V-A-N-D-E-L-L. Karl or Nadia." Then he bit the bullet and said, "There's a human body in the freezer at their house. I'm betting it's Karl Vandell. Send someone over there now."

He'd hung up before she could ask anything more.

"Can't you go faster?"

"What do you think?" he snapped.

Ravinia set her jaw and stared with laser-like intensity out the windshield.

Chloe suddenly spoke, her voice muffled against Nadia's blouse. "You won't hurt me, because if you hurt me, you hurt Mommy. And you love her."

"You don't know anything," Nadia snarled. She shook Chloe hard, put the gun back to her temple, and hauled her over the fence like a ragdoll.

Elizabeth charged forward and Nadia said softly, "Stop," in a voice that froze Elizabeth in her tracks.

"I'll go with you," Elizabeth pleaded. "I want to go with you!"

"Stop lying! You broke it, and there's no going back."

"Nadia, please. Give me a chance to prove my love. What do you want me to do? Just tell me."

She cocked her head to one side. "You want to prove your love? Come on this side of the fence with me."

"I will . . . but I can't until you let Chloe go."

Nadia gave a short laugh. "All I have to do is squeeze this trigger." Her blue eyes danced dangerously. "Very little pressure."

"No . . . no . . . I'll do anything you want. God, please. Anything."

"Then step over the fence." She waited.

The sound of the ocean seemed to fill Elizabeth's ears. She'd stalled as long as she could. She understood that Nadia intended to kill Chloe no matter what she said or did. Chloe was in the way . . . the true object of Elizabeth's love . . .

She moved forward and eased a foot over the rail.

Behind Nadia and Chloe sounded a backdrop of thrumming waves and the occasional loud *phumf* of raging water hitting the rocks below before shooting upward. And from the other direction the sudden squeal of tires.

Nadia cocked an ear and so did Elizabeth who was halfway over the rail.

In that moment, Chloe bit down for all she was worth into Nadia's gun hand, her jaws clamping hard into soft flesh.

The scream that hit Ravinia's ears chilled her blood. She was out of the car and running toward the back of the house, but she couldn't catch up to Rex who'd powered past her toward the women and girl on the other side of the fence. *The other side of the fence!*

"No!" Elizabeth shrieked as Nadia's scream died and she suddenly grabbed Chloe around her throat. Elizabeth leaped forward as Chloe became a whirling dervish, kicking and biting and struggling against her captor, all at the cliff's edge.

Ravinia was yelling, too, screaming anything and everything, as Rex vaulted the fence.

In slow motion, she saw Chloe break free just as Elizabeth slammed her body into Nadia's. Rex grabbed at them as the two women fell to the ground and rolled as one toward the brink. "Elizabeth!" he roared.

Nadia held onto Elizabeth with a vise grip. "We'll be together always!" she cried, jerking her body to the cliff's edge, dragging Elizabeth with her.

Rex lunged for a leg, nearly connected, but missed as the women's bodies were twisting and hurling left and right. Ravinia leaped the fence and grabbed Chloe, stumbling a little, getting an eyeful of churning white waves down, down, down below before pulling back.

Nadia's free hand scrabbled for the gun she'd dropped when Chloe bit her. She slammed it against the side of Elizabeth's head, but she couldn't get any power behind it. Elizabeth was fighting like a wildcat, scratching at the woman's face, screaming and kicking. But they were moving inexorably toward the rim.

"Elizabeth!" Rex shouted, grabbing her leg.

Nadia bared her teeth and sought to aim for him, but Elizabeth was too strong, smacking her hand against the ground, loosening her grip on the gun. Enraged, Nadia clamped herself around Elizabeth and rolled her free of Rex's grip.

And then they started to fall, Nadia's leg and arm over the edge, the momentum carrying them. Chloe screamed in Ravinia's arms and Ravinia was screaming, too.

The wolf came from nowhere. A silver shadow leaping the small fence with ease and launching at Nadia.

Ravinia shrieked, "No!!!" as Nadia and Elizabeth's locked bodies twisted in midair. But it was an illusion.

It was the wolf in the air with Nadia. Rex yanked hard on Elizabeth's leg and pulled her back to safety.

In another slow motion twirl, Nadia and the wolf went over the cliff, end over end, silver fur and blond hair, wildly flinging arms and sinewy, furred legs, a mouth open in a silent scream and sharp incisors sinking into human flesh.

Moments later, a small *thunk* echoed upward, faint amid the loud and restless waves.

Chloe wrenched free of Ravinia's grasp to run to Rex and Elizabeth, the three of them holding each other tightly.

Heart heavy, Ravinia walked to the edge of the cliff and gazed down into the water as another *phumf* of water shot upward. Though her anxious eyes scoured the shore for long, long minutes, there was no sign of either Nadia or the wolf.

CHAPTER 35

The air was lung-freezing cold, the grounds hard as iron around Siren Song in the last week of January. The huge lodge looked down at Elizabeth somewhat balefully, she thought, though she could see it might have an austere charm during the summer. Leaves on the surrounding bushes had been iced by Jack Frost, each vein limned in white. The headstones in the graveyard behind the lodge were cold and gray, brooding under a low, winter sun. Grim, it definitely was, but the women she'd met inside the lodge, her cousins, had greeted her with open arms as if they'd been waiting for her all their lives when she'd walked through the gates.

She stood at the edge of the graveyard beside Catherine and Ravinia, who'd made the trip north with her, though she seemed even more anxious than Elizabeth to get back to California. She was making a life for herself there, bound and determined to be Rex's assistant and partner in the private investigation business. Rex had come with them too, but was in a rental car outside the front gates, not allowed to enter as he was of the male gender, apparently one of Catherine's damn near unbreakable rules.

He didn't like it much, and neither did Elizabeth, but they had listened to Ravinia when she'd outlined the blueprint of what life was like at Siren Song. Both were trying to abide by the strange rules. Now Rex turned his thoughts to the time directly after Nadia fell.

Ravinia grew increasingly uncommunicative since the fight with Nadia on the cliff's edge. She told them it was because the wolf was probably dead, and though neither Elizabeth nor Rex knew ex-

actly what she was talking about, Chloe cried huge crocodile tears and said, "No, he can't be. He just can't be," which seemed to be something they shared between them. There also seemed to be some kind of telepathic connection between her and Ravinia as Chloe had told Elizabeth that she'd called Ravinia and Rex to the house where Nadia was holding them.

When Nadia's death, and the killings before it, hit the news, Vivian was beside herself, feeling halfway responsible for bringing Nadia into their Moms Group. She alternately begged Elizabeth to go back to the gym with her and pleaded with her to attend another Sisterhood session. Elizabeth promised to start back up with yoga, but she wasn't interested in the Sisterhood. Nadia had hidden her true self amongst the other members, and Elizabeth didn't feel comfortable there, anyway.

Detective Driscoll told Rex about the police investigation into Karl Vandell's death and the murders of Channing Renfro and Officer Seth Daniels. It appeared that everything Nadia had said to the women of the Sisterhood was an out and out lie. Her adoptive parents revealed she didn't even like children and didn't intend to have any. Nadia had merely used the multiple miscarriage story to garner sympathy to find a way into Elizabeth's life through Vivian. She'd joined the Sisterhood as a means to enter all their lives.

As for Karl . . . Nadia apparently killed him when he'd stopped being a reluctant assistant to her plans. His colleagues told Driscoll that Karl had initially welcomed her sudden interest in joining a women's group, hoping it would stem her dark spiral down into obsession. He worried that she would become fixated on something to the point of neither eating or sleeping. These colleagues believed that when he discovered her long-simmering, one-sided love affair with Elizabeth Ellis, she finally turned on him. Ligature marks were found around his wrists and ankles where he'd been bound and had struggled to free himself. It was believed he'd been deceased less than a day when Rex found his body.

But who was Nadia, and how did she have gifts? That question remained unanswered.

Ravinia told Elizabeth once again that she should go to Siren Song and meet her cousins and her mother. With the events of the past few weeks, Elizabeth was inclined to take what Ravinia said as truth, so she called Catherine on Ophelia's cell phone and reached the woman who claimed to be her biological mother. That had been a weird and stilted conversation, but Elizabeth also remembered Detective Dunbar's urging to meet them in person and so the trip was arranged.

They left Chloe in the Hofstetters' care for the trip north and heard from Tara that Chloe and Bibi were getting along swimmingly. Without Lissa's influence, the two girls had no problems. As far as Elizabeth knew, Chloe hadn't exhibited any further signs of her gift, so she was hoping that with Nadia gone, the worst of Chloe's "spells" would abate.

Rex stopped his musings to watch Catherine, Elizabeth, and Ravinia as they walked to the graveyard. It was just as Ravinia had said—long dresses and old fashioned style; huge wrought iron gates; an imposing wooden lodge with its blend of time past and modern touches; a long, pot-holed drive; a bevy of blond women; a wild and roaring ocean across a winding road. Catherine, herself, definitely looked like a woman from a different time.

The first meeting between Elizabeth and her mother had been as awkward as the phone call; Elizabeth wasn't one to embrace and hug and neither was Catherine. But their mutual desire for space had worked for both of them, and they'd slowly relaxed in each other's presence.

Many of Elizabeth's ancestors were buried in the graveyard. Catherine walked her between the graves and pointed out different names, giving her a brief history of their lives. Ravinia didn't say much as they wandered around. When Catherine was satisfied that Elizabeth was brought up to date, they walked to the back door of the lodge, but there Catherine had hesitated, looking back once more. Elizabeth and Ravinia stopped, too.

"Declan Jr.'s still out there," Catherine said, turning from the graves toward the west and the ocean.

"You feel him, too?" Ravinia asked, waking up a bit.

Catherine shook her head. "Do you feel him? I just believe we'd know if he was dead."

"I don't know what I feel." Ravinia backed off, turning away.

"You still think Declan Jr. will come after me?" Elizabeth asked Catherine.

"The boys in our family . . . seem to feel the gifts harder, and it becomes more dangerous with age. I don't like taking chances," she answered.

That was enough to give Elizabeth the willies and even Ravinia looked at her aunt and scowled as if she didn't want to hear it, either.

"Come inside," Catherine said, leading the way into the cavernous kitchen. She put a kettle on the stove and poured some loose brown leaves into a tiny basket and began steeping a pot of tea. Elizabeth expected some of her cousins to join them, but when she looked toward the living room, Catherine said, "I want to talk to you alone, so I asked them to give us some time."

"You want me to leave, too?" Ravinia asked. She didn't look happy about it, but sounded as if she would comply.

"No, I want you to hear this, too." Catherine turned to Elizabeth. "I thought Declan Jr. had followed your scent to California, but it wasn't Declan who came after you. It was a woman, which was something of a surprise, but now I think I know who she was. Lost Baby Girl."

"What?" Ravinia had taken a seat at the end of the table. "Lost Baby Girl. What are you talking about?"

"There was a kidnapping a long time ago," Catherine said in her precise way. "A woman who ran a private adoption agency had a baby stolen from her car. She'd put the baby in the car and then the phone rang inside the house. When she went to answer it, the baby was taken."

"No cell phone?" Ravinia asked.

"It was twenty-five years ago," Catherine said dryly.

"This woman . . . who left the baby in the car . . . she was trustworthy?" Elizabeth asked tentatively.

"We'd used her many times." Catherine looked at Elizabeth and then glanced away, and Elizabeth understood this same woman had been instrumental in her own adoption. "She was well-respected around Deception Bay. It happened so fast. No one knew what to think of it."

"Where's this story going?" Ravinia asked, but Catherine ignored her and kept talking to Elizabeth.

"Shortly after the Gaineses adopted you, this woman was brokering another adoption. She was only away from her vehicle a short amount of time, but it was enough for someone to steal the child. A baby girl. She was just gone, and no one ever saw her again. At the time, she was dubbed Lost Baby Girl by the press."

Ravinia demanded, "Why have I never heard of this?"

"Because you don't listen very well," Catherine said to her somewhat sharply.

Ravinia made a leap of consciousness about the same time Elizabeth did.

"Are you saying Lost Baby Girl was *Nadia*?" Ravinia asked. "She's from around here?"

"That's what I believe. The child's mother was a young woman whose father was considered a shaman in our nearest neighboring community."

"Those are the Foothillers," Ravinia said for Elizabeth's benefit. "I told you about them."

Elizabeth nodded. Though some of Ravinia's convoluted tale from the night they'd met had been lost to her, she remembered the Foothillers who lived in the unincorporated town next to Siren Song and were mainly of Native American descent.

Catherine went on, "This young mother had been involved with a man whom we all thought was long dead, but suddenly he was back and . . . creating havoc."

"Who was he?" Ravinia interrupted. Catherine gazed at her hard and Ravinia lifted her hands in surrender. "I just want to know."

"He was a very bad man. An evil man. What his relationship with the child's mother was . . . I don't know. I don't know if anyone really knew." Catherine's tone suggested it could be nothing good. "He was already gone when the baby was stolen, and he wouldn't have cared, anyway. The child's mother wouldn't admit that she'd put the baby up for adoption. It was rumored the shaman prohibited her from even claiming the child as hers. So, after a short, fruitless search, the whole thing was dropped as if it never happened. The local police did what they could, but the shaman and his daughter would not help them. Both of them died years ago, and the story died with them."

"What happened to the father?" Elizabeth asked.

"He's dead," Catherine answered with such finality that Elizabeth could tell there was far more to that story.

Thinking about it, she asked, "Was he related to . . . us?"

A long moment passed and then Catherine said, "Yes," adding quietly, "I'm going to tell you something I've never told anyone before."

Ravinia's head snapped around as if pulled by strings. Clearly, this was way out of character for her aunt. Elizabeth waited expectantly.

"About ten years ago, a woman from Deception Bay was dying of breast cancer and she asked to speak to me. Sheriff O'Halloran came to the lodge and wanted to know if I would go to her. I didn't know who she was, but I went to her at the hospital and she reached for my hand. She had the idea that I could help her. Not save her life, but maybe her soul. I tried to tell her that, whatever she'd heard about us, we weren't priestesses, but she didn't care. She wanted to confess, and she wanted to confess to me, so I let her.

"Her name was Lena and she and her boyfriend of the time were the ones who'd stolen Lost Baby Girl. They'd used a lawyer in southern California, much like my adoption broker did, only the lawyer Lena used didn't require as much in the way of documentation, apparently, and so the deal was done. Much later, Lena learned that the child she'd stolen was the shaman's granddaughter, and though she wasn't Native American herself, she wanted to be absolved by this shaman before she died. She didn't know he'd predeceased her, but when she learned, she then turned to 'the witches of Siren Song' for absolution. When she asked me to help her, she didn't know Lost Baby Girl was related to us through the father. No one did . . . and they still don't know."

"Did you give her absolution?" Ravinia asked curiously.

"I said a few words and told her she was forgiven and she relaxed and died several minutes later." Catherine made a face. "It made me wish I'd done more to help seek out the child, but truthfully, because of her father, I didn't want to find her."

"What was wrong with this man?" Elizabeth asked, even though she could tell Catherine didn't want to talk about him.

"He was my sister Mary's father, Thomas Durant, and he'd been missing for years, so when he showed up, we didn't immediately know who he was. Mary even invited him to the house as a guest, like she did with lots of men, and, one thing led to another. It was after that, that I closed the gates. . . ."

"He was my grandfather," Ravinia said.

Catherine nodded and there was silence for a while.

Then Ravinia asked carefully, "Please don't tell me he was my father, too."

"No." Catherine was positive on that. "And he's not yours, either, Elizabeth. I know you have questions about your father, but I don't really want to talk about him right now. He was a good man, though."

She accepted that with a nod. Eventually, she would probably get all of her history, but she was willing to wait.

"But you think my mother slept with her father," Ravinia said.

"She didn't know who he was, although he knew who she was and didn't care. I believe he was the main reason your mother lost her mind," Catherine said to Ravinia. "He came at me a time or two as well. That's why we had to take care of things."

"What did you do?" Elizabeth asked.

"Made sure he wouldn't hurt anyone again," Catherine said with finality. "He's dead and his bones are burned now. He won't come back to haunt us. But he fathered a number of children in his day, and Lost Baby Girl was one of them."

"Nadia," Elizabeth said.

Catherine nodded in confirmation.

An hour later, Elizabeth and Ravinia said good-bye to the clan of women and were let through the gate by the eldest cousin at the lodge, Isadora. Rex jumped out of the car at their approach and helped them into their seats.

On the road and away from the lodge, he asked, "How was it?"

"The same," Ravinia said.

"Interesting," Elizabeth responded as they turned onto the coast road.

Rex said, "I just got a call from my buddy, Mike Tatum. He says Nadia's body finally floated into one of the harbors."

"Good." Ravinia said. "At least she's really dead."

Elizabeth was glad to hear it, too. She hadn't believed anyone could survive that fall, but when Nadia's body didn't turn up, a terrible question had formed in the back of her mind. She still woke up shuddering most nights, remembering how close she'd come to going over the edge. It was a miracle Rex had saved her, and Nadia had tumbled over by herself. The ocean had immediately pulled her body away and it had been missing for over a week.

"She had a bite mark on her hand," Rex added.

"Chloe," Elizabeth said.

"And there were canine bites on her body, too."

Elizabeth looked at him as they turned east off 101 to Highway 26, the road that led through the Coast Range to the Willamette Valley and the Portland airport. "She was bitten by a dog?"

"By a wolf," Ravinia said, staring out the window pensively.

Epilogue

On Monday, Elizabeth showed Rex Mazie's house and he pronounced it was where he wanted to move. The fact that it was much closer to Elizabeth's home may have been a factor, especially since she'd decided to stay in her house for the time being as the real estate market was picking up and lo, and behold, Staffordshire had actually sold to someone who wanted the Hobbit crèche and was in serious negotiations with Elsa Stafford who was hanging onto those Hobbits for dear life.

On Tuesday, Rex came in to the Suncrest offices and seated himself in Elizabeth's client chair. While she laid out the paperwork and showed him where to sign and initial, his hand had a tendency to slide over and touch hers. When he was finished, she threaded her fingers through his and they looked at each other and smiled like idiots. Love was like that, she realized. Glorious and stupid at the same time. When she and Rex walked out hand in hand, Elizabeth sent Pat a beatific smile, causing the receptionist to frown in consternation, which just made it all that much better.

On Wednesday, Rex took Ravinia to his wireless carrier, put her on his plan, and ordered her a smartphone. She was so grateful and touched that she went silent for a full minute. She then pointed out that as she was currently living at his place until she got a job, maybe he could just give her a job, too. That way she could move out and he and Elizabeth could have some time alone.

He told her he would think about it, which sounded like he was finally going to stop being a pain in the ass and actually listen to her.

On Thursday, Chloe came home from school and skipped up the

steps to watch *Busy Bees and Friends*. Before she tuned in completely, she asked her mom if she was going to marry Rex.

Elizabeth asked whatever gave her that idea, and Chloe said she'd
gotten a message. This immediately sent Elizabeth into a panic.

Chloe gave her a *look*. "Not that kind of message. I can just tell."
She then went on to say that it was okay if they wanted to get married as long as they could also get a dog.

On Friday, Ravinia stopped by the house ostensibly to see Elizabeth, but mostly to see Rex. Given a tiny bit of encouragement, she
was relentless in her quest to get him to take her on as an investigative partner. Rex tried to fob her off, but Ravinia was damn near
unfob-able. Rex then told Chloe that they didn't really need a dog as
they already had a terrier in their mix, and pointed to Ravinia. This
etched a line between Chloe's brows but didn't slow down her beg-
ging one iota.

On Saturday, Rex and Elizabeth left Ravinia in charge of Chloe for
a while. Chloe asked Ravinia if the danger was over, and Ravinia said
it was, though in truth, she'd still been getting faint messages off and
on, but nothing she could quite grasp. She'd certainly gotten Chloe's
messages loud and clear, so she thought they just might be some
kind of aberration. In her heart of hearts, she hoped it was the wolf,
somehow trying to communicate, but she thought that was probably
a fool's dream.

When Rex and Elizabeth returned they brought with them a curly,
black squirming puppy that Chloe squealed over and promptly
named Bentley, the name of the black shepherd from one of her favorite television shows, even though the new puppy was a female.

Ready to leave, Ravinia walked outside, and there he was! A ghostly
silver shadow padding across the neighbor's yard. He turned to stare at
her for a moment, his yellow eyes glowing, and then he moved away.
She was so overwhelmed with relief she almost cried . . . almost . . .
as tears were generally for people who couldn't contain their emotions and that wasn't Ravinia.

Rex and Elizabeth walked out together. He kissed her gently on
the lips before she stepped back inside her house and waved a good-
bye at them. The tender moment made Ravinia uncomfortable and
kind of happy, too. She was a third wheel, no doubt about it, but
once in the car Rex tossed a small booklet in her lap along with some
other papers.

"We start driving lessons tomorrow," he said, as she clutched the booklet close.

For the first time in her life, Ravinia felt truly positive about the future. She was on the right path and absolutely nothing could go wrong.

On Sunday, under the cover of darkness, his physical scars finally healed, Declan Jr. slipped across the border from the wilds of Canada and into Washington State. With blood on his mind and vengeance in his heart, he picked up the signals, thin and weak, that were coming his way. It wasn't his bastard brother trying to get inside his head, it was someone else. Someone a thousand miles or more away . . . a woman who might be needing a little bit of what only Good Time Charlie could give. He could see himself mounting her already, pumping hard, making her scream with ecstasy . . . one of those silvery blond bitches he hated so much.

They thought they'd killed him. Damn near had, but he wasn't done yet. Not by a long shot.

Standing in the center of Podunk, USA, he looked around for any kind of transportation, even a bike would do. Just something that would take him first to Seattle, then Portland, then Sacramento . . . then Los Angeles . . . or maybe San Diego? Somewhere down there she was waiting.

Church bells suddenly rang out, a terrible clanging sound that raked through his brain and made him want to scream. When they finally stopped and he lifted his hands from his ears, he realized that it was Sunday.

Sunday is a day of rest, he thought, then his lips curved into a hard smile.

Or is it?

1-16